EX LIBRIS

Romance
Treasury

Romance Treasury

THE ROMANCE TREASURY ASSOCIATION

NEW YORK · TORONTO · LONDON

ROMANCE TREASURY

These stories were originally published as follows:

ROMAN SUMMER
Copyright © 1973 by Jane Arbor
First published by Mills & Boon Limited in 1973

THE FLAMBOYANT TREE
Copyright © 1972 by Isobel Chace
First published by Mills & Boon Limited in 1972

BLACK NIALL
Copyright © 1973 by Mary Wibberley
First published by Mills & Boon Limited in 1973

ROMANCE TREASURY is published by
The Romance Treasury Association, Stratford, Ontario, Canada.

Editorial Board: A. W. Boon, Judith Burgess, Ruth Palmour and Janet Humphreys

Dust Jacket Art by William Biddle
Story Illustrations by William Biddle
Book Design by Charles Kadin
Printed by Kingsport Press Limited, Kingsport, Tennessee

ISBN 0-919860-24-9

Printed in U.S.A.   A025

CONTENTS

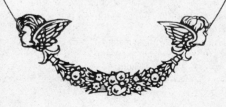

ROMAN SUMMER

ROMAN SUMMER

Jane Arbor

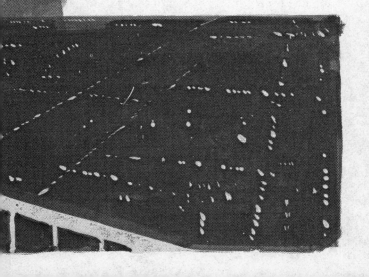

After the tragic death of her husband, Ruth thought she would be immune to the attractions of any other man. Yet, some mad impulse made her answer a newspaper ad that had been inserted by the formidable Erle Nash, the object of her childhood crush.

Ruth soon found herself hired for the job as companion to teenaged Cicely, a likable girl she was to teach the beauty and culture of Rome. When Cicely fell in love with Erle Nash, Ruth did not foresee such a danger for herself.

"The folly of marriage is a heady, distracting adventure I don't need," Erle stated . . . but it was too late for Ruth. For she soon recognized her own hopeless love for him and knew that her only reward would be heartbreak.

CHAPTER ONE

"ARRIVEDERCI, signora! Till Friday, then!"

As if to show her equal command of both Italian and English, little Signora Matteo always mixed her greetings and partings. Ruth, indulging her, would reverse the order and reply in kind, "Till Friday. *Arrivederci, signora*"—and another of Signora Matteo's English lessons would be over.

Today Ruth gave the girl time to patter down the stairway from the apartment, then she moved to the window to watch her emerge onto the pavement of the busy Via Tre Fontane, plunge dangerously into the noisy hustle of scooters and cars, and disappear among the crowds on the opposite side. But though Ruth's eyes were on her pupil, her thoughts were more on the letter that she half regretted mailing three days ago—the letter that had resulted in the peremptory summons to "attend for interview" the Via del Corso offices of a certain Erle Nash at noon tomorrow.

Should she go? There was still time to excuse herself by telephone. No doubt there would be others like her "attending for interview," one of them would be successful in gaining the post of companion to a young English girl, and if Ruth Sargent failed to show up on the Via del Corso her absence would never be regretted by anyone.

She had first seen the advertisement in *La Gazzetta* a week ago, her heart thumping a little as she read it. The name "Erle Nash" jumped out at her from the type though she told herself it had no significance for her now, all the while knowing that, if only for sentiment's sake, it had. But if the advertisement had not appeared for three days' running, showing that the advertiser had not yet found what he wanted, she probably would have done nothing about it. Those three appeals had been her undoing. She had written her own letter and mailed it.

Now, as she ate she folded and propped up today's *Gazzetta* to read while she ate her cold lunch of salami and salad, she remembered why she always saved the paper to read at this meal. It was because, while Alec was alive, it had been their conversation time. Breakfast was always a hurried affair of rolls and coffee; in the evening they'd eaten off trays and watched television or went out to sup at a trattoria or on midsummer nights when the city heat was unbearable, they'd packed a picnic meal and drove their little runabout out into the Roman countryside and walked in the dark.

Today, four years later, there was no runabout. There were other more pressing expenses for a young widow to meet; the problem of earning a living to solve; day-to-day loneliness to combat, without deliberately evoking memories by visiting places where she would never be happy again.

At first there had been friends who had helped. But it was an occupational hazard of Alec's colleagues in the Rome branch of the Far Cathay Travel Service that they moved on at short notice to other fields of work. They came and went to and from the Rome branch, and the ties of friendship rarely stood the strain. For some time now Ruth had had no intimate friends. As time went on her only new contacts were her pupils for English lessons, and they were merely twice-weekly visitors to her home. She was infrequently invited to theirs.

Now the pattern of her days was fairly set. She still had an ache for Alec, but by now it was more a longing for the companionable things they had shared than the deep, soul-destroying hunger it had been at first. Now she could meet the speculative, opportunist look in the eyes of men without allowing invitation to show in her own. Sometimes she wondered if, at 29, she had forgotten what love was. But she hadn't been tempted to learn the bittersweet way of it again, lest circumstance should betray her a second time—as the plane crash that had taken Alec from her had betrayed her once.

Money was tight. She had had the lump sum of Alec's life insurance and a small pension from Far Cathay. She could have earned more in England than she did from giving English lessons and doing some free-lance translating. But she had no ties in England—her parents had retired to Malta. She clung to Rome as a climbing plant to a sunny wall. To her it was home.

She could not have said what had stirred in her at the sight of Erle Nash's advertisement. Curiosity, she wanted to think—a curiosity that was not disloyal to Alec, since Erle Nash had happened to her long before she'd met Alec. Her heart had jumped in that odd way merely because the name had evoked an embarrassing memory of her youth as it had never done so far when it had shouted at her from placards, bills and the Sunday papers. Somehow the advertisement had brought him closer and had put herself into his rarefied orbit. And so, she had sent her letter and now, though she pretended to doubt her intention, knew that she would be going to wait upon the man's pleasure at noon tomorrow. . . .

The address she sought was a block on the corner of Corso and the Piazza Colonna. Her footsteps echoed on the marble floor of the entrance hall; a notice board in black and gold directed her up the graceful staircase to a circular mezzanine floor. Halfway around it the slot on a pair of double doors read, *"Imprese Erle Nash"* and the doors themselves opened onto an outer office, whose walls were covered with signed studio portraits of both men and women—all with the same assured presence. They were tributes of the musical world to Erle Nash, its professional godfather, as it were.

At a desk sat a young man, probably the secretary to "Enterprises Erle Nash" who had written to Ruth. He nodded knowingly as she introduced herself, then asked her to sit down. Signor Nash was in, but occupied. A quarter of an hour, perhaps less, and he might be alerted that Ruth was here.

While she waited she speculated on how Erle Nash might have changed. Her image of a successful impresario was a middle-aged and portly man with a goatee beard, shrewd eyes and fat hands, smoking the best Havanas money could buy. In 15 years Erle couldn't yet be middle-aged, but he might have come to pattern in the rest. And would he recognize her, she wondered, as the ponytailed redhead who—?

She started at the buzz of an intercom from an inner room. The young Italian secretary jumped as if he had been stung; then at the crisp *"Avanti!"* in answer to his knock, he ushered Ruth into the farther room with a "Signora Sargent, *signore*," by way of introduction.

Swiftly Ruth appraised the man who rose briefly, gestured her to a chair, and met her eyes without a glimmer of recognition in his own.

He had hardly changed at all, except that adulthood had deepened the expression lines of his face and there was now a Shakespearean curve to longish brown hair that she remembered as an unruly boyish crop.

He had put on no weight, she judged, noting his easy-muscled shoulders as he sat at his desk, and though he hadn't smiled yet, she knew she was waiting for his trick of lifting an eyebrow at the same time as a corner of his mouth. He couldn't have lost that, could he? It had been the most disarming weapon in his armory. She thought he had probably always known the value of that one-sided smile.

She saw him studying her; the petal cut of her hair; approving, she hoped, the contrast of her white short-sleeved suit with her tan, which was almost a feminine uniform in Rome; the detail of feet in narrow thonged sandals, wrist-length gloves, shoulder bag, and her face—his scrutiny of that, however, the impersonal, businesslike appraisal of a stranger.

He repeated his secretary's introduction, making it a question. "Mrs. Ruth Sargent," to which she nodded and added, "I was born Ruth Anson" then "Charl-wood."

"Charlwood?" He was startled. "You know I was there, you mean? That . . . you were?"

Ruth nodded again and smiled. "At the same time as you were. Though"—making it easy for him—"you wouldn't remember me, I daresay. You were in your last year, while I was still in form four B."

He frowned, musing aloud. "Anson? *Anson?*" He shook his head. "No, I'm afraid it doesn't register. But of course"—making it easy for himself—"between middle and upper schools there was a pretty wide generation gap, wasn't there?"

"Four years—a lot in those days," she agreed.

"And there were hordes of you juniors, it seemed to us. All—" he smiled deprecatingly and the quirk of eyebrow and mouth were still there "—all of you looking more or less alike."

"Yes, I suppose so."

"Or I don't know—" he sat back propping his chin on the ball of a thumb "—I do remember one kid, a girl with red hair in a ponytail and a lot of freckles. She appeared out of a thick fog, dribbling a field hockey ball. But what was I doing on the girls' hockey field on a weekday afternoon? I even had a hockey stick as well, and this infant and I were apparently alone on the field."

Ruth took pity on him. She said, "We were by that time. It was a half-holiday, but people who came to school by bus hadn't gone home at lunchtime because of the fog, and there was to be a school social that night. And the other people who'd been putting in time by fooling about in a scratch game of hockey had given up when they couldn't see the goalposts. . . ."

He nodded, bouncing his chin on the thumb. "Mm, yes. It's coming back now. I said to this wench, 'You've got rusty eyebrows—'"

"And she said, 'If you had hair the color of mine, you'd have rusty eyebrows. They have to match,'" Ruth supplied.

He stared, "How do you—?" Then, his laugh exploded. "You mean *you* were that child?"

"I was 14," Ruth said with dignity.

His glance swept over her. "The hair, yes. Could be. But the freckles?"

"When my face is tanned, they don't show as much. I told you my name at the time. You knew I couldn't help knowing yours, and we got a bit acquainted while we played a one-man-a-side game and—" but she stopped short of the dream that had remained a dream, she'd hoped that at the social he would ask her to dance. He hadn't. And now he was questioning, "Ruth Anson, you said? But what are you doing in Rome?"

"Ruth Sargent now," she corrected, fingering her wedding ring. "I've been here for six years. I'm widowed now . . . but you know that from my letter."

"Ah, I'm afraid I let my chap out yonder screen the letters and sort the sheep from the goats, so to speak. Tell me about yourself, won't you?"

As Ruth briefly sketched her circumstances he interrupted to ask: "You must be pretty billingual now?" And, "When you lost your husband, why didn't you go back to England?" And finally, "Well, I know my job makes me a bit of a nomad between cities, but if you've known that Rome is one of my main bases, why haven't you looked me up before?"

Because, when you love and marry elsewhere, you can afford to forget a hero-worship that's plagued you for years. Aloud, Ruth said, "We inhabited different worlds. Your name is almost a household word. 'Erle Nash presents,' 'By permission of Erle Nash.' The Albert Hall. The Festival Hall. Covent Garden. La Scala—the lot. Besides, I knew you wouldn't remember me. And you didn't."

He turned that smile on her again. *"Mea culpa.* What amends can I make? Give you the job, perhaps?"

She wondered what he would say if she told him she had only used the job as an excuse to contact him. Or had she? Did she want today to be a once only occasion? Playing for time, she said, "If you think I could do it."

"Well, you are my best prospect so far, and I needn't see the others."

"But what does the job entail?" she asked, going in deeper. "I still have obligations to my language pupils."

"You could probably run them parallel to hostessing young Cicely Mordaunt. The position is this: she's nearly 17, the daughter of a lifelong friend of my

mother's, and my mother's goddaughter. Her own
mother is American, wealthy, and anxious for Cicely to
'get culture,' as she puts it. And culture and Rome being
synonymous, who becomes the patsy? Right. Me. So
Cicely descends on Rome for the summer, and that's
where you come in."

"If . . . you mean she would live with me at my flat?"

"Well, she can hardly stay with me in my pad, can
she? That would be a plum for the gossip writers. How
might it go? 'Influential impresario Erle Nash squires
teenager who is sharing his apartment. . . .' No, the idea
was that Cicely should live with her hostess, whoever
she was. You could accommodate her, I hope?"

"I could, yes," Ruth agreed. "My entranceway is so
narrow you could miss it between two shops, but the first
floor apartment has more space than you'd think—two
livingrooms, two bedrooms."

"Well, I'd better see it. Would your local reputation
stand it, as long as I called at a reasonable hour?"

Ruth smiled thinly. "I doubt if anyone would worry,
whatever time you called. I'm not as much in the public
eye as you are," she reminded him.

"Oh, come," he protested lightly. "Not my fault that
the press keeps me well covered. It's the world I move in,
the people I have to know. A new prodigy appears in the
musical firmament, and there's speculation as to how
soon I shall sign up the child. Or a prima donna's tan-
trums threaten to wreck plans for a whole season, and
I'm there at the heart of the storm—".

He rose quickly. "Stella!" he said.

"Stella" came forward throwing a cursory glance at
Ruth on the way. She moved with lithe, practised grace.
Her black hair, stranded with a broad swathe of silver,
was piled like a smoky cloud above her olive-skinned

face, its small features as delicately sculptured as those of Queen Nefertiti. An exotic perfume wafted Ruth's way as the other's smile and extravagantly outstretched arms went for Erle Nash. Her lips went for him too, touching him lightly on the cheek before she chided in Italian, "You sound as if you didn't expect me! I know I'm late, but that's not my fault. Feldini kept me at rehearsal—"

Erle Nash released her hands. "Our date wasn't for today," he reminded her.

"But *caro*, yes! For luncheon."

He shook his head. "Not today. Friday. Look." He flicked the pages of a pocket diary and turned it toward her.

She shrugged and pouted. *"Santo cielo!* Trust you to produce written evidence that you are right! But do you suppose that I don't have to keep a little engagement book too? And mine says, 'Erle. Thursday.' "

"Then it shouldn't, *amica mea.*"

"But I refused Luigi Bernanos, telling him I was lunching with you! Do I take it then that you are more agreeably engaged, perhaps?" Now there was challenge and appraisal in her frank stare at Ruth.

Erle Nash laughed, "Do you expect me to answer that?" he parried. "No, in fact I'm not engaged, and I can lunch. So Luigi won't catch you out. If you'll give me a few minutes—"

"Do you want me to leave?"

"No matter." Sketching an introduction between them, "Signora Parioli, Signora Sargent," he turned to Ruth with a gesture she took as dismissal. "May I phone you at your apartment for that appointment?" he asked.

Ruth drew on her gloves. "Please do. I'm in the book," she said.

"Good. We have a day or two in hand yet. I'll be in touch. Meanwhile, Pietro will show you out."

But as the door closed behind Ruth she found the outer office empty, which gave her a brief chance to scan the photographs on the walls more closely. Yes, as she thought she remembered, it was there—a head-and-shoulders study signed extravagantly, *"Con amore, 'La Parioli,' "* the quotation marks making a slyly confident thing of the name that in the musical world had a mystique of its own, Ruth knew. As Erle Nash was to the business side of that world, so La Parioli was to its cosmopolitan stage. Two stars in their own right apparently in very close accord. . . . Ruth met Pietro returning, carrying a plastic cup of coffee. As she brushed aside his apologies, she wondered if the other woman had had enough curiosity about herself to ask who she was and if she had, what Erle had replied.

He telephoned that evening, apologizing for their unfinished interview and asking if he might come around at once to finalize details.

"Assuming," thought Ruth as she replaced the receiver, "that I'm accepting and it's only details that have to be finalized." But in his office she had said "yes" to him and had said it again just now. Too readily perhaps? That remained to be seen.

When he arrived he shattered another of her illusions about his kind by saying he didn't smoke. But he accepted a drink, carrying it around with him as he inspected the apartment, approving it for his young charge. He paused at the window of the living room, gesturing with his glass at the lemon-colored evening sky above the tall buildings across the street.

"Did you live here with your husband?" he asked.

"Yes."

"Then, though you're pretty well hemmed in, I'm sure he insured you your *soldino di cielo*."

Puzzled, Ruth translated, "A pennyworth of sky. What do you mean?"

"Don't you know? Hadn't you heard the local saying that any lover worth his salt buys for his girl at some time or another the pennyworth of Roman sky that's worth ten thousand lire of sky any other place?"

"No, I've never heard that."

"No? It's common enough." He paused. "Did that hurt? My reminding you of your husband?" he asked with unexpected perception.

Ruth shook her head. "Not now. It once would have."

"How long were you married? Less than three years? So short a time? What happened?"

In the brief, bald words she used for answering such questions from strangers, Ruth told how Alec had been bound for the London office on a routine visit when his airplane crashed and everyone was killed. Then, sparing her companion the conventional sympathy he might feel he must offer, she changed the subject. "Until I saw a news story about you some years ago, I didn't know you were in the musical world at all," she told him.

"It was rather inevitable," he said. "I went to college after Charlwood, and when I finished I joined my father and my uncle who were in partnership as concert agents. But I wasn't content for long with the lesser artistes they dealt with. When I'd had a lucky break or two in placing some star names I began to move into the big time on my own. Of course my beginner's luck didn't hold; but I was cocksure enought to believe that the best plums were there for the gathering, so I bided my time until some of them were ripe."

"Such as Signora Parioli?" Ruth questioned.

"Such as Stella Parioli . . . among others."

"You haven't married." Knowing from his publicity that he had not, Ruth made a statement of it.

"No," he confirmed. "May I—?" At her nod he sat down, stretching out his legs. "No. Looking for a piece of sky on which to squander a *soldino* is no immediate problem of mine. Most of the glamorous, talented women I know are my bread and butter, and while that's so, the folly of marriage is a heady, distracting adventure I don't need."

"You sound rather blasé about women," said Ruth.

He shrugged. "You could say I'm the boy from the jam factory who, when they offered him jam at the Sunday School treat, said, 'No thank you. I works where it's made. . . .'"

"You agree you are blasé?"

"If you like. I prefer to see it as putting first things first—first for me being a career I've worked at like the devil, with the possible entanglement of marriage being a poor second, even if it's anywhere in the field. After all, I have as much of the society of women as I want, and I see no reason at present to invite one of them to shackle me by the wrist." As Ruth flinched at the cynicism of that, he said, "Treading on your dreams, am I? I'm sorry."

She came back at him. "Don't be," she said with spirit. "Personally I'd rather have my dreams trodden on than admit I had no dreams at all."

"Who's admitting to having no dreams?" he countered. "Or is it that being a woman causes every dream to be irrevocably linked to romance?"

"Of course not. But it was your rejection of romance that we were talking about, I thought."

He crooked an eyebrow. "Now *I* thought we were talking about my rejection of *marriage*," he said meaningly and seemed to relish the naïve flush that had flooded Ruth's cheeks. "Meaning that for you they are not necessarily at all the same thing?" she asked.

"Exactly. In other words—that currently I have plenty of jam ..." He allowed his pause to point the meaning of that even more clearly; then he stood up.

"I'll write to Mrs. Mordaunt if I may, telling her we're in broad agreement as to your hostessing of Cicely. She'll be in touch with you, confirming terms. Cicely, by the way," he added, "flies in the day after tomorrow. May I call you as to the time and drive you out to the airport to meet her?"

"Please do." Ruth adjusted quickly to his switch from the provocative to the businesslike, but as he took her hand in parting, his half-amused scrutiny of her face embarrassed her again. "I hadn't noticed until now, but you still have rusty eyebrows," he said.

While they waited for Cicely Mordaunt's aircraft to arrive, Ruth asked how well Erle knew his protégée and what she was like.

"I've known her off and on since she was about ten," he replied. "She and her mother visit my family at intervals. As I remember, she has long blond hair and blue eyes, so she should be God's gift to Italian youth, and you may find your role as chaperon no sinecure. Have you thought out any cultural program for her?"

"Not yet," said Ruth. "I thought I'd find out whether her chief bent is architecture or sculpture or history or whatever and begin with that."

"And supposing her bent leans principally toward the nearest pop joint or the Lido?"

Ruth laughed. "It may well, of course, and I may be hard put to sugar the pill of "culture." But when she goes home, she's going to want to come back to Rome, or I'll know the reason why!"

"Determined to earn your fee, or because you're jealously attached to Rome yourself?"

"Both, I suppose," Ruth admitted. "I only know I'd hate anyone on whom I'd had influence to leave Rome without feeling nostalgia for some unique aspect of it."

Erle leaned back in his chair, regarding her beneath lowered lids. "You're an idealist, aren't you?" he commented. "Or an angel with a flaming sword. Could I have picked better for young Cicely's higher education, I ask myself? Sounds as if, though, I may have to temper the cultural wind a bit by taking her out to the old night-club or orgy. And supposing *I* admitted to seeing Rome as no more than a good central base for my operatings. Would you feel impelled to sell your enchantment with it to me, too?"

Suspecting from his tone that she was being baited, Ruth determined she would not "rise." "It would depend on whether or not I was being paid the rate for the job," she retorted lightly.

He laughed, confirming that he hadn't been serious. "In other words, you wouldn't do it for love?"

"Would you expect me to?" she parried.

"Only for money, hm? Though perhaps you might agree to payment in kind?"

Pretending suspicion of the offer, Ruth said, "What kind of kind?"

"Well, say dinner for two at Alfredo's in exchange for a conducted tour of the Vatican, or a box at the Opera rating a day at the Borghese Museum. What do you say?"

"I think . . . that we're talking a lot of nonsense, and hypothetical nonsense at that," she returned.

He wasn't to be squashed. "Oh, I don't know. What's so hypothetical about it? You may yet find me sitting in at your lectures to Cicely, saving myself either money or kind, and gaining for you two converts for the price of one!" he retorted. But by the immediate announcement of the arrival of the flight they awaited, Ruth was spared having to reply.

It was not difficult to identify Cicely Mordaunt, for she was the only girl coming through alone from the customs hall, and her bright, fair hair lay across her shoulders like a cloak. Moreover, she ran straight to Erle, slinging her purse far up her arm in order to embrace him and plant a kiss firmly on his lips.

"Erle darling, I'm here! I'm here!" she announced unnecessarily, while Ruth was struck by the thought that people have to be 16, like Cicely, or as poised and assured as Stella Parioli, in order to kiss as uninhibitedly as that. She watched as Erle held Cicely off and tweaked her cheek.

"So one sees," he agreed. "Dyed in the wool and a yard wide—"

Indignantly Cicely smoothed her slim hips. "I am *not* a yard wide!"

"All right. Just a figure of speech." He turned to Ruth. "Meet Cicely, will you, Ruth? Cicely, Mrs. Ruth Sargent."

They shook hands. Cicely asked, "I'm to stay with you? D'you know, I'm awfully glad you're young. I thought you'd be the dowager type, or governessy, which would be worse. Does Erle call you Ruth because you know each other well, or because he once knew you at school, as he told Mommy when he phoned about you? And how long ago would that have been, for goodness' sake?"

Erle answered that. "About when you were in your cradle."

"Oh, eons ago! Anyway, may I call you Ruth too?"

"If you want to, I hope you will," said Ruth as Erle led the way to the parking lot.

Ruth had intended to give up the front seat to Cicely, but Erle put the girl in the back, at which she giggled happily, "Talking to me, you're afraid you won't concentrate on your driving!" He retorted cryptically, "Be sure of it, that's it."

Cicely sat forward, and as soon as the featureless airport approach roads were left behind, she became rapturous over a scene where elegant cars purred, where the pavement cafés were crowded with customers, where there was light and shops still open as Rome dressed itself for its gay evening hours.

"I can hardly wait!" she crooned. "I've always heard that Rome is swinging—all those film people who live here, and all those dreamy fashions, 'way beyond beyond. Erle, d'you think you could get us into a really super fashion show? Could you?" He promised laconically, "I daresay I could try," then cocked an eyebrow at Ruth.

"What did I tell you?" he murmured, scarcely moving his lips. "The Vatican and Borghese up against some stiff competition . . . no?"

He left them at Ruth's apartment, saying he would be in touch the next day. Ruth opened the door and went in, but Cicely lingered in the doorway, looking after the car.

"He's dreamy, isn't he—Erle, I mean?" she murmured. "I've been in love with him since I don't know when . . ." Ruth was startled at this extravagant statement and decided it best to ignore it.

She showed Cicely to her room, with which Cicely professed to be delighted, then donned an apron and set about preparing the supper she had planned. She was putting out a bottle of wine when Cicely entered the room, her face falling at sight of the laid table.

"Oh, couldn't we go out somewhere tonight—my first night?" she pleaded. "Somewhere exciting. Wouldn't Erle take us?"

"If he'd meant to, he'd have invited us when we were with him," Ruth demurred.

"I don't know. He might have thought you had something planned for me. Could I phone him and see what he says?"

Ruth thought of the offices she had visited and had begun to say, "I doubt if he'll be there—" when she realized Cicely meant to call his apartment, the address of which she did not know. When told so, Cicely said, "Well, he'll be in the book, won't he? May I look? How do you telephone in Italy anyway? Will you do it for me?"

Ruth got the number for her, handing her the receiver. "If you say '*Pronto*' when he answers, he'll think you've begun to learn some Italian already," she smiled, leaving the room.

When she returned a few minutes later, Cicely, looking crestfallen, had hung up. "I didn't get him," she announced.

"He was out?"

"I don't know. An Italian woman answered. She said '*Pronto*' and then what sounded like her name—Stella

Somebody—and waited. Then, when I said—in English, of course—was Erle there, she said, in English too, but with a foreign accent; 'He is not free' and hung up on me. Shall I try again?"

"I wouldn't, if I were you," Ruth advised.

"Well, will you?"

"No."

"Why not? And who was that woman?"

"Because if he'd wanted me to reach him at his private address he'd have given it to me. And 'Stella,' I think, must be Stella Parioli, a famous singer who's one of his clients. She sings mezzo-soprano roles like Carmen."

"Never heard of her," said Cicely bluntly. "I suppose that makes me a philistine. But what was she doing in Erle's apartment?"

Ruth's gesture was of supreme ignorance. "My dear girl, how do I know? Perhaps she could say he wasn't free because she knew they were going on somewhere."

"Or were spending the evening there, just the two of them," forecast Cicely darkly. "Anyway, what do we do now?"

"I suggest we have our supper as I planned," Ruth said briskly. "And afterward we'll go for a walk around the houses and you can have your first taste of Rome. We won't have coffee here, we'll have it out."

"Oh, okay." But Cicely could not leave her grievance. "In Erle's apartment at night, answering his telephone, sounding as if she owned him! 'He is not free.' " she mimicked the accent cruelly. "So what do you suppose that makes this Stella person? His current girlfriend?"

Ruth said, "Again I don't know." As she went to bring in the dishes she was wondering at her reluctance to define the relationship between Erle and Stella Pariolo. *Jam . . . ?*

CHAPTER TWO

As Erle had warned, Cicely showed no warm interest in the antiquities of Rome. It was the city of luxurious shops, shabby *palazzos* in the district across the river, a thousand fountains, and teeming crowds who lived a large part of their lives on the sunny streets that intrigued her most.

Ruth was disappointed, for it was the blending of the ancient and the modern that fascinated her—the ruins of the Colosseum and the Forum at the very heart of the city center; the noisy scooters and the fussy runabout cars darting about on streets and squares paved and worn to pebble-smoothness by two thousand years of use. Where her eyes were for the majesty and history of age-old things, Cicely's were for people and children and the changing kaleidoscope of the ordinary street scene.

She loved to watch, fascinated, the commonest of Roman sights—a street-corner argument in which gesticulating hands and lifting shoulders were as expressive as the busy tongues, and she would join the audience for a Punch and Judy show in the Borghese Gardens simply for the pleasure of watching children entranced. After a time Ruth realized she must come to a compromise between her duty to Cicely as she saw it and Cicely's own idea of her summer in Rome. But that was after a particularly disastrous morning at the Vatican Museum and following a somewhat heated argument with Erle.

Ruth had warned that their sightseeing would involve, first, a long line-up outside and then at least an hour-long walk through the magnificent Raphaelite galleries, with the prize of the Sistine Chapel at the end of the tour. Cicely had complied, though none too enthusiastically. She took considerably more pleasure in glimpses of the Vatican gardens than she did in the myriad-coloured frescoes and paintings; she even viewed the Sistine Chapel only out of duty, and by the end of the morning her relations with Ruth were considerably strained.

She was sulky at lunch and afterward she said she was going to take a book into the nearby Borghese Gardens. Ruth had a lesson to give to a pupil, who had only just left when Erle called. They hadn't seen much of him since Cicely's arrival and he came unannounced today. He asked where Cicely was and Ruth, explaining, added: "We 'did' the Vatican Museum this morning, and in consequence we're not on the best of terms, I'm afraid."

Erle laughed. "What did I tell you? The child is only 16 and you've probably been cramming culture down her throat."

"It's what her mother sent her here for," objected Ruth.

"You should still dilute the dose."

"But if you're going to see the Vatican Museum, you're going to *see* it, and it takes hours from start to finish. I think Cicely was cross principally because her sandals hurt her. Yet I'd told her to wear sensible shoes."

"And she didn't, and now is 'not amused'?"

"Distinctly not. I'm in the doghouse for 'dragging' her there."

Erle said unsympathetically, "It could be you've only yourself to blame. I wouldn't put it past you to have made out an ironclad itinerary and a rigid timetable, and woe betide anyone who dares to upset it!"

Ruth protested, "Why wouldn't you put it past me?"

"Because, at a guess, you're of the Boy-stood-on-the-burning-deck mentality. Give you a trust to fulfil and you'll fulfil it to its last letter—right?"

Ruth said, "And what's wrong with that?"

"Nothing—so long as it's only yourself you're caging inside a set of rules. Doesn't Cicely ever play?"

"Play?"

"At parties, for instance. You should give one for her."

"I don't know enough people of her age to invite."

"Then I'd better give one. And you could do worse than by taking her to, say, the Piazza Venezia, where she's got half a dozen streets raying out, giving her a city map and telling her to explore by herself."

"I'm supposed to chaperon her."

"Tcha! The letter of the law again. I'm not suggesting you abandon her at midnight, and the only way to learn any city is to walk about it on your own two feet. Which reminds me—can you drive a car in Italy?"

"I used to, and I've kept my driving licence renewed. Why?"

"Because it's what I came to tell you—that I've had another telephone talk with Mrs. Mordaunt and she'd like me to hire a car for you to take Cicely about. So I'm getting a little sports car for you; they're easy to park and you can keep it at the garage around the corner."

"Thank you," said Ruth. "That will mean I can take her farther afield."

"Exactly. Show her the Appian Way, for instance, and dare her to be blasé about driving along the oldest road in the world that's still in use—on the original paving-stones too," Erle advised.

He did not wait to see Cicely, which added to her

sense of grievance when she came in. But on hearing of the projected party and the car, her black mood passed.

Erle invited them to the party by phone. It was to be a restaurant affair. Cicely spent the afternoon at the hairdresser's and emerged with her hair piled high, adding at least three years to her age. Ruth always shampooed her own short hair, but treated herself to an expensive cut. Cicely wore a sunray-pleated lamé dress; Ruth went in one of her two evening gowns, a peacock-green batwing-sleeved *blouson* over a narrow matching skirt.

Erle called for them. He made Cicely, for whom the party was given, his partner for the evening. At the restaurant they and the other guests gathered in a big private anteroom; introductions were made, drinks proffered and the usual party jabber was a Babel of different languages. Watched at a distance by Ruth, Cicely was quaintly possessive of Erle, tucking her arm into his, laughing up at him, making the most of her evening as his particular choice; possibly seeing herself, Ruth thought with a little stab of compassion, as a serious rival of the exotic demanding women who were part of his daily life.

I've been in love with him since I don't know when. Had Cicely meant that to be taken at face value? Or was that mere teenage extravagance? Ruth hoped so. There was no future in laying your all at the feet of a man who claimed that the adventure of marriage was not for him. . . .

The guests did not know who their dinner partners would be until they found their own place-cards at the tables for six in the restaurant. Ruth's partner removed his card and tucked it into a pocket as he announced his name to be Cesare Font. He added when Ruth told him hers, "I do not speak English very well, *signora.* You must forgive me my mistakes!" and saw his dark, grave face light up with relief.

The other people at their table were two strangers, and Stella Parioli and her partner, whom she addressed as 'Luigi.' Was this the Luigi Bernanos whom she had claimed to have turned down in favour of lunching with Erle, Ruth wondered.

The conversation was all in Italian, with Ruth taking less part in it than anyone, though her own partner was attentive enough. At one point Stella Parioli glanced across to Erle's table, where he sat with Cicely and four other young people, to comment, "So eccentric of Erle, to put himself out to see that mere children enjoy themselves." Then, riveting her glance on Cicely in particular, "The young blonde—I don't recognize her. Does anyone know who she is?"

Ruth said, "Yes, I do. She's English—a protégée of Signore Nash. Her name is Cicely Mordaunt, and I'm her chaperon for the summer."

Stella Parioli turned her exquisitely dressed head, looking beneath her lids at Ruth with an air of using a lorgnette in order to bring her into focus.

"Indeed? Her chaperon?"

"Yes," Ruth acknowledged.

The other woman's face cleared. "Ah yes, I remember you now. A week or two ago, wasn't Signore Nash interviewing you for the post of companion—paid companion—to that child?"

The intended slight did not escape Ruth. "Yes, I am being paid," she said.

"As I thought." The reply seemed to give Stella Parioli some satisfaction. She turned to Ruth's partner. "Is your sister here this evening, Count Fonte? I have not seen her yet, if she is."

At Ruth's sharp-drawn breath and glance his way, Cesare Fonte turned a dull red, as if in embarrassment.

"Agnese? She has not come. She does not enjoy such affairs very much," he replied.

"But you enjoy being invited to dine out on occasion?" Somehow the implication was that he was grateful for a bowl of free soup and a charity crust. What a subtly poisonous person the woman was, thought Ruth as Cesare Fonte said quietly, "More than Agnese does, yes."

After dinner there was a concerted move to a night-club for a floor show and dancing. Cars were shared and Ruth went with her dinner partner. Erle signed in his big party; the youngsters took at once to the crowded dance-floor, while other people found tables, watching and chatting over their drinks.

At their table for two Cesare Fonte said suddenly, "You must forgive me, *signora,* for failing to give you my whole name." He took out the place-card he had put in his pocket and showed its wording—'Count Cesare Fonte.' "The truth is that my circumstances are such I prefer not to use my title in my everyday affairs, and my friends, if not my acquaintances, understand this."

Not knowing quite what to reply, Ruth made a non-committal murmur, and he went on. "You see, our hereditary titles are more common than are yours in England, and for a working man to bear one is no help to him. For most purposes, I have dropped it. If I were to marry and my wife should wish to be known as Contessa, that would be different. I should agree, to please her. As it is, my sister and I live in a Casa to the east of the city on the road to Tivoli. It is too big for us but we need the grounds and the stables for my riding-school. That's my work, you understand?"

"I see," said Ruth. "Is your sister not married either?"

"No. She keeps house for us both. She has some help inside, and we both work in the gardens." He paused. "I should be very happy, *signora*, if you and your young guest would visit us one day?"

Liking him for his frankness, Ruth said, "We'll do that, if we may. I want my charge to see the Roman countryside as well as the city. I have the use of a little car, and we could drive out."

"Or if you know our host well enough, he might bring you when he comes himself. He keeps his own mount at my stables. That is how I know him. Do you ride yourself, *signora*?"

But before Ruth could tell him she didn't, Erle was at their table, doing a host's tour of his guests. "Neither of you is dancing?" he asked, sharing the question between them.

Cesare Fonte shook his head. "I am so bad that I haven't dared to ask the *signora*," he said.

"Then may I borrow her?" Erle turned to Ruth. "I've asked the band to play something that my generation understands, preferably a waltz. Will you join me?"

To the strains of the medley they went out onto the floor. Ruth, who hadn't danced for a long time, moved hesitantly at first. But Erle's hand, hard upon her back, guided her expertly and he was patient with her until her feet and body caught the rhythm confidently.

She looked about her at the other dancers. "Where is Cicely?" she asked.

"Probably star-gazing on the terrace thoughtfully provided by the management. With scarecely a word of Italian to her name, she has made some conquests, notably with one Zeppe Sforza, who I've given permission to see her home."

"Oh. Was that wise?"

"Don't worry. Zeppe's father is a Royal Opera artiste, under contract to me, and I know the lad. I've given them a curfew of one a.m. which, with your permission, I'll see that they keep. How do you like Cesare Fonte?" Erle asked.

"Very much."

"You found his lack of English no handicap?"

"He understood my Italian. He tells me you ride, out at his riding-school, and suggested you might take Cicely and me over there one day."

"Good idea. I've been snowed under lately, and I'm in need of a workout. We'll make a date for, say, next week. You'll be impressed with his place, the Casa Rienzi. It's genuine Palladian, come down in the world. But as with a classically beautiful woman, who'll be lovely at eighty, it keeps its grace."

Ruth thought of the perfection of Stella Parioli's features and understood the comparison. No doubt he was remembering it too. Aloud she said, "Does the Casa Rienzi belong to Signore Fonte?"

"To Cesare? No. He rents it for the sake of the stable accommodation. Their own place—he has an older sister, Agnese—is deep in the South, in Calabria, where they have a small vineyard property. They grow grapes and maize, but there are too few people and tourists to merit a riding-school there. So they let that in turn to a local farmer, and came north to Rome. They're both still homesick for their 'ain folk,' I think."

As Erle stopped speaking the music slowed to its end, and he halted, holding Ruth away from him. "Thank you. Why don't we do this more often?" he said in a pantering tone. Probably his favorite closing gambit to everyone he partnered.

He delivered her back to Cesare Fonte, but after the floor show when people were leaving, he came back to drive her to the flat. He parked the car on the empty street and walked with her to the door, at which point she understood what he had meant by asking her permission to see the young people's curfew kept. He expected to be asked in.

Using her door key she fumbled, and he took it from her. He opened the door and followed her in. "You boasted that your reputation would stand up," he reminded her. "But I can wait in the car, if you'd rather?"

"No, come in, please." What else could she say? Besides, it was a quarter to one already and, like him, she didn't think the other two would be late.

Nor were they. At a few minutes after one a car roared noisily up the stone-paved street and stopped outside. After that there was silence—"Saying their goodnights," Erle suggested. Then there was the sound of Cicely's key in the street door; the car drove away and the other two went down to meet Cicely in the tiny hall.

She was a little breathless and prettily flushed. "You see, Erle," she panted, "one o'clock to the minute—right on time. But gosh—" she brushed back a strand of hair which had escaped from the elaborately piled curls— "I'm tired! A lovely evening, Erle—thanks so much." She blew him a kiss and turned for the stairs, her long skirt lifted. "All I want now is my bed. I can hardly prop my eyelids open. Good night, dears—" She went up.

Erle laughed shortly. "Evidently she has been roundly kissed," he said.

Ruth glanced up to the turn in the stairs where Cicely had disappeared. "What makes you think so? How do you know?" she asked.

His gesture was impatient. "My dear girl, you've only to use your eyes! In a woman it always shows. They wear a sort of—well, a glow. A smug glow, granted, but still a glow." He paused, then with that characteristic lift of the eyebrow, "If I knew you better, and the hour being the romantic one it is, I might be tempted to prove it to you. But as things are, you won't need to trouble your mirror to prove it to yourself. Because *this*"—he took her hand and kissed the back of it lightly—"doesn't count. It's just something I've learnt from the locals. . . ."

Another piece of his practised gallantry, thought Ruth when he had gone. She should have had some smart repartee ready, in order to make her ability to fence with words the equal of his. But that was the worst of wanting to believe people always meant what they said. Matter-of-fact yourself to a fault, you couldn't hope to match up with them—ever.

Cicely must have made several friends at the party, for the telephone rang frequently for her. There were some English twins, a boy and a girl, who, like Cicely, were spending the summer in Rome and with whom she went swimming at the Lido; a French girl who took her on a shopping-spree to the notorious "flea-market" in the Trastevere district; and most often the caller, Zeppe Sforza, who, having traveled with his father on singing tours, had enough careful English for Cicely to be able to talk to him. He was a day student at the University, and though Ruth thought he regarded her as Cicely's guardian-dragon whom he had to placate, she felt his awe of her might be a surety of his good faith towards Cicely.

But it was Erle on the telephone or in person whom

Cicely most welcomed, and when he rang up suggesting a day for visiting the Casa Rienzi, she promptly ditched a date with Zeppe so that she could go too.

Ruth protested, "Erle would understand if you explained why you couldn't come. Or you could ask him to take us another day. Why not?"

"No, why should I?" Cicely wanted to know.

"Because you promised Zeppe and you shouldn't let him down."

"Pff! I can go out with him any time. A date with Erle is quite something, and I'm not risking his saying he can't make it another day instead."

Ruth shrugged. "I still think you're behaving very shabbily toward Zeppe, and I won't have any part in it."

"Who's asking you to?" Cicely snapped rudely. "I'm quite equal to turning Zeppe down without help. And anyone would think"—slanting a glance at Ruth—"that you didn't want me along. That you'd rather have Erle to yourself for the day."

Ruth flushed with annoyance. "Don't be absurd," she snapped back. I'm going at Signore Fonte's invitation to meet his sister and to see the Casa. Erle is only giving me a lift because he's going riding. And I can't ride with him. You can."

It was their first sharp difference, and though it wasn't pursued after Cicely's grudging, "I'm sorry. I shouldn't have said that," it disturbed Ruth. Years ago she had known what it was to be grateful for a nod or a word thrown to her from Erle's Olympian heights, and she knew she was reluctant for Cicely to suffer the same growing pains. And that, at the cruel distance between a teenager's dreams and the man of the world that Erle had become.

Cicely, who had done some riding in England, went in some scratch gear—knee-high boots under slacks, and a polo-necked jumper, but Erle criticised her lack of a hat and stopped at an outfitters' to buy her a velvet peaked cap.

"You'd be *brutta figura* without something for your head," he told her.

Cicely wrinkled her nose. "What's *brutta figura*?" she asked.

"In bad taste."

"Oh." Trying on the cap at a rakish angle, "What's the opposite of *brutta figura*?"

"And I am that now?"

He pinched her cheek. "You're adorably fetching in any language," he said. Neither of them saw Ruth's instinctive flinch.

The Casa was about ten kilometers out, standing in parkland, built of brick and stucco with a pillared front-age and flanking wings at either end. There were stables and outbuildings behind the house, opening onto a courtyard. All had an air of having seen better days, though as Erle had remarked, no shabbiness could quite hide the essential dignity of the place.

A short distance away from the house, behind a tamarisk hedge, was a miniature building of similar architecture with a portico on each of its four sides.

"What's that?" asked Cicely, pointing.

"That's a belvedere—a kind of summerhouse," said Cesare, who had joined them. "They were usual features of country-house building in Palladio's day, put to romantic use for the keeping of assignations which couldn't be discreetly conducted in the house, under the eye of an army of servants."

Ruth translated this for Cicely. Then a boy groom

brought out Erle's mount, a magnificent grey, and Cesare took Cicely away to select a suitable one for her. Erle was already in the saddle when she reappeared on a small bay mare. She looked alight with happy anticipation as they wheeled and rode off, side by side.

Cesare stood looking after them. "She is a little in love, the youngster, I think," he said.

Ruth drew a sharp breath. "Does it show?" she asked unguardedly.

"You think so too, then?"

"I'm rather afraid so," Ruth admitted.

Cesare nodded. "Yes, it would be a pity, that. Erle is a fine man—a man's man who is a woman's man too. There are too many of them in love with him for their comfort. For he has charm without heart, and marriage is not in his program, he claims. But come and meet my sister now. She is expecting you."

Before they left the courtyard he stopped to caress the white-starred nose of a horse looking out from its box. "This one belongs to La Parioli. She rides here with Erle sometimes. She was at our table at his party where you and I met, if you remember?"

"Signora Parioli, yes," said Ruth. Then, needing to know, "Is she married?" she asked.

"No, though she has been linked with various names in the musical world—not excepting that of Erle. No, she uses the handle *'signora'* for professional reasons. Our women of standing like hers, addressed as *'signorina,'* would take it as a slight."

Ruth knew it. Knew too that a small hope had died. She had wanted to believe there was a husband in Stella Parioli's background; some man who had rights over her regard and her company; some man other than Erle. . . .

Agnese Fonte awaited them in a high-ceilinged room

that was too graceful to be entirely comfortless. But its furnishing was sparse and forbidding, and Agnese herself, ramrod upright on a hard chair, was as austere as her surroundings.

She was even darker than her brother. She wore her black hair plaited in a coronet around her head, which she held with a dignity that overrode her weatherbeaten skin, thick peasant's ankles and wrists. She was a woman of the south—Ruth recognized the type—somewhat out of her element, lacking the pitiless sun and harsh aridity of her homeland in the "toe" of Italy's "boot." Ruth guessed she must be several years older than Cesare.

He made the introductions, suggesting that when he had shown Ruth the house, she might like some tea and with a nod of her head Agnese agreed.

For a Palladian country house the villa was small, but even so, many of the rooms, including a long gallery on the first floor, were bare of furniture, curtainless and in need of fresh paint.

"We have a landlord who drives a hard bargain," Cesare explained. "He says we do not pay enough rent to justify his keeping the place in full repair. So, as there are only the two of us, we furnish and decorate the four or five rooms we need and keep the others closed." He paused. "It's a pity, really, for it is a house that should have people, children, laughter and comings-and-goings. But there—"he spread his hands. "It has only Agnese and me."

Over the tea which Agnese served, Ruth explained Cicely's circumstances and her own, though evidently the information had gone before her via Cesare, for his sister knew she was a widow and what she did for a living.

It was Cesare who suggested she would like to see the

belvedere, and they went to see it together. It was a dolls' house of a place, all its four tiny rooms connecting. It was designed for the sun, which shone on one of its porticos at any hour of the day. Cesare went to a wall cupboard and brought out a bottle of wine and some glasses and they sat outside while waiting for Erle and Cicely to come back.

Even in Italian Ruth found Cesare easy to talk to. As it had been easy to talk to Alec. As it wasn't with Erle, with whom she felt that both their talk and their silences were a kind of duel, even that he enjoyed it that way. She doubted whether she and Erle could have sat for an hour, as now, chatting agreeably, without a single clash of verbal swords.

When she worried aloud that the other two had been gone a long time, Cesare said, "That's Erle. Anyone who rides with him has to go at his pace and for the time he chooses. That is the secret of his success, I sometimes think—he expects and demands that people strain every nerve to give their best."

"How well do you know him?" Ruth asked.

"Well enough to know that he hasn't much use for amateurs or laggards; nor for women who don't add anything to his public image or his self-esteem."

Ruth commented drily, "You make him sound as if he'd need to be specially kind to his grandmother or to animals, to be a tolerable character at all."

Cesare laughed. "Do I? I think it is that I see him whole—warts and all, as they say, but envy him a little for a steel that I haven't got. It is, as they say also, as simple as that."

When at last Cicely and Erle appeared, Cicely was prettily radiant. She patted the neck of her mount lovingly and went with Cesare to see both horses rubbed down and stabled. Erle and Ruth went down to his car to wait for her.

His arm crooked over the wheel, Erle half turned in his seat. "Well, do you recognize the signs this time?" he asked.

"What signs?" But Ruth was afraid she could guess.

"The kitten-with-the-cream smug look, of course. About Cicely."

"You're telling me that you've kissed her while you were out?"

"No less."

"Was that quite—fair?"

"She wanted me to; it was written all over her. What was unfair about my doing it?"

"Because you must know how vulnerable she is to you."

"No more than to as many other males as want to kiss her for her pleasure and theirs. As the Latin grammars have it, she is 'meant to be kissed' and who am I to slap her ego in the face by turning her down?"

Angry now, Ruth retorted, "Who are you? I'll tell you. You're a man who's twice her age and should know better than to encourage her. She's at the stage where she wants to be kissed seriously, or not at all."

"Phooey. She wants to be kissed, full stop."

"I don't agree. Nowadays they grow up sooner than we—we did, and at seventeen, which Cicely nearly is, they can be jealous and hurt, and they long to know a man is serious—you, for instance, when on your own showing you're just having fun."

"Not just having fun. Saving her face as well."

"At the price of a lot of pain for her when she realizes you aren't serious and never were."

Erle's eyebrow lifted. "I declare you can make a mere

kiss for a schoolgirl with a teenage crush sound like a plighted troth!" he taunted.

"At Cicely's age she could delude herself it *was* a plighted troth."

"For heaven's sake! How many engagements is she prepared to take on at one time? The Sforza boy kissed her the other night, didn't he?"

"You can't know that he did."

"She told me so. So you see—as many kisses as she can collect, so many scalps for her belt, that's all. She's open to all the homage she can get, and no obligations on either side."

Ruth said tartly, "I'd like to believe that. But you haven't seen her jealousy over your other—commitments."

"My other commitments?" His eyes narrowed into a hard stare. "For that sweeping statement you should be made to name six!"

She shrugged. "I'm only quoting your own words— that you enjoyed plenty of jam."

He made a gesture of mock despair. "And to think I meant my little story to show that it's possible to have a surfeit of jam!"

"But you're still willing to use it for your own ends." With an indiscretion quite foreign to her, Ruth added. "I think Signore Fonte is right about you—all your relationships have to add something to your image."

"In—deed?" He drawled out the word. "One short afternoon in each other's company and you get intimate enough to go into a huddle over your friends' shortcomings. Quick work, I must say!"

"It wasn't a short afternoon. You and Cicely were away over two hours. And Signore Fonte—"

"Oh come! Surely you got around to first names?"

She ignored that. "—wasn't critical of you. In fact he admires you for an ability to forward your career that he claims he hasn't got himself." She broke off. "But this is a fruitless argument—we're completely at odds, and all I ask is that you don't hurt Cicely any more than you need."

He straightened in his seat, touched an imaginary forlock. "Yes, ma'am. Noted, ma'am. But if you think I'm going to go all avuncular, with a long white beard—" He stopped at sight of the other two, before they came into earshot. Cicely got into the back seat. "All shipshape and Bristol-fashion?" he asked her.

"Yes. Lovely. We'll do it again, won't we, Erle?"

"Madam has only to command—" He sketched a salute to Cesare and drove away.

At the gate to the road he gave way to allow another car to turn in. It stopped as it drew level. Stella Parioli, in an open-necked shirt and with a silk bandeau round her hair, was driving. She reached across to offer him a hand.

"Leaving, Erle—just as I'm arriving? Won't you turn round and ride with me?"

He shook his head. "I'm sorry, no. I'm playing chauffeur today, as you see."

She thrust forward her lips in a little pout. "Too bad. Then tomorrow perhaps? I am free."

"Tomorrow—perhaps. I'll have to phone you," he promised.

"When? I'm dining out tonight."

"So am I. With Signora Gancia."

"With Clara Gancia? I didn't know she was in Rome."

"I'm hoping to put her under contract for the winter opera season."

"Clara *Gancia?* Oh well—" Stella Parioli tossed her head, "I suppose you know your own business best—" Clearly supposing nothing of the sort, she accelerated and drove away.

To no one in particular, as he set his own car in motion, Erle murmured, "Believe me, I do."

CHAPTER THREE

Of all times of the day, Ruth thought she loved Roman summer mornings best. Noons were fierce, afternoons frenzied and noisy and evenings had to compete with the glare of neon lights. But in the very early morning the city had an air of being washed clean, the streets were empty and quiet as they never were later, and it was possible to hear every "plash plash" of the three fountains which gave the Via Tre Fontane its name.

Cicely was not an early riser and didn't want to join Ruth when she walked in the Borghese Gardens before breakfast. So Ruth went alone, usually striking across the park to the wilder parts where it was possible to believe herself in the heart of the country. Here the sun penetrated the early mist in slanting rays between the trees. It could be temporarily blinding—which was why, on the morning that Ruth almost collided with a soft-shoed solitary runner, she did not realize that the runner was, of all people, Erle.

He was in running shorts and a thin silk T-shirt which hid nothing of his tan and the strong ripple of the muscles of his chest and shoulders. As he held her off from him with an outstretched hand, she thought—funny that I should ever have wondered whether he might have gone to fat. His body is as fit and disciplined and male as when he used to win things at school sports ... Then she was apologizing, "I'm sorry, I didn't see you," and he was saying, "Why—aren't I big enough?"

"It was the sun. I've never seen you here before."

"No, I usually use one of the parks nearer my place, Giulia or Balestra. Do you walk here often yourself?"

"Fairly often, on summer mornings. It clears away the cobwebs. But don't let me stop you, please."

"It doesn't matter. I'd nearly finished the stint I allow myself." He fell into step beside her. "Is this before breakfast or after for you?"

"Oh, before. Cicely wasn't up."

"Then why not finish your own stint by walking back to the car with me and letting me give you breakfast? I parked at the Canestre entrance, so we're on our way."

Ruth hesitated. "Cicely will wonder where I am."

"She won't for long, if she isn't up yet. I'll drive you back on the way to my office."

"You mean—at your apartment?"

He said drily, "That's where I'm in the habit of breakfasting. And as with you, at this hour my neighbours can't suspect me of having sinister designs upon you. Will you come?"

Wanting to accept—she had never visited his apartment—she said, "Thanks, I'd like to, as long as I'm out for not much longer than if I'd walked as far as usual."

"H'm—a tight schedule, but we'll do our best. And I warn you, you'll have to help to *get* breakfast. My daily woman doesn't arrive until after I've left."

When they reached his flat he asked if he could leave her to watch the coffee percolator, heat some rolls, and lay a tray for carrying out onto his tiny balcony, while he showered and changed.

"If you'll show me where I find things," said Ruth. There was something intimate and friendly about coping with his domestic chores. After years of eating alone she was glad, as she had been when Cicely came, to breakfast opposite someone, to be able to pass the butter or to ask "More coffee?" instead of reaching in silence for the dish or pot.

Erle might have read her thoughts, for as she poured coffee and gave him his cup he remarked, "I must say there's something to be said for certain aspects of marriage, such as breakfast for two as a matter of course."

"And someone to get it for you?"

He grinned. "Well, naturally! Though for the sake of something attractively feminine across the table I might settle for getting it myself now and then. But tell me," he was grave now, "don't you ever miss the masculine touch yourself?"

She raised frank eyes to his. "Yes. Often," she said.

"I'm sorry." His hand could just reach hers and it did in a momentary pressure. "Have you ever thought of remedying that?"

"You mean—marrying again?"

"Considering it."

She shook her head. "Not seriously. It wouldn't be the same! You couldn't want it to be. Every deep experience has to be new, not the copy of a prototype. For two different men you'd be different too. What was your husband like?"

How to describe Alec in a few words to another man? At last Ruth said, "Quiet. Modest. Considerate. Reliable as a rock."

"Then don't look for another of his kind. For you'd either be disappointed or forever be drawing comparisons."

She poured herself some more coffee. "I'm not looking," she said with a finality which he seemed to acknowledge, as he let the argument drop.

Presently he asked, "How goes Cicely's affair with the Sforza boy?"

Ruth smiled self-consciously. "I rather think it's off," she admitted.

"Off?" Erle's chuckle was one of triumph. "What did I tell you? You'd have me believe in her grand passion for me, and she's nothing but a butterfly on the flit! Who is the object of her latest amour, then?"

"It isn't an amour. She treats this one as cavalierly as she did Zeppe Sforza. He's an English boy, here with his sister. He's an artist and he takes her sketching. She shows talent too; she's done an awfully good one of the Spanish Steps—."

Erle cut in, "You're talking for talking's sake. Simply to avoid having to eat your own words. Three of us in as many weeks! And to think I half listened to you and have avoided the child!"

Cornered, Ruth took refuge in attack. "And that hasn't been kind of you either. She's worried that she's offended you, and if so, how."

"Well, really!" he protested. "If I see her, I'm to curb my natural instincts to flatter a pretty girl and if I don't, I'm being brutal. You can't have it both ways, my dear Ruth, you really can't!"

"I only asked you not to encourage her. I know she probably tries to set the pace."

"And that's something you should learn about me. In dealings with your sex, I set my own pace or it isn't set at all."

"And that's pretty arrogant of you," said Ruth, though she wondered, remembering Stella Parioli's confident kiss for him. But she was relieved too, as it meant that if Cicely instigated some flirtatious nonsense with him, he had ways of dealing with it.

He shrugged. "Arrogant or not, it's the way I tick," he said. Than, "By the way, though, I don't admit you're right about Cicely. Does she regard you as one of my 'commitments,' ripe for her jealousy?"

Ruth's eyes widened. "Me? Of course not. She has no cause—"

"Then you can tell her you've been to breakfast with me without creating a scene?"

"But of course I can. Why shouldn't I?"

"Why not?" he echoed casually, then looked at his watch. "Time I was moving. And you?"

"Yes, quite." Ruth stacked the tray. "Do we wash up?"

"Heavens no, Maria will do it when she comes. I've just got to collect a few things."

Ruth followed him through to the living room. When she came back from stacking the tray in the kitchen she could hear him in his bedroom. He had left two drawers of a desk wide open, and as she couldn't pass without closing them, she closed the first and was about to close the second. Then she froze, staring at something that was half hidden by some papers lying on top of it.

It was a powder compact. She knew it well. Cicely had complained of having lost it—when? More than a week ago. But what was it doing here, in Erle's apartment? Unless . . . ?

That "unless" made Ruth a little sick. As far as she knew, Cicely, like herself had been to Erle's office, but never here. *As far as she knew* . . . But if Cicely had lost the thing on some clandestine visit here at Erle's invitation, that would account for her lack of worry about it. She had mentioned casually that she had mislaid it. So when could she have been here? Some time when she claimed to have been sketching with Jeremy Slade? Oh, surely not!

Erle was coming back, and full of doubts without any certainties, Ruth did the craven thing. She closed the drawer, leaving the compact where it was, and with every minute that passed knew that it was already too late to accuse him playfully, "Hey, what's this doing here? How come?" to which he might have a totally innocent answer. But again, he might not, and that she shrank from knowing.

They went down to the car and she supposed she made some articulate conversation on the drive to her apartment. She remembered hearing Erle say that he was flying to Vienna to finalize some artistes' contracts with the State Opera, and sending Cicely his love. And when she went in and told Cicely of her encounter with Erle without mentioning the compact in almost the first breath, again it was too late to mention it all.

Or was she pretending it was too late, when in fact it was that she didn't want to learn the truth—about either of them? That Erle was lying when he claimed to have avoided Cicely? That Cicely, accused, would lose face and try to prevaricate? Or might they both laugh in her face, call her frumpish and out-of-date, and claim that girls went to men's apartments alone in these days without a second thought? No, she had to give them the benefit of the doubt, act as if nothing had happened to disturb her. That way she would forget it sooner herself.

But she hadn't reckoned with her watchfulness of everything Cicely said in relation to Erle. When Cicely grumbled, "He didn't tell *me* he was going to Vienna," Ruth's unspoken question was, When could he have told her, if they hadn't met? Nor did she reckon with a rankling inner voice that wanted to know why she cared so much that they shouldn't be lying to her; why it mattered to her that Erle shouldn't cynically add Cicely to his list of conquests. But she didn't consciously answer the voice. For the answer had something to do with that awareness of Erle's virility which she had experienced in the Gardens—like an electric current turned momentarily on, lighting a response within her which she thought had died with Alec. It also had something to do with envy of Cicely's open wooing of his favor, and with Stella Parioli's certainty of it. And the sum of all that was something she would have given a great deal to deny.

Ruth was to find that Erle's advice to dilute the dose of culture for Cicely was sound. Also as he had advised, she sent Cicely exploring on her own, finding she picked up more conversational Italian that way than she would in formal lessons. Her use of it was neither wholly grammatical nor particularly elegant, but she made herself understood.

Between the "musts" of architecture, art and antiquity that Ruth was firm Cicely should see, they went out once or twice a week to Cesare Fonte's riding-school. Cicely persuaded Jeremy Slade and his sister Vivien to meet her there often for riding too. They would go off, a gay party of three, leaving Ruth willing to rest and relax in the garden or on the terrace of the Casa.

Occasionally Cesare or a groom accompanied the riding party, but mostly he allowed them to go alone. Unless he was giving a lesson himself he would join Ruth and they would talk over a glass of wine. Thankfully Agnese Fonte was not often in evidence, for her grim reserve was something of a dampener when she was.

Cesare and Ruth had enough in common for her to think sometimes that being with him was like being with Alec; to speculate on his age—he was probably younger than he looked—and to wonder why so nice a man shouldn't have married yet. As far as she was concerned, he lighted no spark of physical attraction in her; she could have enjoyed the company of another friendly woman as much as she enjoyed his. What had Erle said of the marriage that he meant to forgo for his own ends? That it should be a "heady, distracting adventure," and yes, it should be that and more. She remembered too his warning, right or wrong, that in a second marriage it would be disastrous to make comparisons.

She had little clue as to how Cesare thought of her. She knew he liked her, looked forward to their talks and often deferred to her opinion on all sorts of things. It was Agnese who enlightened her, taking the opportunity one morning when Cesare had been called away.

The day was overcast, threatening rain. Cicely, prepared in waterproof cape and hood, had ridden off with a groom; Agnese invited Ruth into the house for coffee, just as the rain came down. Under the darkened skies the high salon seemed more austere than ever and cold with a chill which, to Ruth's imagination, had no relation to the physical atmosphere.

Agnese was not a woman for finesse. She came straight to her point with, "May I ask you, *signora*, what is your view of this obvious attraction for my brother?"

Ruth stared. "My attraction for him? I don't think I understand you, *signora*?"

"Ah, come! You must know what he feels for you by now!"

"I know that he is friendly, that he likes me, I think. No more than that."

"Well, it is no secret from *me* that it goes further than that; he is in love with you, whether you claim to know it or not."

Ruth said patiently, "How can I know it when he had given me no sign?"

"Bah! A woman always knows these things. She does not need another woman to tell her."

"Then why are you telling me, *signora*?" asked Ruth.

"As I have said, I thought you would not need telling, and I wanted to know how you would answer him if he proposes marriage to you."

"I should be honored, but I should refuse him."

Agnese bridled. "Why? We are poor, but Cesare is a Count of the Holy Roman Empire! His wife would bear the title of Contessa."

"Yes, I understand that, but—"

"Then he *has* spoken to you of marriage?"

"No, he mentioned his title in passing, at our first meeting. But now you know I would refuse him, is that all, *signora*?"

Agnese folded her hands in her lap and sat very upright. She had the air of a judge about to pass sentence. "No, it is not all," she said. "I have to request that if you mean to refuse him, you should not see as much of Cesare as you have done hitherto."

Ruth smiled placatingly. "Oh, really, *signora*! We have contracted for a series of riding lessons for Cicely, and while they continue, I have to drive her over here. She cannot drive herself. And why should I avoid your brother, when I have come to value him as a friend? And he values me, I hope."

Agnese shook her head. "In Italy we do not understand such friendships between a man and woman. If she encourages him as you encourage Cesare, she is not blind to what he has in mind. Cesare understands this very well, and you are giving him hope which you say you do not mean to fulfill. This is cruel of you, and, I warn you, is a state of affairs which I do not intend to tolerate."

"But when he has said nothing to me, what reason could I give him for avoiding him, even were I able to? What do you want me to do?" Ruth asked bewilderedly.

"That I must leave to you," said Agnese with a shrug. "You are an adult, *signora*. You have been married. You must know many ways of discouraging a man."

"Before he has done or said anything that calls for discouragement?" Ruth set aside her coffee cup and stood up. "No, I'm sorry. While matters are as they are between your brother and me, they remain so. I can't do as you ask and you could hardly wish me to tell Cesare that I was avoiding him because you had demanded it of me?"

"I hope that you have more charity than to make trouble between a devoted brother and his sister," said Agnese calmly. "But if you have not, then you must do as you please. Even that would be a small price to pay for Cesare's freedom from a woman who wants him as a lapdog, grateful for her favors, though from whom she means to withhold the ultimate one."

That was too much! Ruth retorted hotly, "If I did as you ask, of course I should not implicate you. But as I am not doing as you ask until Cesare himself gives me cause—"

"And when he gives you cause? After that, what then?" Agnese insinuated.

"That I must decide if he ever gives me cause, and what he wishes himself that I should do, after I have refused him."

"I see. Then there is nothing more to be said?"

"Nothing, I'm afraid," agreed Ruth.

"And it does not matter to you that on my side I shall

do everything in my power to discourage his attentions to you? Even to the point of an open hostility which he can hardly mistake?"

Ruth shook her head a little hopelessly. "That I must leave to you, *signora*," she said. She went towards the door, and turned. "*Addio, signora*," she added distantly.

Agnese merely looked through the window. "It is still raining," she said.

"It doesn't matter. We English are used to rain."

Plunging out into it, but forced at last to seek the shelter of the belvedere's portico, Ruth felt stifled by her own impotent indignation. It was not until later—much later—that she saw a parallel which was distasteful to face. Just as Agnese Fonti had appealed to her she had appealed to Erle not to encourage Cicely, and had met with about as frosty a reception. Were they both meddling do-gooders, Ruth wondered, believing their own case good and thrusting it down the throats of other people. The thought made her feel a little kindlier towards Agnese, who obviously cared for Cesare. But she writhed to picture how Erle must despise her for seeing mischief where—probably—none existed. Then she gave herself a mental shake. She had meant well by Cicely, hadn't she? And if he couldn't see that, why should she care what he thought of her for it?

He was still away in Vienna when one morning there was a surprise in Ruth's mail. An expensive-looking envelope contained a large gilt-edged card of invitation to herself and Cicely to attend a private showing of the *haute couture* collection of Roscuro, one of the best known names in Italian fashion. Smiling, Ruth passed the card to Cicely. "Do you want to go?" she asked.

"Want to *go*? Silly question!" breathed Cicely rapturously, taking credit to herself that the invitation must be

Erle's doing. She had asked him to arrange it, and he had remembered and had done it. "It just goes to show—" she murmured dreamily, though what it showed she did not share with Ruth.

If ever there was a misnomer, they both agreed, it was the description "private" for a showing which had brought crowds of elegant women, with a sprinkling of men, to the foyer of the gracious building on the Via Condotti. Here were housed the display theater and workrooms of the partnership known as Roscuro. Ruth and Cicely were greeted and gathered in, offered drinks or coffee and ultimately shown to their places in the theater, where the audience sat on spindle-legged gilt chairs so cheek-by-jowl that Cicely declared in a stage whisper to Ruth, "If I so much as take a deep breath, I'm going to dislodge this dame next to me!"

The showing began to a medley of Italian voices which stilled to complete silence only when the impact of a particular number galvanized the audience to clap feverishly instead. For the most part its attention was laconic, even slightly bored. The buzz of talk continued unchecked and even a *sotto voce* conversation could not help but become public property.

Such a one was being conducted by Ruth's immediate neighbour and a woman in the row behind. The latter sat forward; Ruth's neighbour craned backwards, with the result that each spoke almost in Ruth's ear. And to her consternation they were discussing Erle . . .

She glanced quickly at Cicely. But the girl was rapt, watching the nonchalant pirouetting of the model on the catwalk, and in any case she hadn't enough Italian to know what was being said.

"I see he is not escorting either Gancia or Parioli today," said the woman behind.

"No, he is in Vienna, one hears. And only La Gancia is here. La Parioli is—where?"

"You think she may be with him?"

"Well, she is not in Rome. If she were, she would not risk not to be seen at a Roscuro."

"No. Then perhaps—though of course one can only guess, and as you and I know, there are half a dozen others who just *might* be in Vienna at the same time as he—There are also, they say, his very pretty English protege and the companion he has found for her."

"And whom, among *his* friends, could he choose to chaperon a young girl, would you say?"

"Oh, I don't think she is a friend of his. Just someone for whom he advertised to shepherd the girl for the time she is here."

"Ah—" With a nod the woman behind Ruth turned to the front again to add her applause for the traditional climax of the collection—a demure wedding gown of ivory lace with a veil merging into a train that ran the whole length of the catwalk behind the model.

Then the audience broke up into chattering groups, and Ruth and Cicely, since they knew no one there, were about to leave when they were approached by the head saleswoman who had welcomed them on their arrival.

She laid a hand on Ruth's arm. "*Signora, signorina*—I have instructions. From Signore Nash, you understand. That whichever design of our collection pleased either of you most should be made to your fitting at his expense." She looked from one to the other. "You were each able to select your favorite one, no doubt?"

Ruth gasped and interpreted for Cicely who, with a whoop of delight, leafed through her program and pointed. "*That* one for me!" she crooned. "That utterly snazzy sailor suit with the bell-bottoms and the round straw hat. Did Erle really mean—? And something for you too! Oh, isn't he a—a positive *lamp-chop*?"

The saleswoman smiled. "We shall send you an appointment for a fitting, *signorina*." She turned to Ruth. "And for the *signora*—?"

As Ruth said nothing, momentarily too nonplussed for words, Cicely cut in, "I know which one for her. That sea-greeny dinner dress with the bishop sleeves caught in at the—" She stopped as Ruth shook her head. "Not that? But you drooled over it when it was shown! Which, then? You certainly fooled me!"

Ruth said, "None of them. I'd rather not choose anything for myself. I will explain why to Signore Nash."

"You cannot decide today? You will be choosing later?"

"No, not at all, I'm afraid. *Addio, signora. Grazie—*" With a hand under Cicely's elbow, hurrying her along, Ruth made her escape. Her temper against Erle sharpened by her enforced eavesdropping, she was fuming within. What did he think she was? Another one added to the "half dozen who just might be in Vienna at the same time as he was?" Didn't he know that one didn't accept expensive clothes from a man unless—? She had to swallow hard upon her indignation in order to answer Cicely's clamourous, "Why on earth not? Why did you turn down Erle's offer like that? Why?"

"Because—"

"Because what?"

"You ought to know. It was an—insult."

"Then why," Cicely argued reasonably, "wasn't it an insult to me?"

"Because he is a friend of your people and you're in his charge." Ruth almost added, "and a mere child" before she remembered that she had argued with Erle that Cicely was mature enough to fall in love. Instead she said, "That makes it different for you."

"And at what point does it become different for *you*?" Cicely asked,

"Why, at the point where he is my employer, of course; where there's no relationship between us except that."

"Though I thought you were supposed to have been friends since you were both so high," remarked Cicely blandly.

"But we'd completely lost touch since then and we met again as strangers."

"Oh," said Cicely, sounding unconvinced. And then, mock-piously, "Preserve me! Just how 1890 can quite sensible people get?"

Inevitably Ruth was to dread her next meeting with Cesare. If she could have confided in Cicely or if Cicely were able to drive the car, she would have been tempted to dodge the issue and not to go over to the Casa. Though that would be to play into Agnese's hands, because she knew she was going to be guarded and watchful of everything Cesare said and did. In fact, if Agnese had wanted only to disturb their friendship instead of ending it, she had certainly succeeded in that.

But on the occasion of Cicely's next riding lesson, Cesare had worries of his own that, to Ruth's relief, had nothing to do with her.

When Cicely had gone out with the groom he confided, "It looks as if I may have an accommodation problem on my hands before long. Our landlord has had an offer from a buyer for the Casa, and he thinks that if the price is right, he may sell. Which could mean—"

"That you might have to go?" prompted Ruth. "But haven't you a lease on the place?"

"For seven years, yes. But it runs out this autumn, and it all depends on whether the buyer would renew."

"And supposing he won't?"

Cesare shrugged. "I can't run a profitable school without stables on this scale, and though we could hardly have a worse landlord, even a bad one plus a renewable lease is better than a good one without."

"Could you find out if the buyer would renew?"

"Not at this stage. So far, I gather, only feelers have been put out, and our man isn't telling much while the affair is still fluid." Cesare went on, "Agnese, of course, is very homesick for Quindereggio, our place in Calabria, and would willingly go back there if we had to. I brought her to Rome hoping to widen her circle. But she doesn't mix easily and it hasn't worked out. She says she would rather be poor in the South than moderately well off in Rome."

"Could you afford to go back if you had to?" asked Ruth.

"Just about, with what I could get for the goodwill of the school and the stock. But me—I do not want to go back. I have more reason that Agnese has for wanting to stay. For instance, friends I value, of whom you happen to be one."

Ruth said, "Thank you. Though you don't have to lose friends by going away."

"One need not. But it happens, doesn't it?"

"Sometimes," she shrugged, remembering how often it had happened to her.

Cesare sighed and looked at his watch. "I must go, I'm

afraid. I have a lesson to give. Will you stay here"—they were on the portico of the belvedere—"or join Agnese in the house?"

"I'll stay here. The sun is lovely," said Ruth, glad of any excuse to avoid another clash with Agnese. Though the other woman seemed to have done nothing yet to carry out her threat to do all in her power to come between Cesare and herself.

A few days later Erle flew in from Vienna and Cicely announced her intention of meeting him at the airport, even though Ruth had to travel to give an English lesson on the far side of the city. "I'll go out by coach, and Erle will have left his car at the airport, so that he can drive me back. I shall also wear my Roscuro and *stun* him with it," Cicely claimed.

But whether or not Erle was duly stunned, Ruth was not to learn without asking the question. For when she returned to the flat Cicely was already there, full of grievance.

"Did you meet Erle?" Ruth asked.

Cicely nodded glumly. "And might have saved myself the trouble. Because who do you think came off the plane with him, *and* all the way back by car? The Parioli woman! I knew who she was, because you had pointed her out at the party Erle gave for me. But he introduced us and—well, she practically patted me on the head! And monopolized him all the way home. Pawed him too, and swivelled her eyes. If he hadn't dropped her first before he dropped me, I'd have thrown up. I swear I would!"

Though the gossips had prepared her, Ruth had to hide her dismay. "Did they—that is, did you gather whether she had been in Vienna too?"

"Not from anything they said—they were talking in

Italian all the while. But after we had got rid of her, I asked Erle, and he said she had been there the last few days—not all the time he had."

"Oh," Ruth changed the subject. "What did Erle think of your Roscuro rig?"

Cicely brightened slightly. "Oh, he liked it. Asked if he could take a swig from the bottle of grog I must be carrying in my hip pocket. He wanted to know what you had chosen too. So I said you'd gone all upstage and refused to accept anything." Cicely slanted an apologetic look. "Did you mind my telling him? He did ask me."

Ruth bit her lip. "No. He had to know. What did he say?"

Cicely hesitated. "M'm, nothing. That is, I don't really remember."

"He must have said something." But suspecting that Cicely was shielding her from whatever caustic comment Erle had made, Ruth pressed the thing no further. If he chose to misunderstand her refusal, he wouldn't have spared her much, she knew.

CHAPTER FOUR

THEY had no further contact with Erle until the day when he telephoned the flat while Ruth was out. When she returned Cicely greeted her with "Erle rang. He plans to take us both to Siena."

"*Siena*?" Ruth echoed. "Why Siena?"

"Several reasons. Because he has to go there next week to hold some auditions. Because he says it's the best-preserved medieval town in Italy and I ought to see it. And because we should be there when they run some crazy horse race all around the main square of the place. Quite something, Erle says."

"Oh yes, the Corso del Palio. It's famous."

"What's a *palio*?"

"The banner that all the wards in the town compete for in the horse race. It's ridden by jockeys in medieval costumes, I believe. But when next week, and for how long? I have lessons to give," Ruth said.

"Leaving on Tuesday, staying three nights. Now you aren't going to make difficulties, are you?" Cicely begged. "You can duck lessons for once, can't you?"

"No, but I may be able to switch them." Ruth found her diary, took over the telephone, and set to work. She found her pupils very cooperative, and when she replaced the receiver after her last call, she felt a little thrill of anticipation. Except for one visit to Malta to see her parents, she hadn't been out of Rome since Alec died. And if Erle prove difficult over the Roscuro dress she had refused, she had Cicely as a kind of buffer state between him and herself. Yes, she was looking forward to Tuesday.

66

Erle drove fast along the motorway; they stopped for lunch on the lake of Bolsano and reached Siena in time for dinner. The narrow streets of the hilltop town were already putting themselves *en fête* for the carnival two days hence; on the day itself every window would be flying flags and tapestries, and virtually the whole population would be on the streets. To Ruth's relief, Erle was his usual urbane self. If her rebuff had said anything to him, he must have forgotten it.

The next day he was occupied, holding his auditions at one of the two music academies, and Ruth and Cicely went sightseeing in the town. In the evening after dinner Erle was taking them to a classical concert at the Chigi-Saracini Palace, an occasion that Cicely was prepared to tolerate for the sake of being able to dress up for it.

It had been a tiring day and Ruth was resting before dressing for dinner. A knock at her door heralded a pageboy with a large dress-box.

Ruth frowned at it. "I haven't ordered anything—"

"With the compliments of Signore Nash," said the boy stolidly.

"For me from the *signore*? You are sure?"

"Quite sure, *signora*. For Signora Sargent. Room 152."

"Very well, I'll take it." Mystified, Ruth gave him a tip and shut the door. She put the box on the bed and stared at it unopened, an intuition what owed nothing to reason telling her what it contained.

She broke the seals and threw back the lid. Yes, there it was, beneath the folds of tissue—the sea green model dinner dress she had coveted from the Roscuro collection.

Her first thought was instinctively feminine—It's *lovely*! Her second—how had Erle contrived to send it to

her? Her third—how dare he—when he knew from
Cicely that she had already refused to accept it? She
could not resist taking it out, shaking out its folds and
holding it against her. Even that cursory trial showed it
had been made to her measurements, and as to how that
had been achieved Cicely might know the answer.

Cicely was at her dressing table in her room when she
called "Come in" to Ruth's knock. Ruth went in and
backed against the door. Without preliminaries she
demanded, "When you told Erle I refused to take a Roscuro model from him, you said you couldn't remember
what he replied. What did he really say?"

Cicely hedged, "Oh dear, has he given it to you?"

"He sent it by a bellboy. What did he say?"

"I didn't like to tell you. You were in a state. He said,
'We'll see about that.' "

"Meaning? All right, I can guess. What then?"

"He asked if I knew your measurements, and I did
pretty well, so I gave them to him."

"Knowing, or at least guessing, what he meant to do?"

"I didn't have to guess. He told me."

"But you didn't see fit to tell *me*?"

Cicely said, "Well, I wasn't altogether on your side,
you see. I'm still not."

"Well, thanks," said Ruth coldly. "Now we know.
Where is Erle, by the way? Have you seen him since we
came in?"

"When you came up before I did, he was reading the
paper in the residents' lounge."

"Good. Let's hope he's still there." Ruth heard Cicely
say "Oh dear" again as she went out, closing the door.

Erle was alone in the lounge. At sight of her he put
aside the paper and stood. "Time for a drink?" he asked.

"Time enough, I suppose. Except that I'd rather not."

"No?" Hands in pockets, shoulders thrown back, rocking slightly on the balls of his feet, he was virile, assured, very much his own man. Against her will Ruth acknowledged it as she snapped, "No, and I've no doubt you know why!"

He laughed then. "Though I don't understand why, I can guess. You disapprove of my gesture, I take it?"

"You should have known I would. Cicely told you, and if you were in doubt you could have come to me."

"And been turned down? I make Cicely a present that she has the grace to accept. In the same spirit I try to make you one, and anyone would think I was bribing your virtue with the Koh-i-noor diamond! As a matter of interest, would you spurn flowers or a box of chocolates with the same dudgeon?"

"Of course not. But there's a very definite line between flowers and *haute couture* models offered to a— mere employee."

"This line being drawn with flowers or a dinner date on this side, and mink on the other, I suppose?"

On the defensive, Ruth muttered, "You know very well that the line is there."

He nodded. "And very proper too," he mocked. "So I'm not to have the pleasure of seeing you wear my gift tonight?"

Reckless with chagrin at his mockery, Ruth said, "I'd rather wear a sack!"

"You wouldn't, and you know it," he retorted. "There's a bit of woman in you that's itching to try that model on. But if a sack is really your preference, probably the management could oblige. Which would you like—corn, coal, or chicken meal? Or all-purpose polythene?" As Ruth flinched he laughed again. "I declare, one is tempted to bait you—you rise so beautifully," he said. Then he came over to her and took her by the wrist. "Now listen to me—"

She tried to twist free, but he held fast, steering her gently but masterfully to a chair. "Sit down and listen and see reason if you can," he ordered. "Think back to our first interview. Supposing I'd found you suitable as a hostess for Cicely in every particular, except for your appearance, what might I have done?"

"Turned me down, I suppose."

"I said 'all other things being equal,' didn't I? As it was, your taste in clothes didn't need any prompting, I judged. But if it had, I'd probably have suggested you take a cash allowance or run an account in addition to your salary, as your right."

"Well?" said Ruth unhelpfully.

"Well, this. If we'd arranged things so, I would have been picking up the bills, wouldn't I?"

"You wouldn't have sanctioned *haute couture* models for me."

"That's beside the point. You'd have bought some things on my account, or if you want to split hairs, on Mrs. Mordaunt's account. And if I choose to order a model gown for you for a special occasion, what's so improper about that? And for me tonight happens to be a special occasion. I'm well known in Sienese musical circles, and I'd like my womenfolk to do me proud. And so, will you bury that stiff pride of yours and wear the dress tonight?"

Ruth saw that she must give in. "You make it very difficult to refuse," she said.

"Good. And now the pipe of peace in the shape of a drink?"

But Ruth, who had had a sudden resolve, excused herself. In her room again she rang the hotel hairdresser to get an immediate set and evening styling, and when that had been done to her satisfaction she set about as exotic a toilette as she had ever achieved. If he wanted her to do him credit, she would do just that or die in the attempt!

Eyebrow pencil and mascara; a touch of green shadow to emphasise the green of the eyes which were the complement of her russet hair; color, no more than the faintest blush for the cheeks; pale lipstick; no jewelry but pendant earrings—and the dress, its corsage caped, its skirt tiered, its graceful fall entirely flattering.

She was giving herself a final appraisal at her mirror when the pageboy knocked again. This time he brought a square perspex box containing a spray of orchids tinged with green at the petal-tips. With it was a card— "A peace-offering. If your conscience needs salving in accepting it, note that I am sending one to Cicely too." The signature was "Erle."

Ruth couldn't remember when she had last had a gift of flowers from a man. Certainly not since she had been widowed, and these were the first orchids she had ever been given. They were the final touch the lovely dress needed. Pinning them on, she went out to meet her Cinderella evening.

It was long past midnight when she was again in her room. First she had gone with Cicely to her room to talk over the dinner, the concert, and the party of Erle's friends afterwards. But now she was at her own dressing table, her reflection looking back at her as her thoughts ranged over all that the evening had done for her . . . to her.

It had begun with a look in Erle's eyes which, turned upon her, she had never chanced upon before. She had seen them laughing, coolly appraising, mocking, reflective, but never wide with admiration of her, as they had been at his first sight of her tonight.

And in the instant of meeting them with her own and having to look away, she had learned something about herself. She hadn't gone to all her trouble to create an effect of which he would approve, out of bravado or pique. She had done it in the hope of earning just that unstinted look, wanting it to say more than she knew it could, wanting him to know how dearly she valued it.

That meant his admiration was important to her—that he had become important, too important, to her life. She could remember the glow of first knowing that she was in love with Alec, that he loved her in return and that if he asked her to marry him their life together would have the makings of a happily fitted jigsaw puzzle. Tonight there had been no such confident glow. Instead there had been a heady, nervous excitement to her awareness of Erle as another man she could love— *had* once loved in an immature, adoring way? It was an extension of that woman-to-man response to him which she had experienced in the Gardens. It was a magnetism, working only one way, which for her peace of mind she ought to resist, and could not. For on his own admission, for Erle Nash there wasn't a consummate love for any one woman; only the "jam" of a passing pleasure in the company of many of them; that, and the expedience of cultivating them for his professional ends.

And between herself and him there was not even that necessity. What was she to him but a convenient appendage to his sponsorship of Cicely? He had admitted that even his gift to her had had an ulterior motive—

that under his escort she should do him credit with his friends.

She had seen the danger of Cicely's falling for him. Why hadn't she seen it for herself? Because, she supposed, she had thought she was immunized against a second love. But she hadn't reckoned with a capacity to love which hadn't died with Alec. Nor with her woman's need to give and to share and to partner that had been starved since Alec's death. More than once she had doubted that she had it any longer. Only tonight had she rediscovered it in full measure. It was an ache in the heart, a hunger that had to be endured.

She rose from the dressing stool and slowly began to undress. There were all the tomorrows of the summer to be faced. For only when Cicely went home could the link with Erle be broken. Though just how much, she wondered, did she want it broken? When the days to autumn could be counted on her fingers, would she do the counting eagerly—or with pain?

The preliminaries of the Corso del Palio were afoot early the next day. The shops were shut, but outside booths were set up for the sale of snacks and drinks. The central square, the Piazza del Campo, where the historic horse race would be run, was ringed about with seating stands, and all the overlooking windows and even the rooftops were at a premium. Ruth and Cicely heard that because the race had some remote religious connection, each horse and jockey competing would be blessed with holy water before the start. Each of the seventeen town districts had an entrant; the betting ran high, and long before the race was due the jockeys were in their colorful costumes of doublet, breeches and hose, mingling with and being toasted by the crowds. Though the race itself would be a headlong stampede around the arena, lasting only a few minutes, the whole day was given over to a carnival that would last far into the night.

Erle's influence had obtained good viewing seats for his party and after making a morning's tour of the side-shows, they were seated in time for the parade of runners and riders before the race. They had placed their bets, Erle playing safe with the favorite, Ruth and Cicely hoping to win with outsiders.

Suddenly Cicely was staring across the arena and nudging Ruth. "Look over there—who's that? It can't be. Why, it is! It's Jeremy. Keep my place—" She was out of her seat and darting through the crowds to accost the young man in scarlet shirt and black jeans whom she had pointed out to Ruth.

Ruth identified him for Erle. "It's Jeremy Slade, the English boy I told you about," she told him as Cicely brought the young man over, plying him with questions and offering him six inches to sit down on.

"He hitchhiked all the way from Rome," she told them. But I've said he can have a lift back with us. That's all right, isn't it?" she appealed to Erle.

"Of course. We've got a spare seat, which he could have had on the way up, if he'd asked. What brought you?" Erle asked the boy.

"Well, Vivien—my sister—went down with a bit of a sore throat, and with Cicely away that left me on my own. So as I knew there's a special Sienese school of painting, I thought I should see it and at the same time make some sketches of the Palio that I can translate into color later on."

"Just to look and sketch? I hoped you'd say you came because I was here," Cicely teased him.

"Well, I did wonder if I might run into you."

Erle asked, "Where are you staying?"

"Oh, just a cheap youth place behind the Cathedral."

"But you'll join us now and have dinner with us tonight?"

"Thanks, sir. I'd like that," said Jeremy, and edged in beside Cicely, his precarious hold on the narrow slice of seat necessitating his putting his arm around her waist.

They all concentrated on the arena, where the horses were being maneuvered into position for the start. In that confined space it hadn't the slightest chance of being a fair start, but once a ragged lineup was achieved, the signal for the start was given to a deafening roar from the crowd. The race was a short mad rush. The winner, Leo, who had led all the way, had been Cicely's choice. As soon as they could edge through the crowds, she and Jeremy went off to collect her winnings.

Watching them go, Erle commented drily, "Do you really believe that story of single-minded dedication to his art? I'm afraid I don't."

Ruth laughed. "You think he really came to see Cicely?"

"Well, don't you?" Erle countered. "And what do you bet we don't see much more of them until they turn up for dinner?"

Nor did they, until Cicely and Jeremy reappeared for a meal for which no one had changed from day clothes, as the "done thing" for the evening was to tour the town on foot to see the various street parties that each district held for its particular competing jockey. After dinner Cicely and Jeremy again went off on their own and Erle and Ruth joined a party of the hotel guests for an evening on the town. It culminated in the ward which had won the banner and where the winning horse as well as his rider were being fêted at a long supper table in the main street. The banner was displayed at the head of the table and the whole scene was lighted by flares and lanterns hung from the buildings.

Afterwards Erle and Ruth strolled back towards their hotel across the Piazza del Campo, comparatively deserted now that most of the inhabitants were scattered to their own district's partying. Erle halted suddenly, pointing to the dominating tower of the Palazzo Publico, one of the main buildings on the square.

"What about taking a bird's-eye-view?" he suggested.

"From the tower? Will it still be open?" queried Ruth.

"Tonight, I should think so."

They tolled up the stairs and emerged onto the top platform where, for the first time that day, they found themselves alone in a public place. Ruth had expected that others would have had the same idea—to view the lighted town from far above its streets. She hadn't thought to be isolated there with Erle, too vividly aware of his physical nearness, while in everything else he was as remote from her as a distant star.

They moved to the parapet and stood, elbow to elbow, looking down at the lighted island that was the town. The streets were narrow canyons, beaded along their length by the light of lamp standards; the noise of the revelry, muted by distance, could still be heard.

"There are going to be some thick heads in the morning," Erle commented.

"Yes. I hope Jeremy doesn't keep Cicely out too late."

Erle said, "I wouldn't worry. He seems a fairly responsible youth. But what happens now to your theory that Cicely has an incurable crush on me? I must say she greeted the boy as if he were manna from heaven."

"Oh, she can be charming enough when she pleases; she was, with Zeppo Sforza until she dropped him." Privately Ruth thought Cicely had been using Jeremy as a foil—showing Erle that someone appreciated her, if he didn't in the way she wanted.

He said next, "I wonder you haven't been to Siena before. Did you have to wait for me to bring you?"

"I haven't been about very much at all since I've been a widow," Ruth said.

"That's a mistake. Life has to go on. And friends, travel, the odd party now and then ought to help."

"Except that a widow makes uneven numbers at parties, and anywhere she goes alone men tend to see her as fair game."

"Oh, come! You can't blame an unattached man for chancing it with an attractive widow."

"Except," said Ruth again, "that he isn't often as unattached as all that."

"The wolf type, eh? I'd judge you to have poise enough to keep that kind at a distance. And you can't run away from all men, just to escape the nasty few. That way you could become so—desiccated that you could forget how to respond to the real thing when it happens again."

Ruth hesitated. She hadn't meant the exchange to take this personal turn. For her it was dangerous. "Sometimes I think—" She stopped. Since last night the present tense wasn't honest. "There have been times when I've thought I'd already forgotten," she amended.

"You should keep in practice by giving even the most unlikely affair a chance to develop for you." Erle turned to lean back against the parapet, so that he faced her. "In that regard," he said, "I wonder if you know why I suggested we come up here, hoping we'd be alone?"

She was trembling a little. "Why did you?"

"For curiosity's sake."

"Curiosity—about me?"

"About all this," he nodded. "To see whether you're really as detached as you appear and as cloistered as you claim to be; whether your lack of the girl-tricks that most women employ—all eyes and invitation—means that you've indeed gone cold. And about that, there's only one way I know of for a man to find out—"

As he spoke, his hands went out to her shoulders and about her, drawing her to him. She drew a sharp breath, panting, her lips parted, as his mouth found hers in a long searching kiss which merged with another . . . and another to which she responded with all the pent-up, starved emotion of years. Yet not only because she was hungry for love but because, though he didn't know it, he was her love, the one man now alive who could rouse her so. Her body willow-bent to the pressure of his arms, she gave herself up to the moment; her hands wandered over his back—and clung as urgently as his until the engulfing tide of feeling ebbed; cold sanity returned, and she wrenched herself desperately free.

She smoothed down her dress and thrust back her hair. "That was—" she began.

"Unfair? Yes." Erle stood, his hands limp at his sides, his breath coming as deeply as a runner's. "I'm sorry, I shouldn't have invited it. But I didn't know—"

"Didn't know what?" she echoed sharply, afraid.

"Just how much need you've had to keep dammed up . . . bottled inside you behind the calm face you show to the world."

"You claimed that it was what you kissed me for—to find out," she accused him.

"I never expected to spring a mine at your feet. After all, I'm just any man to you. Yet that was neither an iceberg nor a lukewarm response. It was the kind of answer you'd give to a lover, and I shouldn't have probed something that has so little to do with me."

So she hadn't betrayed her secret to him after all! It gave her spirit to say distantly, "For mere curiosity, no. And what makes you think you betrayed me into the kind of answer I'd give to someone who loved me?"

"Just that, supposing I were a man with hopes of you but no certainties, I'd have been—encouraged."

"You were putting on an act. Doesn't it occur to you that I was entitled to do the same?"

His scrutiny of her face was calculating, as if he were weighing that up. "If you say so, then I hope so," he said. "I'd rather not think of your showing that degree of cooperation to any Tom, Dick, or Harry who made an experimental pass. So where do we go from here—into a state of war?"

"How can we, placed as we are in relation to Cicely? If I can forget a lack of appalling taste, I would hope you can do the same."

Erle said, "Agreed. I only asked because in war, they say you can't afford to blunder twice, and I wanted you to know that I've no intention of offending you again."

"Good," said Ruth. "Once was enough for something as meaningless as that."

Without replying, he turned with her and went ahead of her down the stairs.

CHAPTER FIVE

RUTH supposed it must be Erle's experience with temperamental women stars that enabled him to put the overnight incident behind him. She played her part too, and on the journey back their relationship could not have been more matter-of-fact.

For some time after that Erle virtually disappeared into his own circles and Ruth's and Cicely's days took up their former pattern. Then, one evening when Cicely was out and Ruth was alone in the flat, she answered the door to find Cesare there.

"Are you engaged?" he asked diffidently.

"No, I'm alone. Come in, won't you?" Ruth invited.

"Thank you."

In her sitting room he looked about him. "I've never ventured to call on you here before," he said.

"No. Will you have a drink?" For something to say in the slightly uneasy atmosphere, Ruth added, "Cicely is out, exploring on her own. But she's been gone rather a long time. I hope she'll be back soon."

"Thank you. Just a sherry." Cesare looked up at her before she sat down with her own drink. "I'm glad you're alone. That's how I hoped I might find you. Ruth—?" he said, and stopped.

"Yes?" she prompted.

"This. Don't be offended by my asking, but was Cicely with you on your trip to Siena with Erle Nash?"

Surprised, Ruth said, "Why, yes. It was to show her Siena and the Corso del Palio that Erle took us. Why?"

Cesare looked relieved. "Because Agnese heard somewhere that it was you alone whom Erle took with him."

Not believing that Agnese had heard anything of the sort, but had made it up in order to vilify her in Cesare's eyes, Ruth remarked, "Why on earth would he have done that?"

"Well," Cesare said uncomfortably, "one knows that Erle enjoys the company of women—"

"And has plenty, without wanting mine on a business trip to Siena," put in Ruth. "Yes, exactly. I didn't think it likely, and I'll certainly warn Agnese against passing such a story on." Cesare paused and sighed. "I am worried about her. Every day now she tries to persuade me to go back to Quindereggio, refusing to see that I must wait on the chance that either the Casa is not sold, or if it is, that the new landlord will renew my lease. If not, I must get the best price I can for the goodwill of the stables, and return to Calabria with the capital."

"Even then, would it be wise to live on capital?" queried Ruth.

"I think we shouldn't need to. With capital behind us we could expand our vineyards and our maize farm. If only Agnese would have a little patience!" Cesare took a drink, then said, "Ruth—?" and stopped again.

This time her heartbeat quickened a little at the appeal in his use of her name. "Yes?" she said at last.

"Don't you know?" He set aside his glass and sat forward, his hands limp between his knees. "You should. I'm not good at hiding my feelings, my hopes. You must know what I am trying to say?"

His look, his manner were too intense for her to pretend she didn't understand. She said, "If you mean you've grown fond of me, too fond, I—"

"Oh, Ruth, more than that! Fondness is for friends, but I *love* you. And if Agnese knows it of me, you must too!"

Ruth said, "Of course I've known you like me as a friend. But no more than that. Does your sister know you've come to say this to me tonight?"

"I didn't tell her so. But we are very close, she and I, and she knows it has been in my mind for some time."

"Without *my* knowing, and ... I wish with all my heart you hadn't said it now."

"Why not? To know yourself loved must be a little pleasing to you at least?"

"It is. I'm grateful and—touched. But to *be* loved isn't enough for marriage, if that's what you are asking of me. One must love in return, and I—don't."

"Why not?" he asked again. "Because you see the thought of a second marriage as a disloyalty to your first?"

Though she knew it wasn't so she clutched at the straw of that. "I don't know. Perhaps—"

He shook his head. "I don't think a husband who had cared for you could grudge you a love like mine—after years. Or is it that you really don't know, and I've rushed you? Telling you before *showing* you—As I can, if you'll let me."

He rose as he spoke and went over to her, taking her glass from her and drawing her to her feet. Then his arms went round her and he kissed her long and tenderly on her lips, her throat, her brow, evoking no pulse of response in her, no stirring of the blood.

At last she said, "Don't please—" and turned aside her head. He stood back from her, though not releasing her hands. His face looked suddenly old. "No?" he said. "It's not that I've rushed you or that you need time to learn to love again? You're telling me that there's nothing there for me at all?"

She shook her head. "Not—like that. But I like you so

much. Believe that, please. It's the rest—the rest that you want from me that isn't there."

He drew her to him again and she leaned against him gratefully. "It's not your fault. You can't help it. But I had to know," he said, his voice rough.

"Yes. Will you tell Agnese what has happened between us?" Ruth asked.

"Yes." He hesitated. "I don't like to say this to you, but I think she may be—relieved."

Remembering her pledge to know nothing of Agnese's hostile fears, Ruth said, "You think she wouldn't want you to marry me?"

"I think she doesn't want me to marry at all. She is afraid of losing me to another woman."

"And I suppose you'd rather I kept away from the Casa as much as I can in future?"

"Kept away? Oh no, that mustn't happen. I can control myself, I promise you. Say you will come again as usual?" he pleaded.

She smiled at him. "Very well, I'll come." (If he was generous enough to want her without strings, she wouldn't let Agnese drive her away!) She disengaged herself gently and stood apart from him. Just in time, as it happened, to save them both embarrassment as the door opened and Cicely, followed by Erle, came in.

"We met in the Trastevere. I was lost," Cicely explained. The two men exchanged nods and a word or two and almost at once Cesare excused himself.

"You haven't finished your drink," Erle pointed out.

"Oh—no." Cesare swallowed it at a gulp and Ruth went down with him. "Must you tell them that you have refused me? I have my pride," he said at the door, and looked relieved when Ruth said she would say nothing about it.

Cicely had gone to her room, leaving Erle alone. He refused a drink, saying he wasn't staying. "By the way," he added, "when I told you I wasn't suggesting you should send Cicely out on her own at midnight, I wasn't implying that you were free to get rid of her at any hour *up* to midnight for your own convenience."

Ruth stared. "For my convenience? What do you mean? I didn't send Cicely out anywhere."

"No? Well, I must say Fonte made as hasty an exit as if he'd been caught in a guilty assignation."

"You're implying that I got rid of Cicely because I'd made a date here with Cesare and didn't want her around?"

"Seemed likely, I thought, when we found him here, and neither of you particularly at ease. Just standing, as if you'd sold all you chairs."

"He was on the point of leaving," Ruth lied.

"And left—like the proverbial scalded cat. However, if you say so, I'd better believe that it wasn't by your design that Cicely was wandering in a maze of alleys in the Trastevere as nearly as not after dark. If I hadn't happened by in the car, she might have been there still."

"But she left here in full daylight, ages before Cesare arrived—with*out* my expecting him."

"Just chanced to call in, h'm?"

"More or less."

"Or less . . . It'd be my bet that he was hoping Cicely wouldn't be here. But why all the dudgeon? You're an attractive woman, and with all the time you spend together, you can't expect him not to have noticed it."

"All what time we've spent together?" Ruth demanded. "Just while Cicely is out riding!"

"I was quoting Agnese Fonte—that you and her brother frequently find the belvedere handy for its original purpose. She probably thinks you have designs on his title. Have you?"

"Agnese Fonte thinks nothing of the sort!" Ruth added, "And that's about as impertinent a question as you've ever asked me!"

"As if I expected you to answer it! Or as if you haven't a perfect right to entertain Fonte here if you choose."

"To hear you accuse me, no one would believe you allowed me the right," Ruth retorted.

"Ah, that was when I suspected you might be making a pawn of Cicely. I misjudged you." He paused, scrutinizing her in the way she always found disturbing—eyes narrowed, that one brow lifted. "And I ask myself, who am I to grudge you that look you were wearing when we came in?"

"What look do you mean?" But she had flushed hotly, knowing.

"The one that tells tales. The one I described to you once as a smug glow—that time, of Cicely after a session with her current boy-friend. Remember?"

He didn't wait for her answer to that. Mentally writhing, Ruth knew that it had given him the last word.

The next time she went to the Casa, Cesare was not there, but Agnese sought her out, standing before her, an agressive figure, to demand, "So you have refused my brother, he tells me?"

Ruth looked up at her. "Yes. You'll remember that I told you I would."

"Yet until he asked you, you continued to come here. And now that you have refused him, you still come! Have you no shame, *signora*? No heart? If you stayed away, he would soon forget you. I can promise you that."

"But I told you, if you remember, that if he asked me and I had to refuse him, I should do what *he* wished, and he particularly asked me to come as usual with Cicely. And as I should find it difficult to make other arrangements, I was grateful that he did," replied Ruth.

"Tch! I am not troubled by your embarrassments," Agnese snapped. "Of course Cesare is hoping you may change your mind. That's why he wants to continue to see you, and if you will not, you are being unfair to him."

Ruth said, "Isn't that for him to say? Besides, it can't be for very long. In the autumn there won't be any problem, for I shan't be coming after Cicely has gone back to England."

"The autumn! Let me tell you, *signora*, that if Cesare would listen to *my* good sense, we should not be here ourselves until then!"

Ruth tried an olive branch. "Then if the time is even shorter than I think, could you try not to see me as an enemy until then? After all, if I accepted your brother without loving him, I should do him a much greater wrong, should I not?"

But Agnese was not to be placated. "That is an 'if' that you claim has never arisen for you. You do him quite enough harm by continuing to put yourself in his way, and I warn you I shall not spare you in consequence."

"That, I wish I hadn't to believe of you," said Ruth. "But you didn't spare me, did you, in telling Cesare that I had gone alone with Signore Nash to Siena? Fortunately I was able to tell him myself that it wasn't so."

"I thought the facts were as I said. After all, for Signore Erle Nash, it wouldn't be the first time—"

"But with me, at no time," Ruth denied crisply. "And

I'd have hoped, *signora*, that you would be above such empty slander."

Agnese looked beyond Ruth's shoulder. "It depends on what one has at stake," she said loftily. "For me, it is Cesare's happiness."

It was clear that she honestly believed so. But when Ruth said quietly, "I care about that too," she spoke to the empty air. Agnese had stalked away.

It was about a week later, when Cicely was out shopping with Ruth, that Cicely lingered at a street newsstand, walked on a few steps, then turned back.

She fingered a flamboyant, glossy magazine from a pile. *"Vorrei questo. Quanto?"* she asked the news vendor. He told her the price; she paid him, and brought the weekly to Ruth.

Ruth said, *"Lo Sussurro?* It means *The Whisper.* It's a scandal sheet—usually seven or eight articles, mostly all conjecture and all pretty scurrilous. Even Royalty doesn't escape. What do you want with that?"

"This," said Cicely, showing the cover, at which Ruth gasped. She was looking at a blown-up flashlight photograph in colour of herself and Erle at a restaurant table, the pupils of their eyes pinpointed by the flash, their heads close together. They were laughing.

Cicely said, "I thought it would stop you in your tracks. It must have been at Siena."

"But—but—! You were there as well, two nights, and Jeremy and you the other!"

"They seem to have cut me out. It was the second night. Look, you're wearing the Roscuro dress you were so prickly about," Cicely pointed out.

"Yes, I remember. But we were all laughing just then. This makes it look—" Ruth read the caption—"Who is the attractive redhead with Erle Nash at Siena's Annual Palio? See inside for all that *Lo Sussurro* knows of the answer." Then she handed the paper back to Cicely. "All right, I can wait for nonsense like that until we get home," she said tersely.

"They might have taken *me* with Erle," Cicely mourned.

As soon as they reached the flat she produced the magazine again for Ruth. "What does it say inside?"

Ruth found a paragraph on a gossip page. Under the heading, "Our Cover Picture," she read aloud, "The lady is the latest newcomer to Erle Nash's circle, though not of it in the professional sphere. She is English, a widow; *Lo Sussurro* understands she is his childhood friend, now vividly returned to his life. She is currently playing hostess to his protege, a very young blond. They are both often to be seen in his company, and *Lo Sussurro* is curious enough to wonder which of milord's favorites may expect to take a minor place in order to make room for one of them or both. Or can he keep them all happy?"

Cicely said, "So they do know about me. A very young blond, indeed! I wonder who told them all that?"

"Who knew we went to Siena with Erle?" Ruth asked.

"Well, the Fontes, Jeremy and Vivien Slade. Or Erle may have told a lot of people," Cicely offered.

"And they can make—*this*—out of it. How dare they?" Ruth exploded. "They know so much about Erle that they must know what our connection is, and that it's perfectly innocent!"

"Making trouble for trouble's sake," agreed Cicely. At the sound of a car stopping, she looked out of the window. "Erle. Coming here. Now we'll see what he has to say about it all!"

She went down to let him in and bring him up. Erle said, "I've brought you two tickets for the open-air *Aida* at Caracalla tonight. It's the most ambitious opera they do there, all color and spectacle and a huge cast. So don't turn up your pretty nose Cicely love, just because you think it will be highbrow. It's something that your mama will expect you to have seen."

"Aren't you coming too?" she asked.

"No. Sorry. I've got to go to hear a new singer of *lieder* at the Eliseo Theatre, with a view to signing her up." Noticing the magazine on the table where Ruth had discarded it, he picked it up. "*Lo Sussurro,* eh? Whose bedside reading? Yours?" he asked Ruth.

"No. I bought it," Cicely told him. "Look at the cover, if you want to know why."

He flicked back to the cover and emitted a longdrawn "We—ll!" He glanced at Ruth, turned to the inside paragraph, and read it through quickly, then skittered the magazine from him.

"Seems I'm supposed to have added some reserves to my alleged harem," he commented.

"Can't you do anything about it?" Cicely demanded.

He shook his head. "Freedom of the press, and the Italian Press is more free than most. *Lo Sussurro* practically writes its own license for that type of speculation. Besides, it manages to sail just the safe side of the truth. I did take you both to Siena, and as I have to be seen to enjoy showing off my professional clients in a social way, both my public and private lives are anybody's business, making it inevitable that there'll be guesswork as to how far my intimacy with any woman goes." He looked across at Ruth. "I'm sorry you had to get involved, but that's your penalty for mixing with a piece of gossip-fodder like me."

"It isn't your fault," Ruth said a shade grudgingly. "But how do they get their news and pictures? Do they follow you round with a camera or something?"

"Well, when their newshounds heard about our Siena jaunt, they would have got their local correspondent to angle a picture so that it fitted the story, I suppose."

"But how would they hear about your movements?"

Erle shrugged. "Anyone's guess."

"For instance, would they accept the information from anyone of the ordinary public who told them?"

"Probably, yes. *And* be willing to pay for it, if they thought they could make something spicy out of using it. Why?"

"I only wondered," said Ruth with studied careless- ness. But her question had had purpose. She knew now that she had indeed made an enemy of Agnese Fonte. Agnese, Ruth felt sure, hadn't been content to tell her garbled story to Cesare, she had found a much wider audience for it.

Two weeks later, on the eve of Cicely's seventeenth birthday, Ruth went shopping for a present for her.

She knew what Cicely would like and where to buy it—a Parigi cameo brooch from a jeweler on the Spanish Square, and she was selecting one from the tray pro- duced by the salesman when she was aware of the woman being served at the next showcase-counter. It was Stella Parioli. She looked up and across as Ruth did; their eyes met and Stella acknowledged Ruth with a nod and a patronizing smile. But a minute or two after she had turned back to the spread of jewelry before her, she beckoned with an exquisitely gloved finger.

Surprised, Ruth excused herself to her salesman.

"So kind of you, *signora*," murmured Stella. "I am having difficulty in choosing, and it always helps to have the opinion of another woman, don't you think? Now, which would you select, supposing you were making the choice for yourself?"

Ruth looked in some embarrassment at the cushions and trays, displaying a dozen or so jeweled sprays and clasps. "I think it would depend on what I wanted to wear it with, *signora*," she said.

"Oh—for the lapel of a suit, or to light up a plain black gown, you know? I tried this one; and this—" Stella allowed the assistant to hold each of two sprays against her suit "—but somehow they lack something. Oh—that? Yes indeed—" as Ruth touched a gleaming spray of leaves and flowers, each flower with a tiny pearl at its heart "—that's quite lovely, isn't it? I think—"

"Allow me, *signora*—" the salesman addressed Ruth as he held the spray against the breast of her sundress to enable Stella to judge it.

"Yes indeed," she said again. "I'll have that. How much is it?"

The man named a price at which Ruth barely suppressed a gasp. "I'm afraid I've chosen something very expensive for you," she said.

"It shows your good taste. Thank you, *signora*. I am grateful," Stella said graciously, and then to the man who had asked if the sale was to be cash or account, "Neither. It is a present to me. I was to meet Signore Nash here to choose it. But he is late and I have an appointment to keep. So put it aside, will you, and when he comes in, tell him I've chosen and ask him to collect it?"

"Of course, *signora*." She was bowed out with some

ceremony, and Ruth returned to her own counter. Puzzled at first, she now felt it likely that Stella had wanted her advice rather less than she had wanted to advertise the fact of Erle's gift. Ruth had chosen Cicely's cameo and was waiting to have it wrapped when Erle came in, looked about him, noticed her, and came over to her.

"I was supposed to meet Parioli here at noon. Have you seen anything of her?" he asked.

"Yes, she—" Ruth began, but stopped to allow Stella's assistant to explain what had happened. He produced the spray in its case for Erle to see. Erle said, "All right. Very choice. I'll pay cash," and took out his checkbook. As he wrote, "You say you did see Stella?"

"Yes, I was buying a brooch for Cicely. It's her birthday tomorrow."

"I know. There'll be flowers and a present—an evening bag—for her by messenger in the morning. Were you and Stella speaking to each other? You met at the party I gave for Cicely, didn't you?"

"Yes, and she called me over, asking me to help her to choose your present to her," Ruth told him drily.

His eyebrow quirked up. "Did she indeed? Propping open the lion's jaws in readiness for my head with a vengeance!"

"What do you mean?"

"Well, you disapprove heartily, I take it? Expensive trinkets being very much on the wrong side of that permissible line which you draw between chocolates and mink?"

"By my code, yes. I've no right to judge for anyone else."

"But you're judging like mad, all the same. Your very backbone is rigid with censure. But if you've finished now, may I drop you anywhere? My car is just outside."

"If it's not out of your way you can drive me home," Ruth told him.

"Right."

They had reached the flat and she was getting out when he asked, "What's Cicely doing to celebrate tomorrow?"

"Jeremy is taking her and his sister to dinner, and to a nightclub to dance."

"And you?"

"I shall have a quiet evening to myself. I shall probably wash my hair."

He turned in his seat and looked up at her, standing by the car. "Don't wash your hair," he said. "Ask me to come round instead."

"You? Of course, if you— Why?" she asked in surprise.

"Not with any motive that *Lo Sussurro* could find suspect. May I come? What time are the youngsters leaving?"

"At about eight, I expect."

"Then I'll come some time after that. Don't plan to feed me, I shall have dined. O.K.?"

She nodded yes and he drove off.

Ruth was in a flutter of nerves before he arrived, as she went about plumping cushions and putting out drinks. She couldn't think why he should actually invite an evening of the flippant exchanges into which he and she were usually drawn.

When he came he accepted a drink and walked about with it, as he had done on his first visit to the flat. Ruth watched him, feeling, as always, the distance between them to be immense. As if beyond all reason, she loved some one on the far side of a great gulf! Someone she knew only by sight and in daydreams; someone who didn't know her at all.

At last he took a chair and sat facing her. "You know, it's a pretty rare experience for me to spend an evening with a woman I feel I can talk to, and she to me, without the undertow drag of the man-woman thing between us," he said.

"You hope that of this evening, you mean?" said Ruth.

"With you, yes. It's a rapport that no Latin women understand. For them it has to be charged, however slightly, with allure, felt, if not by both, at least by one. Or perhaps I'm wrong; perhaps for any woman the sexual challenge bit has to be got out of the way before she can relax into friendship with any given man. As you and I could be said to have got it out of the way at Siena, don't you think?"

Ruth reddened deeply at the shaming memory. "Did we?" she said.

"I understood so. You dismissed it as meaningless, and in that context, I agree it was. It was an experiment I shouldn't have made, and it's behind us. But supposing I said that, if I knew you better, I feel I could talk to you as I would to a man, would you be flattered or offended?"

She knew the answer to that. "I'd be flattered," she said.

"And I'd mean it that way. But most women would be outraged—they'd conclude that I was implying they had no sex appeal, and label me as a boor. Fortunately I got the message pretty early in my professional career, and I've exploited it successfully ever since. I've learned how and when to turn on the male-versus-female heat."

"You make yourself sound very calculating and cold-blooded," said Ruth.

He shrugged. "Just self-preserving. I've a living to get that's all-dependent on my management of people, particularly of women. And though I may be case hardened by now, I enjoy my work—don't get me wrong about that."

Ruth thought for a moment. "You know, I doubt if I'd react very favorably to what you admit is so much—technique," she said.

He smiled his one-sided smile. "Ah, I don't let the working part show!"

"And isn't there a risk that so much of what you once called 'jam' could—sort of—warp your aptitude for . . . the real thing?"

"If by 'the real thing' you mean love and marriage, why not say so?" Without answering her question, he laughed. "Do you realize how busily we're proving my point? That even you and I, pledged to a platonic evening, are already launched on a classic he-and-she argument? I think instead you'd better fill me in on what happened to you after you left Charlwood. It'd be safer."

His laugh and his words were a cool breath of sanity which she ought to have welcomed, and could not. She longed to tell him that, proud as she would be to feel herself treated like a man-friend, at heart she was no different from his "most women," as fully aware as they of that man-to-woman pull which he admitted to exploiting.

But she managed a shrug and a smile as she said, "By your standards it was all rather dull. I only ever had one job—in the foreign section of a bank. That was how I met Alec—across the counter when he used to come in on business for his firm. We fell in love and then we married and came out here. Circumstances were difficult at first—the language, no friends, shortage of money—but essentially nothing was difficult. We used to—." She had meant to give Erle the merest précis of those years, but suddenly, her memories of them were vividly pictorial. She found herself describing them with tenderness and wry humour.

When she finished speaking Erle said, "You're describing a completely different world from mine. You did nothing spectacular; you went hardly anywhere, except on the beaten track; asked if you could pick out one highlighted event or one particular day, I doubt if you could name it, could you?"

"Of course I could. There were plenty of those," she said. "But it was all the ordinary days, the ones that rolled over our heads without our noticing them and that I couldn't name now, even by the years they were in, that made our happiness—until it stopped."

"Well, thank you for telling me," said Erle. "Is your husband's grave in Rome?"

She shook her head. "No. It was—" She checked, her lip quivering, and Erle looked away, until she said with forced brightness, "And now don't you owe me your life story?"

"Another time, perhaps. Not now. It's longer than yours, for one thing, and I couldn't expect you to appreciate the necessity for some of the details." He nodded across at her small record player. "Have you got some good records? May I hear some?"

"If I have anything you like. Come and choose," Ruth invited, reading his change of subject as a deliberate switch-off from the personal.

They spent a companionable hour or so, listening to

and discussing music. Of various famous and eccentric conductors and star performers Erle had some anecdotes which hadn't reached the newspapers, and their talk didn't touch anything personal again until Erle was about to leave.

He took Ruth's hand, weighing it lightly in his own. "You know, I ought to have been better acquainted with you when you had freckles that showed all across your nose," he said.

She shook her head. "The Sixth didn't want to know about Form Four B."

"Was there anyone in your lot who used to walk you home from parties and put notes in your desk?"

Ruth dimpled at the memory of a contemporary admirer whose very name she couldn't recall. "Yes, there was someone," she said.

"Then perhaps it's as well I didn't make contact. I might have been jealous."

"Of freckles and a ponytail and rusty eyebrows? Not you!" she scoffed.

"Oh, I don't know. I was young enough to be romantic, and I wasn't as wary of entanglements as I am now."

"Meaning you couldn't be jealous now if you tried?"

He considered the question. "I suppose not. I hope not. Jealousy is a deplorable waste of spirit anyway, isn't it?"

(She would not betray to him that she knew how cruel—and how demanding of spirit jealousy could be.) "I don't really know," she said. "Alec never gave me any cause."

"Then we're two lucky people, aren't we? We belong to ourselves." Erle dropped her hand, adding, "Meanwhile, thank you for a blessedly detached evening. They're rare."

When he had gone, Ruth leaned her head back against the wall of the tiny vestibule. They hadn't quarrelled; they had hardly even skirmished, and she could go to bed in the warm glow of his praise of her as a friend. She wanted more, but if that was all he had for her she must settle for that. Tomorrow she would wake up happier than she had for a long time.

CHAPTER SIX

CICELY was to take a poor view of Erle's evening with Ruth.

"Why couldn't he have come when I was here?" she wanted to know.

"It was probably one night that he happened to have free," said Ruth. "By all accounts he doesn't have many."

"But what did you talk about? What did you do?"

"We talked about all sorts of things. About school for one. And we played some records. I asked him if he would stay until you came home, but he said that would be too late to keep me up, so he left at about 11."

"What a mad, mad whirl!" said Cicely in a sour grapes tone. "I must say that was a nice birthday for me, that was. Jeremy and I had a fight, and we aren't speaking now."

"But he saw you home, I hope?"

"Oh yes. We dropped Vivien at their *pensione* and it was on the way here that we had the fight. What happened was that Zeppe Sforza was at the same nightclub with a party, and we joined forces. One reason was that we needed a boy for Vivien, but Jeremy said I danced with all the others much more than with him. I said he knew what he could do with silly jealousy like that, and he said he ought to have known what a lightweight I was, the way I'd dropped Zeppe when he came along, and he wished me luck with my next, or with Zeppe again, if Zeppe was fool enough to have me. Anyway, *he* was through. I said some more in the same vein, and that was that. I suppose Vivien will take his side. But who cares? Erle hasn't gone riding with me since I took up with them, so now I'll make the earliest date with him that I can."

Ruth said mildly, "It's a pity about Jeremy though. You seemed to have a lot in common. And choosing between Zeppe and Jeremy, I'd say there was a good deal more future in Jeremy. He's English, for one thing. You wouldn't have to leave him behind."

"And who has to choose between Zeppe Sforza and Jeremy? They're not the only males in Rome. And who wants a future—at seventeen? Look—*that* for Jeremy Slade and all his works!" Cicely raged petulantly as she ripped from her sketching-block a black-and-white drawing of the Fountain of Trevi, and tore it up.

The next news Ruth had of the rift came from Jeremy himself who caught her up one morning in the city. Hands in trouser pockets, he slouched along beside her, making an earnest business of keeping one foot on the pavement, the other in the gutter. He broached the subject first. "What's Cicely doing with herself these days? Has she taken up with that lout Sforza again?" he wanted to know.

"Not that I know of," said Ruth.

"With who, then?" Jeremy demanded with a fine scorn of grammar.

"She hasn't mentioned anyone or brought them home. Is there no hope the two of you could make it up?"

"Not while she's got this fool thing about older men." I suppose you know she's carrying a torch for that uncle figure, Erle Nash? I tried to laugh her out of it once, by telling her she'd only got a yen for him because he was a sugar-daddy who was out of reach. But she said that was all *I* knew; that he kissed her when they went riding together and that he'd welcome her at his apartment any time. Is that true? *Does* she go to his rooms?"

Remembering the evidence of Cicely's compact in Erle's desk drawer, Ruth felt a little sick. "Neither of them has ever told me so," she said.

"Well, would they, if—?" Jeremy doubted. "I mean— sorry if he's a friend of yours, but he is supposed to have a reputation, isn't he?"

Ruth took him up on that. "Either you think Erle is out of Cicely's reach, or you suspect him of playing around with her. You can't have it both ways. I'll certainly ask her is she's ever been to his apartment alone, but I think she'll say no."

"Then why did she tell me she had?" said Jeremy unarguably as they reached the shop Ruth was going to. They parted.

When Ruth put her question there was a moment's pause. Then Cicely said, "No," convincingly.

"Well, I met Jeremy this morning, and he says you told him you were always welcome there," Ruth told her.

"Oh well—" Cicely's shrug admitted it. "What if I did? He'd insulted *me*, so I let him have it. Anyway, if he wants to know anything about me now, why doesn't he come and ask me himself?"

"Would you be glad to see him if he did?"

"No."

This exchange, whatever it did for Jeremy's chances, satisfied Ruth that Cicely's denial had been the truth and that her boast to Jeremy had been just so much empty air. There was still the mystery of the compact, but Ruth decided against appearing to throw doubt on the girl by confronting her with it.

So matters rested until, returning one evening from

giving a late lesson, Ruth found that Cicely was still out. There was nothing remarkable about that, if she could have been with Jeremy or Vivien, or had left a note saying where and with whom she was and when she expected to be back. But there was no note. Ruth looked at her watch. It was nearly ten o'clock and it was dark. Ruth made herself a light meal and ate uneasily, sitting on the edge of her chair.

Whom could she ring for advice or in search of Cicely? Erle, obviously. The Slades. Zeppe Sforza's home? Cicely's French girl-friend had gone home a week or two ago, so she was "out." The Casa? No, Cicely couldn't have got there without the car and she wouldn't have gone at night. Anyone else?

Before she rang anybody, Ruth went to see if, by elimination, she could find out how Cicely had dressed. The answer seemed most likely to be wedge-heeled evening sandals, velvet evening slacks, and the embroidered halter-top she usually wore with the latter. So she was not in day clothes and in that rig must have gone by taxi. But where?

Ruth's call to Erle's apartment elicited no answer. Next she rang his office, expecting no result, and got none. When she rang the Slades' *pensione* Vivien came to the telephone. She was concerned but surprised that Ruth should ask. Neither of them had seen Cicely, as Ruth must know, since the night of her birthday. Jeremy was out, but Vivien knew where he was and Cicely certainly wasn't with him.

Ruth cradled the receiver. Where next? The police? The hospitals? She rejected the idea for the moment. She would ring Erle again—and again. He had to come home some time, though she feared it might be in the small hours. Meanwhile, Cicely would surely come back safely; apologetic, Ruth hoped, but with some reasonable excuse. A second and a third call to Erle were both abortive. Ruth fidgeted about the flat, listening, tensed, for every car that sounded as if it might be stopping. None did. The time became 11 o'clock; then half-past, then midnight. Vivien called back once to see if Cicely had returned, and then, much later, the telephone rang again.

Ruth snatched at it. It was Jeremy, his voice staccato, sounding annoyed.

"I was in bed," he said. 'The night porter had to bring me to the phone. Cicely—"

"Cicely? Wh—where?"

"At Erle Nash's apartment."

"But—but she can't be! I've phoned there more than once and there's been no reply!"

"Well, that's where she is. Says she's been there all evening, and they're having a whale of a time."

"I don't believe it! And why should she call you?"

"To get even, is my guess. She knew I didn't believe her when she said she was on those terms with him. I suppose she wanted to show me, and made it nearly one o'clock in the morning as sure proof."

Ruth said, "I'm sure she can't be there with Erle. He wouldn't have kept her until this hour."

"He may think you know where she is, and so wouldn't worry."

"He'd still answer his own telephone."

"You'd think so," Jeremy agreed. Then, "I thought to warn you that Cicely sounded a bit—odd."

"How—odd?"

"As if. . . .Well, her words were a bit slurred, and she was giggling." Jeremy sounded embarrassed.

Ruth took his meaning. "Oh no!" she breathed. "Erle

can't have allowed her to—" She broke off. "I'm going over there," she said.

"At this hour? Do you want someone with you?"

"No. Go back to bed. I'll go in the car. It'll be something I can do, instead of sitting about and worrying myself sick. Good night, and thank you, Jeremy. I'll phone you in the morning."

There was still plenty of traffic in the streets. On summer nights Rome never slept. As Ruth drove, though her worry was uppermost, she knew that for all her protestations to Jeremy, she was almost equally revulsed by the fear that she might indeed find Erle and Cicely together, both of them in a state of no particular concern for her. For one thing, how could Cicely possibly be in Erle's apartment if he weren't there? She couldn't have got in.

When Ruth reached the building the mystery deepened. To her knocks on the door of Erle's apartment there was no answer and no sound from within. Back in the street again, she reconnoitered; none of the windows on that level was lighted. At last she drove back by the way she had come and put the car in the garage. She was using the key on her own door when suddenly it was opened from within and Erle stood there, a figure of granite.

"Where've you been?" he demanded.

Too taut with anxiety to show relief at the sight of him, Ruth retored, "And were have *you?* I've been over to your apartment. Where's Cicely?"

"In bed." He stood aside to allow Ruth to pass and closed the door behind her.

"In bed?"

"Sleeping it off."

"Sleeping *what* off?" But Ruth thought she knew.

"Her flirtation with my liquor cabinet. She knows her

limit is about one glass of wine, but she seems to have had herself a ball."

"And you let her? How could you?" Ruth accused.

"Let her?" he exploded. "I wasn't there!"

"You must have been! Otherwise how could she . . . !" He made a gesture of exasperation. "Come up, and I'll give it to you—in words of one syllable, if necessary."

He followed her up into the living room, where she took off the cape she had flung over her shoulders, and turned to face him.

"Now," she said belligerently, "you invited Cicely for the evening; you may or may not have known she didn't tell me where she was going, but you let her drink too much; you let your telephone ring, and whether or not you were there all the time, you must have been there some of it, because she couldn't have got in otherwise."

Erle's small push on her shoulder surprised her and thrust her into a chair. He remained standing.

"That's all you know," he said. "At some time or another I must have told Cicely that my woman goes back in the evening, to cook for me if I'm going to be in or to set the table and leave something for me in the fridge if I'm not sure. Tonight Cicely arrived, says she persuaded Maria that I was expecting her, and when Maria left, Cicely stayed on. That would have been—"

"Something before ten, which was when I came home," supplied Ruth.

"Oh, long before ten. She admits to have been there for nearly five hours, waiting for me. Expecting me every minute and afraid it might be you looking for her; she didn't answer the telephone when it rang two or three times. She mixed her drinks well on an empty stomach, trying a little of everything I had and not liking any of it except a *crème de cacao* liqueur, which tasted of chocolate. I, incidentally, was dining with Parioli, and after taking her home arrived back about half an hour ago to find Cicely drowsy and maudlin. And if you think I roused her with a 'Sleeping Beauty' kiss, you're wrong. I *shook* her awake and got the story out of her. Then I brought her home—your car and mine must have crossed on the way—and maneuvered her to the point of bed if not actually into it."

"Did she tell you," Ruth asked, "that well after midnight she rang Jeremy Slade to tell him that you and she were whooping it up together?"

"I tell you," Erle repeated, "I wasn't back until around one o'clock. Anyway, why should she do that?"

"To impress him, Jeremy thought. He phoned me to tell me where she was. And even if—" reaction from strain was working Ruth up "—even though she did the whole thing herself, you're not entirely without blame, you know."

"Indeed? How come?"

"You should know. I've told you. You've encouraged her, flattered her, kissed her, then dropped her flat for a while after I'd protested. You—you turn charm on and off like a light. You *use* it on people."

"And on whom do I practise this electric exercise?"

"On Cicely, for one. And she can't take it. She lets herself believe all it seems to say. So she thinks she has only to show willing, and you'll take it further."

"And make herself a thorough nuisance to all concerned. Look—tonight it was on the cards whether, before taking Parioli home, I took her first to my place to collect an opera score she'd lent me. What would she have thought of finding Cicely there?"

"I'm sure you could have reassured her. After all, it's a hazard you must have encountered before now."

Erle's expression hardened. "And what the merry hell do you mean by that?" he demanded.

"Well, you make so little secret of the number of strings to your bow that you must expect to get your lines crossed sometimes." Quite reckless now, Ruth added, "And while we're on the subject, this isn't the first time you've had Cicely in your apartment, is it?"

"Alone—the only time she has been there was tonight."

"Then how did she manage to leave her powder compact there? A blue enamel-and-silver square thing—I saw it in a drawer of your desk the morning you asked me to breakfast."

Erle's stare was hostile. "You saw it there, and you didn't have the honesty to ask me about it?"

"I've never asked Cicely either."

"Why not?"

"I didn't want to watch either of you lying."

"But you didn't forgive us. You stored it up, making a canker of it. I wish you were of an age to be made to write out the *'Honi soit qui mal y pense'* bit 100 times. It might teach you charity. In fact, I found that thing in my car one day; threw it in the drawer, meaning to return it to Cicely and forgot it until now. Does that satisfy your moral fears, Mrs. Grundy?"

Ruth flared at that. "You put Cicely in my charge, and it's not grundyism to care what happens to her!"

"Well, she's in no danger from me, and never has been. I refuse to shoulder blame for her adolescent crazes—they'll have to burn themselves out. I don't collect scalps—of teenagers or anyone else for the sake of counting them on my belt. I look for some poise and balance in the women I cultivate as my friends, of whom, incidentally, I thought you were one. Seems I was wrong. Or perhaps it is that the most stable of women can call on the vituperation of a fishwife when they have a grievance and a whipping-boy handy. Up to men to make allowances, I suppose."

His tone withered Ruth's like a frost. "You don't have to make allowances for me," she said. "When I'm in the wrong, I'm not above making my own amends. I'm sorry I misjudged you on both counts. But the evidence I had tonight seemed against you, and up to date that other time, I think your encouragement of Cicely had given me cause."

She waited. But when he didn't offer her any matching generosity of his own, she stood up. "Will you go now, please? Before I go to bed myself, I'd like to see that Cicely is asleep and comfortable."

As she moved toward it, he put himself between her and the door. "I hope you'll do nothing of the sort," he said. "Leave her alone. You've had your say with me; your beef with her can wait until the morning."

"I wasn't going to—" Ruth protested. But not waiting for her to finish, he turned on his heel and left her.

The street door slammed, the car moved off, and Ruth stood, fighting a lump in her throat. It threatened to well up in tears of strain and self-pity and regret for something lost to her that she could have kept, if only she had bridled her tongue—Erle's regard.

After a difficult scene with Cicely, Ruth exerted her authority by insisting that Cicely should phone Jeremy herself.

"I promised to," Ruth told her. "But you'll do it instead."

Cicely grumbled, "Why should I?"

"To apologize for getting him out of bed in the middle

of the night to tell him a pack of lies," Ruth replied crisply. But she thought it tactful to absent herself when Cicely went to the telephone and Cicely didn't volunteer what had passed between Jeremy and herself.

That evening, from Erle to Cicely there were flowers—a tight posy of pink rosebuds—which she dismissed as "the least he could do after the way he treated me last night," but which Ruth suspected she was willing to take as his closing of an incident she was only too glad to forget. There was no message for Ruth, and the next news they had of him was a telephone call, which Cicely took, to say that he was flying to New York that night and would be in touch when he returned.

While Cicely was not seeing Jeremy, she was willing to give more time to "culture" and Italian lessons from Ruth. But on a morning when Ruth had planned a visit to the art galleries of the Casina Borghese, Cicely asked diffidently, "Would you mind very much if I went sketching with Jeremy in the Trastevere instead? We could go to the Casina another time, couldn't we?"

"Why yes," Ruth said, and then, "When did you two make up?"

"I don't know that we have. He'll have to watch his step. But he and Vivien were having coffee at the next table on Vittorio Veneto yesterday, and he came and asked me, and I said yes, if *you* were willing. So shall I go?"

"Do," said Ruth. "The El Grecos, the Titians and the Rubens have been in the Casina for a good many years now, and I guess they can wait a bit longer."

That same morning, while Cicely was out, Vivien Slade called to see Ruth. "Jeremy doesn't know about this," Vivien said. "But he wouldn't go riding at the Casa while Cicely was mad at him, in case they met there. And now he'd like to go again, but he won't ask her if you'd give us a lift again, in case she snubs him. So I decided to ask you myself. Only must you tell Jeremy I have? I mean, could you ask us—sort of out of the blue, you know?"

Ruth laughed. The intrigues of the young, designed to "save face!" "Of course," she told Vivien. "I'll ring you tonight and suggest we go over tomorrow. Will that do?"

"Oh thanks," said Vivien. And then. "By the way, did you know that the Casa was to be sold?"

"Yes. Cesare Fonte told me some time ago."

"And that Erle Nash has bought it?"

Ruth's head jerked up in surprise. *"Erle?* No! How do you know?"

"It was in the paper this morning. Just a paragraph. What paper do you take? It'll probably be in yours too."

Ruth said, *"La Cazzetta.* But it isn't delivered. We collect it, and I haven't been out. What did yours say?"

"Just that he was 'understood to have acquired' the Casa Rienzi for an 'unnamed sum in the region of—' oh, I don't remember, but billions of lire, and then a bit of history about the Casa, and that was all. But I thought you'd know," said Vivien.

Ruth shook her head. "It must have only just gone through. Erle is in New York now, and as Cicely twisted her ankle and couldn't ride, we haven't been to the Casa for two weeks. But I'll ring you, and if Jeremy is willing, we'll all go over tomorrow, and Cesare will tell me, I'm sure. Wait. If you're going, I'll come with you and collect my paper. I'd like to see what it says."

Evidently the item of news had been syndicated, for the wording in *La Gazzetta* was identical with Vivien's version, as far as it had gone. Ruth's first puzzled reaction was to wonder why Erle should be interested in buying the Casa at all; her second, to wonder how the sale would affect Cesare's future.

But this even Cesare did not know. When the three youngsters had gone off with the groom, he said, "I've been waiting to let you know that it was Erle who was in the market for the place, and now the sale has gone through."

"He hasn't mentioned his interest in it to us. Why do you suppose he bought it?" asked Ruth.

Cesare shrugged. "As an investment, perhaps. He could more than treble his money any time, if he sold or developed the grounds for building. Although—"

Ruth cut in, "But how will you stand? Is he willing to renew your lease?"

"He won't say either way yet. He is within his rights of course, until my lease does run out in the autumn. I shall press him to let me know before then, but he can't throw me out *until* then."

Ruth remembered the point at which she had interrupted earlier. "You began to say 'Although—something,' " she prompted Cesare.

"Yes," he agreed. "I was going to mention that last week before I had heard the sale was clinched, I had a surprise visit from Signora Parioli."

"But she rides here regularly, doesn't she?"

"Not this time. She said she had a favor to ask of me—she wanted me to show her over the house. Well, not knowing then who the prospective buyer was, I asked her if she was interested from that point of view. At which she laughed and said no—that she was only acting from a woman's curiosity and from having promised a friend that she would give her opinion of the property. That being so, she knew she was asking a favor, but she hoped I would agree."

"And did you?"

"Well, of course, though I needn't have done, as she hadn't come with any authority." Cesare smiled ruefully. "I'm afraid she didn't think much of the interior. The rooms were cold, and the decorating deplorable. I went on the defensive for it—pointed out that it needed much more gracious living than Agnese and I could afford for it. And somehow, from the way she continually said, 'I would do—this, or that,' by way of changes, I got the impression that she had a good deal more particular interest than mere curiosity."

"She had also said she was viewing it for a friend," Ruth reminded him.

He nodded. "Yes, that too. And when I heard later that Erle had bought it, a possible reason for her coming to view it clicked into place in my mind."

Ruth suppressed a little shiver of apprehension and jealousy. "You think Erle may have sent her?"

"It's difficult not to think so. She certainly had the manner of a woman who might be planning for her own future comfort and pleasure."

Thinking back to Erle's gift of jewelery to Stella, Ruth protested, "But she couldn't possibly accept a *house* from Erle!"

"No. Unless—" Cesare stopped, and Ruth had to force herself to meet his unaware gaze.

"You mean—unless he's going to marry her and install her here?"

"At the moment, that seems a probable explanation," he agreed. And couldn't know, she thought, how much her own question had cost her.

Later she was to reflect painfully that if she hadn't wantonly destroyed Erle's impression of her as a friend he could talk to he might have confided in her his change of heart in the matter of marriage. Even that—almost—might be preferable to the gulf that yawned between them now. When he came back to Rome, for appearances' sake and for Cicely's, they would meet and talk *across* Cicely, as it were. There would be nothing else to link them. Nothing.

It was on a day when the papers had carried a picture captioned, "Erle Nash, in New York on professional business, entertains a cosmopolitan party of friends at the Stork Club," that Cicely, having pointed out to Ruth that Stella Parioli was of the party, suddenly announced, "You know, I think I've had enough of Erle."

"Had enough of him?" Ruth echoed.

"Had enough of him as a pin-up, I mean. Grown out of him, if you like. I had a monumental crush on him and I haven't any more. You have to work so hard at crushes for just crumbs in return. It's a sort of one-way traffic. Or haven't you ever had one? Wouldn't you know?"

"Yes, I've had one," said Ruth. "A long time ago."

"And suddenly, or perhaps not all that suddenly," Cicely pursued her theme, "it's brought home to you that you're getting nowhere fast. That if they notice you at all, they're only being kind. That they pinch your cheek or pull your hair and even kiss you as they'd kiss a six-year-old. Take Erle—I've even stopped being jealous about him. He could take up with my best friend tomorrow, and I shouldn't care. Odd, isn't it?"

"Odd?" thought Ruth. "The understatement of the year where I'm concerned! I, wholly wrong about the depth of your feeling for him; he cynically right. I, shielding you from him at the cost of his friendship for me; he, knowing that it was only calf-love which you'd soon forget. As, out of sight of him, I did myself. Though mine took longer to forget, and, in sight and sound and touch of him again, has come back full circle. . . .

Aloud she told Cicely, "I think it's a stage in growing up. It's apt to happen when you find something less one-way to put in its place."

"You mean when you find someone you can communicate with? Someone who seems to communicate with you?"

Ruth said, "How your generation does overwork that poor word 'communicate!' But yes, I suppose so, if by it you mean speaking the same language, which was our way of putting it, I remember."

"As Jeremy and I begin to, I think," Cicely mused.

"Communicate, I mean. As I never could, quite, with Erle. Can you?"

Ruth hesitated. "Not always. But you need to remember he has to be something of a diplomat, manipulating people and situations as he does. And diplomats can't always afford to tell the world all they're thinking."

"All the same, Erle could let up a bit with his friends," Cicely judged. "But there it is. I'm not bothered any more. I'm cured of him—just like that."

"Able to put, say, Jeremy in his place?"

But Cicely was not to be drawn wholly on the subject of Jeremy. "Could be," she said carelessly. "At least we start equal, which I suppose I never did with Erle. But do you know what I'd like to see one of these days?— Erle falling flat on his face for someone quite ordinary! Without any talent or any glamor or anything at all that he could *use*. How would that be for a laugh?"

Ruth said quietly, "You are disillusioned about him, aren't you? I hope you're not going to show it too plainly when he comes back. After all, you owe him quite a lot—this summer in Rome, for one thing."

Cicely's shrug dismissed any debt for Erle. "If he hadn't done it for me, I suppose somebody else would," she said. "Anyway, he knows what I think of him. I told him, the night I was at his apartment."

"Oh—what did you tell him?"

Cicely had the grace to blush. "The worst of it was, the next morning I couldn't remember what I had said," she admitted.

Ruth laughed. "Just the *crème de cacao* talking, eh?"

"The—what?"

"The liqueur that was the only thing you liked among Erle's drinks."

"Oh, *that*. Yes, well—whatever I said must have been scathing, for I do remember that he looked quite taken aback. And for anyone as self-assured as Erle to be stopped in his tracks is quite something, wouldn't you say?"

"Quite," Ruth agreed, reflecting that Erle, nonplussed even momentarily, was a scene she had never yet witnessed.

CHAPTER SEVEN

Now the city was in the grip of its torrid late August heat. As usual at this time of year Ruth and her language pupils took a month's holiday; she and Cicely went often to the Lido to swim and to escape from streets where even the stone walls were fiery to the touch.

Erle rang once to say he was back from America, but made no further contact for some time. His work of organizing his clients' winter seasons of concert and opera engagements was at its height, he had said when he telephoned. From then on every social contact he had was likely to have some professional purpose behind it.

From behind Ruth Cicely had prompted, "Tell him we know he's bought the Casa, and see what he says." But she was too late. Erle had already rung off.

Then, one afternoon when they came home from the Lido, his car was parked on the street and he was pacing urgently up and down. "I've been trying to phone you for hours," he said.

"We've been out at the Lido since this morning."

"All right. But let's go in now. My mother has called from England with some rather bad news."

Cicely looked at him sharply. "Bad news for you? Or do you mean—for me?"

He nodded. "None too good, little one. But take it easy." Ruth had opened the door by now. With a hand on Cicely's shoulder Erle propelled her up the stairs. In Ruth's living-room she turned on him. "What is it? Not—Mother?"

"I'm afraid so. She was in a taxicab smash last night, and she's in the hospital."

116

"Wh—why? What's wrong? What's happened to her?"

"A broken leg, and they suspect some internal injury which they aren't willing to confirm yet. She was still unconscious when my mother got in touch with me."

"Unconscious? Oh no!"

He put an arm round her and she turned her face into his shoulder. He signalled to Ruth, "A drop of brandy, I think," then put Cicely into a chair and knelt by it, holding both her hands.. "Do you want to go home, little one?" he asked.

"Oh yes, yes! Can I? I mean—how soon?" she pleaded.

"Tonight. How about that? I've already provisionally booked a flight for you. It only needs confirming by phone, and I'll come with you, of course."

Her eyes filled with weak tears. "Oh, Erle, you're good! Will you really? I thought you were so hideously busy just now."

But he was already at the telephone, saying over his shoulder to Ruth, "Is that all right with you? Can you get her ready and give her a light meal if she can eat it?"

He phoned the airport, booked a call to his mother, and rang several other numbers. Cicely declared she couldn't eat, but did manage most of a plain omelette Ruth cooked for her. She said to Ruth, "Jeremy and Vivien—you'll tell them I've gone home?" And reflectively, when it was just about time for her and Erle to leave, "And that's a pity too. Jeremy told me the legend about the Fountain of Trevi—that if you throw lire into it, it's a sign you'll come back to Rome. But I meant to put if off until the night before I was really leaving, and now it's too late."

"Do you want to come back?" asked Erle.

Her face lighted up. "Do I? It's been heaven—or nearly."

"Then on the way to the airport, what do you say to our making a detour from Tritone to take in Trevi? Have you got any small change handy?"

"Oh, Erle, bless you!" She turned to give Ruth a bear hug and a kiss on each cheek. "Thank you for every—thing," she murmured. "And may I come back?"

Across the room Erle, collecting her luggage for carrying down to the car, commented drily, "Mission accomplished, it seems."

Cicely looked round at him. "What do you mean?"

"Just that, before you came, Ruth threatened that when she had done with you, you'd want to come back—or else!"

"Did you? Did you really?" Cicely appealed to Ruth.

Ruth nodded and smiled. "I'm glad it's worked out," she said. Then they were both gone, leaving an emptiness and a finality behind. For it was already so near to the end of Cicely's time in Rome that she was unlikely to come back this year. And with Cicely's going, there weren't even days to be counted to the severing of the link with Erle. It was surely broken now.

On the evening of the next day there was news from England. Erle phoned to say that though Mrs. Mordaunt was out of danger, besides her broken leg she had some internal hemorrhage from a crushed rib and a degree of concussion. She would be in the hospital for some time. Cicely sent Ruth her love. It would probably be a week before Erle came back.

Before he returned Jeremy and Vivien Slade, who were leaving themselves, came to say goodbye. Vivien was going to a domestic science college in the autumn,

Jeremy on an advanced art course. They would pick up the threads with Cicely again, they promised themselves, and "Jeremy is really going for her," Vivien confided to Ruth when they were alone. "He's going to be completely shattered if she takes up with anyone else." As if, thought Ruth, at nineteen and seventeen Jeremy and Cicely ought to plight their troth for good. But perhaps they had. Who knew? It had been known to happen.

Left alone, Ruth found herself with unwanted time on her hands. She was used to the heat of Roman summers and didn't mind it. Alone, she preferred the country to the Lido beaches, where family parties and couples shouted and laughed and swam and sunbathed together. So she packed picnic lunches and a book and, beyond the city boundaries, took any road which offered, using the car until when, Erle returned, and with Cicely gone, she would have no further right to it. She window-shopped on foot and took herself to the last nights of open-air opera at Caracalla, one among ten thousand people, neighbours for a night, who would scatter to the far corners of the earth when their holiday was over.

Cicely wrote happily of her mother's improving condition, and Erle telephoned. He had left England, but was doing some business in Paris before he came back to Rome. Then one day Ruth had an unexpected visitor— Stella Parioli. Surprised and puzzled as to what the other woman could want of her, Ruth asked her in. To which Stella merely said "Thank you" and followed Ruth up to the apartment.

It was midmorning. Ruth offered drinks. Stella refused them. She sat, graceful and poised, laid her bag and gloves on a table beside her, and waited while Ruth unplugged and removed the vacuum cleaner she had been using. Then she said, "I do hope, *signora,* you will understand that it's a certain goodwill towards you that has brought me to see you"—a remark which, in explanation of her guest's errand, left Ruth none the wiser.

She echoed blankly, "Your goodwill, *signora?* Well, thank you. But am I in any particular need of it, do you think?"

Stella nodded slowly. "I'd say so. Reject it or misunderstand it if you like. But in view of—this"—taking a printed cutting from her bag and handing it over—"don't you agree you are in need of all the charity of your friends and acquaintances that you can get?"

Ruth took the cutting, experiencing the all-over chill of gooseflesh as she thought she recognized the layout of the print, the gloss of the paper. *Lo Sussorro* again! Or a similar rag to it. She longed for the moral courage to hand it back, to refuse to read it. But that was beyond her will, and she read it through, while Stella watched her.

Head lowered, apparently still reading, she was silent until Stella prompted, "Well? You read Italian well enough, I suppose, to understand what it says?"

Ruth said slowly, "Indeed I know what it says—that I am in the habit of visiting Signore Nash's apartment very late at night, alone and after midnight in one instance. But that's not to agree that my friends could possibly believe the implication behind it. Nor, if I may say so, *signora,* do I appreciate the 'goodwill' that bothered to bring it to my notice. Won't you explain?"

Stella's delicate brows lifted. "But surely? After all, someone would have done so, if I hadn't. And by no means everyone, believe me, would be concerned enough to beg you to be more discreet in future."

"You are worried lest these lies should harm him as much as me? As if any real friend of his or mine could care!" Ruth scoffed.

"But haven't your names been linked in a similar way earlier?"

"At least once before that I know of."

"With some cumulative effect, no doubt, even if they are proved to be lies—"

"Which they assuredly are," Ruth cut in. "I have *never* visited Erle Nash's apartment for the purpose that's hinted at here."

"Nor very late at night at all?" Stella insinuated.

"Never. That is—" Ruth had remembered her abortive errand in search of Cicely.

At her check, Stella pounced. "Ah, then you have on occasion? You would do well to realize, *signora,* how much can be read into a small amount of truth like that!" she advised.

"Once only," Ruth said tautly. Not for anything, she resolved, would she reveal Cicely's silly escapade to a sophisticate like Stella Parioli. "Signore Nash wasn't even there," she added.

"Tch! So you had a fruitless errand? But how unfortunate for you that on that one occasion you should have been seen by some interested party! Seen to arrive, that is. Not seen to leave, as I think it says there?" Stella's nod indicated the cutting which Ruth still held.

Ruth said, "Yes. Though my leaving happened a very few minutes later, when I found Erle Nash wasn't at home."

"Sadly for you, the informant didn't wait to see."

"Or chose to suppress, as it made a better lie that way." Ruth handed back the cutting, which Stella folded and dropped into her bag. Ruth went on, "I can't help thinking that you are as concerned as you are, because you feel that this sort of thing involves not only Erle Nash and me, but reflects indirectly on his circle of friends as well. In which case, though it's no fault of mine, I'm sorry."

Stella smiled thinly. "Thank you. And you are very perceptive. I do care, as Erle will, that scandal spoken of him does no good to intimates of his.'

"Intimates such as yourself?"

Stella took a mirror from her bag, tilted her chin to examine her face from several angles, then put the mirror away and rose.

"Such, perhaps, as myself," she agreed, and then, "Tell me, *signora,* how would you describe your own relationship with Erle?"

Ruth said, "As his friend, I hope, we first knew each other many years ago, at school in England."

Stella nodded. "Yes, that he told me. Not, then, as his *good* friend, with all that the film stars have taught us to understand by that?"

Ruth flushed. "Certainly not," she said.

"I thought not. He speaks warmly of you of course. But I'm afraid he may not understand at all how you could be careless of your own good name and his as to make gossip of this kind even remotely possible. You are not a child, *signora.* You should certainly know by now how readily one's enemies talk!"

It was Stella's parting shot. It left Ruth raging, and in no doubt whatsoever that wherever Stella's "goodwill" was directed, it certainly wasn't towards her. Stella was only concerned that through her own association with Erle, she shouldn't be seen to be "touching pitch."

But who, this time, could have witnessed her visit to

Erle's apartment, Ruth wondered. True, the streets were still full of people, but Agnese Fonte would not have been among them at that time of night. Who else then had enough malice towards her to make up such a story? It was a question still unanswered when Erle returned to Rome.

He phoned to say it was important he see her, and after asking him for news of Cicely and Mrs. Mordaunt, Ruth suggested a time that afternoon. When he arrived he threw a copy of *Lo Sussurro* on the table. "You'll have seen this," he stated, not asking her.

Ruth said, "Yes, Signora Parioli saw to it that I did. She brought it to show me."

Erle nodded. "So she told me, feeling you ought to see it. The point now is—what is to be done about it?"

"The last time they concocted the same kind of lie, you said there was nothing that one could do," she reminded him.

"Ah, nothing negative, I agree."

"Negative? Such as?"

"Well, demanding that they apologize or retract in print. This time it's obvious they picked on the night you came to my place in search of Cicely, and as in the Siena story, there's enough truth in each to allow them to plead justification. Their strength is that they don't accuse us of immoral goings-on; they only hint, and a retraction of something that hasn't even been said wouldn't be worth the paper it was printed on. Quite apart from the fact that rebutting this latest story would involve Cicely, and that we certainly don't want."

Ruth bit her lip. "No. What, then? Do we have to let it go as we did before?"

"I doubt if you can afford to. One isolated story didn't matter. That's why I dismissed it. But two begin to smell of a concerted attack and before it turns into a campaign against your reputation it had better be stopped. With some positive action that they'd have to understand. Even be happy to, is my guess."

"By 'positive' you mean go to law? Sue them? That they would enjoy the publicity that would afford them?"

Erle shook his head. "Nothing like that. To sue would be only one step beyond asking for a denial and just about as efficacious against a libel that hasn't even been made. No, the positive action I have in mind would be mine, and needing your full agreement." He paused, looking straight at her, holding her glance. "In short, I'm suggesting that you allow me to announce our engagement forthwith."

For a moment the words didn't register with Ruth. Then they did, reuelly and incredibly, since no one would propose as bluntly as that. Hearing her voice as if it weren't her own, she echoed, "Our *engagement?* Yours to me? What do you mean?"

"Just that. We announce our intention to marry at some future date which can be as vague as you please. As a public gesture only, of course. Emotionally it needn't mean a thing to you."

"And to you—though you can't possibly be serious?"

"I am. For me you could say it's a front I'm prepared to put up for your protection."

"For my protection! What could it do? The lies have already been told!"

"About an alleged roué—me, and a new woman in my firmament—you. In those roles, meat and drink to the gossip columnists. But if there's anything the Italians relish fully as much as scandal, it's the promise of a wholesome love affair on its way to fruition. Offered that, they'd be prepared to forgive and forget all and be happy to speculate instead on a likely wedding date and who will be there as our guests."

"But it wouldn't be true! It isn't going to happen!"

"Which they're not to know—until, after a decent interlude, the length of which would be your choice, we decide to tell them."

Ruth protested again, "It's an unthinkable suggestion. Quite, quite impossible. For one thing, no one would believe it of—of you and me. For another—" But Ruth stopped short of telling him she knew he must have sent Stella Parioli to look over the Casa Rienzi with a purpose.

He took her up. "Who cares what anyone believes of the hard fact of an announcement in *La Gazzetta* or *Giornale e'Italia?* It's there to be read and accepted. But by your 'for another thing' do you mean it's impossible because you're already bespoken? How do matters stand between you and Cesare Fonte?"

"I've told you, I like him. We're friends."

"Is that all? By all the signs the man is in love with you. But so far you haven't committed yourself?"

"No."

"Why not?" At Ruth's quick frown Erle laughed shortly. "All right—I'm being impertinent. I apologize. But you do see that if you already had ties there, this operation wouldn't be possible? Whereas—"

"It isn't in any case," she broke in. "My friends—yours—all know there's never been any question of marriage between you and me. The English papers will copy the news, and Cicely and your family—"

"Ah, I can't surprise my family by now. And Cicely has already forgiven me the gallantries which you found so sinister. She has told me so herself."

"Your own friends, then—what would they think?"

"After the initial shock, I'm going to acquire a new image in their eyes. As a potential marrying man, and not the hard case they've always thought me. And when, in the fullness of your own time, you throw me over, imagine the flutter of new interest there'll be! I'm going to enjoy that, and so will they."

At the flippancy of his tone Ruth frowned again. Watching her, his expression changed and he came over to her. He said gravely, "I'm serious, Ruth. Your own code is so rigid that you drive me to defend my motives with idiotic banter like that. But you've got to appreciate that, as I see it, I owe you this. It's the only way I know to shield you from scurrility which you would never have invited if you hadn't swum into my orbit again. Yours is a private world; mine is public, and though the gossip-mongers have to have their way with me, if I know anything about it, they're not having it with you. What's more, you owe it to me to allow me to protect you from possibly worse to come."

"It needn't—if we didn't meet at all again."

He shook his head. "Too late for that. They've got their teeth in and they'll hang on. The next thing would be speculation as to the whereabouts of the hidey-hole in which we were continuing our suspect affair out of the public eye. No, I got you into this, and I'm getting you out of it, if you'll let me. Say you will?"

Ruth said nothing, blaming herself for weakening, yet knowing that she would agree to anything he asked of her with such sincerity. But she still demurred faintly, "It wouldn't work. I'm no good at playing a part."

"It'll be up to us to *make* it work," he countered. "We'll need to be seen about together. Oh, and you'll have to have a ring—"

But from that she recoiled with such a passionate "No" that Erle looked at her, eyebrows raised. "No to the whole idea? Or no to the ring?" he asked.

"To—to the ring. I won't accept one under false pretences."

"Aren't you rather straining at a gnat, while agreeing to swallow a camel? You must have a ring," he said.

"But not one bought for the purpose. I couldn't. I have an antique pearl and opal ring that was my great grandmother's. I'll wear that if I must."

"You must, I'm afraid. And for the rest you'll take your lead from me?" At her dumb nod to that he went on, "At this point we ought to seal the agreement with a kiss, which you wouldn't like. But if the press boys expect us to lay on some public affection for their benefit, you'll be tolerant of that?"

"I—suppose so."

"Good. I'll make things as easy for you as I can, and let's hope they'll switch off the limelight in favor of the next hint of scandal in higher places than ours." As he made ready to go he added, "I'll phone the announcement to the papers as soon as I get back to my office." But that brought another "No" followed by a pleading "No—please" from Ruth. He halted. "It has to be announced," he said.

"I know," she agreed. "But not in tomorrow's papers, please. I couldn't bear—That is, I wouldn't care for Cesare Fonte to hear of it that way. I must tell him myself."

Erle looked at her from his distance across the room. "So?" he said meaningly, and then, "All right. I'll hold everything until after you've seen him. Let me know."

Ruth said quickly, "May I keep the car for the

moment?" But she knew he hadn't heard. He had slammed out of the room.

As it happened, however, she didn't need to dread facing Cesare for longer than until evening, when Erle telephoned to suggest he should tell Cesare the news himself.

"If you did it," he said, "I imagine you'd find it as distasteful to your conscience as you say you would accepting my ring?"

"Yes," she agreed bleakly.

"Then give me permission, and I'll do it for you."

"Tell my lies for me, you mean?"

He avoided agreement with the crudity of that. "I'd handle it better than you would, involved with Fonte as you are—"

"Only as a friend to whom I'd hate to lie for no better reason than to shield myself from ugly scandal," she retorted.

"Yes, well, don't forget you're scotching it for me too. But a scruple like that makes it my duty to do this for you. I'll send Fonte to you afterward, and the way I'll have done it should keep him as your friend."

Tired of fighting, though ashamed to feel relieved, Ruth gave way. "Thank you," she said wearily.

"As a friend—until you decide you want him as something more," Erle added, and rang off. When Cesare came to see her, Ruth realized that living the masquerade of her engagement was no easier for his having heard of it first from Erle. Cesare was so openly generous in his wishes for her happiness that she was sorely tempted to entrust him with the truth. And though, with the announcement already sent to the papers it was too late, at least she made herself answer some of his questions with honesty.

For inevitably he asked, "You were in love with Erle already when you refused me?" To which she replied simply, "Yes."

"You're convinced of loving him enough, in spite of all the women with whom his name has been linked?" To which she said yes again, and then, because she had to know, asked, "What did Erle tell you about—caring for me?"

Cesare smiled wryly. "I think he knows what I feel for you too. So he let me down lightly. He said, 'You could say it's a case of: boy meets girl; boy loses touch with girl for too long; boy meets girl again; happy ending.' Good of him, I thought, to play down his feeling for you instead of forcing me to compare it with mine, knowing you had found mine wanting."

Ruth longed to confess, "He wasn't playing it down. It doesn't exist. In order to shield me he was simply being adroit with words." Aloud she protested, "It was mine that was wanting, not yours. Yet you—you're generous enough to wish me well. We can still be friends?"

"For as long as you want me, though after a while it may have to be at a distance. Because obviously now Erle won't renew my lease on the Casa, which means Agnese and I will be returning to Quindereggio after all," said Cesare.

"Why 'obviously now?'" Ruth queried. "Why do you think he won't?"

"Don't you know? Surely because he must have bought it with the idea of making it your future home? Hasn't he told you so?"

"No. We—we haven't discussed any future plans like that," she replied evasively. "Besides, you must be wrong. If he were thinking of it for me, he wouldn't have sent Signora Parioli to check it over, would he?"

"Ah, but it's there that I was wrong. Misheard her, or misunderstood her, or, not crediting that she would have come without his knowing, jumped to the conclusion that he must have sent her."

"I jumped to the same conclusion," Ruth pointed out.

Cesare laughed. "Hoping, but not knowing so short a time ago that he was going to propose to you? Oh, Ruth, my dear, what does it feel like to be so infinitely lovable to at least two men, and yet so modest as not to know it?"

She looked away. "I always knew that you liked me. Also that, though we disagreed on a lot of things, Erle did too—in his fashion." Feeling herself on dangerous ground, she changed the subject to ask, "Supposing Erle did only want the Casa as an investment, would you still expect him not to renew your lease?"

"Ah, I'm not asking him to renew it. I've definitely decided to sell and go."

"You have?"

Cesare nodded, "For reasons I don't think you will make me explain, beyond saying that even if you and Erle aren't at the Casa, you will be here in Rome whenever he is himself."

Guiltily Ruth understood. Erle's piece of quixotry on her behalf was like a stone thrown into a pool, creating ever-widening eddies as it dropped. Now it was uprooting two people, one of them courageously cutting his losses by going, the other only too glad to snatch at the opportunity. She said, "I suppose Agnese is happy about your decision to go?"

"More than happy. Triumphant that what she chooses to call 'wisdom' has prevailed. I'm afraid I may have another name for it if I don't sell at a good profit. But she is already packing up in spirit, as it were. Which reminds me. . . . Cesare paused. "She brought to me the other day another peice of scandalous gossip about you and Erle. But perhaps you have seen it?"

"In *Lo Sussuro?* Yes," said Ruth. "But you didn't believe that what it implied was true?"

"*Santo cielo,* no! I realized at once what it sprang from, and told Agnese so. Some busybody of a reporter must have seen you on the night that you went to Erle's apartment, expecting to find Cicely there—wasn't that the real truth of it?"

"Yes," Ruth looked her surprise. "But how did you know about that?"

"From Cicely. How else"

"Oh. I hadn't expected she would tell anybody about it, since it didn't show her in the best of light. Jeremy Slade knew, of course. And Vivien. But—"

"Well, she made it into a good story against herself to Agnese and me one day, and naturally I reminded Agnese of that." Cesare looked at his watch. "Do you think I could ask you to lunch with me, without the gutter press deciding that I'm double-crossing Erle?" he asked.

Ruth managed a smile. "I think we could risk it," she said. But she spoke mechanically, her thoughts churning.

She hadn't, after all, been *seen* to visit Erle's flat that night. It had been Agnese Fonte again who had turned Cicely's innocent story into the evil trash it had become in her own and *La Sussurro's hands!* Well, thought Ruth, she had been warned. Agnese had threatened to use any chance to injure her that offered. This was Agnese's own stone thrown into the pool of other people's lives—touching Ruth, her self-sought enemy; Erle, and even Cesare with the inevitable backwash of the circles that it made.

CHAPTER EIGHT

As soon as the news broke—in small paragraphs in the serious newspapers and as double spreads in the popular press—Ruth began to savor the distasteful truth that a falsehood told often enough gradually becomes easier to tell and more credible to the teller. The first time she said "We" of herself and Erle she felt a pang of guilt; by the tenth time she had to say it in answer to questions her qualms of conscience were less and the pretense that they planned a future together seemed less of a sham. Sometimes she even allowed herself the fantasy of "If he were really in love with me, the things I'm doing and saying would be true"—which lent her a mirage of peace while she indulged in it, though she hated herself for doing so.

Seemingly, if Erle had ever had any such misgivings he had quashed them even before she had. He played the lover, the happily engaged man to perfection. In order that Ruth should not be harried at her apartment by reporters he called a press conference in his office, where he parried awkward questions about the secrecy surrounding his courtship, put his arm round Ruth and kissed her warmly as the enthusiasm of the photographers demanded, and made a good story of their original teenage meeting in the fog of an English winter day.

All of which was reported lovingly, with romantic trimmings; with, even in *Lo Sussurro* and its kind, never a backward glance at the sour insinuations of a week or so ago.

What Stella Parioli's reactions were to Erle's engagement Ruth did not know. Erle did not tell her and she scorned to ask. Presumably, whatever his relations with Stella, he intended they should continue within the limits set by his public committal to Ruth. It was as if, Ruth felt, they had tacitly agreed that the subject was taboo between them. The future of the Casa Rienzi was another; Erle hedged by saying he had thought it a wise investment. He agreed blandly with a questioning reporter that it would make an ideally luxurious home for a bride, but did not discuss it with Ruth beyond saying that he could make no firm decision while the rights of Cesare's lease had still some weeks to run.

"Cesare told me that he won't ask you to renew it. He has decided to go south again," said Ruth.

"So? Well he hasn't told me as much, and the wind may have changed for him by then," was all Erle said.

There was an expensive cable from Cicely:

Well, you could have fooled me, you dark horses. Thought you only went hand-in-hand for my sake. Tell me the date of the wedding and I'll play bridesmaid. Or matron of honor to Ruth if I beat you to it. Joke, ha-ha. Mother won't hear of my being engaged to Jeremy until I'm eighteen. Love to both, Cicely.

There were warm good wishes and some coy curiosity from Ruth's language pupils. Little Signora Matteo in particular took to herself some reflected glory from her connection with Ruth. "I tell all my friends that I learn the English from *la fidanzata*. And that my husband who, as you remember, *signora,* is a stage-hand at the Opera House, often sees and speaks with *il sposo*, Signore Nash," she claimed with pride.

There were, for Ruth, the inevitable canvassings of photographers, couturiers, stationers, confectioners, and travel agencies, offering their several wares—from stu-

dio portraits to the guaranteed privacy of far-flung honeymoon spots. And Erle, busy as he was, gave her time
and attention—as much as she could have asked if they
had really been engaged and more than her conscience
told her the false situation deserved.

But it was all so public. At parties that he gave for her,
once the introductions were made, they mingled sepa-
rately until the last of the guests had gone. And at
bigger, restaurant affairs they were parted by the length
of the long table. Ruth supposed that people assumed
they had their private times together before the parties
and theater visits and after them, though it wasn't so in
reality.

Once, when he drove her back late from a concert
after which they had gone backstage to meet some
artistes of international fame, she tentatively asked him
in.

They were still in the car. He hadn't put on the courtesy light and she could not see his expresson as he said,
"Don't tempt me. I might accept," and kept purposeful
hands on the steering wheel, ready to leave as soon as
she had gone.

She had laughed then, and so had he. *Both of us knowing how little there is to tempt him, tête-à-tête with me,
even after midnight*, she thought as she got out of the car.
She hadn't asked him since.

She wondered how long he though the charade should
continue. "A matter of weeks? Or months?" she had
asked him. To which he reminded her that he had promised to leave that to her, though an engagement broken
too soon might bring all the sour speculation down on
them again. If she could stand the strain, a few months
rather than weeks would be his advice. After which . . .
He had left the end of that remark in the air.

After which, Ruth foresaw, she wouldn't be able to stay in Rome. It wouldn't be possible for her to slip straight back into obscurity, and she wondered that Erle seemed to think she could. She might not have to leave for good. That remained to be seen. But escape she must, for a time. From the commiserations of her friends, from the triumph of her enemies, and most of all from an Erle who must be avoided. Where would she go to? To England, alone? Or Malta, to her parents? She did not know, and procrastinated in making a decision.

It was from Signora Matteo that she was to hear of trouble in Erle's professional world. Ettore Matteo, the *signora's* husband, had his ear well to the ground in opera circles, and according to him, she told Ruth, the rivalry between La Parioli and Signora Clara Ganzia threatened to come to a head.

Signora Matteo said, "They are both prima donnas, and although there are not so many mezzo-soprano leading roles, they both expect to be offered what there are for the winter season. They are saying, so Ettore tells me, that Imprese Baptisti is bidding for the management of their affairs against your *fidanzato, signora,* and that if he, Signore Nash, cannot suit them, they may leave him and go to Baptisti. But how can one know? It may only be backstage talk."

Whether it was or not, Ruth knew Imprese Baptisti for an impresario, second in influence to Erle, but in keen rivalry to him for the top operatic names. She rather doubted the gossip. She thought Erle must surely be guarded against either star's right to break her contract with him at short notice. But she would have given much to know that if she were to him the platonic friend he had once claimed she was, he would confide such troubles to her. He had said, hadn't he, that he felt he could talk to her as to another man and had let her take pride, however briefly, in that? But he told her nothing, and it wasn't until she had seen a hint of the news in a serious musical journal that she broached the subject with him.

He shrugged it off. "Where did you get the idea?" he asked.

"From *Il Mondo Del Musica*. It said—"

"I know what it said. Wishful thinking, that's all. Baptisti is the editor's second cousin or something. These negotiations always are on a knife-edge of chance, this way or that. But both Parioli and Ganzia know very well when they're well off, and that's with me," he said dismissingly, very sure of himself in his dealings with both stars, and for more than professional reasons, with Stella Parioli at least, Ruth supposed.

Now that she had no longer to take Cicely over to the Casa, she was glad to be free of that embarrassment. Sure as she was that Agnese Fonte had been *Lo Sussurro's* informant, without proof she had neither the right nor the wish to accuse Agnese, and she could only hope that until Cesare and his sister left for the South, they need not meet for more than a formal few minutes.

Chance, however, was against that. In going for luncheon in the crowded restaurant of a department store, she was shown to the one vacant chair at a table for two by a harassed waitress, who asked the permission of its other occupant for Ruth to share it with her.

The other woman, her face in the deep shadows of a pillar, murmured, "*Prego*," and Ruth, nodding her thanks sat down oppostie Agnese.

She noted that Agnese had finished her meal and was lingering over coffee and a cigarette. So the ordeal need not be too long . . . Agnese said a cool *"Buon giorno, signora,"* Ruth returned the greeting, adding something banal about the weather which Agnese ignored, and Ruth concentrated upon the menu, though only too conscious of the dark eyes upon her.

She had ordered and was eating when she noticed with dismay that Agnese had lighted a second cigarette. Agnese, under cover of the clatter about them, said abruptly, "So. I think you and I have not much small-talk, *signora*, but please allow me to congratulate you on your recent engagement," and, cutting short Ruth's murmured thanks, went on, "And I congratulate, rather than wish you well, because you *are* to be congratulated, I'd say. Wouldn't you?"

Ruth said, "In England we usually congratulate the engaged man, not the—"

Agnese nodded, "It is so with us too—usually. But I chose to congratulate you on the piece of strategy which ensnared for you Signore Nash, while dallying with my brother's sincere devotion to you—keeping him dangling until you thought yourself sure of the other. You understand me, no doubt?"

Ruth defended herself, "I understand you very well. You think I was playing one man against the other. But as I told you before, I refused your brother as soon as he asked me to marry him. At that time I had no idea whatsoever of becoming engaged to Signore Nash."

"Pff! I am not concerned with dates or befores and afters," Agnese scoffed. "Only with what is very clear now—that you weighed the drawbacks of becoming a poor *contessa* against the advantages of becoming a rich businessman's wife, and of course chose the latter, though still continuing to see Cesare as before. But I wonder, *signora*," pausing to touch the tip of her cigarette on the ashtray, "whether you will find it as much of an advantage as you think, being chosen for reasons which are rather obvious to other people, if not to you?"

"Now I don't understand you, I'm afraid," said Ruth. "What do other people know about my engagement that I don't?"

"Why surely?" Agnese queried. "That it is—as his marriage to you will be—merely a refuge for Signore Nash, a bolthole from all the glamorous women who are snapping at his heels, competing not only for his professional attention, but for the marriage that he has so far escaped. One hears of him that he is a man who insists on doing his own wooing, that he will not be pursued. But can you be quite sure, do you think, that his wooing of you was for the reasons that any woman must want?"

Ruth put down her knife and fork, afraid that her shiver of apprehension had betrayed itself in her shaking wrists. She had feared that by some chance Agenese would learn that her engagement was a false front. But this was worse. For it could—just—be true. In moments of misgivings she had allowed herself to question Erle's insistence on the chivalry of protecting her name by engaging himself to her. At such times, as a motive it seemed too thin for belief. And though in killing the scandal it seemed to have worked, supposing it had never been his motive in the first place? Supposing he had only been seeking a temporary escape from, say, Stella Parioli's assumption that he was her property; that she had only to call whatever tune she liked, and he would dance to it? Ruth had heard him claim once that he knew very well what he was about in managing his own affairs. Was this then his way of heading off an importunate woman wanting marriage when he did not, by pretending engagement to another woman—herself?

Oh no! Not Erle! her heart protested. He couldn't callously have made use of her so! Yet, while the doubt was there, the pain was also. Doubting, she could hardly face him, but, loving him, she was afraid to know for sure. She needed time to think, to plan, to rehearse—She became aware that Agnese had stubbed out her cigarette and was standing, ostensibly waiting for her bill, but really waiting for a reply to her question.

Ruth made a supreme effort. With a pride that had Agnese known it, was only surface deep, she said, "As to that, I think I'd rather trust my own fiancé than all the people who may think they know differently." At which Agnese shrugged, "As you will. You should know, of course," and left her.

After she had gone Ruth made a show of continuing her meal. She was thinking that she might have confounded Agnese by daring her to prove that she had not carried false information to *Lo Sussurro*. But that would be to sink to the level of Agnese's malice, which she scorned to do.

She had a date for a party with Erle that evening. At such short notice she couldn't break it without embarrassing him, but she rang his office and left a message with his secretary to ask him to call for her earlier than they had agreed. On such occasions she was usually ready to leave with him as soon as he came for her, but tonight, she asked him in.

Except in public he never offered her any gesture of endearment, and tonight he lounged easily on the window seat as she sat across from him, her hands clasped tautly in her lap.

He said, "You summoned me to a tête-à-tête?"

"Yes. I decided today that all this—" she paused— "can't go on."

He sat staring at her, but clearly understanding.

"That's nonsense," he said curtly. "It has to go on."

"You promised that the right to end it at any time should me mine," she reminded him.

He stood then and paced the room back and forth, past her chair. "But for heaven's sake—within some bounds of reason!" he exploded. "How long has it been now? Just three weeks—no more. What good do you suppose it's had the chance to do in that time? On. Off. Blow hot. Blow cold—hardly before the ink has dried on the announcement in the papers! Why, we should be the laughingstock of Rome, if not worse in store for you."

"And it matters to you that you shouldn't be the laughingstock of Rome?"

"It matters that *we* shouldn't, for a whim of yours which, at this stage, I dare you to justify," he retorted.

"But you said—"

He cut in, "All right. I said the privilege should be yours. But I stipulated there should be a decent interval before you claimed it, and do you really suggest that three weeks' duration is either decent or sensible? Or fair?"

"Fair?"

"By the conditions which I thought you'd accepted. Even, if I may mention it, by a certain obligation to me."

"Meaning," Ruth said slowly, "that if you'd thought I would break it off as soon as this, you wouldn't have offered me the protection of an engagement? But was that—" she paused, then plunged recklessly "—was that your real or your only motive behind it?"

He halted opposite her chair. "And what are you implying by that?" he demanded.

"That it has occurred to me it wasn't very credible or sound reasoning on your part—"

142

"What was wrong with it? So far as it's been given a chance to date, it's done, hasn't it? But do you mean 'occurred,' or 'was suggested' to you, I wonder?"

"It was suggested."

His eyes glinted angrily. Then you've confided the truth of it to someone? To whom?"

Thrust on to the defensive, Ruth expostulated, "No. No, it was someone who believed our engagement to be a real one—"

"Who?"

"I'd rather not say. Don't make me. But in talking about it they implied that you hadn't been sincere in entering upon it with me."

"And what did you say to that?"

"I—said I thought I could trust you. What else could I say?"

"H'm—lip-service loyalty to a man and a bargain you've since decided to ditch. This busybody's argument must have impressed you. What was it?"

"It wasn't very creditable to you, but you must see that I had to defend you?"

"Against what, for goodness' sake?"

"The suggestion that our engagement had been a way of escape for you from your entanglement with your other—commitments."

She was completely unprepared for—and disarmed by his shout of derisive laughter. "And you were ready to believe that?" he queried.

"I didn't want to. But when I thought about it, it seemed a more likely motive than the other. Or an additional one, perhaps."

"To juggle with a proverb—taking two stones to kill one bird? My dear girl, when I need to shelter behind one woman, in order to extricate myself from the toils of another, or from several, I'll opt out from both public and private life, for I'll have lost my touch beyond recall. Satisfied?"

"Then it wasn't true? Your only reason was to protect me from any further scandal?" Ruth could not keep relief out of her tone.

He tilted his head, as if in thought. "Supposing I'd offered you any other which happened to occur to me, would you have cooperated?" he parried.

"I don't know. What else could you have offered me?"

"Well, say some motive which would be to my self-interest, rather than to yours?"

"I—think so, if it were something which seemed worthy of you," she said gravely.

"Ah—but worthy by your standards, or by mine?"

"By mine, I suppose. Though wouldn't you say the standards of most honest people are much the same?"

He laughed again. "One of those loaded questions to which I claim the right not to answer! In return, I'll agree to leave my own 'suppose' question dangling. Meanwhile you're resigned to our continuing our compact?"

Ruth moved restlessly. "If you think it's necessary," she hesitated.

"You *know* it's necessary for longer than this," he countered with vigor. "Necessary to give it a chance to complete the job it's begun tolerably well. Necessary, when you decide its time is up, for it to appear like an engagement that has run reasonably long enough to have been found wanting. Necessary too—and here's a test of your good faith—that at this particular stage of my business affairs, I shouldn't be hounded by all the snoopers there'd be, chanting 'Why?' and 'How come?' and that *you* shouldn't be harassed by your pet busy-body's snigger of 'What did I tell you?' Well, fair enough? Anyway, what did you mean to do, if I'd agreed to your breaking with me now?"

So he had realized there wouldn't be room for both of them in Rome when the break did come, thought Ruth. "I'd have gone away," she said. "I must still go when—"

"Where to?"

"I hadn't decided. Perhaps to—" But at the thought which struck her then, she checked. "Don't you think it might be better if, when the time comes, you could tell people truthfully that you didn't know?" she appealed.

"Better?"

"Easier, then."

He looked at her thoughtfully, as if he were weighing the point. Then, "Yes, I suppose it would," he agreed, and utterly perversely Ruth could have burst into tears.

His facile agreement made her feel let down, abandoned. In that difficult time of their public parting, she would be alone, and he ought to want to know ... to *care* where she went and what became of her! At least he could have argued the issue. She might have told him of her tentative plans, and confirmed whatever they were when, in the future, she did have to leave Rome. Or again, she might not. *But he should have wanted to know.*

Before the news broke publicly the Opera House grapevine had it, and Signora Matteo brought it to Ruth. Clara Gancia was to star in the winter season in Rome; Stella Parioli would be going to the Metropolitan in New York. Both valuable contracts had been negotiated by Erle and both ladies were understood to be well pleased. There was now, Signora Matteo reported, no more talk of Imprese Baptisti. As always, there was more prestige for an artiste with Signore Nash than with any other impresario in the profession.

Ruth's reaction was a glow of pride for Erle, mingled with speculation as to how Stella's absence in America would affect his relationship with her. Probably very little. In these days it was possible almost to commute between Rome and New York; more than likely he would see her nearly as often as now.

As soon as the papers had the news Ruth rang him to congratulate him. Beneath his nonchalant thanks she sensed an elation which she longed to have the right to share with him. As it was, her voice would be only one among the many there would be, praising the success of his coup.

A few days later he came to see her at the apartment. "We're going to have to give a farewell party for Parioli," he announced.

She questioned the "we."

"You and I," he explained.

"You, but why me?" With rare tartness she added, "Because, in the circumstances, it would look better?"

He glanced at her quickly. "Don't be waspish. It isn't in character. No, because that—" pointing to the antique ring on her engagement finger "—makes us a team in people's eyes, and it will be expected of us. Don't worry, I'll handle the whole thing from the office. All you'll have to do will be to look charming and be gracious with our guests. Parioli has her own ideas as to the form the party will take. *Al fresco* and different, she stipulates."

"How—'different?'"

"Different from the run-of-the-mill cocktail crush or the dinner-and-nightclub thing, I gather. Open-air, because she wants us to give it in the grounds of the

Casa; and different by way of keeping it in period with the place."

Caustically Ruth wondered who was giving this party—Erle or Stella. Erle went on, "She took the idea from some Watteau paintings in one of the galleries—of the *fêtes champêtres* of the French aristocracy. All pastoral simplicity, the guests playing at being shepherds and shepherdesses and dressing the part. Sounds crazy, I agree, but the lady must have her way."

Ruth said drily, "It's novel, at least. But can you give it—the party—until the Fontes have left the Casa?"

"Oh, we can't wait for that. Parioli is leaving for rehearsals in less than a fortnight."

"Will you be going with her?"

"Not *with*—I shall probably go over later. It depends. No, as Fonte is still technically in tenancy, I'll have to get his permission to stage the thing next week. Would any day suit you?"

"As far as I know. The idea is that we all go in costume?"

"That's it. Open-necked shirts, pantaloons, and humble forelocks for us men, and something fetching in shepherdess-cum-milkmaid tradition for you. You can leave all the arrangements to me. We'll choose Thursday week, if that suits you."

Not much relishing the role of hostess to Stella as guest of honour, Ruth was nevertheless challenged to play it in authentic detail. To this end she studied the catalogues of the Rome galleries that contained paintings by Watteau, and visited them in turn.

In one of them she found what she wanted—a pastoral scene of the seventeenth century, where country boys and girls were disporting themselves all over the canvas.

Some seemed to by playing a version of Kiss-in-the-ring; a group of seated girls were making daisy-chains; a few sheep grazed in the foreground and some couples were coyly flirting in the shade of some middle-distance trees. A pillared building in the misted background was so characteristically Palladian that it might have been twin to the Casa Rienzi. Grudgingly Ruth acknowledged that Stella had been original in her choice both of setting and costume for her farewell party.

Ruth chose one of the dresses and memorized it faithfully—full panniers over a ballet-length petticoat, a cross-laced bodice with puff sleeves and a sunbonnet slung by its strings like a cape on the wearer's back. In a shop she found some coarse striped material for the ballooning panniers and some flower-sprigged muslin for the under-petticoat and bodice. A children's department produced a sunbonnet which was too small for her, but which she needn't wear on her head. By trial and error and several hours of rough stitching she contrived a tolerable and quite becoming copy of the original.

When Erle called for her on the evening of the party he was informal in shapeless white trousers, a full-sleeved open shirt, and a gaudily patterned cummerbund, and they agreed they were as typical of a Watteau peasantry as the twentieth century could achieve.

With the passing of August the fierce heat had mellowed to a golden, windless warmth. As they drove out of the city, east towards Tivoli, the westering sun was on their backs, casting long shadows on the road ahead and dappling the shade of wayside trees. When the red ball finally disappeared, it would be dark in less than an hour.

"Are Cesare and Agnese coming?" Ruth asked.

"No. Fonte has had to go down to his place in Calabria for some days." Erle glanced at her. "I thought you'd know?"

She shook her head. "I haven't seen him."

"And Agnese prefers to hold aloof from anything in the nature of whoopee. She wasn't too willing for her brother to lend us the park, until I promised that the caterers should set up their tents and barbecues and things as far from the house as possible. It seems she has an obsession about intruders and she sends Cesare on a police tour of the house and the stables every night after dark. The stables are empty, by the way. I had all the horses shipped to a livery stable in Tivoli for twenty-four hours, in case they took fright at the fireworks display that's being held."

"It's meant a lot of work for you," said Ruth.

"Oh, I've only played major-domo. I've handed everything over to Rolli's, the caterers, and they've done the lot." As Erle turned in at the gates of the Casa, he added, "I must have them warn people that the belvedere is out of bounds to us, as well as the house. Seems a pity, as it's part of the Palladian scene, but I made that concession to Agnese too."

He parked the car and directed her to the tent which was the ladies' cloakroom, arranging to meet her again in the central tent where they would welcome their guests.

They had arranged to arrive early, and for a little while Ruth had the cloakroom to herself. As she looked at the ranks of well-lighted mirrors and the sample bowls of powders and perfumes and tissues on each dressing table, she wondered where, at this party, the seventeenth century was supposed to take over from the twentieth. Certainly not here. Nor, from what she had seen of the main tent, with its specially laid dance floor, the big supper tent, and the palpably modern bar, anywhere else.

As she went to meet Erle she was thinking that if it had been her party she would have tried to keep it in period. She would have held it in the daytime, on the greensward of the park. No carefully boarded walks between the tents. No tents, in fact. No massed banks of hothouse flowers. No electric barbecues. No bar. If they danced, they would dance on the grass, dew-wet feet or not. They would cook over wood or charcoal, and they would drink the wine of the country from . . ..

She was still deep in fantasy when suddenly Erle was there, flicking a finger and thumb before her face, as before a sleepwalker's.

She laughed self-consciously. "Sorry. I was miles away," she said.

"Where?"

"In another century."

He cocked an eyebrow. "With Watteau and his nymphets? Deploring the compromise we've had to make?"

"Thinking it's a pity, perhaps. As a *fête champêtre* it isn't all that rustic, is it?"

"Not so's you'd notice. Especially considering those characters down yonder."

She looked to where his nod indicated. At the far end of the tent was a group of men with cameras slung on shoulders and wrists—unmistakably photographers.

"All this and the press too. Did you have to invite them?" she asked.

"Of course. Stella's privilege. When a prima donna appears at a farewell party, it ranks alongside a farewell performance and has to be honored as such."

Ruth glanced from her own costume to his. "I wonder why we bothered," she commented a little sourly.

He laughed. "So do I. But when I pointed out that the arrangements she was demanding weren't exactly in period, Stella said, '*Caro mio*, my idea of fancy dress was only a gimmick for a bit of extra publicity. We don't have to go slumming as well!' Hence the décor and the amenities that friend Watteau wouldn't recognize, you see."

"And publicity is All, of course," Ruth murmured.

"For the star names, yes. Without it and people like me, they wouldn't become star names or stay that way for long. You shouldn't knock publicity just because of the raw deal it handed out to you and me through no fault of our own." Erle took her hand and held it down by his side. "Time we were appearing as a welcoming host and hostess. Our guests are beginning to arrive," he said.

They came, at first in a trickle, then a stream, then in a flooding crowd. Though some of their ideas of period dress were odd, they had all entered into the spirit of the invitation. They were all carelessly ragamuffin according to some past age or other. And it *had* been a novel notion to get the party going, Ruth admitted. Presently the glasses were clinking to a babel of voices, laughing, criticizing costumes, gossiping, flirting.

Like Ruth, Stella had done her period homework well. She was in sunflower yellow smock, the skirt slashed into ragged petals, the bodice a mere crossover of black shawl. A flat-crowned straw hat, encircled with daisies, was slung from her wrist by its ribbons, and her magnificent hair with its swathe of silver was in studied disarray. She came with Luigi Bernanos, whose name

Ruth had first heard in Erle's office and who had part-nered Stella at Erle's restaurant party for Cicely. As usual Stella was able to make an importance of her entrance, the crowds parting for her as she came down the floor to Erle and Ruth. Her greeting for them was identical—a kiss on each of their cheeks for them both, with, for Erle a murmured, "You make a very virile peasant, my friend!" and for Ruth, "So charming of you to humor my little whim. We must all start equal, I thought—" which to Ruth sounded about as subtle a piece of condescension as she had ever heard.

The party was under way. Groups formed and reformed and moved on. People danced, adjourned to the bar and back again. Ruth now knew enough people in Erle's circle to be welcomed by them, though the friendlier they were the more heavily her deceit. But she supposed Erle was right. She must carry it through now to the point—how distant might it be?—where her break with him could appear to be a considered decision on her part. If she could handle it well and then slip away, these good people needn't ever know they had been duped. It would soon be forgotten, just one of those things that happened.

The reporters and photographers were busy, corner-ing "lions" and probing for snippets of copy. One of them caught Ruth when she was alone, wanting to know the probable date of her wedding to Erle, and their plans after it. She dealt as vaguely as she could with his persistence. All their plans were fluid, depending on Erle's commitments for the autumn, she told him.

"And the spot for the honeymoon?" he asked.

"Now would you really expect me to know that at this stage?" she parried, and escaped.

Still alone, she wandered outside the circle of light and the frenzied activity. In the distance across the park there was a single dim gleam to be seen. Leaving the party behind and going nearer to identify it, she saw it was from one lighted window in the Casa; all the rest of the building was in darkness. At the thought of Agnese alone there, Ruth experienced a fading of her rancor. She hadn't ever wanted to make an enemy of Agnese. That had been Agense's choice, and since she was unlikely to make any conciliatory move, Ruth was tempted to make one herself. When Agnese and Cesare went away it would be too late.

Erle had said that the Casa was out of bounds to the party. But to one woman alone, on a peace mission? Ruth ignored the ban and went purposefully ahead.

When she reached the house she realized in sudden panic that she hadn't rehearsed what she meant to say to Agnese. How would she deal with the rebuff she might very well invite? She stood irresolute under the colonnade of pillars, then decided she must play it by ear, and lifted the great knocker on the door.

There was no response from within the house. She knocked again, and was about to do so a third time when she checked. Silly of her to suppose that Agnese, objecting to the invasion of the grounds and alone in the house, would answer the door at that time of night! Giving up, Ruth sent a last glance to the one lighted window, then turned to go back the way she had come.

It led past the belvedere, dark behind its shielding tamarisk hedge. When Ruth had passed it before, all had been as silent there as at the house. But now on the far side of the hedge there was a rustle of movement which halted her, alert, listening and a little frightened.

A night animal running for cover from all the

unwanted light and noise in the park? No. People? Moving on, she reached the free end of the hedge and looked around it. Two figures, a man's and a woman's, had approached the little retreat, the man already in the deep shadow of one of its porticos, but with his hand outstretched behind him to guide the woman. Ruth's eyes, accustomed now to the darkness, had view enough of her before she too slipped into the shadows.

Stella! Her remarkable hair, the yellow of her peasant dress unmistakable. Stella, keeping rendezvous with someone. Who was he? But even without the glimpse of light shirt-cuff above that backward stretching hand, Ruth guessed. After Erle had made public the limits of the party area, only he was likely to have defied his own ban, in order to be alone with Stella, knowing that they would not be disturbed. The belvedere, as an illicit meeting-place for lovers, had come into its own.

Knowing she had no right to be hurt, that Erle had broken no given promise to her by philandering with Stella, Ruth turned away. By absurd comparison the crowds and the clamor of the party appeared to her as a refuge, and she was anxious to get back to it. There was a shortcut through the stable yard and she took it—only to freeze in her tracks again as she realized she was not alone there either.

Behind the weak nimbus of a hand-torch a tall figure in black was moving from empty loosebox to loosebox, unbolting their half-doors, looking in, closing them again. Agnese! So that was why she hadn't answered the door of the Casa. She must have been on her way down here—trusting no one, intent on doing Cesare's nightly security patrol herself. As Ruth stood in the shadows, not caring much for the thought of Agnese's reception of her if she revealed herself now, she saw the torch fade out; heard the "click, click" of Agnese's finger on the button and her exasperated "Ah—" as she thrust the dead torch into a pocket of her jacket and reached for one of the oil storm lanterns which Cesare kept for emergency lighting, hanging on a wall.

She set it on the floor of the shed adjoining the loose-boxes, took matches from her pocket, crouched to open the talc door guarding the lantern's wick, struck a match—and with an awkward movement of arm or body knocked the lantern over. Kneeling low now, with her free hand she reached to retrieve it. Between the fingers of the other hand the lighted match was still alive, burning down to the point where, nearly spent, she flung it from her with another sharp "ah" of annoyance.

But on the floor the tiny dying flame took new life, flared, licked greedily and surely along some path which might have been laid to feed it. *Spilt oil from the lantern when it keeled over!* Ruth had time to think before the flame spread, on and wider and back to Agnese, now on hands and knees, beating wildly to quell it. It caught at her skirts—she must be kneeling in oil—and as Ruth reached her, knocking her flat beneath the weight of her own body, an explosion cracked and cracked again. Within a foot of their prone bodies, from a shapeless bundle leaning against a wall, new flames spurted and grew. The bundle itself detonated and suddenly fell apart, blazing. And then somebody else was there, straddle-legged for balance, a bucket in either hand.

Water for the bundle, dry sand for the path of oil and for their two prostrate figures. Another bucket each of the same and Erle—*Erle?*—was helping them to their feet.

An arm supporting each of them, he looked down at Ruth first.

"Ruth—my love, my *love*—what gives?" he murmured, stabbing her through with a heady delight which quickly turned to pain.

Putting on an act, even here and now! He must have made a habit of this public claiming of her, for how could he possibly think Agnese, in these circumstances, could care how amorous or close their relationship was?

What was more, there was no longer any wonder in her mind as to how he came to be there. From the distance of the belvedere no one could have mistaken the menace of that first explosion, whatever its cause. And he had been at the belvedere. With Stella. *Hadn't he?*

CHAPTER NINE

ERLE'S question went unanswered, for at that moment Agnese sagged and would have fallen but for his support. He released Ruth in order to hold her upright. "Had the fire reached either of you?" he asked.

Agnese tried to draw herself up and free of Erle's hold. "No, no, it was foolish of me and careless," she said grudgingly. "I tried to light the lantern and knocked it over. I did not know anyone was near."

"Lucky for you that Ruth was, though she shouldn't have been," said Erle. "And may I ask why you were out here yourself, *signora?*"

"I wanted to make sure that all was safe."

"After I had promised you I would patrol the whole place myself? Anyway, even if you didn't trust me, why an oil lantern? Why not bring a torch?"

"I had one. I have it." She touched her pocket. "But it went out and the lantern would have served if— "

"If you hadn't knocked it over and spilt oil among this sort of fire hazard." Erle kicked at the scattered debris from the canted bundle. "Fireworks, no less."

"*Fireworks?*" Ruth echoed, peering down. "Then that was the explosion and the smaller ones which followed! I couldn't think what— But why were there fireworks?"

"That I don't know. But I will, before the night's out," Erle promised grimly. He broke off as Agnese began to shake uncontrollably. "Shock," he said briefly, and as Ruth nodded agreement he told Agnese, "I'm going to get you back to the house. Carry you there, in fact, for warmth and brandy and bed."

156

Momentarily she managed to stiffen. "That's not necessary nor—seemly, *signore*. I can walk—,"

But, a hand under her knees and an arm round her shoulders, he was already balancing her considerable weight as easily as if she had been a child. "My torch," he said to Ruth. "I threw it down when I dived for the fire buckets. On that sack over there—will you bring it along?"

They set out, skirting the tamarisk hedge when they came to it without Erle's throwing the belvedere a glance. At the explosion which had alerted him to danger, he must have sent Stella back to the party for safety, Ruth decided. He knew the place would be empty now. In her hand she weighed the big torch she was carrying for him and wondered that he should have brought it with him. She would have expected them to perfer the anonymity of the darkness.

At the house Agnese told Ruth where to find cognac and blankets, and then there arose the question of leaving her for the night. Erle drew Ruth aside.

"I'll drive you back straight away if you'll give her a bed at the apartment," he suggested.

"Of course I will—if she'll come," Ruth said doubtfully.

"Why shouldn't she? I shall make it an order and fetch the car. I'll tell the assembled company as little as I can and come back to the party myself, after seeing you both safe. A pity about the anticlimax for you, but we'll make up for it—some time," he added.

While he was away Agnese grudgingly allowed Ruth to find her night things and a change of clothes, and when he came back he brought Ruth's cloak with him. When they reached the apartment, he telephoned

Cesare at Quindereggio, telling him what had happened and promising that Ruth would keep Agnese as her guest as long as necessary. Which could be about as short a time as she can bring herself to accept my hospitality, thought Ruth, overhearing. But she didn't say so to Erle.

She made up a bed for Agnese in the room Cicely had had and went to shed her grimy peasant dress and to take a bath. She meant to see Agnese comfortably settled before she went to bed herself, but Agnese forestalled her by coming to the door of her room as Ruth emerged from the bathroom.

"May I speak to you before you go to bed?" said Agnese, her gruff tone making it a demand rather than a request.

"Of course. I was coming in to see you anyway. Won't you get into bed?" said Ruth.

Agnese did so, sitting bolt upright against the pillow's, staring at her big hands outspread on the quilt.

"You saved my life," she announced

Ruth shook her head in deprecation. "Oh no," she said.

"*Yes.* I was afraid. I lost my nerve. If I had got to my feet I should have run in panic and that would have fanned the fire. Instead—"

"Instead, I knocked you flat and sat on you," said Ruth, smiling, "Forget it, please."

"No. This is not all I have to say." Agnese rubbed a hand anxiously across her brow. "How was it that you were there?"

"I had left the party a little while earlier. I had seen your light in the Casa and I had gone there to see you. But you weren't there, and I was on my way back, using the stable yard as a short cut."

"To see me? What for?"

Ruth looked down at her own hands in her lap. "Well, in case we didn't meet again, to say goodbye to you without ill-feeling," she admitted.

"And if I had repulsed you, what then?"

"I'd have been sorry, but at least I should have tried."

"As I must try now. I am proud, and it is difficult. But I have to tell you, *signora,* that I have deliberately slandered you, blackened your name in public for my own ends. Because you had encouraged and then scorned my brother, I twisted what I knew to be the truth. I told those false stories to the gutter press—"

Ruth nodded slowly. "Yes, I know," she said.

"You *knew,* and—?"

"That's not quite true. I didn't know for certain, though I thought it must be so."

"Because I had warned you I would stop at nothing to revenge myself on you?"

"Yes. But I think I realized how hurt you were, and when I went to the Casa tonight I did mean to try to convince you that I had never knowingly encouraged Cesare and that he knows and accepts the reason why I couldn't marry him."

Agnese nodded. "Yes, he has always been more generous than I. Or perhaps more easily deceived. For he says you have told him you are entirely happy in your engagement to Signore Nash. Yet, as I have taunted you myself, with such a man, how can you be sure he means as well by you as you by him?"

Ruth colored. "How can one ever be entirely sure of another person's affection? One can only hope."

"Only, sometimes, to be cruelly mistaken." Agnese looked away across the small room, as if at a scene beyond its confines.

Ruth ventured, "You know, perhaps, what it is to be so misled, *signora?*"

Agnese brought her gaze back to the present. "Once, yes. But it is a long time ago now; an old story not worth the telling. I have forgotten the effect of it. Now I have Cesare to care for, and I am well content."

"And if he should marry for love, as I hope he may?" Ruth asked.

Agnese drew herself up. "That is his right as a man, and I shall not stand in his way," she declared stoutly. "But I will *not* have him scorned because he is poor or wanting in the courage to prove his worth, or see him encouraged and then rejected for a lesser man." She paused. "All this I believed of you, and it made you my enemy in consequence. You understand?"

"I think so. I'm glad you told me," said Ruth.

"Even though you say you knew some of it already?"

Ruth smiled. "The results. Not the full cause, and that I do now understand. Cesare is fortunate to have you for a sister." She stood up and laid a hand over one of Agnese's. "You have forgiven me now, *signora?*"

"And you me?" Agnese added diffidently, "All happiness in your coming marriage, *signora.* I must wish you that."

"Thank you," said Ruth, almost tempted, as she had been with Cesare, to confess that there was no happiness in store for her in marriage to Erle. But she said nothing. Cesare, Agnese, everyone would all know soon enough that there was to be no future to their engagement, and until then she must keep her promise to Erle.

The next morning Erle telephoned to say that a doctor would be coming to see Agnese, and asking Ruth to keep her until then. "As I remember," he added, "you haven't explained what had taken you down to the stables last night?"

"I hadn't much liked the thought of her alone, and I'd been over to the house to see her," said Ruth.

"Against orders?"

"As hostess, I felt I was privileged to break them. But I missed her, and I was making my way back to the party across the stable yard." Wondering what he would say if she enquired how *he* had managed to be so promptly on the scene, she asked instead, "Have you found out how the sack of fireworks happened to be where it was?"

"Nobody wants to take responsibility for it. But from my sifting of the evidence I deduce that it may have been delivered at some time when the caterers weren't on the site. It had been dumped there instead of being added to the main stock they had on hand."

"I'm sorry I missed the display. Was it a good one?"

"As spectacular as most, with the superlatives tending to run out before the grand finale."

"What time did the party break up?"

"In the small hours, with its objective achieved. Stella prounounced herself enchanted with its success as a last appearance of the season for her, and made me her proxy for thanking you for giving it."

"It was your party for her," Ruth reminded him.

"But in the circumstances, generous of you to cooperate."

Did he mean generous in view of her false role as his fiancée, or generous to a more favored rival, she was wondering as he went on, "Either the doctor or Cesare Fonte may beat the other in descending on you and

Agnese. When I spoke to him—he rang me again last night—Fonte said he was coming back to Rome, leaving Quindereggio at dawn. He should have news for you. I think."

"News for me?"

"And for his sister. But news I imagine he'll want to give you. I instructed my agents to make him an offer for the goodwill and the stable stock of the Casa, and he has accepted my figure."

Completely surprised, Ruth asked, "But what do you want with a riding-school business?"

She heard Erle laugh. "I don't," he said.

"Then why buy one?"

"Say that when I have a major project in mind, I believe in clearing my decks first." He laughed again as he rang off.

In fact, the doctor had pronounced Agnese only in need of rest and quiet some hours before Cesare arrived. He was anxious to hear all the details which Erle had not given him, and when Ruth protested that she had "done nothing," said he preferred to take Agnese's version of the affair. Before he arrived, Agnese had said, "I think we should not tell him that we already know of his settlement with Signore Nash"—a suggestion which would not wantonly spoil the other's fun. So they showed admirable surprise, and there was no doubt of the pleasure it gave Cesare to make scoop news of the transaction. "The papers making the offer were sent to me at Quindereggio," he said. Turning to Ruth, "You have a phrase in English—'beyond the dreams of avarice'—and Erle's figure goes beyond my furthest hopes of anything I could ask or get elsewhere. It means everything—" He checked, frowning. "No, not everything. But ease, freedom from worry for a very long time to come, until Quindereggio is on a footing which will serve Agnese and me very well."

"Though one questions why he should pay such an inflated price," demurred Agnese, looking at Ruth. "Do you not know why? As his *fidanzata,* you should," she ruled.

But Ruth, remembering that they had agreed to know nothing of Erle's plans until they heard them from Cesare, was able to say with truth that Erle had confided none of his motives to her. It was not until Agnese had gone to collect her things, preparatory to returning to the Casa with Cesare, that he showed he had come to his own conclusions on the matter. He said wistfully to Ruth,

"Obviously, having both the Casa to make it your home with him, Erle wouldn't want a riding-school to be run from the grounds. Nor even for me to continue there for as long as I might need to bargain with other purchasers. He is rich. He could afford to buy me out and sell the goodwill to no one else. The stables he will keep up privately and you, Ruth, will have to learn to ride!"

"I don't know. Perhaps—" she said noncommittally, agreeing privately with Cesare's reasoning, though not with his conclusion that it was she whom Erle meant to install as mistress of the Casa. He intended it should become a private home again. What otherwise could he have meant by "clearing his decks?" But when all was done, though he might live there himself, it would not be with her as his wife. Not with her.

Cesare said goodbye to her then, while they were alone. He took both her hands in his and, humble and self-effacing as ever, he said, "The one thing I wanted of you, you couldn't give me, but I still have a lot to remember and to treasure. And though I am jealous and envious of Erle now, I wouldn't choose not to have known you—and loved you. You understand?"

Ruth nodded. "Nor I—not to have known you."

"And you will be here, as my friend, when I come back to Rome—as I shall?"

But she had to find an evasive answer to that. Where, when he returned to Rome after a time, might she be herself? She didn't know, and after he and Agnese had gone, she questioned why he should be grateful to her. For the only service she was able to do him was a negative one, of which he must never know. In his eyes, Agnese might have failings, but she had no feet of clay. He did not guess the lengths she would go to in pursuit of an enemy, and Ruth was determined that, if she could help it, he never would.

However subtly offensive Stella Parioli could be when she chose, she did not lack the veneer of social good manners, in that she telephoned Ruth to repeat her thanks for the Casa party before she left for New York.

"Such a success you and Erle made of it for me," she crooned. "A thousand pities that you weren't able to enjoy the end of it with us, but I told Erle he mustn't *fail* to let you know how appreciative I am for your having given it for me."

"Thank you," said Ruth, and with too vivid a memory of the belvedere rendezvous, couldn't resist adding, "Certainly the papers gave a great deal of space to it the next day."

"Oh, *them*." Stella's tone dismissed the whole Italian press. "Of course they are always rather avid for anything about me, though I assure you I told any reporters I spoke to that they should give full credit to Erle and you too."

"Which they did," said Ruth drily.

Stella agreed, "Yes, and I was so glad. Because though it was Erle's idea to give me a farewell party, it was mine that it should be at Rienzi. A nice touch, I thought, that you should give it as your first party in the grounds of your future home."

At Ruth's ambiguous murmur in answer to that, Stella went on blandly, "Which reminds me, I do have a small quarrel with you, you know. Because it was so very soon after Erle asked me to look over the Casa that *you* denied to me that there was any romance between you at all. Do you think that was quite fair?"

Ruth said stiffly, "At that time there *was* nothing between us, and I think you must have known that, *signora.*"

"Ah, I thought I did, but with Erle one never can tell. He has such universal charm. Rather too universal, I'm afraid, for a young wife to tolerate easily. . . . You won't have to mind too much if, after marriage, he appears to—and even does on occasion—neglect you for other women. Not really the marrying kind, Erle, and later he could feel trapped. And if you are thinking it morbid of me to warn you, do remember, won't you, how well I know him myself, and have done for years?"

"I'll remember it," promised Ruth. As if she would ever need warning against entrapping Erle in marriage! Opportunity, they said, was a fine thing. . . .

Stella murmured, "So wise of you not to resent advice. And I speak from experience; never, for all our closeness, letting Erle fear that he wasn't free as air—even to indulge an urge to marry, which isn't *him,* you understand? Though of course one can only hope for you—"

"Which I am sure you will be charitable enough to do," put in Ruth.

"Of course! Though—forgive me—just an instance of how, for your own sake, you shouldn't claim Erle too much, too early. Naturally he will be coming over for my debut at the Met. But unless it is so soon after your honeymoon that he can scarcely refuse you, do wait, won't you, for him to suggest you accompany him? And if he does not, try to make light of whether you are to come to New York with him or not?"

To which Ruth said, "I see what you mean. And though of course Erle will want to see your debut in America, I think you may take it—safely—that I shan't be there."

Stella drew a sharp breath that could be heard on the line. "Safely?" she echoed, catching at the deliberately chosen word. "Ah, that means you are offended, jealous! Though I assure you—"

But Ruth had had enough. She hung up.

CHAPTER TEN

STELLA duly departed, after being fêted in the airport V.I.P. lounge, laden down by bouquets, and pursued to the departure gate by reporters.

Erle held auditions, put out feelers towards new contracts, and consolidated existing ones in a tight schedule of flights to Paris, Milan, Vienna, and Berlin.

Ruth's life continued while she considered a time—or such an interval of it as she supposed Erle would consider "decent" before she broke their false engagement.

Then one evening when she was to dine with Erle at a restaurant, he postponed ordering aperitifs, saying he was expecting two other guests, some people on a visit to Rome.

"Then I haven't met them before?" queried Ruth.

"You know one of them—" As Erle spoke he rose, offering both hands to the two women who were approaching his table. Ruth gasped, her first swift thought one of reproach that he should have inflicted *this* upon her; her second, that he probably couldn't help himself. For coming ahead of a beautifully groomed older women was Cicely—all smile and open arms, first for Erle and then for Ruth herself.

"Surprise, surprise! Isn't it? I made Erle swear he wouldn't tell you!" Cicely caroled. "Mother, meet Ruth and congratulate Erle on getting her. Fancy! They must have had a growing yen for each other all the time they were coping with me. But not so much as a whisper out of either of them. Why not? You may well ask. Search *me,* though there was a time when I admit I shouldn't have been amused—Ruth, meet Mother. Isn't she mar-

167

vellous? Only convalescent a week, and suggesting we come out here to thank you for all you did for me! We're staying at the Salvatore—fabulous! How's Cesare Fonte? And that grim Agneses? Erle, what are you giving us for dinner? I'm *starving!*"

From such eager twitterings Ruth and Mrs. Mordaunt, smiling at each other, took it that they were introduced. Erle ordered drinks and they chose their meal, and presently, to all appearances, they were as happily normal a group as any in the room. Even Ruth forced herself to behave as if it were all true, wanting to believe it was; trying not to look at the inevitable aftermath of continuing lies and evasions until Cicely and her mother went back to England and the lengthening "decent interval" which this re-meeting with Cicely must entail. After this, she and Erle couldn't break with each other yet. He might carry it off. But she knew she could not, if she were ever to look the girl in the face again.

Cicely's gaiety was infectious, the people at nearby tables watching and laughing with her, indulging her youth. Mrs. Mordaunt was a much-traveled American, urbane and drily amusing, and Erle was, as always, a perfect host. The evening was hilarious, but not a late one, the price of Mrs. Mordaunt's surgeon's having allowed her make the trip being her promise that she would always be in bed by midnight, Cicely jealously saw that she kept it.

They parted, arranging to meet for shopping, for sightseeing, for a return dinner party before the fortnight of the Mordaunts' holiday ran out. Erle first took them back to their hotel, then came back for Ruth. As she joined him and he started the car he said, "You're thinking that was an unlooked-for complication, but I assure you I couldn't avoid it. Didn't see why I should—particularly," he added, as if by afterthought.

Ruth was wearily, "Why not? I see that you couldn't. But you should have wanted to try—for my sake."

"What would have been the use? You know perfectly well that Cicely, in Rome again, would have looked you up. And you were glad to see her and to meet her mother, weren't you?"

"Of course I would have been—in any other circumstances. As it was, it was the most embarrassing experience I've had since—"

"Since we got engaged? Well, bless you for a good actress. No one would have guessed."

"I've had enough practice, the last month or two. But that didn't make this evening any the less hurtful." Ruth looked out of the car window at an unfamiliar street. "Where are you going? Isn't this an odd way to take me home?" she asked.

Erle turned a corner. "I'm not taking you home—yet," he said.

"Not? Where then? Please—I've had enough. I'm tired."

"You can be tired later. We're going out to the Casa. I've a fancy to serve you a nightcap in the belvedere."

She sat upright, outraged. "*Not* at the belvedere!"

"Why not? You'll like what I've had done to it. The Fontes never furnished it, except as a summerhouse. But I've had some rather nice pieces found for it—"

"I—I wonder you dare!"

"Dare furnish my own property? Why shouldn't I?"

She was convinced he was deliberately baiting her. "You know quite well what I mean!" she accused him. "The—the associations it has!"

He threw her a quick glance. "But I understood from

Fonte that you turned him down. That being so, I didn't suppose the belvedere would have all that many nostalgic associations for you."

"It hasn't any," she snapped "You know I meant— for you!"

He shook his head. "None for me—so far."

"No? Then I suppose it's oversensitive of me to hope you'd have scruples about asking *me* there, after the use you made of the place on the night of Stella Parioli's party?"

He looked at her again and she saw he knew she was serious. "I made no use whatever of it that night. I'd put it out of bounds," he said.

"To everyone but yourself, maybe. Perhaps that was why—"

She watched his hands tighten on the steering-wheel. "The ban was at Agnese's request. I told you so at the time," he said coldly. "Except on my way over to the stables to check the whole place, as I'd promised her, and when I carried her back to the house, I wasn't within shouting distance of the belvedere all evening. So just what are you implying?"

"I'm not implying. I'm stating what I saw for myself— you, taking Stella into the belvedere in the dark."

He laughed then though not amusedly. "My dear girl, with the whole of the amenities of Rome available— hotels, restaurants, nightclubs, not to mention a lot of shadier joints; nor, come to that, my apartment or hers— do you suppose for a minute that I'd need to skulk into a neglected summerhouse to keep an assignation with *grande dame* Parioli? Use your reason, do!"

Ruth found she could not look at him. "But it *was* Stella, and it must have been you. After you had announced the ban, nobody else would have dared."

"It wouldn't have deterred Stella, if she fancied some private dalliance. And if you're right, someone else must have done."

"I—I thought it was you. Stella's costume was unmistakable, and I saw your hand, your cuff, your sleeve—"

"Not mine. What about trying, say, her friend Bernanos for size? Or even some smaller fry? She collects worshipping fans by the dozen and occasionally extends one of the handsomer ones a regal hand."

Ruth watched her suspicions begin to disappear like receding pain under a drug. "But if you weren't at the belvedere, how were you able to get into the stable yard as quickly as you were?" she asked.

"Oh dear, I though you understood that too." He spoke with firmer patience. "I've told you, I'd promised Agnes Fonte I'd do the rounds, so I had a powerful torch ready with me at the party, and was nearly there when I heard the fireworks explode—and ran."

"O—oh—" she murmured, defeated but briefly happy.

"So—o," he mimicked her long-drawn word. "Then I take it you can bring your self to look over the belvedere in its new dress?" When she did not reply, he went on, "The house must wait for a while. Architects and decorators first. After that, I want to give time and money and all the professional skill I can command to make it a house to be proud of—and a home."

"*Your* home? Is that why you bought out Cesare at what even though was an inflated price—to keep it as a private property?"

"Partly, yes. For the rest, I rather wanted to see what a sizeable lump of capital might do for his prospects with you."

Ruth worked that out. "He'd told you I had refused to

marry him, but you thought that if he had more money, I might change my mind?"

"If you had, I'd have crossed you off my visiting list for a gold digger. But I had to find out. I mentioned, I think, that I always need to clear my decks?"

"Even of other people's affairs which don't concern you?"

"Ah, but this did concern me very closely."

"As to whether or not I married Cesare? Why should it?"

"Suppose you guess—?"

But he didn't wait for her to answer that, alighting instead to open the locked gates of the Casa and to close them again behind the car. In his seat again and moving on, he said, "Well? Or shall I put it another way? Why do you think I've brought you to a kind of mini-housewarming of the belvedere tonight? You, just you. No one else?"

Ruth was aware only of the deep thudding of her heart. "Perhaps for something of the same reason you sent Stella Parioli to check over the house for you—you want the woman's angle on the facelift you've given the belvedere?" she suggested.

There was silence. Erle pulled up alongside the tamarisk hedge and helped her out. "I never asked Parioli to look at the Casa," he said.

"Well, she came, before Cesare knew who'd bought it, and depressed him immeasurably with her comments on it."

"Not with my authority. I hope I have better manners than to ask one woman's advice on the décor of a house I hope to share with another." He had put a hand beneath Ruth's elbow to guide her, and at the low step to the portico he paused.

"Some ceremony called for here? Or no," he answered himself, "That's for a bride—the carrying across the threshold bit. It can wait."

He unlocked the door to the first of the tiny rooms, touched a switch with lighted fat electric candles in waist-tall, floor-standing gilt sconces, casting attractive light and shadow on chair seats embroidered in grospoint; on a gilt loveseat, on twin couches, button-studded and covered in old velvet; on dark wood and circular carpet.

His arm went around Ruth's waist, drawing her to stand very close to him. "Well, suppose you try to guess now?" he said gently. "To begin with, why I wasn't over-concerned that you should have been embarrassed in front of Cicely tonight. I've been worried for you before, but not tonight. Doesn't that say anything to you, my Ruth?"

Frightened lest she thought she knew and didn't she said. "Wh—what did you want it to say?"

He gave her a little shake. "Come! *I'm* asking the questions. Don't you know that I meant it should be the last time you should suffer conscience, or have to hedge or lie by omission? The last time for me too— Not that any of it was ever a lie for me. I've *meant* our engagement, Ruth, all along. And hoped, even before that. On my side none of it was false or without a future—the hope of being allowed to claim you; of making a home to share with you. If not here, then anywhere you would come with me." He turned her to face him, looking deep into her eyes. "Do you understand what I'm saying? Asking?"

"If—" She broke off, then found words slowly. "If it were anyone but you, I think you would be asking me to marry you. But you've always poured such scorn, said that marriage wasn't for you that you didn't need it, that it would cramp your style."

"Ah, the wilder ravings of a bachelor about to succumb to the most maddening woman on his scene, my love!"

"Me—maddening?"

"Uh-huh. Maddeningly detached. Maddeningly honest. A fighter—frequently with no holds barred. And quite maddeningly lovable."

"I've only fought you when you've fought me!" Ruth disclaimed.

"Ah, but *how*—when you did! All claws out for your defense of Cicely's honor; for your own integrity—remember your affront over the Roscuro dress I gave you?—and even against your need of love, if not mine, when I kissed you at Siena. That night I was frightened for you, Ruth, and despairing for myself, lest, being as hungry to be loved as you seemed, you might be tempted to snatch—and not at me."

"Yet you didn't trouble to find out where I wanted to snatch?"

"How could I? Once your control took over again, you rejected me; said the whole thing was meaningless, that you were putting on an act."

"Because *you* had said you were only curious, experimenting."

"Oh, come! A guy has to have some kind of opening gambit. Especially against opposition like yours."

Shyly she looked down and away. "Except that there wasn't any opposition. I was snatching at you with all I had."

Erle drew a long sigh. He stroked her hair, lifting a strand of it. "You say that now? And mean it?" he queried.

She nodded. "As much as I did then, though I think I didn't admit it until Siena."

"Nor I, until I realized I was learning what jealousy was. I'd never experienced it before."

"*I've* known for a long time. But you dismissed it once as a mere waste of spirit," she reminded him.

"I was whistling in the dark, denying it was on my very heels. I never did know how things stood between you and Cesare Fonte, until I asked him straight out and he told me. And who was there for you to be jealous of in paricular? I'd *told* you my alleged harem was as innocuous and necessary to my job as—as porridge is to a Scot!"

"I've been jealous of Stella Parioli, for one. And with cause, I think."

"Nonsense. With almost every word I've spoken to you about her, I've shown you I've taken her measure. She's glamorous—"

"As I can never be."

"As you don't need to be. You're a honey as you are. And she's talented, and ambitious, and as singleminded as her profession demands. And going places, with the sky as her limit, through *my* good services to her. You don't grudge me my star pupil, surely?"

"*Only* your star pupil? You give her valuable presents!"

"On the wrong side of your rigid line?" Erle laughed. "That was petty of me, I admit. To pay you out for scorning my present to you, I deliberately didn't explain that that bit of jewelry nonsense was to mark the anniversary of Stella's début as a professional singer—a kind of birthday present, no more. And if it had been anything less than expensive, she'd have taken a very poor view, considering all the money I make out of her."

"I—see."

"I hope you do now. But I must say I got more than a spark of malicious fun out of watching your dear disapproving face." He led her to one of the couches, went to pour drinks, brought one to her, and sat beside her.

She said hesitantly, "I don't understand. When did it all begin for you?"

He spread a hand. "Who knows where love begins? It could even have been on a hockey pitch in a fog."

"Not for you then."

"Probably not. I forgot your name. But there has to have been a morning when I woke—or perhaps a night before I went to sleep—when I said to myself, 'I mustn't let this girl get away from me,' and began my campaign."

Ruth laughed at him over the rim of her wine glass. "You didn't let it show!"

"I dared not. You were so becalmed in your widowhood. You'd come to terms with it, and I felt I had to hasten slowly. But that night when I said that you and I could afford to ignore the man-woman thing, I was just one ache of desire for you."

"And you left me feeling wrapped around with your friendship—which I destroyed when I doubted you about Cicely."

"Yes, you were pretty obtuse about Cicely. But it didn't do you any harm to be a little bit jealous."

Ruth reddened. "I *wasn't* jealous of Cicely!"

Erle laughed. "I'd like a shrink's ruling on that!"

"Well, perhaps I was a little envious of her," Ruth admitted. "She was able to reach you so easily and so gaily. Whereas I—"

He laid his free hand over hers in a tight clasp. "I think, my darling girl, you wouldn't admit to jealousy of a new love because that implied a betrayal of the old—your first, Alec. You say you were hungry at Siena. But you were guilt-ridden too, perhaps?"

But Ruth shook her head. "No I think I'd accepted by then what you had put into words. I knew that loving a man as different from Alec as you wouldn't be any real disloyalty to him. What I had of him I've still got and shall always keep. He'd understood that, I know."

"And I shan't trespass," promised Erle, "You won't be forced to comparisons, please God. And I'm going to imagine that he's glad for you."

"I must too. Our last words to each other whenever we parted, even for a few hours, were, "Be happy," and I am. I *am!*" Ruth stirred her hand within his. "But if you've loved me as you say, why didn't you make our engagement a real one, instead of—?"

"Because you were still so aloof; because Fonte was still hovering and I was too craven to try my luck and find I'd lost. And for a more practical reason; supposing I did win, I wanted you to experience a kind of trial run—to learn just what committing yourself to me would entail."

"You mean—?"

He nodded. "I thought you'd know. All the differences. The social stuff. The brittle contacts. The razor edge between success and failure. Show business from behind, instead of in front. The sporadic traveling, hither and yon. The temperamental stars male and female—Do you realize, my Ruth, that round and about me there'll always be Pariolis and Grancias and their like? And accepting that, you can still be very sure and content that I chose *you,* and none of them? Never even considered one of them as a wife?"

"You said you considered no one as a wife. But I think I can."

"Only 'think'?" he urged.

"No. More than that. If you want me, I can take it—all of it. Though I can't help remembering how hurt I was that when we parted in the future and I left Rome, you wouldn't have wanted to know where I went."

"But that was your decision—that I wasn't to know."

"I still felt you ought to care enough for me as a friend to want to know."

Erle feigned a sigh. "The irrationality of even the dearest of women! I only agreed because if we had reached that point—of your turning me down—though I'd have cared like the devil, I'd have preferred not to know, lest I'd be tempted to come after you, only to take my punishment all over again. Cutting my losses, d'you see?" He set aside his glass and took hers almost roughly from her. "What are we doing, holding inquests on the past when we've got a *now?*" he demanded. "We're wasting good time, even if we've plenty of the same ahead."

He pulled her against him. His hands moved caressingly, touching her hair, making a frame for her face, drawing her closer, then holding her off.

"You know," he said, as if in awe of the discovery, "I've gone through most of the motions in dealing with women, but I've never known before this need to have and to hold . . . to love and to cherish—and the rest; never felt as caveman-fierce as I do now. Of course I realize what's happened to me. *You* have. But it's a new experience for me and I may overplay it. So are you going to bear with me, my all-in-all, if I need to show the world pretty blatantly that you're mine, my woman, *my* prize?"

She laid her head in the hollow of his shoulder, equally in awe of a nearness to him in spirit and in body which she had never thought would be hers by right of love. She said a little fearfully, "I can't believe it's happening, but if it is, I think I'd be sad and worried if you didn't want to claim me—like that."

"Or like this?" A forefinger under her chin turned her face up to his, but then softened to a response that was all acceptance, all tenderness, all gift of herself.

For a long time after that they said nothing coherent; spoke only by look and touch and smile and little wordless murmurs of delight and promise to themselves of the ultimate mastery and sweet surrender to come.

Then they were spent, and only holding hands like children. Erle stood, drawing Ruth to her feet. He fingered a pocket, took something from it, and tossed it in his palm, then showed it to her.

"My soldino," he said. "For your pennyworth of sky that I have to give you. Come and see which bit you'll have, and be sure to choose one with plenty of stars."

Laughing, she went to stand on the portico with him. Head on one side, she pretended to consider the expanse of the sky. "I *think*," she said slowly, "I'll have the bit that's east o' the sun and west o' the moon."

"And which bit is that?"

"How do I know?" she teased. "A good astronomer could probably tell you."

"The book says I have to afford one *soldino's* worth of sky. Astonomers come too expensive and they aren't thrown in," he retorted.

"All right, skip the astronomer. Suppose *you* choose?"

"I was hoping you'd ask me." Putting his arm round her, he turned her in the direction of the dark mass of the Casa, just discernible against the horizon. He said, "I'll go for a short-term bargain. I'll buy you the whole of the dawn sky on just one morning—the day that we first make this place our home, yours and mine. Would you regard that as value for money, my Ruth of the Biblical name and the eyebrows that got left out in the wet until they rusted up?"

She smiled up at him, enjoying the whimsey. "I couldn't ask for more, and as a present from you I'd settle for a lot less," she said, and offered him her lips again.

THE FLAMBOYANT TREE

The Flamboyant Tree

Isobel Chace

Frances was understandably nervous about her new position in Tanzania. Not that she wasn't a fully qualified and capable doctor, but she was very conscious that the hospital would be in her sole care. In England someone else had always been there to take the final responsibility; here there was no one.

To make matter worse, she was faced with Simon Abbott's sharp antagonism. It had been evident right from their first meeting when he'd learned who she was.

"So you're Dr. Whitney!" he had exclaimed angrily. "And you turn out to be a woman. That's all we needed. Well," he added, "you won't last ten minutes!"

CHAPTER ONE

THE air was lighter in Nairobi. Frances Whitney looked about eagerly, but it was too dark to see much but the bright stars in the sky and the hanging disk of the moon. London seemed a long, long time away; yet it was only that morning that she had been there, struggling with the nervous qualms that had assaulted her as she had stepped into the enormous cabin of the jet that had flown her to Africa. There had been one brief stop at Entebbe, Uganda, when, although it had not been too hot, she had felt the dampness of the atmosphere flood into the airplane. Nairobi had too high an altitude to be damp. Someone had told her that fact long ago, when she had first thought of coming, but they had failed to tell her that the air was heady like wine and scented with sunshine and sweet-smelling plants.

The taxi took her straight to her hotel. There was very little she could see in the darkness. She had an impression of wide, clean streets and small groups of people walking along the pavements. Then, before she was ready for it, the taxi had zoomed up a steep slope and had deposited her at the entrance to the hotel.

The foyer was large and comfortable. A souvenir shop was straight ahead of her, and the desk, manned by several pretty young women, was on the right. Frances hesitated, looking behind her to see if the porter had brought in her battered suitcase.

"Can we help you?" one of the women asked her.

"I—I have a reservation for the night," Frances managed. "Dr. Whitney."

The receptionist was surprised, but she did her best to

hide it. "Yes, Dr. Whitney," she said flatly. "Will you fill in this form, please?"

Frances struggled in her purse for her passport and copied the number onto the form together with all the other information that has to be supplied on every occasion when one travels.

"You are going on to Arusha tomorrow?" the receptionist confirmed with her.

Frances nodded. "I'd like to spend longer here," she admitted, "but they're expecting me immediately."

The receptionist smiled. "It will be a surprise, too," she said gently. "They were expecting a male doctor!"

Frances laughed. "Oh no! They must know! I never made a secret of my being a woman. The offer was open to any qualified doctor."

The girl smiled. Her hair had been beautifully set, and she was quite one of the prettiest women Frances had ever seen.

"I don't think anyone will mind, doctor. The village needs a doctor. There are very few who will give their services to the young countries for even a year or two. We were all told to make you very welcome."

"But this is Kenya," Frances reminded her. "The village is in Tanzania."

The woman shrugged. "We can still be glad of your coming," she said. She reached behind for one of the room keys, decorated by a large carved lion to prevent the guests from pocketing it by mistake. "The porter will show you to your room. Shall I arrange transport to the airport tomorrow morning?"

"Thank you," Frances said gratefully. "I think the flight leaves at 11 o'clock."

She turned away from the desk, looking for the elevator. It was half-hidden behind the souvenir shop, and she might not have seen it had it not been that someone else was waiting to go up in it. A tall man, dressed in drill trousers and a safari jacket that had seen better days, pressed the button a second time with a touch of impatience. His face had been burned brown by the sun. He had the nonchalant look of a man who had everything he wanted. Frances found his very presence gave her a jolt. It was, she thought wryly, the first time she had really seen a man for a very long time.

Medicine had long been a family affair with the Whitneys. Frances's father and mother were both doctors, and no one doubted that their daughter would also train in the same hospital and eventually enter the family practice to work with her parents.

There had been a time when Frances wondered whether or not she really did want to be a doctor, but as there was nothing else she could think of to do, she had settled down to the long years of training and had done well.

It had been during the year that she had been working for her finals that she had fallen in love. She had flattered herself to begin with that no one would ever know—certainly not the man in question! He had been one of the registrars at the hospital; looking back now, she could see that he was a thoroughly unlikable young man. He had done nothing to deserve the short but devastating publicity he had briefly shared with her. Frances's work had gone to pieces just when it mattered most, and she had borne the aftermath of her parents' united wrath.

Somehow she had scrambled through her finals and had worked another year in the hospital, but she had not made the mistake of losing her heart again, not to anyone or anything. Then had come her great moment of rebellion. Her parents had concluded that she would join them immediately, but Frances had refused with a stubbornness that had surprised them all, herself more than anyone.

"I am not in need of money immediately," she had said firmly. "I'm going to volunteer to go abroad."

"But you don't know anything about tropical medicine!" they had argued with one voice.

"I don't know very much about *any* medicine!" she had retorted bitterly.

She had gone about making her preparations with dogged efficiency. She had read an article about the self-help villages of Tanzania, where the population worked together in a kind of cooperative for their mutual benefit. And, before anyone could stop her, she had volunteered to go to one of these villages for a period of two years for no more than her keep and some pocket money to keep her going while she was there.

Mrs. Whitney had said dolefully that she really had hoped to retire; her father had looked disappointed and had talked about all the money he had invested in her career. Frances, who knew quite well that the grants she had received had only covered the bare necessities of her training, had tried to explain to him her own need for new surroundings and a respite from the bitterness that had grown like a living thing within her. It was a hopeless task.

"Anyone would think you'd had an unfortunate love affair!" her mother had sighed, forgetting all about the events of more than a year before. It was a constant annoyance to her that Frances showed no signs of attracting a husband, or even that she saw marriage as a desirable state in life.

"If I were a man you'd think it was a good idea for me to see something of the world before I settle down!" Frances had protested.

"But what will you do?" her mother had wailed. "All alone in a primitive village and not a soul to talk to."

"I'll learn to be a doctor," Frances had said. "And a damned good one at that!"

Her mother had frowned at her. "Don't swear, dear," she had said automatically. But, for some reason, neither of her parents had tried to dissuade her any more after that. They had even helped her to pack her bag and had driven her to Heathrow to catch her plane. She would always be grateful to them for that.

The man leaned against the side of the elevator and looked her up and down with appreciation. Frances tried to pretend that she hadn't noticed, but the slight blush in her cheeks gave her away.

"Just visiting?" he asked her.

"Yes," she said.

The elevator doors opened and the man stepped out into the corridor swinging his key back and forth between two fingers.

"All alone?"

"I don't mind my own company," she retorted.

His eyebrows lifted slightly. "Good hunting!" he drawled.

The elevator doors closed again, taking her up another floor. It had been a humiliating thing for him to say, she thought, as she tried to stir herself to anger. But the truth was that she didn't mind as much as she ought to.

She felt alive and faintly excited; she had liked the strong look of his face.

It took her hardly any time to wash her hands and
face and change for dinner. She wore a black dress with
a very low back and a small sequinned bolero over it.
She thought it suited her, for the plain black highlighted
her very fair hair. Catching sight of herself in the mirror
she saw that she was pretty, with large vulnerable eyes
and an uptilted nose that belied the strength of her
mouth. Even so, she did not much care for eating alone
in a public restaurant, so she hunted around in her suitcase for the book she was reading to take down with her.

With an almost Gallic gesture, the headwaiter showed
her to a table. He then produced an elaborate menu and
took her order in the pauses in the great roar of sound
coming from the band. Frances took out her book and
tried to read, but she felt dazed by the volume of noise
that gushed out of the loudspeakers, shaking the very
cutlery on the table. Several couples were dancing, most
of them European and probably on holiday. But there
were several Indians as well, and Africans too, and even
a number of mixed couples, lending a pleasant, cosmopolitan air to the room.

Frances abandoned her book and watched the dancers instead. A white-coated waiter brought her some
soup, serving her with infinite care from an enormous
cauldron on a trolley.

"May I join you?"

Frances jumped and looked up to see the man from
the elevator standing beside the table. He too had
changed and was wearing a cream-colored dinner
jacket, set off by a scarlet cummerbund. He looked more
sure of himself than ever.

"Please do," she said faintly.

He sat down at right angles to her, shooting his long
legs out under the table.

"So you're still alone?" he asked dryly.

The color started up her cheeks. "It seems not!" she smiled with gentle irony.

He gave her a surprised glance. "Would you care to dance?" he asked abruptly.

She nodded and stood up, saying nothing because the band had reached a crescendo of sound that was difficult to compete with. It was strange to feel his hand in the small of her back, or the hand of any man for that matter; even more strange to find that he danced well and that she had no difficulty following him. It had always been one of the things that she most disliked about dancing. At hospital dances she had been teased again and again for refusing to follow her partner's lead. But then the doctors there, valiantly crossing off their "duty" dances before they went back to their girlfriends, had not been at all like this man who would brook very little interference in anything.

He held her closer, slipping his hand up beneath her bolero and finding her bare skin. She wanted to object, but she could not. Instead, she closed her eyes and allowed the music to become part of her very being. She felt his cheek against hers and wondered at herself for not pulling away from him. When he kissed her just beside her ear it seemed a natural part of the dance. Her heart hammered in time to the beat of the drums that crashed beside her.

When the dance came to an end, he led her back to the table and held her chair politely for her as she sat down.

"How do you like Nairobi?" he asked her.

"I've only seen this hotel," she said.

"And some of the local characters," he added for her.

"Do you live here?" she asked.

He shook his head. He picked up the menu as the waiter approached their table, then gave his order in rapid Swahili.

"Shall we have some wine?" he asked her, in English, in the middle of the flood of incomprehensible words.

"There's no reason for you to—"

"I'd like to," he cut her off. "We can drink to the possibilities of our meeting!"

Frances felt his speculative eyes watching her and pretended an interest she was far from feeling in the dance floor.

"Shall we dance again?" he suggested.

She was afraid he would think that she had been silently asking him to dance again with her, but she couldn't bring herself to refuse. What had come over her?

"If . . . if you like," was her hesitant reply.

"I like it very much!" he answered smoothly.

It was scarcely a dance at all, she thought afterward. The music had changed while the band took a short rest, and there was only a single trumpeter playing softly to himself. This time he put both arms about her and held her so close that she could scarcely breathe. Never in her whole life had she been so close to anyone, and yet it didn't seem at all strange to her. He smelled nice and his hands on her bare back were cool and firm.

When he kissed her on the lips, she stood quite still and allowed it. It was balm to her bruised spirit. She didn't even know his name and he knew nothing about her, and yet he obviously found her attractive. He had even sought her out, and that was something the man she had loved had never done. He had kissed her once, clinically and efficiently, she remembered bleakly. She had objected, and he had immediately let her go and had turned elsewhere. This man, on the other hand, wouldn't have let go even if she did object. She didn't know how she knew that, but know it she did. And she didn't care. She was more than happy to kiss him back.

"Mmm, you taste nice!" the man murmured in her ear.

"It's the soup," she smiled.

"Maybe." He kissed her again. "Do you have a name, by the way?" he asked her.

"Frances. My friends call me Fran."

"Simon," he muttered briefly, kissing her again.

She ate the rest of her meal in a dream. He supplied her liberally with wine, his eyes watching her flushed face.

"It's a good place to come for a holiday, isn't it?" he teased her. "Aren't you glad you came?"

She lowered her eyelids, refusing to answer. She didn't like his watching her, though she couldn't put her finger on the reason. He was like a large, lazy lion waiting to pounce on his prey.

"You must never be afraid in Africa," he warned her. "You've come so far in search of adventure, you can't turn back now."

"I'm not afraid," she said steadily.

"Good. After all, I'm not very frightening, am I?"

She longed to tell him exactly how frightening he was, but she had no wish to antagonize him. The truth was that she was quite enjoying being a little afraid. She found that it added a spice to the evening she had never known before. It was like an intricate game when neither of the players could afford to make a single mistake.

"Well, am I?" he repeated.

She shook her head. "I think you like your own way," she hazarded timidly.

"And are you going to oblige me?" he asked blandly.

She felt suddenly stifled, her throat dry and her hands ready to tremble. "No!" she burst out.

"Why not?"

Frances shook her head. "I don't believe in casual affairs," she said, her voice gruff with embarrassment.

He accepted this with unblinking calm. "Of course I will do everything I can to change your mind. The night is young and I can wait!"

"And I won't have any more wine, thank you," she said abruptly.

He said nothing, but his eyebrows shot upward. Frances hesitated, on the brink of telling him that she had given up men for a long, long time to come. But common sense told her that he would not believe her, or, if he did, that it would merely present him with a challenge he could not resist.

"Do you come here often?" she asked him brightly.

"Every now and then," he answered easily.

"But you live out of town?"

His eyes met hers, a touch of amusement in them. "What do you want to know? Whether or not I'm married?" He laughed shortly. "I'm not. I spend most of my time where I don't see a girl from one week's end to another—"

"So I imagined!" Frances observed dryly.

He looked significantly at her left hand. "Nor are you married," he reminded her.

"No."

"But not lacking in experience?" he suggested mockingly.

She smiled demurely. "I'm sure I'm not in the same league as you."

"I've never found women slow to learn!"

"Then I have a surprise for you, Mr.—er—Simon. I learned my lessons only too well. It's not a path I care to travel again."

His expression was mildly contemptuous, "I suppose you came out here to *forget?*"

"Not entirely," she said. "I came here so that I could be myself—"

"Oh no!" he exclaimed.

"Is it so difficult to believe?"

"Frankly, yes. You haven't the courage to be yourself, Frances Whoever-you-are! You're one person when you're dancing and quite another when you're sitting here congratulating yourself on your prim, schoolgirl morality—"

Frances stood up, her cheeks scarlet. "At least I don't set out to deliberately hurt other people!" she informed him with quiet dignity. "Nor do I use people for my own ends. I may be prim, but I'm not stupid!"

He stood up too. "Anything else?"

"Yes!" she snapped. "I'm a better loser than you are! Nor do I stoop to personal abuse when my charm fails to have the desired effect!" She bit her lip, suddenly, horribly aware of what she had said. "I mean . . ." she began, hoping to retrieve the situation. "I mean. . . ."

"Yes? Please don't spare my feelings, will you?"

"I shouldn't have said that," she admitted penitently. "I'm sorry."

His eyes held hers with a force she couldn't define. "You're younger than I thought," he said harshly.

"I'm *very sorry*," she said again. "I . . . I think I'll go to bed."

He laughed suddenly. "You should never allow yourself to feel guilty, you know," he told her conversationally. "It gives me an advantage that I don't deserve."

"Oh?" she breathed uncertainly.

"Definitely. If I were to kiss you now, you'd be afraid of hurting my feelings all over again, so you'd kiss me right back!"

Frances swallowed. "But—"

"Come on. I'll take you up to your room and leave you at the door." His eyes glinted. "Tomorrow is another day!"

He finished the wine in his glass in a single gulp without bothering to sit down again; then he escorted her through the crowded dining room, nodding a greeting here and there when he recognized someone he knew. They walked down the small flight of stairs to the foyer, where he paused at the souvenir shop. He pointed to a single glass on which had been engraved a large bull elephant, with the famous steamed pudding shape of Mount Kilimanjaro in the background, strikingly displayed against black velvet.

"I'll take that," he said to the uniformed clerk in the booth. He paid for it and watched it being wrapped; then he took the box and placed it in Frances's hands. "No ill feelings?" he asked her.

"But I can't accept—"

"Why not?" he cut her off.

"It's expensive and . . . and—"

"Most good things are expensive." He took her arm and led her away toward the elevator.

"That's why I can't accept it," she said, almost with relief. "There are strings attached."

"None that you don't agree to of your own free will," he assured her.

"Then . . . then why?"

"Because you're pretty," he laughed at her. "And because I'd like you to have a good holiday."

"I haven't come on holiday."

"No," he remembered, "you've come to be yourself!"

She allowed herself to be shepherded into the elevator, annoyed with herself for being so conscious of his presence beside her. The elevator hurtled upward, giving her no time to arrange a good night speech in her mind. Then she remembered that she had scarcely thanked him for the glass. She turned toward him impulsively, just as the doors of the elevator slid open.

"I'll always treasure it!" she said warmly.

He stepped out and smiled at her, taking her key and glancing down at the number. He walked briskly along the open corridor, put the key in her door and opened it. He even turned on the light.

"Simon—"

"Uh-huh?" He stood in the doorway, blocking her way into the room. He took her bag and the box with the glass in it, putting them down on the built-in desk just inside the door.

"Simon?"

His arms slipped around her and his mouth descended on hers. Any protest she might have made died on a single sob. She made a last, desperate attempt to break free, an attempt that ended in her putting her arms around his neck and pulling him closer still.

It was he who brought the kiss to an end. It was he who pushed her through the open door and closed it with a sharp click. It was like waking from a pleasant dream to an unpleasant reality. Frances tore the door open again, but he had already gone. There was no doubt about it. The final victory had been his.

As soon as she was dressed, Frances went out onto the balcony for her first look at Nairobi in the early-morning light. The mauve blossoms of the jacaranda trees were everywhere. They almost totally surrounded some rather ugly pink apartment blocks just opposite her room, and she could see yet other mauve drifts of color further down the street. The traffic was already beginning to build up, pouring into the city from the surrounding suburbs where most of the people lived. Frances glanced at her watch. She had plenty of time to go out and take a look at the city before breakfast.

She packed her suitcase with care and left it near the door to be carried down later. There was no one about except for an African who was busy taking early morning tea trays to rooms on his floor. He approached her, concern on his face.

"Would you like tea now?" he asked quickly.

Frances shook her head. "No, I'm going out!" she told him.

He merely grinned at her.

She felt very good as she walked down the road. She had never seen a more lovely place in her life. The wide streets, lined with banks of flowers; the soft, cool air that was full of sunshine; and the cheerful greetings people made to each other.

Frances walked past the Anglican Cathedral, which looked remarkably like an English country church, and the main post office. Farther on, she caught a glimpse of the Roman Catholic Cathedral, half-hidden by large blocks of offices and a fairly big bookshop. She would have liked to have explored more, but she grew nervous that she might get lost, so she walked slowly back to the hotel again, stopping frequently to admire the different-colored bougainvillea along the way.

Breakfast was being served by the time she returned and, feeling hungry, she found herself a table and sat down quickly. Perhaps, in England, they had once served similar breakfasts, but she had never known such a time. She gazed with awe at the center table, loaded with fruits and cereals from which one could help oneself. And that was only the start. There was a choice between eggs, bacon and sausages, fish cakes, smoked haddock, or anything else one cared to think of, followed by crisp golden toast and a choice between marmalade and honey.

When she had finished, Frances went to the reception desk and paid her bill, asking that her luggage be brought down to her.

"We'll call you when the taxi comes, doctor," the receptionist promised. "Where will you be?"

"I'll wait here," she said. Several chairs were arranged in little groups in the foyer, and she pointed to one in the shadows where she intended to sit.

She saw Simon long before he saw her. He was dressed again in a safari jacket, stained red with the rust-colored earth. He too went to the desk and paid his bill. She wondered where he was going, a little surprised that he should be leaving so soon. Then he turned and saw her. He came over and sat down in a nearby chair.

"I should have thought you would be out seeing the sights!" he greeted her.

"I've been out," she said.

His lazy eyes glinted dangerously. "Couldn't you sleep?"

"Oh yes! I slept like a log!" she lied casually. "I think flying all day must be more exhausting than one imagines."

"So they say," he agreed dourly.

"I see you're checking out," she went on conversationally. "Didn't you find what you wanted here?"

"Unfortunately I have to earn my living," he drawled. "I'm going home. The Masai are moving their cattle and I don't want them anywhere near my animals!"

"Of course not!" she agreed mildly.

He made an impatient gesture. "They don't believe that their cattle are infectious, but unfortunately it's only too true!"

"And I suppose you have a vast investment in your own cattle?" she asked him sweetly.

He looked at her for a long moment. "Not in cattle," he said.

She let the subject die. She didn't know why she wanted to goad him, but she was disappointed that he should be checking out without a single thought for what had passed between them the night before.

There was a flurry of activity by the door and one of the porters ran over to where they were sitting.

"Daktari! Daktari! Your taxi has come!"

They both stood up together, colliding into one another. Simon recovered first and pushed her back into her chair.

"I'll be saying goodbye, Fran," he said simply.

"But it's my taxi!" she claimed indignantly.

He shook his head. "Daktari means doctor in Swahili," he explained kindly.

"I know! That means me!"

"I'm a vet—" He broke off, staring at her. "What is your name?" he demanded. "Frances what?"

"Frances Whitney."

He clapped a hand to his brow. " That's all we need! Dr. Frances Whitney! And you turn out to be a woman!"

"I'm still a doctor!" she said, hurt.

"You won't last ten minutes!" he retorted.

Her temper fired up. "Just watch me!" she said icily.

He glared at her, the kindliness gone. Indeed, his dislike could not have been plainer. "Unfortunately I shall have to!" he said.

CHAPTER TWO

THEY rode in silence to the airport. Frances pretended she was interested in the scenery. They passed the entrance to the Nairobi National Park, where the visitors can see wild animals in their own habitat in what is also practically a suburb of the city. There was also a drive-in cinema, with an immense screen, and room for literally hundreds of cars. It was the first one Frances had ever seen.

"Simon—"

"Dr. Whitney?"

"Do you live at Nguyu?"

"You don't have to look so worried. I won't bother you. *That* I can assure you!"

She lapsed into silence. Tears jerked into her eyes. It was unreasonable of him to be so cross. She hadn't tried to hide her identity. Nor had it been she who had accosted him the evening before, thus getting them both off on the wrong foot!

"I didn't realize you were a vet," she said at last, making conversation because the silence was unbearable.

"No," he said.

"I . . . I don't even know your name."

"Simon Abbott," he growled.

"Oh," she said.

The taxi drove up to the reception lounge and Simon jumped out quickly and paid the driver before Frances had time to object. He marched ahead of her into the departure booth, pulling his passport out of his pocket. Frances followed more slowly, uncertain of what to do. She paid the airport tax that the clerk demanded of her and accepted an immigration form for the Tanzanian government to be filled in on the plane.

Simon was waiting impatiently for her when she reached the other end. He signaled to a porter to take away her luggage with his and then proceeded to ignore her. Oh well, she thought, he would have to work it out for himself. But it hurt all the same.

Their flight number was called and there was a rush toward the numbered door that led out to the concrete apron where the Dakota was waiting for them. A smart stewardess in a leopardskin cap escorted them across to the plane, watching them anxiously as they climbed the steps and entered the small cabin of the now ancient airplane. The floor of the cabin sloped steeply uphill, making it difficult to get into the well-used seats. Frances stared about her with horror. She did not like flying at the best of times, but this plane must have come out of the Ark!

Simon Abbott flung himself into the seat beside her, his lazy eyes watching the emotions flitting across her face.

"I hope you're a good flyer, doctor," he drawled. "This doesn't boast a pressurized cabin, you know."

"I'm thankful that it boasts two wings!" she exclaimed.

"More or less," he added.

"Are you frightened too?" she asked him before she could stop herself.

"Are you frightened?" he countered. "I thought I told you that it didn't pay to be scared in Africa."

She tried to relax but found it quite impossible. A steward came running up the steps, a check list in his hand, and counted the passengers twice over, his pink turban nodding as he ticked each name on his list.

"How long is the flight?" Frances asked nervously.

"About an hour. Calm down, doctor, I won't let anything happen to you!"

"You won't be able to prevent it," she pointed out reasonably. "And I wish you wouldn't call me doctor. It makes me nervous!"

He found that interesting. "Does it indeed?" he asked dryly.

She blushed. "How would you like to be called vet all the time?"

"They call me *daktari* most of the time," he said placidly.

"But that means doctor," she objected.

"I'm an animal doctor!"

"Yes, but it isn't quite the same, is it?" she said demurely. "What will they call me?"

He shrugged. "So you think you're superior to a mere animal doctor?"

"No!" she denied hastily. "Only you wouldn't be called doctor in England, would you?"

"Are you?" he riposted.

She looked at him seriously. "I'm fully qualified," she said.

"To practise among the coughs and colds in England, I daresay. What do you know about the sort of thing you can expect in Nguyu, Dr. Whitney?"

Her eyes fell. "I expect to be better than nothing," she said.

"If you were a man, you might be! But Nguyu Hospital is no place for a woman. And don't expect my help, because I'm only an animal doctor!"

"I won't!"

The Dakota moved forward in a sudden movement, taxiing along the runway and smoothly up into the air.

Frances froze in her seat as she watched the wheels leave the earth. The wings creaked in an air pocket, causing momentary discomfort, but the plane rose eagerly higher until the airport buildings disappeared behind them and the scorched gray-brown of the earth stretched out beneath them for as far as she could see.

"What do you have against a woman being a doctor?" she asked slowly.

"Nothing. If you want to know, it's *you* being a doctor that I resent!"

She was startled into looking at him again. *"Me?"* She licked her lips. "But why?"

"Don't be silly, Fran," he said tersely. "I had other plans for you."

"Oh, *that!*" She dismissed it lightly, for she really couldn't see why her being a doctor should matter one way or the other.

"Yes, *that.* I'd have flown back to Nairobi in a day or so and who knows what might have happened then. Now I've got you around my neck for the next two years—"

"I see," she said. "Love them and leave them?"

"I like to have the choice," he agreed without apology. "Nguyu has a decidedly restricted social life and we have to get along with one another whether we like it or not. That isn't easy with any woman—"

"I've managed!" she interrupted him abruptly.

"Heartwhole and fancy free?" he mocked her.

She thought of the one love of her life and stared out at the scenery below them. The only sign of human habitation was the occasional ring of huts; otherwise there was nothing but the gold-gray earth.

"Once I thought I had fallen in love," she admitted.

He put his head back and she was glad not to feel his

eyes watching her. "And what happened?" he asked.

"He didn't notice me," she said.

He shot forward. "Now that I don't believe!"

"Why not? I'm quite ordinary, you know," she managed. "It happens all the time."

"So it does," he agreed more gently.

"So you don't have to worry about my getting in your way," she assured him. "I'll be busy with my own work."

"With no kisses on the side?"

She shook her head. "I've never done that before," she explained earnestly. "I can't understand what came over me last night!"

He gave her a doubtful look. "I wish I didn't know what came over me!" he answered shortly. He was silent for a moment. "All right, Frances," he said at last. "We'll try it your way."

The plane went through a series of air pockets, dropping several feet and rising again. Frances began to feel decidedly ill and hoped that she would manage to last until their arrival at Arusha. She had never traveled in an unpressurized cabin before and she had not known what the difference would be. It meant an aching head and a sinking feeling in her stomach that she feared would lead to her being physically sick. She gritted her teeth and stared out the window. An enormous mountain came into sight in front of them. For an awful moment she thought they were going straight into it, but they wheeled at an extraordinary angle in the air, and a few seconds later they landed safely on the rough grass of Arusha airfield.

It was hotter than it had been in Nairobi and the few passengers hurried across the field and into the airport buildings. A uniformed clerk leisurely stamped their passports and collected up their immigration cards. Others brought the luggage across from the plane and loaded it into trolleys ready for the customs officer to cast a casual eye over it. Neither Simon nor Frances were asked to open their suitcases, the officer contenting himself with carefully forming identical symbols in chalk on every suitcase in front of him.

Simon picked up their cases and hurried out of the building, throwing them into the back of a waiting Land Rover. The driver snapped smartly to attention. The effect was somewhat spoiled by his shorts, which had become thin and torn around the hem, and his old army boots, which had no laces.

"*Daktari,* I have brought your car!"

Simon shook him by the hand. "Hop in the back, will you?" he said with an easy air of command. "The *memsahib daktari* will sit beside me in the front."

The driver's curious eyes shot around to look at Frances and he wiped his hands on his torn shorts. Frances held hers out and he shook it timidly. "*Jambo, memsahib,*" he said.

"*Jambo,*" Frances responded warmly. "*Hebari?*"

The man's nervousness left him and his face broke into a smile. "*Msuri sana!*" he laughed happily. He jumped into the back of the Land Rover, leaning forward to hold the door open for her.

"Where did you learn your Swahili?" Simon asked her, as she struggled into the high seat beside him.

"That's all I know," she told him. "I have a dictionary in my luggage, though, and I try to study a little every day."

"Very commendable," he grunted. "Abel," he shouted to the man in the back, "this is *mama* Whitney."

"*Mama daktari,*" the man said with a grin.

"Abel comes everywhere with me," Simon went on. "He has a twin brother called Cain—"

"And he's still alive?" Frances couldn't resist interrupting him.

It was Abel who laughed. "Very much alive," he answered in his deep voice. "Cain would kill nobody. He's afraid of the animals."

Simon said something to him in rapid Swahili and the man nodded. "Cain will be your servant," he went on agreeably. "I will tell him that the *daktari* has said it is to be so."

"But I don't need a servant!" Frances protested. "I've always looked after myself—"

"You won't have time at Nguyu," Simon told her. "Cain will suit you very well. Abel will see to that, won't you?" He turned with a quick smile to the man in the back.

"Cain will work very hard," Abel agreed with such decision that Frances could only feel sorry for his unknown brother.

"But—" she began.

"I suppose you know that you will be running the hospital single-handed with only the help of a nursing aide?" Simon interposed.

"Even so," she said.

He ignored that, merely confirming the arrangement with Abel that his brother Cain would work for the *mama Daktari*, translate for her, and generally do everything that was needed. Abel only nodded. He sat back, leaning against the suitcases, and shut his eyes, dropping off to sleep almost immediately.

Frances had never felt less like sleep. They came into the town of Arusha, past the buildings that housed the offices for the East African Common Market, past some shops and out again from the main part of the town to the market. The women, brightly garbed in vivid blue and the mud-colored red so much favored by the Masai, sat in groups, their wares set out before them, bargaining and gossiping under the hot sun.

When they were right outside the town, they stopped by a clump of trees to eat sandwiches and drink coffee from a thermos that Abel had brought with him. Simon was in a hurry to keep going, however, so there was no time to explore the small village nearby. Frances could only catch a glimpse of the banana plants that stood around the doors of the huts, and the hard, beaten-down paths that led hither and thither without any apparent pattern.

Soon there was nothing but the flat savanna lands. The slopes of Kilimanjaro towered upward behind them, but the summit was lost in clouds. Somewhere beside that mountain an international airport was being built that would mean that the great planes from Europe and America would be able to fly directly into the main tourist area of Tanzania, without having to go to Nairobi first.

Frances knew immediately that they had passed from the lands of one tribe to another. The agriculture became less sophisticated the farther they went, and the land grew poorer. Where, at first, there had been solid fields of maize and fat hump-backed cattle, now there were only expanses of grassland, which had been deliberately set on fire to encourage the new growth that the rains would bring.

They turned off the main road and started down a long dusty road to Lake Manyara. The dry weather had corrugated the surface and a great cloud of dust ballooned out behind them. Whenever anything came the other way, it was impossible to see the road ahead for seconds at a time; the dust was everywhere, settling in a fine coat of red over the seats, the dashboard and the luggage.

Once a flock of ostriches, ridiculous-looking creatures with long hairy necks and outsize feet, made a concerted dash across the road, then slowed down and stalked with great dignity back to where they had come from. Abel woke up at that, smiled at the sight, and nodded off to sleep again.

"What is Nguyu like?" Frances asked Simon, more to keep awake than to start a conversation. The heat was strangely soporific and, combined with the rumble of the tires traveling quickly over the corrugated road, it was practically irresistible.

"What do you want to know?"

"Anything," she said. "I hardly know anything about this place, except that it has a hospital and a school. I didn't even know there was a vet!"

His lazy eyes never left the road. "I'm only there at times," he told her. "I spend much of my time in the Serengeti and Ngorongoro and Lake Manyara. Nguyu is a convenient center because it isn't far from any of the national parks."

"But do they need a vet in the national parks?" she objected.

"Sometimes. Most often when the poachers have been at work. But I do other things as well. I like to study the movements of the animals—I'm doing some research for the government on that sort of thing. The tourist industry depends on the animals, you see, which is a good thing, for man is the most selfish animal of all; the industry has a much better chance of survival if tourists bring in vast sums of money!"

"That sounds rather cynical," Frances said with disapproval.

"Does it? It wasn't meant to be. It's little more than the truth. The animals were practically all killed off at one time. It was a fight to get the game reserves going and even more of a fight to keep them. But, since independence, because of the new airplanes, the tourists have started to come and they're managing to save the animals for the whole world."

Frances sighed enviously. "It must be interesting, working with animals," she said.

"Your work must be pretty interesting too," he consoled her.

"Coughs and colds in England?" she mocked him.

"You'll have something else to sharpen your scalpel on here—if you last. The conditions are not exactly what you're accustomed to."

"I'll survive," she said.

They came then to the Rift Valley, the great crack in the earth's surface that stretches from Israel in the north all the way down to Lake Nyasa in the south. In Africa it formed the rift in which the soda lakes lie. In Kenya, the valley has two sides, in Tanzania only one. The eastern bank slopes gently toward Lake Manyara and the national park there, and then rises in a steep, almost perpendicular, cliff at the top of which are some of the most superb views in the world.

"We'll have tea at the Lake Manyara Hotel," Simon suggested. "Your last taste of civilization for a while!"

"I could do with some," she agreed. "The dust is pretty awful, isn't it?"

"Wait until it turns to mud!" he grunted.

He set the Land Rover into a low gear to enable them to grind up the steep hill. A great baobab tree stood on the left of the road, looking exactly as it was supposed to look, the upside-down tree, the tree with its roots in the air. Only now the tree was in full bloom, its great cream-colored flowers hanging absurdly on the stumpy branches.

When they gained the top, they could see the local air strip and, soon after, the place where the road branches off for the hotel. A zebra trotted out of a private garden to look at them, his stripes glinting in the sunlight. Behind him was the first green grass Frances had seen in Tanzania. And flowers were everywhere, exotic flowering bushes as well as the more ordinary flowers such as gladioli and roses.

Simon parked the Land Rover just outside the door and sauntered into the hotel where he was greeted by shrieks of welcome. Apparently he was well known throughout the district. Frances stood some distance behind him, shyly watching the scene as he slapped palms with everyone in sight.

"How's business?" he asked them.

"Good," they grinned. "The lions have been seen yesterday and today. They are sitting in the trees quite near the entrance to the park."

Simon glanced at his watch. "We haven't time now," he said regretfully. "This is the *mama daktari* who is going to Nguyu. I'll bring her back some other time to look at the lions."

The men didn't slap palms with her, Frances noticed. They shook her gravely by the hand, irrepressible smiles on their faces.

"*Mama daktari* has come from England?" she was asked politely.

"Yesterday," she said. Could it really have been only yesterday? It seemed such a long time since her airplane from London had touched down at Nairobi Airport.

"We would like tea, please," Simon requested. "We'll be outside by the swimming pool."

"Ndiyo, bwana," came the answer, slipping back into the more familiar Swahili.

Simon put his hand on Frances's elbow and guided her through the hotel bar and out onto the patio. Some people were playing around the swimming pool, laughing and joking. Others, a little older, were seated at the numerous little tables that stood a little above the bowl in the cliff where the swimming pool was situated. Beyond, lay the Rift Valley, the thick trees that concealed much of the national park, Lake Manyara, and the hills, which looked blue in the distance.

But none of these captured Frances's eye. She was riveted to the spot by a single spreading tree that bowed towards the hotel. It was covered in scarlet blossom, radiant and fiery in the afternoon sun. It was not a flame tree, for she had seen pictures of those and, anyway, they seemed mean in comparison with this cloud of color.

"What's that?" she asked Simon, pulling at his sleeve.

"That?" He looked amused. "That's the famous flamboyant tree. It's a native of Madagascar, but it does well here."

"I think it's the most beautiful thing I've ever seen," Frances exclaimed in awe.

Abel came and stood by her shoulder, a little puzzled by her admiration for what was, after all, only a tree. "I will get you a small one to grow at Nguyu," he offered.

Frances turned to him, her face alight with enthusiasm. "Will you really? I'll plant it somewhere where we can all enjoy it?"

"The *daktari* has a garden beside his house," Abel told her. "Cain is a very good gardener."

"Then he can make a garden for me!" Frances said excitedly.

The two men grinned at each other in mutual understanding.

"So you will employ Cain after all," Simon drawled.

Frances blushed. "To make a garden, yes," she said.

Nguyu was very remote. The road actually bypassed the small town, but a battered signpost pointed it out down a narrow lane through a plantation of acacia trees. The town was built on the grid plan and was a series of square mud houses, most of them with roofs of corrugated iron. Between the houses were narrow paths of earth, hardened by thousands of footprints. Here and there, the houses opened up and it was possible for a car to ease between them. At one end of the town was the marketplace, with long counters placed at right angles to each other, under high thatched roofs that afforded some shelter from the heat of the sun. The market place was seldom empty; even so late in the afternoon, huge hands of green bananas hung around the posts that held up the roofs.

"The hospital has received a coat of whitewash to honor your coming," Simon told her, pointing out a building that, to her confused eye, looked exactly the same as every other.

"It doesn't look very big," she responded nervously.

"You won't have many in-patients," he said easily.

"Won't I?" She looked concerned.

"Most of the sick people prefer to be looked after in their own home. They have to be very ill indeed to want to stay in the hospital. Probably that's why most of them think that if one goes into the hospital one will die there."

"But that's terrible!" Frances exclaimed, horrified at the misconception.

"No, it isn't," he said seriously. "I think most medicos are of the opinion that curative medicine is too expensive, generally speaking, for poor countries like Tanzania. We have to concentrate on preventive medicine." He smiled ironically. "We haven't reached the stage when we can choose to keep sick people alive and afford to have fine, healthy children as well. There isn't the money available."

"Does one have to choose?" Frances asked uncomfortably.

"One has to choose one's priorities if one is working on a shoestring," he answered.

The Land Rover came to a stop outside a small group of houses a little way out from the town. Abel jumped out from the back and clapped his hands loudly. A small group of children, curious to see the new doctor, came running out of the bush and stood absolutely still, staring at her out of their large, dark brown eyes. Few of them were completely dressed. Some wore no more than a flimsy shirt, but all were clean, their faces lively.

A man, so like Abel that he could have been none other than Cain, came out of one of the houses, and grasped the handles of the suitcases in the Land Rover. Abel spoke to him quickly in his own tongue and Cain nodded respectfully.

"*Mama daktari,* come this way," he growled at Frances. "House ready now."

Frances glanced at Simon, but he was not looking at her. This was a moment, she realized, that she was going to have to face alone, and she wondered why she should be so hurt by his apparent desertion. Surely this was what she had come for?

She turned on her heel and followed Cain down a narrow path toward the most distant of the small group of houses. The leaves of the banana plants slapped her on the face as she walked. They smelt as they looked— green and earthy.

"This is your house, *mama*," Cain announced. He ducked his head to enter the open doorway into the almost dark interior.

Frances followed him more slowly. The mud walls smelled damp and small patches of rust fell from the roof onto the furniture down below. Not that there was much furniture for it to fall on. There was a table and a couple of chairs in one room, and a bed and another table in the other.

"*Choo* outside," Cain announced.

"*Choo*?" she repeated.

He beckoned her to follow him. They walked down another path that went around behind the house and there, sure enough, was a small outhouse from which emanated a revolting stench.

"*Choo*," said Cain.

Frances glanced inside at the simple hole in the ground around which flies buzzed in an ecstatic kind of dance.

"I can't use that!" she gasped, then shook herself mentally for overreacting.

Cain nodded his head. "*Choo*," he repeated stubbornly.

"Perhaps some disinfectant—" Frances mused. "There might be something in the hospital. I'll have a look first thing tomorrow."

"Yes, *mama*," he said obediently.

The house, when she got back to it, seemed cleaner, if only by comparison, and she sank thankfully onto the nearest chair. A rooster with a remarkable lack of timing, heralded the sunset immediately outside her window. Cain opened the window and shouted at the bird, but it was not to be deterred by anything or anyone and went on crowing into the rapidly approaching darkness.

"*Mama* not eat here tonight," Cain told her cheerfully. I go home now, be back tomorrow."

She stood up, anxious to sort out exactly what his duties were to be and how much she would be expected to pay him; but before she could attract his attention, he had given her a cheerful wave and was gone, whistling some obscure pop song under his breath as he vanished down the narrow path.

Left alone, Frances decided that the first priority was to find a lamp. She looked in the only cupboard she could find and was pleased to discover a pressure lamp, like one she remembered her grandmother having. But this was much harder to light. She found some matches and, turning the screw at the side, she held the flame hopefully somewhere near the mantle. It lit, but as soon as she began to pump, it flickered and died. It was a long time before she discovered that the knack was to leave it alone for a few seconds and then pump like mad, while the light grew brighter and brighter, searching out the dark shadows in the corners of the room.

Triumphantly, she bore the lamp over to the table and put it in the center where it was less likely to be knocked over. It had a wobbly bottom, she noticed. She tried to straighten it with her fingers and, while she was doing so, a black shape shot out of one of the corners of the room, uttering piercing sounds that froze her blood.

Frances dropped the lamp back on to the table and ran as fast as she was able out of the house. The black shape followed and disappeared into the trees. Nothing would have induced her to go back into that house by herself. She ran blindly toward the only light she could see, coming to a panting standstill outside the lighted window. Inside was Simon and a woman of about her own age. The woman appeared happy and was laughing up at him. And, even while Frances watched, Simon stooped his head and kissed her lightly on the cheek.

CHAPTER THREE

"IT was only a bat," Simon said easily.

Feeling more than a little hysterical, Frances gave way to sheer fury. "A *bat*? I won't have bats in my house! Why, everyone knows they're full of fleas and very likely other things as well—"

"I kept saying that you should have somewhere decent to live," the strange woman maintained stoutly. "And I didn't know you were a woman then! You'd better come and live with my brother and myself."

"She'll stay where she is!" Simon said sharply.

The woman made a face at him. "Why? We don't live far away!"

"Because this house was specially built for her," he answered flatly. "She'll get used to it."

The girl shuddered. "Well, I wouldn't! There are beetles in the roof. If I were you," she went on earnestly, "I'd move my bed into the middle of the room and stand the legs in tins of paraffin. I'll come and help you, if you like."

Frances thanked her warmly. "It's very kind of you," she said.

"Rubbish. Women have to stick together out here or we wouldn't survive at all!" She glared at Simon. "What are you laughing at?"

"The idea of your not surviving anywhere," he chuckled.

"Oh well, I'm different," the woman said casually, half agreeing with him. "I've always lived here." She shrugged. "If you had any manners at all, you'd introduce us!"

"Okay," Simon said obligingly. "Dr. Frances Whitney, Miss Elspeth Peissel. Elspeth lives with her brother on the other side of the hill. They grow coffee in their spare time and make their money taking photographs of animals."

"Better than killing them!" Elspeth said flippantly. "What brought you here, Dr. Whitney?"

"A love affair," Simon put in dryly.

Frances went scarlet. "I . . . I shall eventually join my parents' practice," she explained. "It all seemed too easy. I w-wanted to give something first. That sounds trite, I suppose—"

Elspeth nodded agreeably. "I'd probably have done the same. Only with us, it was our parents who up and left us. They shot off back to Europe and the fleshpots, while Mark and I took over here!"

Frances tried not to look as shocked as she felt. "I suppose your brother is older than you are," she said. Elspeth fairly hooted with laughter. "He's 19!"

But how could they leave him?" Frances demanded, abandoning any pretense at tact.

"Easily," Elspeth assured her. "They were helped along because we're Tanzanian citizens and they're not—"

"How complicated!" Frances swallowed.

"Not really," Elspeth said judiciously. "I'm a much better farmer than my father ever was!"

"Not too difficult a feat!" Simon put in wryly.

"No," Elspeth laughed. "But then one can't afford to sit on one's bottom and watch the money rolling in any longer!"

"If you're staying, Frances, you'd better sit down," Simon drawled, pushing a chair nearer her with his foot.

She remembered the scene that had greeted her eyes

through the window. "I . . . I don't want to interrupt," she began uncomfortably.

Elspeth stared at her. "No chance of that. I kiss Simon whenever I can. He kisses me only when he feels like it."

"Oh," said Frances. "I see."

Elspeth grinned. "One would go mad if one didn't do *something*!" she said wickedly. "You're lucky, you'll have your doctoring to keep you sane!"

"If the bats don't scare you out of your wits first!" Simon added, an amused edge to his voice.

Elspeth stood up and stepped over Frances's outstretched feet. "Don't you go doing this," she warned Frances. "Walking over people is considered very bad manners in Tanzania. I do it all the time, of course, but then I don't pretend to have any manners!"

"I'll remember," Frances said with a smile.

"Good. Goodbye you two. I must be going." She turned briefly to Frances. "I'll take you home for dinner and a bath if you like."

"I'd love it!" Frances replied immediately.

"She can't," Simon answered simultaneously.

Frances frowned at him. "Why not?" she demanded. "Cain says I can't eat in my own house. Not that I'd want to! I'd probably find something even nastier than the *choo*!"

Elspeth giggled. "I'll bring you some disinfectant tomorrow," she promised.

Simon smiled slowly. "Nguyu has arranged a party to greet the new doctor tonight. They'd be hurt if you stood them up."

"But nobody told me!" Frances protested.

"I'm telling you now," Simon grunted.

Elspeth looked aghast. "What will they give her to eat?" she demanded.

Simon shrugged his shoulders. "How should I know? I expect the women have been preparing *pombe* all day in her honor."

"But she can't drink that!"

"Why not? I do."

"Oh, you! You don't care what you swallow, but I assure you I couldn't!"

Simon's eyes became stern. "Nevertheless they'll be offended if Frances doesn't try it."

"What is *pombe*?" Frances put in.

They both stared at her. "Local beer," Elspeth explained. "A mucky poison that doesn't kill you— quite!"

"It isn't as bad as that," Simon said pacifically. "The trick is to pretend to gulp it down, but actually take tiny little sips."

"I don't like beer," Frances said flatly. "*Any* beer!"

Simon laughed. "That lets you out! You'll have to drink lemonade."

"Thank God for that!" Elspeth sighed piously. "I'll leave you to it! Good night!"

When she had gone, the room seemed suddenly empty. She wasn't a large woman, but she bounced with sheer animal vitality that more than made up for her rather plain features and her stringy fair hair that was neither long nor short.

Frances sought for something witty to say, something that would relieve the tension building up within her in the face of the lengthy silence that followed Elspeth's departure.

"How long have you known her?" was the only thing that came to mind and, before she could stop herself, she heard the words tumble out of her mouth.

Simon eyed her lazily. "Quite a while."

Frances recovered herself with difficulty. "She's nice. I like her," she said. She met Simon's eyes bravely and was quite cross to see his gleeful amusement. "I. . . ."

"You should have stayed in Nairobi," he told her.

"Why?" she retorted.

"I'd have thought it was obvious!" he drawled lightly. "In Nguyu we have to pretend to be quite indifferent to each other's charms, or we wouldn't survive at all. You keep to your house and I'll keep to mine."

"I suppose that's the arrangement you have with Elspeth!" she answered fiercely, annoyed that he had read her feelings so accurately.

"Elspeth is an old hand at the game."

"Oh?" Frances tried to sound cool and disinterested.

"So you'd best keep that jealousy of yours under control," he added for good measure. "Your job is waiting for you, Dr. Whitney!"

She turned and left his house without another word. It was painfully black outside, lit only by the great jeweled stars in the sky and the flat-topped orb of the moon in a strange sky. She had left her door open, and now she shut it with a bang from the inside, putting off the moment when she would have to look around to see if there were any more bats concealed in the rafters. To her infinite relief, there were none.

She sat down on one of the wooden chairs and looked about her. There was a great deal that would have to be done to make her house as comfortable and as cheerful as Simon's. His was as neat as a new pin, and he had hung a variety of posters all over the walls. Well, she could do that too. She hadn't any of the colorful reproductions of wild animals that he possessed, but she was sure she could find something that would be better than the bare mud walls.

It was so silent outside that, paradoxically, she could hear sounds that the company of another would have obliterated. Was it a dog that howled like that? And those soft, padding footfalls? She was sure it must be a lion or a leopard at the very least. Supposing it found a way in? She leaped to her feet and barricaded the windows, and tried to lock the door, only to find that there was no key. Tomorrow, first thing, she decided, she would have Cain put a bolt on the door—it wouldn't only be to keep the animals out!

To give herself something to do, she unpacked her things. There was a cupboard of sorts in which she could put her clothes, but there was nowhere suitable for her medical books, so she put them back in the suitcase until she could get a box made for them.

The next task was to tackle her bed. She thought Elspeth's advice was probably good, but there were no empty tins in the kitchen that she could fill with paraffin to stand the legs in. For tonight at least, it would have to be enough to heave the bed into the middle of the room and hope for the best.

She had barely finished when someone rapped sharply on her door. She pushed her hair back out of her eyes and went to answer it. She was surprised to see Abel, wearing the remnants of his old military uniform, his buttons polished so that they shone in the light of the hurricane lamp he was carrying.

"The party is ready to start," he told her proudly.

Frances put a hand to her mouth. "I'll just be two minutes!" she exclaimed. "I want to put on another dress."

He nodded, smiling broadly. "I will wait," he said.

Frances thought that if he had gone to the trouble of dressing up for the party it was obviously expected that she should do the same. She put on the same dress that she had worn the night before, adding a soft white chiffon scarf and some zircons that her father had had made into a necklace for her; they flashed satisfactorily in the indifferent light. When she was quite sure she looked well, she went back to the door and the waiting Abel.

He marched down the path with her half-running behind him.

"Where are we going?" she asked breathlessly.

"We have taken the hotel for the evening," he said grandly. "All the elders are waiting there to meet you. We are very pleased to have a doctor in Nguyu."

The hotel was in the middle of the town. The building was identical to all the others, but painted across the outside wall in wavery letters was the legend "Hotel Tanganyika. Proprietor Mr. Ndendulu Esquire."

"He is my cousin," Abel explained concisely. "Please come inside."

He pushed aside the shabby curtain in the doorway and she stepped into the crowded room. It seemed to her that there was a wall of faces all looking at her. Very few of them were young and there were no women at all.

Frances blinked at the gathering, forcing a smile, unwilling to admit even to herself that she was a little afraid of them. She noticed that most of them were wearing aged dinner jackets, one of which had long since lost its once elegant sleeves. One or two pairs of trousers had been rescued at the same time as the jackets, but some of them had had to make do with trousers of another color, or even with shorts. Only three of them wore shoes; tennis shoes that had once been white, with holes in their toes and laces that had been knotted and lovingly mended by their proud owners.

"This is Mr. Ndendulu," Abel began the introductions. "Mr. Biboko, the headmaster of our school; Mr. Mbulu, the headman—"

Frances shook hands with each one, wondering at their remarkable dignity. She would have liked to have slapped palms as Simon did, but she remembered in time that she was a woman and expected to behave as such.

"Do you have many pupils in your school, Mr. Biboko?"

"We have many. This year our students are going to take the exam for the first time. I am trying for the exam too, but it is hard work studying and teaching too."

Frances wondered what the exam was. "It must be," she said warmly.

"I can pass in Swahili and in English, I think," the schoolmaster went on. "But I am not easy in my mind about English history."

"Do you have to take that?" Frances asked him, impressed.

He nodded his head sadly. "The examination papers come from London," he explained. "I am taking English medieval history because I have been told that it is more like our own history, but I find it very strange."

"I should think so!" she exclaimed.

He laughed without bitterness. "It is easier," he confided, "than the science subjects. They are always giving examples that we don't have here. Either the trees don't grow here, or we haven't the chemicals to make the experiments. It is a very great handicap that no one takes into consideration. How can we explain how a ship sails on the ocean when we have never seen the ship or the ocean?" He sighed heavily. "We had an American who came to teach in a school near Arusha and he told us many things." His eyes opened wide. "He had a *degree*, but he taught in a school just like mine for a whole year."

Mr. Mbulu flashed a wide grin. "Mr. Biboko is hoping that you will give some lectures in his school," he put in slyly.

Frances blinked. "I suppose I could," she said reluctantly.

"Very good thing for Nbuyu," Abel said with finality. "Lots of good health!"

"Y-yes," murmured Frances.

She was more relieved than she could say when the curtain was pulled back and Simon entered, dressed, she noticed with something like delight, in full evening dress, including a row of medals on his chest. It was, she thought, almost indecent to be so pleased to see him, especially when she thought of the ungallant way he had dismissed her earlier.

He sat down on the long bench that lay along the opposite side of the room, a slight smile his only acknowledgment of her presence.

"*Daktari!*" a few of the men greeted him with satisfaction.

He slapped palms with the man next to him. "What do you think of our pretty doctor?" he asked him.

The whole room peered at Frances out of the corners of their eyes, nodding their heads agreeably.

"She is going to teach in my school," Mr. Biboko said importantly.

"Is she indeed?" Simon grinned.

"Well—" Frances began.

"It is a good thing. Very, very," Mr. Mbulu interrupted her.

Several women came in together, their print frocks faded from constant washing, and greeted the men with shy smiles. They carried large bowls, which they put down on the table, together with a tray of assorted cups and glasses. Frances sat up very straight so that she could just peep into one of the bowls. It was full of a gray, bubbling liquid, covered with an off-white foam. This, she thought, must be the dreaded *pombe*.

Mr. Mbulu picked up one of the glasses, which he dipped into one of the bowls, handing it to her with a courtly, charming gesture. "This has been made by my wife," he told her. "She makes the best *pombe* in Nguyu."

There was an immediate outcry at this claim, and the women giggled at the shouts of denial from their husbands.

"I'm not very fond of beer," Frances began bravely.

"Drink! Drink!" the men pressed her.

She took the cup, convinced that the evil mixture was bound to poison her, and put it to her lips. The *pombe* tasted like sweet mud and was as horrible as she had expected.

"Ugh!" she said involuntarily.

They roared with happy laughter. "Women are no good at drinking!" They grinned at her. "With our women it is just the same!" They had no reservations about their own capacity, however. They opened their throats and poured the *pombe* down, smacking their lips appreciatively.

As a concession to Frances's presence, the women stood grouped by the door, exchanging comments with one another in their own language. Occasionally a child's face would appear from behind her mother's skirts, only to be gently chastised and pushed outside again.

"This is a very good party!" Mr. Ndendulu, the owner

of the hotel, announced after a few minutes. "Very, very good party!"

Mr. Biboko leaned forward and dug Simon in the ribs. "Does she enjoy herself?" he asked in an audible undertone. "Is this party like the ones she is used to?"

Simon's eyes wandered over Frances's dress and face. "She's never been to a better party!" he assured the schoolmaster affably.

"She will like the food better than the *pombe*," the schoolmaster went on. "Tell her, *daktari*, that she will like the food!"

"I'm sure I will!" Frances said quickly.

Mr. Mbulu broke into hearty laughter. "The *daktari* will be seen more often in Nguyu these days! Now that *mama* has come among us!"

Simon laughed as hard as any of them. "I want a woman in my house, not one who is working at the hospital or teaching in school!"

"Ayee! The *daktari* is a wise man!" Mr. Mbulu sighed.

"I think that shows a thoroughly selfish point of view!" Frances put in, nettled.

The old men stared at her. "Someone must cook and watch the children," they said.

To Frances's surprise, it was Abel who came to her defense. "Since *Uhuru* women are doing many things," he remarked carefully. "*Mama daktari* can do all these things. She would not have come all the way from England if she wanted to stay inside the house."

"The difficulty is to do all these things at the same time!" Simon said dryly.

"I can try!" Frances flashed at him.

"Not as my woman you don't!" he retorted, and they all laughed again.

The women went out again and returned carrying

trays laden with food. There were not enough plates to go round, so some of them shared with their neighbor. A great dish of rice was put on the table, another of meat, and a third piled high with vegetables buried under a hot peppery sauce.

Someone gave Frances a spoon and invited her to help herself from the various dishes. She thought she had never tasted better rice and the meat, too, was delicious. Most of the vegetables were strange to her and the sauce brought tears to her eyes, but Mr. Biboko had been quite right—she did like the food.

The others took the pieces of meat with their fingers, cramming them into their mouths hungrily. It was only then that she realized what this party had cost them. Each one of them had contributed something toward it, bringing his own plate and cup. Only she and Simon had brought nothing with them.

The women sat in a huddle, their babies asleep on their knees or feeding at the breast. One by one, the children pushed their way into the room, careful to keep out of the way of their elders, intrigued to see this strange white woman who had come to live in Nguyu.

The bowls of *pombe* on the table were emptied, leaving only a few black seeds in the bottom of the bowl in a sea of unappetizing-looking mud. Looking about her, Frances thought it must be pretty potent stuff. There was a distinct air of conviviality in the room that had not been noticeable before. Only Simon looked as sober as he had been when he came in. He winked at her.

"Dr. Whitney has been traveling all day," he said, smiling. "She will fall asleep where she is, if she doesn't go home soon!"

The old men laughed raucously. "*Mama* should have drunk more *pombe*!" they teased her.

"You must be very careful when you go into your house," Mr. Mbulu told her ponderously. "The rains are coming soon and the spiders like to come inside—"

"Spiders!" she exclaimed. "As well as bats!"

"Bats too," he agreed. "It is very difficult to keep them out of the house."

"Doesn't your wife complain?" Frances asked him.

He laughed and said something to one of the women seated on the floor. She laughed and stood up, pulling her child away from her breast, and buttoned up her dress.

"My wife is violent against bats!" Mr. Mbulu stated. "She will walk home with you and shift them all out of your house for you."

"But I don't want to take her away from the party—"

"It has been a good party! Very, very!"

She smiled, suddenly liking them all very much. "Yes," she agreed.

Everyone looked so pleased that she was touched. "Perhaps when I am more settled we could have a party in my house," she said, afraid that they wouldn't like the suggestion. But their eyes gleamed.

"We will all come!" they assured her.

"So will I!" Simon said.

"You will have to make the *pombe*," Frances told him, wondering why the others all collapsed into laughter.

"That's woman's work," he told her.

She gave him a flustered look. "But I can't possibly make it. . . ."

Mrs. Mbulu swung her baby onto her hip and smiled across the room at Frances. She said something to her husband, which he translated, grinning. "The women will show how it is done if they can come to your party too. They will show you anyway," he added more sternly. "We cannot have a party without *pombe*!"

"But of course the women must come!" Frances exclaimed. "It wouldn't be a party for me without them!"

Mr. Mbulu chuckled appreciatively. "Mr. Ndendulu has two wives!"

Frances strove to keep a straight face, failed, and found herself laughing as heartily as everyone else.

"He is a rich man," the schoolmaster said. "He makes a lot of money keeping the hotel."

"He must." Frances said admiringly.

Mr. Ndendulu laughed as much as anyone. "Sometimes I make 50 shillings a week!" he boasted.

"He is a rich man," Mr. Biboko repeated.

The night air seemed cool and vital after the stuffy atmosphere inside the hotel. Frances took a deep breath and laughed out loud.

"Mama?" Mrs. Mbulu's gentle voice inquired.

Frances tried to think of a single word in Swahili that would sum up her feeling of general well-being. She was so very glad that she had come. But any words that she had memorized had fled from her mind. She shrugged her shoulders helplessly and followed the tall black woman as she swayed gracefully along the path ahead of her.

Her front door opened at the merest touch. The lamp was still alight on the table, covered by a blur of moths and other flying insects. Their less lucky brethren lay dead on the table. Frowning at the sight, Mrs. Mbulu swept them onto the floor with the side of her hand. She picked up the light and held it up high into the corners of the ceiling. There was nothing there. She smiled in quiet triumph and disappeared into the bedroom. In a few seconds she was back, chuckling softly in the back of her throat and shaking her head. She hitched the baby higher on her hip and put the lamp back on the table. Then with a soft word of farewell, she walked out of the door, pulling it shut behind her; Frances could hear her bare feet disappearing down the path between the banana plants.

If there were no bats, there were plenty of spiders to keep her occupied as she began to get ready for bed. That was another thing she would have to ask Elspeth, she decided. There must be something that would discourage this excess of animal life from making her life a misery.

She was just on the point of finding a book to read when she heard a knock at the door.

"Yes?" she called out.

"It's me, Simon. I only wanted to make sure you got home all right." He stuck his head around the door and she held her practical dressing gown closely about her. The towelling material felt rough beneath her fingers.

"Yes, thank you," she said.

"Nice party?" his eyes looked straight into hers. "They were pleased to be asked back, you know."

"I want them to come," she said. "I think they all must have contributed to the feast tonight."

"They did!" he agreed cheerfully. "Can I come in? I brought a bottle of good old-fashioned whisky with me!"

Without a word Frances managed to find two glasses. She had not expected him to visit her so late at night.

"Only a very small one for me," she said.

He made a face at the whisky bottle. "The taste of *pombe* is apt to linger longer than I like," he told her. He poured out the two drinks and handed her one of the glasses. "Here's to you!" he said.

She took a careful sip of neat whisky. "Do you still think I should have stayed in Nairobi?" she asked him sweetly.

Simon stood in the doorway, hunching his shoulders and glowering at her. "From whose point of view?" he retorted.

"I think they need a doctor pretty badly here," she said evenly.

He drank his whisky at a single gulp. "I'm going on safari tomorrow. I'll be away for about a week. If you want to know anything, ask Elspeth, or better still her brother—"

"I might at that," she agreed. "He's more likely to tell me the truth about you!"

"Don't rely on it!" he said dryly.

"Why not?" she asked.

"He happens to like me," Simon answered.

"So does Elspeth!" she shot at him.

"Yes, I believe she does," he agreed calmly. He set his glass on the table and put his hands on her shoulders, ducking his head to kiss her on the lips. "That's to keep you sweet while I'm away!"

Frances stiffened, dismayed by the shock of pleasure the brief contact gave her.

"Oh no, Mr. Abbott," she said. "You can't have it both ways." She picked up the bottle of whisky and put it in his hand. "You stick to your house, remember? And I'll stick to mine!"

"And Elspeth?" he asked her, amused.

Her temper flared. "You can kiss her as often as you like as far as I'm concerned!"

He touched her cheek with infinite gentleness. "Good night, Dr. Whitney," he said.

"Good night, Mr. Abbott."

She waited until he had gone, and then she flung herself into bed, turning out the lamp with a flick of her wrist. At least he would never know that she spent the first night in her new home crying herself to sleep.

CHAPTER FOUR

THE sun had just risen when she heard sounds in the next room. A few seconds later Cain knocked on her door and entered carrying a tray of tea and a glass of freshly squeezed orange juice.

"You weren't at the party!" Frances accused him sleepily.

He shook his head. "No. I not speak much English."

"Abel was there," she said.

"Abel with *daktari*," Cain growled. "Both gone safari."

He left the room again, shuffling his feet. Feeling very spoiled, Frances poured herself a cup of tea and sipped the orange juice. In a few minutes, she decided, she would get up. The first thing she would do was find a place where she could plant the sapling of the flamboyant tree that Abel had brought for her. She would plant it outside her door, so that when it grew big enough it would shade the front of the house and keep the inside cool.

Cain had cooked her breakfast by the time she had dressed. She sat at the table and ate the scrambled eggs and bacon, wondering where he had learned to cook so well. She was just beginning her second cup of tea when someone came to the door.

"*Mama! Mama daktari!*"

Frances put her cup down, spilling some of the tea in the saucer. She leaped to her feet and pulled the door open. A small boy stood outside.

"*Mama?* Come quickly!"

She needed no second bidding. She stopped only to

236

grab her medical bag, and then hurried after the boy as he ran down the path and into the narrow maze of houses beyond.

When they arrived at his family's house, the boy plucked at her skirt and pulled her in through the open doorway. A bevy of children fell over one another in their anxiety to make room for her.

"I am so sorry, doctor, to bother you so early in the morning," Mr. Mbulu's voice greeted her. "I have stepped on a thorn—"

Frances looked quickly down at his feet. She had not seen them the night before, for he had been one of the few to wear shoes. She saw now that his foot was badly swollen and full of pus.

"Why didn't you tell me last night?" she exclaimed, horribly aware of the pain that the man must have been in all night.

"It was a party last night," he explained. "It was not right for you to start work until today."

She dropped on her knees and examined his foot with care. "The thorn is still there," she told him.

"I think so, too," he said.

"It will have to come out. . . ."

He nodded. "It is a poisonous thorn. Shall I come to the hospital?"

Frances hesitated. It was very dark in the shabby little house, but, on the other hand, she didn't want to move the old man unnecessarily.

"Perhaps your wife could boil some water for me."

Mr. Mbulu called his wife and firmly told her what to do. Frances smiled at her and the woman smiled back.

Opening her bag she made ready an injection with a local anesthetic and slipped it into Mr. Mbulu's leg almost before he was aware.

"You're a bad man," she chided him. "Don't you realize that you might have lost your leg if you had left it
much longer?"

Mr. Mbulu smiled sleepily at her. "*Daktari* says you
are a fine doctor!"

"It wouldn't have mattered if I had been or not!" she
rasped him. "Besides, he doesn't know whether I'm a
good doctor or not."

Mr. Mbulu nodded judiciously. "The *daktari* is a very
wise man. He can make all the sick animals well again.
It is known that one medicine man can always recognize
the power in another."

Frances let him go on talking while she worked on his
foot, pressing out the pus that had formed all around the
thorn and, finally, picking out the inch-long white-cen-
tered thorn and holding it up for them all to see.

"Eh, eh!" Mrs. Mbulu exclaimed.

Her husband gazed longingly into Frances's bag.
"Will you be putting on a bandage?" he begged her.

She chuckled. "A *huge* bandage!" she promised him.

He grinned, watching her every movement as she
applied the bandage and pinned it neatly.

"Come and see me at the hospital tomorrow," she told
him.

He stood up and hobbled with her as far as the door,
still smiling. "I shall tell *daktari* that you are a very good
doctor! With soft, gentle fingers!"

Frances pushed the hair back out of her eyes, more
than a little put out. "I don't think he will be at all interested," she said.

But Mr. Mbulu thought he knew better. "We have all
seen him looking at you!" he chuckled. "Of course he is
interested!"

Frances felt decidedly harassed as she walked back to her own house. Frank speaking was something she had always professed to admire, but when it came to her own emotions it was suddenly quite different. A decent veiling seemed highly desirable, even from herself. Simon Abbott had never pretended more than a mere passing fancy for her to keep him amused for an hour or so. She would be nothing but a fool to take him seriously. And she wasn't a fool. At least, she didn't think so. She decided to not even think about him. She would be glad that he was away and that would be that.

Satisfied, she hurried into the house and found the flamboyant tree sapling. Cain watched her curiously as she took it out of the plastic bag that Abel had wrapped it in. The sapling drooped sadly over her hand.

"I've never done much gardening," she began.

Cain took the sapling from her. "I plant," he said with decision.

Frances was relieved that he, at least, seemed to know what he was doing. He loped off down the path, reappearing a few minutes later with a *panga,* a kind of machete and the universal tool of Africa, with which he began to dig a hole a few feet away from her door. He was busy filling the hole with water, when a Land Rover rumbled through the narrow streets of the village. Frances looked up immediately, sure that it was Simon who had come back for some reason, but she saw at once that it wasn't. She became conscious of the most unbearable feeling of desolation. It was Elspeth, accompanied by two men, neither of whom Frances had ever seen before.

"Hi there!" Elspeth called. "Is Simon about?"

Frances shook her head. "He's gone on safari."

"Funny," the other girl said. "He didn't say anything to me!"

"Does he have to?" one of the men asked her.

"No, but he always does!" She glanced across at Frances. "This is my young brother, Mark. Dr. Whitney. And this is Baron von Rahner, a friend of ours."

The baron stepped out of the Land Rover and bowed jerkily in Frances's direction. "I am most happy . . ." he began with a strong German accent.

"Klaus is interested in coffee," Elspeth went on, just as if he hadn't spoken at all.

"Which is more than can be said about me!" Mark Peissel put in cheekily. He was very like his sister to look at, with the same, rather flat features and colorless eyes.

"No one is interested in you either!" his sister informed him bossily. "If I hear any more about you climbing Mount Kilimanjaro, I shall go mad!"

"If you don't hear about it from me, you'll hear it from Klaus," Mark said reasonably.

"I know," Elspeth sighed. "You both go on and on and on! You'll have to rescue me, Frances, by having dinner with us tonight."

"Thank you very much," Frances accepted promptly.

"Meanwhile, I've brought you the disinfectant," Elspeth said. "What are you doing out here anyway? Admiring the view?"

"Planting a tree," Frances said.

"*Disinfectant*?" Mark muttered. "Isn't that rather like taking coals to Newcastle?"

"Mind your own business!" Elspeth snubbed him. "It's for her *choo*!"

"Enough said!" Mark agreed. "Is it awful? Mind if I take a look?"

"Help yourself," Frances said.

"Don't mind him," Elspeth advised her. "He's crazy!"

"No, no, not crazy," Baron von Rahner said gently. "He is very interested in hygienic matters and plumbing. It is one of the comforts of staying with the Peissels—everything of that nature works."

"How nice," said Frances, trying not to laugh.

"It is," he assured her with enthusiasm. "It is indeed."

"You'll find out!" Elspeth muttered darkly. "Can we come in for a visit?"

Frances glanced at her watch. "Of course," she said. "I shall have to be off to the hospital fairly soon though. I haven't seen it yet and I want to check on the facilities before I start arranging hours and so on."

"Mark can go with you," Elspeth said brightly.

"But will he want to?"

His sister looked surprised. "Of course he will want to! He'll make everything work for you."

"He is a highly intelligent young man," the Baron put in gravely.

Elspeth gave him a positively skittish look. "I suppose that's why you visit us so often!" she said tartly.

"Of course," he returned politely.

Cain gave them all a hostile glare as they entered. "*Chai,* Cain," Elspeth commanded, not noticing the look.

Cain's eyes swivelled to Frances, who nodded quickly and hoped for the best.

"Were you in the middle of your breakfast?" Elspeth asked, looking with distaste at the still-unwashed dishes on the table. "What a mess this place is!"

"I was called out on my first case," Frances told her, not without pride.

Elspeth chuckled. "I see you had a good bash at the spiders! I brought you something for them as well."

"You didn't!" Frances exclaimed. "I can't tell you how grateful I am. How did you know?"

"I know Simon's house," Elspeth reminded her. "We had the same trouble there, until I found that this did the trick."

"We?" the baron inquired, his eyes twinkling.

"Well, you don't suppose Simon suffered alone, do you?" Elspeth retorted.

"No, no," he agreed. "He has, as you English say, what it takes."

Elspeth smiled complacently. "I wonder if it's true that he's kissed half the pretty girls in Africa south of the equator?"

"You should know if anyone does," the baron said dryly.

Elspeth wrinkled up her nose thoughtfully. "Jealous?" she asked him.

"Me?" He sounded surprised. "No, my dear, I am not jealous of Simon. I like him far too well." He stood awkwardly in the small room, waiting for the two women to sit down. "How many rooms have you?" he asked Frances. "It seems to me it is not a very comfortable house."

"There's the bedroom through there," Frances told him.

"But no proper kitchen? And no bathroom?"

"Simon's house isn't much better," Elspeth drawled.

"But that is how he chooses to live, or so I have heard. Dr. Whitney must have been shocked to have come to such primitive surroundings!"

"No, I wasn't," Frances assured him. "I didn't know what to expect, but I was warned that the accommodation wouldn't be at all luxurious. . . ."

"The roof is rusty!"

"I know," she said. She looked and felt embarrassed. "But I wouldn't like to live at a much higher standard than everyone else in the town."

Elspeth blinked "Well, that's telling us!"

"Yes, but you're not the doctor here," Frances almost apologized.

"They won't understand what you're about any more than I do," the other girl warned her. "You realize that?"

Frances didn't answer.

"But I find it quite understandable," the baron said. "At first I did not, but you have come to be a part of Africa, have you not?"

"For two years," Frances said lightly.

He smiled. "I wonder if it is something you can set a time limit on," he mused. "Africa makes up her own mind who her children are."

"She is going to work for her parents eventually," Elspeth said quite sharply.

"Indeed?"

"They are both doctors too," Frances found herself explaining.

Mark came in through the open doorway, and smiled sheepishly at his sister. "Have I kept you waiting?" he asked.

"No," she said indifferently. "Cain is making us tea."

Mark's face brightened. "I've got rid of the flies, Frances," he told her shyly. "I don't think you'll have any more trouble. They hadn't.. . ."

"Don't bother to explain!" Elspeth begged him.

"No," the baron agreed. "I have this very sensitive stomach and I need to be spared the realities of life!"

Mark grinned at him. "Says you!" he jeered, and pretended to be winded by the German's retaliatory punch in his ribs.

Frances was glad of Mark's company when she went to the hospital. She was quite nervous of her new responsibilities. She was very conscious that the hospital was in her sole care. In England there had always been someone else to take the final responsibility, but here there was no one, no one at all!

"The thing is," Mark said solemnly, "that you'll have to get things organized right away. No one will know when you'll be at the hospital unless you have some kind of set hours. I'll work out a timetable for you."

Apparently he knew his way around the hospital quite well. The refrigerator, he told her, had been used mainly for keeping Simon's beer cool, but there was plenty of room to store various medicines in it as well. The operating room was a bit primitive, but Simon found it adequate for dealing with his animals. He had even managed to treat some of the local people, not with the expertise that she would bring to the job, of course, but still it had been better than nothing. The consulting room had been useful for putting up Simon's friends—male friends, because he usually went to Nairobi, Arusha, or Dar es Salaam when he wanted female company.

"And the waiting room?" Frances asked him coldly.

Mark grinned. "There isn't one. They have to wait outside. But Simon planted a few trees to keep the sun off them. . . ."

"While they line up to see *him,* I suppose!"

"Well, there isn't any other doctor for miles around." He went into the building ahead of her, excited by the prospect of showing her around. "Elspeth had the place built," he told her proudly, "though she told me not to tell you that!"

"Why ever not?"

"She's funny that way," he said. "She admires what the Nguyu people have been able to do for themselves. They have very little money, you know, and yet they managed to build their school in their spare time, everybody contributing towards it. Elspeth supplied the materials for the hospital, but they did quite a lot of the actual building themselves. Even the schoolchildren came and put in their stint after school. Self-reliance, we call it here!"

"I wonder what Simon calls his doctoring." she said dryly.

Mark looked anxious. "I wouldn't make a thing of that," he told her. "It was he who recommended that Nguyu should have its own doctor. In fact, you wouldn't be here if it weren't for him!"

"Poor Simon!" Frances exclaimed.

Mark looked puzzled. "I don't see why," he said.

"He wasn't expecting a woman," Frances explained.

Mark's flat face broke into laughter. "Nor did Elspeth, come to that!" he said wickedly. "She's used to having Simon all to herself, at least when he's in Nguyu. And," he added with a touch of gallantry, "I must say the competition is pretty hot!"

Frances chuckled. "Thank you, kind sir," she said.

"Not at all!" he responded.

The hospital was very well fitted out, Frances discovered. The equipment was not the latest, nor was it the most sophisticated of its kind, but it had been well chosen and she became confident, as she came to the end of her tour of the building, that she would be able to cope with most things that arose. In case of a greater problem a call could be put in to the Flying Doctor service to have the patient flown to the nearest large hospital.

As well as her work in Nguyu, she also had a large area to cover each week, visiting the various nearby villages and holding a clinic in each one. To help her to do that, she had been assigned a medical orderly who had recently retired from the Tanzanian army. He was an immensely tall man and a devout Moslem, coming originally from another part of the country. His name was Mwete.

"*Jambo, memsahib*. The *daktari* left instructions that your Land Rover was to be put in good order. I am to drive you, he says, as well as assist you here in the hospital."

"Do you mind working for me?" she asked him frankly.

Mwete laughed. "I am a very good medical man, very! I like to work with a medical woman. You will make people well and I will help you."

"No love potions!" Mark frowned at him.

Mwete looked innocent. "No, *bwana*."

Mark waited for him to leave the room. "His father was a witch doctor," he told Frances. "He probably learned all the arts from him, but I don't suppose he practises much these days. The army doesn't smile on that sort of thing."

Frances felt rather shaken. "A witch doctor!" she exclaimed.

Mark smiled. "He won't do you any harm," he said.

It was the beginning of a long day. Frances began to think that everyone in Nguyu had decided to visit the doctor that day. They stood outside the hospital, gossiping happily. They didn't seem to mind how long they waited. This, she thought with a satisfaction she had never known before, was doctoring at its best. For the first time since she had qualified, she felt really needed.

She even began to ignore Simon's invisible presence in the consulting room. She was shown scars, remnants of gashes that he had sewn up, and presented with pills that he had handed out for minor ailments that hadn't warranted calling in the Flying Doctor. He had made a pretty good job of things too, though she swore she would never tell him so. In the future, he could stick to his animals!

At lunchtime, Mark opened a couple of bottles of beer from the refrigerator and showed her the posters he had made. They invited attendance at the hospital for the prenatal clinics, for vaccinations against this and that, or merely for consultations with the doctor on such subjects as family planning, nutrition and hygiene.

"You're going to be kept pretty busy!" he told her.

Frances nodded happily. She pinned the posters up on the walls, then stood back to admire the general effect.

"Very nice!" she congratulated him.

Mark sipped his beer thoughtfully. "I think we'll put up a nice photo of the queen there, and one of the president just beside her. What do you think?"

Frances nodded her agreement. She glanced out of the window and saw Mr. Biboko, the schoolmaster, walking quickly toward the hospital.

"Do you think he's coming here?" she asked Mark.

"Looks like it," the boy said. "I'll make myself scarce. I'll go and have a chat with Mwete."

But Mr. Biboko was already outside the door, perspiring freely as a result of the speed with which he had come. His eyes went immediately to the posters and approval was plain on his face.

"These are very fine!" he said admiringly. He wandered around the room, examining each one closely. "You are busy now?" he asked.

"No," Frances said.

He smiled nervously, taking a pair of dark glasses out of his pocket and balancing them on his nose. "I have been thinking, *mama*," he said in a little burst. "I mean, it is necessary for the prestige not only of myself, but for the whole of Nguyu, don't you think?"

"What is?" Frances asked him gently.

"The exam!"

Frances blinked. "Oh yes?"

He slammed a book down on the table in front of her. "If you are not busy, *mama*, will you tell me about Henry II?"

"Oh," said Frances. "The exam!" She turned the pages of the history book idly, wondering what use to him a knowledge of the Plantagenet kings of England could possibly be. "All right," she said at last. "I'll teach you about them in the evenings—when I have time."

Mr. Biboko beamed at her. "It is very kind! Very, very! I will bring some of my boys also. . . ."

"You can't tonight," Mark reminded her from the doorway.

"No," she agreed. "I can't tonight. . . ."

"Tomorrow night!" Mr. Biboko said with determination. "We will come tomorrow night!"

Frances gave him a helpless look. He snatched off his dark glasses and wiped his face carefully on a snowy white handkerchief.

"Mr. Biboko," she said, "I don't know very much history myself. . . ."

"Oh, yes, I think you know a great deal!" he said sincerely. "I am very interested in the Black Prince. Do you know about him?"

Frances smiled, completely defeated. "Yes," she admitted, "I know about him." She hesitated. "Will you teach me about your history and customs in exchange?" she asked him.

Mr. Biboko nodded, looking very happy indeed. "It will be a fair exchange," he grinned. "A very fair exchange."

"If you go on like this, you'll never have a minute to call your own!" Mark told her as they drove out of Nguyu toward his sister's house.

"I don't mind," she said.

"Simon will have something to say about it—"

"It's none of Simon's business!"

Mark raised his eyebrows thoughtfully. "Ho, ho," he said.

"You forget," she went on quickly, "I have other interests beside Simon Abbott. Besides, I hardly know him!"

Mark grinned. "Elspeth will be relieved!"

"She's welcome to him," Frances said belligerently.

"Don't you like him?" Mark asked, surprised.

Frances tried to stop herself from blushing. "I . . . I don't know if I like him or not," she managed. She thought of the glass he had given her, which she deliberately had left in the bottom of her suitcase together with her medical books, and hoped that nobody would ever know that she had accepted it from him. "I don't find him a very interesting topic of conversation!"

They covered the ten miles to the Peissel coffee estate in less than half an hour. The coffee trees spread out from the house and gardens like a fan. At one end was a collection of sheds, where the beans were dried and sacked ready for transport; at the moment the sheds were empty and awaiting the next crop. The house and gardens could have been transported straight from Europe. The drive was lined by ornamental trees and the flower beds were a blaze of color. Behind the soft green of the well-watered lawn stood the house, tall and built of rough-hewn stones, with a tiled roof and latticed windows.

Elspeth had heard the Land Rover and came out of the front door, her dogs at her heels, to greet them.

"Dinner will be at half-past seven," she told Frances. "Meanwhile you'd probably like a bath. Take as long as you like and really enjoy it. Mark will show you where the bathroom is."

It was a beautiful bathroom, full of pretty tiles and well-lit mirrors. The pale lemon bath was full of hot, scented water, and the towels had come straight from the warm airing cupboard. It was bliss and sheer, exotic luxury, and Frances enjoyed every minute of it. She emerged, fresh and thoroughly clean, about half an hour later. She wandered down the stairs to find the others in the sitting room.

The baron looked at her with amused appreciation. "If you are going to visit here often, I shall have to come more often myself! You are looking very beautiful, doctor!"

"I'm afraid I could never look that," Frances said with a laugh. "but isn't it wonderful what a bath can do? I wonder if I could persuade Mark to put one in for me at Nguyu?"

"I expect he could fix you up with a shower," the baron smiled. "I am told that Simon has one in his *shamba*. It takes the worst of the dust off, even if the water doesn't get very hot."

The dinner was as good as the bath had been. It was a treat to eat perfectly cooked food and be offered the right kind of wine with every course.

"I wonder that your parents could bear to go back to England," she said to Elspeth, "when they had all this here."

Elspeth laughed. "I'm afraid they think the best days are over," she answered. "They only let Mark and me stay on here because they couldn't get a good price for the place. Mark is going to England next year to attend university, but I shall stay here until I die!"

"If your husband will allow it," the baron suggested.

"Why shouldn't he?" Elspeth demanded with genuine amazement.

"He might have a career of his own," he said mildly. "Or he might wish to live somewhere else."

Elspeth's eyes darkened. "Then I shan't marry!" She turned on him angrily. "Would you rather live somewhere else?"

The baron smiled deprecatingly. "I am not likely to be your husband," he pointed out. "If I were, I wouldn't mind staying here some of the time."

"And I could stay here on my own while you climbed your horrible mountains," Elspeth teased him.

"But I am not a marrying man."

"Then I shall have to marry Simon," Elspeth sighed.

"If he'll have you!" Mark put in with brotherly candor.

Elspeth smiled a secret smile to herself. "He'll be here until he dies, too," she said.

"Yes," the German agreed rather sadly, "in that respect you are two of a kind."

Whereas in two years' time, Frances thought, she would be starting again in England in the comfort of her parents' practice—and she would hate it! Every minute of it!

CHAPTER FIVE

FRANCES had been in Nguyu for a whole week and Simon was still away. The flamboyant tree at her door had put out its first green shoots as a reward for her constant attention, morning and night, loving it and watering it and hoping that it would grow rapidly into a tree like the one at the hotel at Lake Manyara.

It was Sunday and she had just been to church. The service had been taken by the local catechist, for the priest only came once a month. It didn't matter what sect one belonged to for in Nguyu everyone went to the same church. Even Mr. Ndendulu had been there, accompanied by both his wives and his flock of children, and he had sung the hymns more loudly than anyone else.

Cain came out of the house, and he was actually smiling. "Lunch ready, *mama!*" His smile grew broader. "*Mama* no go to *memsahib* today!"

"No," Frances agreed ruefully.

"Good, very, very!"

Frances chuckled. "It makes more work for you!" she said. Cain did not make a particularly good servant, but she had realized after the first day that she couldn't possibly have managed without him.

"*Mama*—" Cain urged her.

"I'm coming," she said.

They both heard the car coming at exactly the same second. Frances hoped that it wasn't Elspeth. She didn't feel inclined to be with anyone that afternoon. She was tired and she wanted time to herself.

"*Daktari!*" Cain wagged his head happily.

The Land Rover came to a stop outside Simon's house and a moment later he ran up the path, pushing aside the banana leaves with impatient hands. He looked, Frances thought, quite wonderful.

"Cain!" he roared. "Cain! Is Abel back yet?"

Cain's eyes grew large and frightened. "Abel?" he said dazedly.

Simon was unexpectedly gentle with him. "Is he back yet?" he repeated more slowly.

Cain shook his head. "Abel gone with you!"

"Yes, he went with me," Simon answered him. "I sent him to the game warden's house the day before yesterday. He was going to make his own way home from there. Have you seen him?"

"Abel not home," Cain said positively.

"You're sure?" Simon shot at him.

Cain trembled. "Abel not here," he repeated.

"What could have happened to him?" Frances asked Simon. She could feel his anxiety as strongly as if it were her own.

"I don't know. I'm going out to look for him!"

"I'll come with you," she said quietly.

His eyes flicked over her. "You'd better stay here. Cain can come with me."

"Cain would be worse than useless," she told him briskly. "I'll get my bag."

She thought he was going to argue with her, but he didn't. He waited impatiently while she checked the contents of her medical bag.

"I don't know how long we'll be gone," he warned. "Are you sure you want to come?"

"You forget. I'm a doctor," she reminded him.

"And a woman! Especially in the middle of a game

park! I'm staying out there until I find him. There won't be any turning back when you get tired!"

"I wish you wouldn't shout at me," she objected mildly. "When I start to complain, you can shout all you like, but until I do. . . ."

He smiled reluctantly. "Aren't you afraid to be alone with me under a tropical moon?" he asked her.

"Not a bit!" she said cheerfully.

Cain fluttered around the room, making sandwiches and putting them in a bag for her. He may have looked ineffectual, but Frances knew that she would never have thought of taking any food with her.

"I'll fill up some cans with water and petrol," Simon said abruptly. "Come along to my place as soon as you can."

She wasn't long behind, clutching Cain's sandwiches in one hand and her bag in the other. She had pulled a cotton hat well down onto her head to keep the sun out of her eyes, but otherwise she had come exactly as she was. She climbed into the passenger seat of the Land Rover and tried to catch her breath.

"Is it very serious?" she asked Simon timidly.

"It could be," he grunted.

"Was he on foot?"

"He liked it that way! He's walked it a dozen times before! He knew what he was doing—"

"I wasn't blaming you," Frances said humbly.

His shoulders sagged a little. "I know," he said abruptly. "I suppose I blame myself."

"We'll find him!" she said with a confidence she was far from feeling. "After all, you know which route he must have taken, don't you?"

"Yes, but—"

"Of course we'll find him!" she said heartily.

They tore through the narrow streets of Nguyu. The old women in the market, guarding the goods they had for sale, ran with unexpected agility to the side of the road to see them go past.

"*Daktari!*" they called out.

Simon replied something that was quite unintelligible to Frances, but she caught Abel's name and the long-drawn-out, piercing gasps of the old women. "Aieee! Aiooo!"

Simon's face looked bleak. "They think he is already dead," he told her.

"Dead?" somehow she had not thought of that.

"Abel's not the kind to die easily," Simon said roughly.

"No," she agreed, clinging at straws. "He's very different from his brother, isn't he?"

"They're aptly named," Simon agreed. "Abel loves and understands all animals, whereas Cain abhors them. Cain is the gardener. One day he hopes to have a small market garden of his own."

"Yet it was Abel who gave me my flamboyant tree," she reminded him.

"And Cain who planted it."

"How do you know?" she retorted. "I might have planted it myself!"

He laughed. "Is it growing?" he asked her.

"Of course!"

"Then Cain planted it! That man can make anything grow!" He cast her a quick look, his eyes not lazy at all. "Thanks for coming, Fran."

She felt herself blushing vividly and wished she had more control over herself. "Oh," she said lightly, "I have my professional moments. You might need a doctor after all."

"Is that the only reason you came?"

She felt a tight constriction in her throat. She had to keep it light no matter what, she thought. "Actually the Plantagenets had quite a lot to do with it," she told him.

"Mr. Biboko?" he said at once.

"He works so terribly hard!" she said. "I never imagined that there was so much to be learned about England in the Middle Ages."

"What does it have to do with you?" he asked quietly.

She turned to face him. "Oh, Simon, he *needs* help. He and those pupils of his are starved for information. They come for an hour's study and often they don't go home until the small hours. And there they all are the next morning, running to school just as if they had spent all that time at home in their beds!"

"And you? Are you running to the hospital too?"

"No," she admitted. "But if they can do it, so can I!"

"I hope you're right, my dear. They're used to the climate, don't forget. You've only just got here."

She dismissed the warning with a laugh. "I'll survive," she said. "I'm tougher than I look."

His hands tightened on the steering wheel. "You'll need to be! You have the softest, silkiest hide of anyone I know!"

"And you know so many!" she said tartly.

"That's none of your business, Doctor Whitney."

"None at all," she agreed quickly. "Just as my skin is none of yours!"

"If you feel like that," he said gravely, "you shouldn't wear a certain delicious black dress that reveals so much of it—"

"I'm not wearing it now!" she snapped defensively.

"Just as well for my peace of mind. Will you take the wheel in a moment, Fran? We can start looking seriously any time now."

They rushed on down the narrow dirt track, traveling downhill all the way until they came out onto the flat savanna lands. It was possible to see for miles in all directions; only a few thorn trees broke up the skyline. The grass was thin, harsh and burned gray by the sun. The bushes, too, were gray-green and grew in patches in the deep red earth. At frequent intervals termite mounds, gaunt and hard as pottery, topped the bushes. Mongooses peered out of any that had been abandoned by the white ants, making good use of the cool passages that the termites had fashioned for their own use. There had at one time been other trees, but the elephants had knocked them over, stripping away their bark and leaving them dead and silver on the ground. It was hard to see even the fleet dik-dik, the smallest of all the antelopes, often weighing no more than a few pounds, as they darted away from the track.

Simon brought the Land Rover to a stop and changed places with her.

"Which way do I go?" she asked him.

He pointed along a track that was overgrown from lack of use. "That's the shortest way to the game warden's house," he said. "We'll go that way. If we don't find him, we'll come back the long way."

She nodded, not wasting her breath on speech. She was nervous of driving the Land Rover under Simon's critical eye. She knew there were two sets of gears, depending on whether or not one wanted to use the four-wheeled drive; she wasn't at all sure which was which. She found it was easier than she had expected and made a fairly smooth start. Simon breathed a sigh of relief and climbed into the back seat, lifting the roof up so that he could see better. He stood on the seat, staring through the binoculars at every likely spot, yelling at intervals for her to go faster, or slower, or even to stop altogether.

Frances had little time to look at anything but the track ahead of her, but she did see some elephants in the distance and became so excited they very nearly left the road.

"Can't you do better than that?" Simon roared at her.

Frances jumped up and down in her seat. "But do look, Simon! Look at those elephants!"

"Shut up!" he shouted at her.

"I will not!"

"Fran, for heaven's sake, they're only a few elephants! And that big bull looks as though he's in trouble. Keep away from him and *get back on the road!* You're the worst driver I've ever come across!"

"I am not!" she exclaimed loudly. "I've never seen an elephant before—at least, only in a zoo, and they don't look at all the same there. They look much smaller, for one thing!"

"Possibly because they're Indian elephants," he suggested sweetly.

Frances accepted this. "What is wrong with that one that's going off by himself?" she asked.

Simon trained the glasses on to the enormous animal. "It could be that he's got some safari ants up his trunk," he said. "He's making for the nearest water to get rid of them. They're a pest in the wet weather. I've seen elephants completely maddened by them. They can even die in the end."

Frances's heart was wrung. "But this one won't die, will he?"

Simon shook his head. "Not he!" he grunted.

With some difficulty Frances set the car back on the road and drove along it, a thick wall of dust rising up behind them.

"I wouldn't like to walk along here by myself," she said after a while.

"Abel has lived around here since he was a baby," Simon told her. "The first job he ever had was herding cattle on these plains. He never knew anywhere else until he went into the army."

The track was badly rutted a little farther along. Frances tried to avoid falling into them, afraid of what Simon would say if the vehicle overturned. Her extreme caution, however, led to other difficulties. The sides of the ruts caved in under the weight of the tires, turning to dust in which the wheels spun helplessly.

"Frances!" Simon yelled, exasperated.

She roared the engine, her face set. "If you can do better, you drive!" she said stormily.

"Don't do that! Reverse, woman. Reverse! I don't believe you have the faintest idea what you're doing!" He ducked his head inside the vehicle, stepping down from the back seat, reaching over beside her and slamming the gear lever into reverse. "Now try!"

"I can't!"

"Frances!"

"And don't shout at me! I can't think when you shout at me."

He pulled her bodily out from behind the wheel and deposited her on the passenger seat. In a few seconds he had eased the Land Rover into reverse and onto some harder ground.

"I suppose you have driven a car before?" he said evenly.

She sniffed, very close to tears. "Of course I have!"

"And you actually passed your test?"

"At the first attempt!" she said defiantly.

"Well, it doesn't mean you can drive! Heaven help you when the rains come and you have to do some real driving! And don't cry!"

"I'm not crying!" she denied. "And," she went on, getting angrier by the moment, "in England we have proper roads to drive on, not a . . . dust bed! And we have cars that go, and are even comfortable! And we don't yell at each other all the way down the highways just because we feel like it. I think you're horrible!"

"My God!" he said.

"And what does that mean?" she demanded.

"It means that you'd better shut up!" he said.

Frances sniffed again and searched her pocket for a handkerchief. She couldn't find one and blinked hopefully to keep the tears from spilling over down her cheeks. She must have a handkerchief somewhere, she thought with a touch of desperation. She always had a handkerchief!

Simon held his out to her in silence. She accepted it gratefully and blew her nose violently. "Why?" she said crossly.

"Why what?"

"Why should I shut up?"

He stopped the Land Rover and pulled his bush hat low over his eyes. "Because this isn't England, and a dust track is not a highway, and because if you don't shut up, I shall forget you are a doctor and do you a violence that we shall both regret!" He eyed her lazily. "Is that enough to begin with?"

"Yes," she said.

"Then you'd better try your hand at driving again and watch where you're going!"

"All right," she said sulkily. "Only don't shout at me."

"I won't," he promised. "Next time I'll try kissing you instead. At least you kiss better than you drive!"

She ignored that, blinking nervously as she took his place behind the wheel. Her hands were trembling as she pushed the gear lever forward and started the Land Rover down the track again. She was determined that she wouldn't say another word to him—ever! Other women might welcome these verbal assaults from him, and other assaults too, come to that, but she had better things to do with her time and energies. She would show him that there was at least one woman in the world who saw him as he really was. Not a charmer who could take what he wanted, when he wanted, but an arrogant brute who didn't warrant a single thought from anyone who had any self-respect!

"What's that?" she burst out, seeing a large gray shape on the road ahead of her.

"Rhino," he said briefly.

"W-will it move?" she asked, her voice trembling despite her.

"It may. You'd better stop."

She did so, with a jerky movement that nearly dislodged Simon from his perch on the back seat.

"I'm s-sorry," she said.

He didn't answer. He rested his elbows on the roof and looked at something for a long time through the binoculars.

"Can you see anything?" she asked him.

He grunted. "There's another rhino over there," he said. "She has a baby with her."

"Oh, let me see!" Frances pleaded.

Simon handed her the glasses. "Over there," he pointed.

She adjusted the sights and trained them on the two animals in the distance. The mother was lying on her side, a small trickle of blood running from her shoulder. The baby stood a few feet away from her, his horn as yet only a tiny bump above his prehensile lip, and he was trembling.

"She's hurt!" Frances reported.

"That's what I thought," Simon drawled. "I think I'll get out and take a look."

"But you can't!" she protested. "This one will see you!"

He dropped down into the seat beside her. The rhinoceros ground its teeth on a thorn bush, sniffing the air, its shortsighted eyes peering at the Land Rover.

"Do you think you can drive this thing over to that tree?" Simon asked Frances in an undertone.

"I don't know," she confessed.

"Take it slowly," he encouraged her. "Ease her over that hillock and let her drift down between that tree and the rhinos. And for heaven's sake don't get between the mother and the *toto*. Rhinos are as unpredictable as any other females!"

"Thanks a lot!" she retorted.

"Let's go."

Frances did as he had told her. She drove the Land Rover off the road in a wide sweep toward the tree. At the top of the slope, she switched the engine off and allowed the vehicle to drift down, coming to rest immediately under the thorn tree that Simon had indicated.

The rhinoceros they had left behind on the road ran off into the bush, its ungainly gait carrying it away from them at a great pace. Rhinos seldom congregate, and this one had no great interest in the mother and baby it had left behind.

Frances put on the brake with her hand. The ratchets ground against each other, and the mother rhino raised her head, snorting with fear and anger.

"She's hurt all right," Simon said.

The rhino heard him speak and, with a great effort, got to her feet, swaying. Frances thought she heard a groan from the tree and looked up sharply.

"*Daktari!*" a voice breathed faintly.

"It's Abel!" Frances exclaimed.

But Simon was not listening. He opened the door of the car and seized the heavy bore gun on the back seat. The rhino came a few unsteady steps toward him and then stopped, pawing irritably at the ground.

Simon stepped away from the Land Rover and raised the rifle to his shoulder. It was easy to see where the poor beast had been hit before and where someone had tried to hack away her horn of matted hair, probably hoping to sell it later at an inflated price—there were still people who believed that rhino horn is an aphrodisiac.

Frances never knew what instinct made her know when the rhino gathered herself to charge. Without thinking, she found she had started up the engine and had swung the Land Rover between the rhino and Simon. A second later, two tons of rhino collided with the Land Rover, tossing the vehicle into the air. Frances held onto the wheel with all her might, not daring to look at either the animal or at Simon. The car crashed back onto the ground and she wrenched the wheel around again as the mother rhino retreated toward her baby. Then she turned to rush the Land Rover again.

Simon threw himself flat on the ground and fired the rifle. The rhino, already rocking on her feet, met the full impact of the bullet and keeled slowly over. Simon jumped to his feet and walked over to her, firing again as he went. The great animal shook under the blast, pulled her feet up in an instinctive movement, and died.

Simon stood for a long moment looking at her. Frances wondered what he was thinking and if he shared her pity for the huge, armor-plated animal who had only been trying to defend her young.

"What will happen to the baby?" she asked. Her voice sounded strange to her ears.

"We'll take it back to Nguyu," he said. "Elspeth will bring it up."

Frances could feel herself shaking. "She can't have it!"

"It'll starve if we leave it here," he said, pushing his hat on to the back of his head.

"I could look after it! Cain will help me," she said.

He came and stood beside her, throwing the rifle back into the Land Rover. He put both his hands on the open window, his lazy eyes studying every detail of her face. Then, just when she was least expecting it, he kissed her hard on the lips.

"What was that for?" she asked him. She felt cold and she had started to shiver.

"That's because you can drive a damned sight better than I thought!" he said gruffly. "I'll have to rope the *toto* and put it in a sack—"

"But what about Abel?" she demanded.

"Abel?"

"He's up in that tree. I can't think how he got there, and I can't think how we're going to get him down."

Simon stared up into the flat-topped thorn tree. It was hard to see anything against the sun, but he could just make out the shape of a man curled up in the branches.

"Abel!"

There was a long silence and the man moved his hand. *"Daktari,"* he whispered.

Simon pushed the Land Rover back under the tree with his bare hands and leaped up onto the roof. He swore vividly as the thorns caught at his clothing.

"Is he all right?" Frances called.

"No," he said briefly. "It looks as though the rhino got him first."

"I'm coming up," Frances said. She grasped her medical bag firmly in one hand and climbed onto the hood of the Land Rover. "Let me see," she commanded.

Simon shook his head. "Get back in the car, Fran. I'll do what I can for him, and then I'll get him down somehow."

But Frances only shook her head. "You're in my way!" she said sharply.

"Fran!" he pleaded.

She tried to make a joke out of it. "You're the animal doctor, remember?" she said. "This is my job."

"It isn't very pretty—" he began.

"Nor is an accident on the highway," she retorted.

"I suppose not," he agreed. He pulled her up beside him. "What are you going to do?" he asked her.

"I'm going to give him a shot that will put him out for a while. Will you hold my bag?"

She was pleased to see that her hands were completely steady as she broke the seals on the tube of morphine and filled the hypodermic syringe. She concentrated fiercely on the task, not allowing herself to think, even for a minute, of the great, gory wound in Abel's side that was hanging wide open, exposed to the flies and the fierce afternoon sun. Only when she had slipped the pain-killing needle into Abel's muscular arm did she turn her attention to the gaping hole.

"I'll have to operate as soon as we get him back to Nguyu," she said abruptly. "I can't do much here."

"Getting him down will hurt him," Simon pointed out.

"I know," she said. Her voice broke dangerously. "I'm going to climb up behind him. Otherwise we'll just tear him to pieces on those thorns."

She had never been much good at climbing trees and the thorns tore at her flesh and hurt her badly, but at last she was able to wedge herself against a handy branch and lift Abel's head and shoulders into a more comfortable position. Happily, he was already unconscious and, in a few moments, she was able to roll him out of the tree and into Simon's waiting arms.

Simon laid him on the roof of the Land Rover and jumped to the ground.

"Now, what about you?" he asked her.

"I can't move!" she cried.

"Try jumping," he suggested.

"I can't!"

"Look, stop saying 'I can't' to everything and jump! You'll be all right! I'll catch you!"

"I can't even see you!" she panicked.

"*Jump!*" he yelled at her.

She fell out of the tree rather than jumped. He caught her, more or less, and deposited her without ceremony on her feet beside the Land Rover.

"My, my," he said, "you do your doctoring the hard way, Miss Whitney—"

"Oh, Simon!" she wailed. She picked a thorn out of the palm of her hand and whimpered against him. "Please don't tease me now," she said. "I can't stand it!"

"No," he said gently, "I can see you can't. Get in the Land Rover, Fran, and I'll put Abel in beside you. He'll do until we can get him back to Nguyu. He isn't bleeding too much."

She was too tired to argue with him. She sat heavily on the canvas-covered seat, feeling bruised in body and spirit. Simon lifted Abel into the seat beside her, lying his head against her knee.

"I'll take the *toto* in the front with me!" he grinned at her.

She nodded wearily, barely aware of what he was doing as he roped the tiny rhinoceros and tied it tightly into the front seat. Then, without a word, he climbed in himself and drove back to the dirt track, easing the vehicle onto the rutted surface, and on, back to Nguyu.

CHAPTER SIX

THE baby rhinoceros kicked ceaselessly.

"Hush, *toto*," Simon said soothingly. He laid a hand on the hard skin of the baby's back and patted him gently. "Hush, *toto*. You've got a brand new mama to look after you now. You're a lucky beast!"

Frances watched his hand reassure the young animal and felt it again in her imagination flat against her own back. It was ridiculous to be jealous of a small orphaned creature, but she was. She shut her eyes and refused to watch him any more. Why should she care? She knew he didn't.

Simon caught a glimpse of her nodding head in the driving mirror. Abel was groaning faintly; he had lost a lot of blood and was in shock from his injuries.

"How many men have you kissed?" he asked Frances out of the blue.

She sat up indignantly. "How many women have you?" she retorted.

"Enough to tell the difference," he said dryly.

"What difference?" she asked sourly.

"Ah well, if you don't know, my love, you can't have kissed very many."

She thought he sounded unbelievably smug, and she disliked him very much.

"I told you . . . why I came here," she said in a throbbing voice.

"So you did!" he goaded her. "Tell me some more about this lover of yours. I see him as tall, handsome and very rich. Probably clever as well, or he would have bored you sooner or later. Did he have the masterful touch?"

"He wasn't in the least bit handsome!" Frances denied, and was surprised to discover for the first time herself how much this was true.

"Ah!" Simon teased her, "Your taste is improving!"

She blushed. "He wears glasses," she said irrelevantly.

"But he was still rich and had the masterful touch?"

"N-no," she admitted.

"No to wealth or to the other?"

"No to both," she said faintly.

"Poor Frances! What kind of a man was he? He sounds a cold fish to me. Whatever did you see in him?"

"He's a very good doctor!" she said with spirit.

He looked at her in the driving mirror. "Is that all?"

She refused to answer, but when she thought about it, that *had* been all. The whole romance had amounted to nothing more than that she had admired Rodney as a doctor! She thought back to the single kiss he had ever given her, on which she had built so much, and remembered it now as a rather uncomfortable experience in one of the hospital's well-lit corridors, with the distant sounds of the hospital dance punctuating the hurried embrace.

"I really believe that was all!" Simon said, trying not to laugh.

"Well, it wasn't!" she said crossly.

"I'll never believe that his brand of kisses made your heart beat faster!"

"You can't possibly know!" she pointed out with mounting indignation.

"Oh yes, I can!" he answered.

"How can you know?" Frances asked unwisely.

"Because I know the difference," he said solemnly.

"And I don't?" But she did! She had known immediately when he had touched her and had danced with her exactly what the difference was. With Rodney, she had admired him terribly and had secretly tried to pick his brains so that she would be as good a doctor as he was. She had talked herself into being in love with him, because everyone she knew had been in love with *somebody*, and she had begun to think that she didn't really want to be a doctor anyway. With Simon, it had indeed been different.

"Do you?" Simon asked.

She thought of denying it. She thought she might even pretend that she didn't know what he was talking about.

"There wasn't *only* Rodney!" was what she actually said.

"No?" he prompted her.

"No," she said, goaded into still further indiscretion. "You couldn't expect it, could you? A qualified doctor has to be of a . . . a certain age. You couldn't expect me not to have had any experience. I'm not an adolescent any longer!"

His laughter mocked her. "I like the bit about being of a certain age!" he said.

"You don't believe me?" she protested sharply.

"Not a word of it!" he replied promptly.

"Well, I believe everything I've heard about you!" she retorted.

"Good for you!" he congratulated her.

"Especially about all the girls you've kissed!" she added, much aggrieved. "And not only kissed, I dare-say."

"Does that bother you!" he asked.

"Why should it?" Her voice trembled dangerously. "It's nothing to me what you do!"

"No, of course not," he said dryly.

"I knew you were a flirt the first moment I set eyes on you!" she assured him.

"Of course," he murmured, "your vast experience would tell you that!"

"Quite," she agreed.

"Did it also tell you that girls of a certain age shouldn't flirt at all if they have no interest in the object of the exercise?"

"I don't flirt!" she denied furiously.

"Don't shout," he reproved her. "You'll disturb Abel."

"I'm not shouting!" Frances said in a more moderate tone. She looked at Abel with concern. He looked very ill indeed. "Oh, Simon! I don't like the look of him. Can we go any faster?"

"Another half hour," he answered abruptly. "Will he last?"

She examined the unconscious man more closely. "Yes, but I don't want to wait any longer than necessary. I'm going to operate the moment we get to Nguyu. Cain will have to give him some blood to keep him going."

"Is the operating room ready?" he asked her.

She nodded. "I'll have to ask you to act as anesthetist for me. Mwete isn't ready for that."

"No, probably not," he agreed easily. "Are you doing anything about training him?"

"What I can. He had a lot of practical experience in the army, but he hasn't had much real training. He ought to go away to a hospital somewhere and be properly trained as a qualified nurse."

"He has his wife and family to consider," Simon informed her.

"Does he have a wife? I didn't know." She supposed

that she ought to have made it her business to find out, but she had been so busy all week there had not been much time for the kind of gossip that would have told her that sort of thing. Whenever she had seen him, there had been urgent things afoot, like putting the hospital into a state of readiness for emergency. Ah well, it was just as well she had done that! Poor Abel would not have stood much chance if she couldn't operate immediately, not that his chances were very good as it was. She was beginning to think that he was bleeding somewhere inside where she couldn't staunch the flow, but his heart still beat strongly beneath her monitoring fingers. He had all the toughness of the land where he had been born and brought up.

"Is Abel married too?" she asked.

Simon shook his head. "He's still getting the bride price ready. He has his eye on an expensive little piece from another tribe on the other side of the Rift Valley. I'm afraid this will set him back quite a bit."

"I think it's terrible that women are still bought and sold!" Frances exclaimed.

"It's a kind of insurance for her future," he said. "If he treats her badly, her father will soon interfere—if he cares about her at all."

"And if he doesn't?" she asked.

"It's the custom of the country."

"It doesn't set a very high value on women, does it?" she said in a small voice.

Simon laughed. "I really believe you think you're worth more than a few cattle and the odd goat!" he teased her.

"Well, don't you?" she wailed.

"I don't know," he said thoughtfully. "I shall need notice of that question. How's he doing?"

"Not very well. How much longer now?" she asked.

"A few minutes. Nguyu is just over the hill."

She sighed with relief. When she thought about the operation ahead of her, she felt very raw and inexperienced. She only hoped that Simon wouldn't guess quite how inexperienced a doctor, as well as a woman, she was. She wiped her palm on her skirt and winced with sudden pain. It was nothing more than a scratch from the thorn tree, but it was painful. She noted dully that she had others all down her arms and it was difficult to tell which was her blood and which was Abel's.

The sun hung low in the sky. She was surprised to see it was already evening, and she, despite Cain's sandwiches, had eaten nothing since breakfast. She should eat something while she could, but the thought of food revolted her.

"Simon, there aren't enough lights!" she worried aloud.

"I'll fix some up. Don't look so anxious, love, you'll pull it off! Abel's as tough as they come!"

Frances bit her lip. "Just as well!" she muttered.

There was no twilight. The sounds of night were already in evidence when Simon drew up outside the hospital and stepped wearily out of the Land Rover. Mwete rushed out, bringing a portable stretcher with him. His calm competence was a joy to Frances, as she watched him place the stretcher along the seat beside Abel and slide the unconscious body onto it. He and Simon carried Abel straight into the operating room, leaving her to follow, clutching her medical bag in one hand.

Simon was as good as his word. While she was scrubbing up and laying out the sterilized instruments she would need, he rigged up a lighting system that was more than adequate, even if it was noisy and flared up in the slightest breeze.

He stood beside her, tying up her gown and holding out her gloves, snapping them onto her torn hands with a gentleness that made her feel soft inside.

"Turn around and I'll tie your mask," he said.

"What about yours?" she asked.

"Mwete will see to that."

Frances crossed to her patient and began to expose the long wound in his side, staunching the blood that had begun to seep through the temporary bandages she'd put on earlier. It was going to be a long job, she thought.

Without a word, Simon adjusted a mask over Abel's face and dripped the only anesthetic they had onto a piece of gauze.

"Okay," he said.

"Has Cain come?" Frances asked him.

He nodded. "Mwete is getting a pint of his blood now. He'll fix it up as soon as he can."

"Good," she said.

Surprisingly, now that the moment had come, she found that she was quite confident and knew exactly what to do. Shutting out the noise of the lights and Simon's disturbing presence, she concentrated her attention on the job in hand. She could almost hear the surgeon whom she had often assisted in London talking to her as she worked. She barely noticed when Mwete brought in the pint of blood he had taken from Cain and Simon slipped the needle into Abel's arm adjusting the bottle on the cradle over his head. She did notice that Abel improved after that and she cast a quick look of triumph at Simon. He grinned at her behind his mask.

"Clever girl!" he said.

"That ought to be worth more than a few cattle and a

goat!" she retorted. "Can you fix up a saline drip now. I won't be much longer."

"Take your time," he said calmly. "He's doing fine."

She threaded her needle with care and began to stitch up the wound. When she had finished, she had a neat line of stitches holding the edges of the skin closely together.

"I'm glad to see you can sew a fine seam!" Simon remarked.

"I take pride in it," she smiled. "Don't you? I mean, when you operate on your animals—"

"I do my poor best," he agreed. "Are you through?"

Frances dropped a dressing over the wound and strapped it firmly in place.

"That's it!" she confirmed.

"Good. Mwete and I will get him to bed." He tore off his mask and smiled at her. "A very nice job too, if I may say so, Dr. Whitney. Congratulations!"

Frances felt weak at the knees and more tired than she had felt in a long time. She watched the two men as they lifted Abel carefully onto the trolley, Mwete holding the bottle of saline as though it might bite him at any moment. Simon wheeled the trolley out of the light and into the shadows beyond. She heard them come to a stop in the tiny ward that was attached to the hospital. Abel groaned faintly as they tucked him up in the high hospital bed.

Suddenly, she thought she was going to be sick. It was due to the sun and the heat and having little to eat all day, but it was humiliating. Then she thought that she might faint first, and sat down quickly on the nearest chair, desperately swallowing the rush of saliva that came into her mouth.

"Does it always take you this way?" Simon asked her cheerfully, as he entered the room and noticed her somewhat green complexion.

"Oh, Simon!" she protested.

"So much for you in the role of the impregnable doctor!" he muttered.

"Oh, go away!" she besought him.

"And leave you to pass out on your own? No, no, I'll see you to your bed, my love. You'll feel quite different in the morning!"

"I'm going to sleep in the hospital," she said wearily. "I have to stay with Abel."

"Mwete will be with him. You are going to sleep in your own chaste bed and knit up the unravelled sleeve of care, or whatever. You've done enough for one day." He smiled at her. "More than enough for an inexperienced girl who doesn't know puppy love from the real thing!"

"Oh, Simon!" she said again.

"Mwete!" Simon's voice roared through the hospital. *"Mama* doesn't feel well. I'm taking her home. Will you clear up in here?"

"Ndiyo, bwana."

Frances made a helpless gesture of protest. "I can't expect him to—"

"Will you walk, or shall I carry you?" he asked her civilly.

She was obliged to smile. "You couldn't carry me all that way," she said. "You're not Samson."

"Then you'll walk?"

She gave in to the relentless pressure of his hand on her arm and stood up shakily. "I don't want to go home," she said tearfully.

"You'll do as you're told for once!" he told her.

She winced. "Must you shout at me all the time?"

"It seems to be the only thing you understand," he said wearily. He put his hands on her shoulders and pushed her out of the operating room, out of the hospital and into the warm night air of Nguyu.

Simon walked quickly while she staggered along by his side feeling sorry for herself. He would never want to kiss her again! He would despise her for the weakness.

"Simon, I can't go this fast!"

He tucked her hand into his arm and pulled her along. Cain was waiting at her door, a large piece of sticking plaster decorating his arm where the needle had been. A wide smile replaced his normal scowl. *"Mama,"* he said, followed by a flood of words she couldn't possibly understand.

"Mama is going straight to bed!" Simon said masterfully.

"Ndiyo," Cain agreed. "But *mama* must eat something first!"

Simon gave Frances a push toward the bedroom. "I'll give you two minutes," he said, "then I'm coming in whether you're ready or not!"

Frances was ready, if only just. She lay against the pillows and eyed him mutinously. "I'm hungry," she said.

He laughed. "Cain is bringing you something to eat in a moment," he told her.

"What about you?" she asked. "Aren't you hungry too?"

"I'll have something later." He came close to her bed and looked down at her enigmatically. "Thank you for all you did for Abel, Fran. He wouldn't have made it if you hadn't been here. But don't dwell on it. Go to sleep, and pleasant dreams to you! Good night!"

She clenched her fists under the bedclothes. "Where are you going?" she demanded.

"Me?" His eyes twinkled with suppressed laughter. "I'm going to Elspeth's for the night. I'll see you in the morning."

She shut her eyes and refused to answer. At that moment she hated him more than anyone else on earth!

Frances was almost asleep when she heard the knock on the door. She flung herself out of bed and, carrying the lamp in her hand and clutching her dressing gown around her shoulders, went to see who was there. The Baron Klaus von Rahner blinked at her in the sudden light.

"I am sorry to disturb you," he said. "I had not thought it to be too late to call."

"It isn't," Frances said frankly.

"But you are already in bed!"

"I've had quite a day," she said dryly. "Won't you come in?"

The baron stood transfixed to the spot. "What is that peculiar noise?" he asked.

Frances listened. "I expect it's the rhinoceros," she said. "I forgot to ask what happened to him."

"A rhinoceros?" he echoed.

"A very small one," Frances confirmed. "You see, Simon had to kill his mother—"

"Do you have him inside your house?" the German asked reasonably.

Frances bit her lip. "I didn't want Elspeth to have him!" she explained.

The baron stepped into the room and looked about him. "Do you think Elspeth would harm him?" he asked.

"No, of course not!" Frances answered quickly. "But . . . well, he's mine!"

"I see," he said, and perhaps he did.

"I'm afraid I can't even offer you a drink," she continued hastily. "At least not unless I go and steal some whisky from Simon!"

"Is he still away?" the baron asked.

Frances stared at him. "N-no," she said. "As a matter of fact he's gone over to Elspeth's. You must have passed him on the way here."

"Probably wants a bath," the baron muttered.

That's what he thinks, Frances thought wryly. Simon wouldn't drive ten miles for a mere bath and, if that was all he had wanted, he would have taken her with him. She could have used a good soak to get the prickles of sweat out of her skin, and out of her spirit too.

"Perhaps you wouldn't mind fetching the whisky?" she asked the Baron. "I have a patient at the hospital and I really ought to look in and see how he is."

"In your nightdress?" the baron objected.

"Well, no, I thought of getting dressed, actually," Frances assured him, her cheeks a little red.

"Good," he said. "Then I don't mind getting the whisky."

Frances found some clean clothes and put them on while he was gone. She tied her hair back with a ribbon and put on lipstick to make herself look a little less tired.

"Shall I pour you out some too?" the baron called out.

She left the bedroom and smiled at him. "Yes, please."

He studied her for a long moment. "Do you mind my coming to see you?" he asked then. "We seem to have seen very little of you since you came to dinner that once."

"I've been busy," she said lightly.

"Is that possible in Nguyu?"

"It is for a doctor. Things seem to go wrong so easily here. Even a small scratch often has to be lanced—"

"And this takes all your time?" he insisted.

"It's what I'm here for," she said.

He shrugged his shoulders. "It is not for me to advise you, Miss Whitney—"

"Won't you call me Frances?" Frances interrupted him uncomfortably.

"If you will call me Klaus." He waited for her to nod before going on. "I have been coming to Tanzania for a great many years. I like to climb mountains, you see. Particularly, I like to climb Kilimanjaro. Did you know that during the war there were some Italian prisoners of war who escaped from their camp to climb Kilimanjaro?"

"And did they?" she asked.

"Oh, yes, they climbed right to the top. And then they turned around and went back to their prisoner-of-war camp. But perhaps you cannot understand such enthusiasm." He smiled blandly. "Mark understands," he added.

Frances frowned. "I don't want to climb mountains myself," she confessed. "But there are other things I want to do—"

"Like being a doctor in Nguyu?"

"That," she agreed. "And other things."

"Exactly!" He gave the word a curious stress that made it sound very German. "So you must not bury yourself altogether in your work. It will be good for you to come out to see us every now and then."

Frances flushed. "I prefer to wait until I'm asked," she said.

"I am asking you now," he pointed out.

"Yes, but Elspeth hasn't asked me."

He was silent for a moment. Then, "Why don't you like Elspeth?"

"But I do!" Her protest didn't sound very convincing even to her own ears. "Besides," she went on, "I think she and Simon have a right to be alone together some times."

"Is that a hit at me?" he asked quaintly. "I stay with the Peissels very often, you know. I am at home there, as you English say."

"I think perhaps Simon is too," she said sadly.

But the baron only shook his head. "Simon does not admire the civilized," he said flatly, "But you? You are different, I think."

"I've never known anything else," she said.

"Until now," he reminded her.

"Until now," she agreed. "Now I don't know what I want. All I know is that I want something more than a pretty tiled bathroom—"

He laughed easily. "You will want what your husband wants," he accused her.

"But I don't have a husband!" she said smugly.

The baron sighed heavily. "You are a nice girl, Frances," he said. "Elspeth is a nice girl also, but she will want her husband to want only what she wants, and for a man that is a hard thing to accept."

Frances couldn't see Simon accepting it at all! "Perhaps they will want the same thing," she said.

"Perhaps." She was surprised by the bitterness in his voice and forced herself to smile at him. "Then we shall have nothing to do but to console one another." He looked her straight in the eyes. "Does it surprise you that I am in love with Elspeth?" he demanded.

It did, but she didn't want to say so.

"Why don't you take her climbing some time?" she suggested. "You'd be standing on your own ground there!"

His eyes narrowed thoughtfully. "Perhaps I will try," he said. "And you will come out to visit us soon, and more often?"

"Yes, I will," she promised.

When Klaus had left, she walked over to the hospital and let herself quietly in through the back door. Mwete was asleep in a chair, his head cushioned on his arms that were spread over the desk in front of him. Frances tiptoed past him, unwilling to disturb him, and went into the ward by the side of the operating room.

Abel was still asleep but as she watched him, he opened his eyes and grunted.

"How are you feeling?" she asked.

His eyes grew muzzy and she realized that he was not really awake yet. She checked the drip over his head and pulled the blankets up over his chest in case he should feel cold.

"*Faru!*" he said loudly.

She wondered what he was talking about. "If you like," she said.

He laughed weakly. "It was a rhinoceros, *mama*. The poachers had tried to kill her for her horn, but she chased them off. She thought I was a poacher too."

"Hush," Frances said. "You mustn't talk now. I'll give you something to make you go back to sleep."

"I fired at the rhinoceros, but my aim was no good and she still lived. She came again and tossed me up into the thorn tree—"

"You mean you didn't climb up it?" she asked, horrified.

"I don't climb thorn trees," he said distinctly. "Did the *daktari* kill the rhinoceros?"

"Yes," she said.

"And the *toto*?"

"Is mine." She prepared an injection and gave it to him quickly. "Try to sleep, Abel. The *daktari* will be in to see you in the morning."

His fingers clung to her wrist. "*Mama*," he whispered, his voice already growing sleepy. "Thank you, *mama*." His eyes fell shut and he drifted into sleep. "*Mama daktari!*"

Mrs. Doctor! Frances snorted down her nostrils disparagingly. She turned down the light over Abel's head to the merest glimmer and walked away from his bed. Mwete was still asleep when she went into the office. She found a pillow in the cupboard and placed it under his head to make him a little more comfortable. She felt more content than she had for a long time. Whatever happened, she was needed in Nguyu, and at that moment that was enough for her.

CHAPTER SEVEN

FRANCES discovered that the baby rhinoceros had a very sweet tooth. She succeeded in making him come to her by offering him small portions of chocolate. He would stand quite still and suck on them, making the most extraordinary noises. Abel was very interested in his progress and, to keep him in his bed, Frances allowed the baby rhino to go to him, ignoring Mwete's pleas that he should be left outside and Simon's jeers that she was nothing but a sentimental female.

"What name have you given him, *mama*?" Abel asked her.

Abel put out a hand and patted the rhino's head. "You cannot call him baby forever!"

"Well, no," she admitted. "I'll ask Simon for some suggestions."

Abel grinned. "Whose rhino did you say it is?" he teased her.

Frances refused to answer. "You are getting better!" she told him.

"As good as new," he agreed.

"And then you'll be getting married, I suppose?"

He chuckled. "As the *daktari* would say, women gossip, gossip, gossip!"

"You mean you're not getting married?" she demanded.

"Oh yes, I am," he agreed. "Just as soon as I can find six cows and a dozen goats. I plan to get married the next time the priest comes around."

"Is she a Christian too?" Frances asked innocently.

"She doesn't know it yet," he said moodily. "When will you get married, *mama*?"

285

"Goodness knows!" she exclaimed. "I don't know anyone who has enough cows and goats and chickens to even think of marrying me!"

"The *daktari* has all the animals of Africa," Abel observed.

"And half the women as well!" she said crossly.

Abel laughed heartily. "You will have to buy a love potion from Mwete. He will sell it to you very cheaply because he likes working in your hospital. His love potions are very successful. Did you know that his father had 32 wives? It takes a whole pile of magic to keep all those women happy!"

"Well," said Frances, "it sounds a fine advertisement for his father's magic, but I don't see that it says anything for Mwete."

"Mwete is a good Moslem!" Abel told her.

Simon came into the hospital and pushed the baby rhinoceros firmly out of the door with his foot. "Mwete doesn't have to buy his wife with goats!" he grinned at Abel.

"You leave *toto* alone!" Frances reproved him. "You hurt his feelings when you shut him outside."

"Rubbish, woman! And if you feed him any more chocolate, you'll rot his teeth!"

"Yes, *daktari*," she said submissively.

He looked at her suspiciously. "How's your party coming along?" he asked.

She had thought that he had forgotten all about her party. "I'm going to ask Elspeth to help me with it," she answered him.

To her surprise, he frowned. "Don't you have enough helpers already?" he demanded.

"I thought she might feel left out," she tried to explain.

"Elspeth?"

Frances looked embarrassed. "Klaus thought she might be," she amended.

Simon shrugged. "You can ask her if you like, but I don't think it's exactly her cup of tea. I'd like to see her drinking *pombe* out of a paint tin!"

"Why not?" said Frances.

His eyes glinted. "I should have thought you would have seen that for yourself," he told her.

Abel pulled himself up higher in his bed. "Everyone is hoping to be asked to *mama's* party!" he grinned. "The women have been talking about nothing else for days!"

"I thought they had all been talking about your approaching nuptials!" Frances teased him.

"That too!" he agreed complacently, smoothing down the sheet over his chest.

"My goodness," Frances said admiringly, "you're as conceited as the *daktari*.!"

The two men laughed together. "But not as conceited as a certain female of my acquaintance!" Simon retorted.

Frances flushed. "I'm not conceited!" she denied heatedly.

He nodded gravely. "She thinks she is worth more than a few cattle and a goat," he pronounced solemnly.

"I wish you wouldn't be so ridiculous!" Frances flashed at him.

"Why not?"

"It isn't ... seemly," she said with considerable dignity.

Simon's eyebrows shot up, giving his face a comical expression. "My dear girl, I don't feel particularly seemly when I think about you. Would you have it otherwise?"

It seemed she would never learn not to cross swords with him, she thought, no matter what promises she made to herself.

"I must be going," she said in a voice that sounded decidedly strained. "The clinic is waiting for me."

"Is Mwete going with you?" Simon asked.

She shook her head. "I want him to help Abel out of bed—"

"Then I'll drive you," he rapped.

"I'm quite capable of driving myself!" she said smugly.

"Must you argue with everything I say?" he shouted at her. "Have a look outside and you'll see it's going to rain at any moment!"

"What if it does?" she asked.

"My dear girl—"

"I am *not* your dear anything!"

"—if you think I want to spend the night looking for you when you've got yourself stuck in the mud, you're dead wrong!"

"No," she agreed bitterly, "I'm aware you have other uses for your evenings! Only I won't get stuck in the mud!"

"Oh, go and get your bag!" he roared.

"And I refuse to be shouted at!"

"Then don't be such a pigheaded ninny! I'll be around the back, waiting for you. I'll have a check on their cattle while I'm waiting for you."

She shook her head at him. "You don't even know where I'm going," she wondered at him.

He grinned, "Oh yes, I do! I know your schedule as well as my own, my love. You're off to Msasa, and I'm going with you!"

The first drops of rain were falling out of the leaden sky when she went out to the Land Rover. She went back inside to fetch her rainproof cape and threw it over her shoulders, pulling the hood up over her hair. It was exciting to see the first of the rain falling on the parched ground. Each drop stayed intact and covered with dust, bouncing up and down on the hard earth, and the sound of it striking the tin roofs was like the noise of applause. But a few seconds later it had stopped, as suddenly as it had started, and the sun came out again.

"It doesn't look as though I shall need my cape after all," she said to Simon, about to return into the hospital to hang it up again.

"Probably not," he said unhelpfully.

"Or you to drive me," she added, unable to resist the temptation of annoying him once more.

"Frances," he said, "I am a patient man—"

"May you be forgiven!" she interposed.

"All my life," he assured her, grinding his teeth, "I've been a patient man, but that was before I met you!"

"No doubt!" she chuckled. She stepped daintily up into the Land Rover and folded her hands on her knee, pleased to know that she was irritating him as much by her sudden docility as she had by arguing with him.

"Some day, someone will wring your neck for you!" he told her.

"That will be someone else's privilege," she said comfortably. "Someone who rates me higher than a few cattle and a goat."

He laughed abruptly. "More like a few goats and a cow!" he said nastily.

"I see my value is going down all the time," she complained.

"Blame it on your shrewish tongue!"

She blinked, aware that her cheeks were wet and thinking it was the rain. She put a hand up to her face in a quick gesture of surprise and quickly wiped away the unbidden tears. If she allowed Simon's remarks to get to her she would be quite undone!

"Well?" he prompted her. "Aren't you going to say anything to that?"

"No," she said.

He looked at her sharply. "Are you crying? If that isn't just like a woman to take refuge in tears when she's losing an argument!"

"I'm not crying!" she swallowed. "I've ... I've got something in my eye!"

"Let me see!" He stopped the Land Rover and held the nape of her neck so that he could see better. She tried to back away from him, but his hands were too strong. He smiled very gently. "There's nothing there, is there?"

She shook her head, humiliated.

"Poor Frances," he said. "It isn't a very fair battle, is it? And you do fight very hard!"

"Why isn't it fair?" she asked in a voice that caught in the back of her throat.

"Because I'm destined to win in the end, and you to lose."

Frances struggled away from him. "I don't see it that way!" she said proudly.

He touched her nose with his finger. "No?"

"Certainly not!"

But when he kissed her she made no further effort to escape, not even when his hands found their way beneath her rain-cape and caressed her. He kissed her hard and long, but finally pulled away from her, smiling at her rather shakily.

"I'm sorry," he said at last.

Frances took a deep breath, determined to answer him lightly. "You don't have to worry that I'll take you seriously," she said, forcing a laugh. "I know you have your reputation to consider!"

"*My* reputation?" he yelled.

"There is not the slightest need to shout," she went on waspishly. "I quite understand you are only keeping up your head count. You see, I do know the difference after all!"

"Are you implying that *that* meant nothing to you?" he demanded.

Her heart pounded. "S-something like that," she murmured.

He switched on the engine and crashed the gears. Thoughtfully moving her knee out of his way, she watched him in silence as he began again. The engine stalled and she began to laugh helplessly.

"Frances, I swear I'll murder you . . ."

She restrained herself with difficulty. "Would you like me to drive?" she offered.

Simon's only answer was to start up the engine again and drive much faster than she liked down the slippery road.

"One day," he said, "I'll make love to you until you cry for mercy! And don't expect any gentleness from me, Dr. Whitney, because I don't feel gentle. This isn't Nairobi. This is raw Africa. And don't say I didn't warn you!"

"You can warn me all you like," she said with dignity, "but I don't see that it makes any difference where one is. Klaus comes here often enough and he respects—" She stopped, biting her lip. The expression on Simon's face frightened her into silence, and she began to wish she hadn't begun to say anything at all, not about Klaus, for he had nothing to do with this gulf between them.

"I . . . I mean . . ." she began.

"Don't be childish, Frances," he said.

She swallowed, "But you scare me," she told him. "A little."

"And you scare me one hell of a lot," he said flatly. "You don't even begin to know—"

"I can't help being inexperienced," she muttered, with renewed spirit. "It isn't a crime!"

"No," he admitted. "But it's a trifle disconcerting—especially as you look so sleek and woman-of-the-world—"

"That was what you thought in Nairobi, wasn't it?" she said.

To her surprise he laughed. "When you've quite grown up," he said, "I'll tell you exactly what I thought in Nairobi. Meanwhile," he glanced across at her and smiled, "meanwhile, I shall try not to think of you at all!"

Well, she thought, he wouldn't find that very difficult. She knew exactly how often he went to Elspeth's at night. She couldn't help knowing, because she could hear the Land Rover going past her door and coming back in the morning.

"But you will come to my party, won't you?" she said suddenly.

"Try and keep me away!" he said.

They were more than an hour late arriving at Msasa. A small group of people sat by the side of the road. Most of them were women, their babies playing around them. They were quite unperturbed by the lateness of the doctor. They were accustomed to waiting and did so easily, without fretting, knowing that Frances would come when she could. They knew she had a long way to come and that any emergency might have overtaken her on the way.

They stood up and waved when they saw the Land Rover approaching, adjusting their voluminous garments with one hand and soothing their babies with the other. They preferred to wear very bright colors, the more vivid the better, and most of them covered their heads with square pieces of the same material. Those few who were bare-headed had their hair cut as short as any boy's, if they didn't shave their heads altogether.

"*Daktari!*"

Frances stood back from force of habit—she had grown so accustomed to hearing Simon being called by this name. But these people were calling to her. They burst into a flood of Swahili, of which she could only understand a small part, all of them wanting her attention at the same moment.

"Shall I leave you here while I go and see this herd of cattle?" Simon asked her, a little amused by her gratified astonishment at her sudden importance.

"I won't be very long," she said.

"Then I'll wait," he answered, "It will be my turn to show off in front of you when I catch up with the cattle."

She chuckled. "All right," she said. "That's fair."

Simon grinned. "I'm glad you think so. So far all the glory has been yours!"

"Oh, Abel!" she said.

"Abel and other things," he agreed lightly. "I'll be in the Land Rover when you want me."

Frances managed to persuade the women into a line and began the long business of finding out why they had come to see her. Sometimes it was only curiosity that

had brought them, sometimes they were genuinely concerned about their children. One had come to consult
Frances about some obscure disease her husband had
contracted, slaying him all the while with her tongue
because he had not come himself. On one boy's hands,
she detected the telltale early signs of leprosy and made
a note that he would require treatment immediately if he
was to be cured. The thought that such illnesses could
still strike and be left undetected for so long depressed
her. Of all the major tropical hazards, yaws had had the
greatest medical success—it could be easily cured—and
yet there were still places where people suffered and
died, not knowing that health could be obtained a few
miles away and at the cost of a few pennies.

The babies were a delight to Frances. Whatever they
lacked materially, few of these children were deprived of
affection. They responded accordingly, placid and loving in their turn, sure of themselves and the love of every
adult around them. Frances played with them happily,
advising their mothers about feeding problems and trying to persuade them that keeping a three-year-old
breast-feeding was unlikely to prevent them from having another baby, no matter what they had been told by
the old women in their villages.

Then, when the clinic was over, the women gathered
together their few possessions and walked away into the
bush, leaving Frances alone on the side of the road, feeling suddenly lonely without their chatter.

Watching her as she stood there, Simon thought how
vulnerable she looked. He drove the Land Rover up
level with her and opened the door, stretching across the
vehicle to do so.

"Two years of this won't be enough for you, whatever

you might say," he observed as she climbed in beside him.

As this was almost exactly what Frances had been thinking herself, she was put out by the remark.

"They need doctors at home too!" she said.

"Oh, certainly," he said indifferently.

"And my mother wants to retire," she added defensively. "She's longing for my father to find himself another partner."

"And it has to be one that he himself has begotten?"

"I don't think he would put it quite like that," Frances said, "but that is the general idea. It was a foregone conclusion even when I was in the nursery."

"I take it you have no brothers or sisters?"

"No," she said, "there's only me."

Simon drove as fast as he was able along the dirt track toward a nomadic African settlement, which, to Frances's dismay, they could smell long before they could see it. A small circle of shelters had been built out of mud and dung, the spaces in between them filled in with a barricade of sharp-pointed sticks. Inside the cattle were kept safe at night. By day, they wandered across the open land, competing with the wild animals for their share of feed, guarded by boys who were not yet old enough to be taken into the most junior grade of warriors.

"Are these the famous Masai?" Frances asked in dismay.

Simon shook his head. "I'm afraid these are only a poor imitation. The Masai live for their cattle, and often build up very fine herds. These people care only for numbers, with the results that you can see."

The cattle looked thin and unproductive, more dead

than alive, and the elders were suspicious of Simon's presence. Only a few of them spoke Swahili, which made the proceedings long and complicated, and even more open to misunderstanding.

Simon picked out an animal here and there apparently at random, and ran his hands over the beast, an expression of ferocious anger on his face. On one of them he swatted a fly and held it out on the palm of his hand with a touch of triumph.

"What is it?" Frances asked him.

"Tsetse. It will have to be reported." He said as much to the old men, who merely looked hangdog and stubborn.

"Stupidity is very hard to deal with," Simon said to her in English.

"Well, I don't suppose they've had a day's schooling between them," Frances excused them.

"That, my dear, has nothing to do with stupidity, I regret to say. If it had one could eradicate the mutton-headed with remarkably little trouble!"

She laughed. "True. What are they being particularly stupid about? Doesn't the tsetse fly carry sleeping sickness?"

"It so happens," he told her, "that we have much cause to be grateful to the tsetse fly. If it hadn't been for it, there wouldn't be a wild animal left on these plains. It was the tsetse fly that kept the domesticated animal away. Now, with modern controls and so on, the nomadic tribes press closer and only the national parks protect the wild animals."

"But these cows aren't sick from the tsetse fly, are they?" she asked, studying the limping beasts more closely.

"No," he said briefly. "Foot and mouth. If they move

from here, they could spread it right across the Serengeti."

"What are you going to do?"

"Keep them corraled up here. That's why they're so angry. They know that the *Askaris* who will come out to see that they stay will be of a different tribe and that they won't be able to bribe them. Serves them right! It's cruel to keep cattle under these conditions."

Frances looked about her and saw the women bent double under their enormous burdens of firewood. The men she noticed were mostly drunk and very much at their ease.

"It's cruel to keep women under these conditions too," she said.

He chuckled. "Women and cattle! They're often treated much the same in Africa!"

"So I see," she said dryly.

"And draw the proper conclusion, I hope!" he drawled softly.

"That I'm not so sure about," she answered, half-laughing. "Tell me, are those heavy things they wear around their necks and ankles to make them look beautiful, or merely the badge of servitude that they look?"

He laughed. "A bit of both. I must say, until you pointed it out to me, I hadn't realized that it gave quite such an impression of a chain gang! Perhaps there is something to be said for a more equal approach after all!"

Frances's eyes sparkled militantly. "Definitely," she said.

They were obliged to wait until a police sergeant arrived in answer to Simon's call on the radio, and by that time the sun was at its zenith and the world was stilled to a drowsy buzz of insects in the golden grass.

"Are you in a hurry to get back?" Simon asked as he settled himself back in the Land Rover.

Frances shook her head. She wondered what he was going to suggest and her heart shook within her, yet she was oddly excited.

"Then I'll show you one of the grandest sights in Africa," he promised. "I never miss it if I can help it, but it will mean quite a long drive. Do you mind?"

She stretched her muscles, smiling slightly. "I'm ready for anything," she said.

He shot a quick look at her and away again, and she bit her lip, hoping that he had not misunderstood. She couldn't bear to have another brush with him quite yet; she was still too sore from the last venture.

"I mean I'd like a long drive and something else to think about," she amended her statement.

He smiled easily at her. "Right," he said. "So be it. 'Truce, gentle love, a parley now I crave. Methinks 'tis long since first these wars begun—' "

Frances stopped him with a gesture, quite overcome that he, of all people, should quote poetry at her. Though why shouldn't he, after all? But she would have liked to see Rodney doing anything of the sort, not that he would have known any poetry in the first place. Quite suddenly she liked Simon very much indeed, if only because he didn't think it unmanly to be well read.

"Simon, have you always lived in Africa?" she asked him.

"Yes, why?" he countered.

"I don't know. Because you're not quite like anyone else I've ever met."

"I should hope not!" he said indignantly.

She struggled with herself for a few seconds. "I meant it as a compliment," she confided.

He flushed, which surprised her, for surely he was

accustomed to women saying nice things to him. "Then I'm complimented," he said awkwardly. "You're a nice woman, Frances. A very nice woman."

And now what, she asked herself.

"And now we'll go and take a look at the animals," he added kindly.

Standing high above the plains they could see the great herd of gnus gathering for their annual migration. The smell of rain was in the wind and instinct drove the gnus toward the new grass where they could bring up their young in relative plenty. From where Frances and Simon stood, it was hard to believe that these animals belonged to the same family as the antelope and were not some relative to the domestic herds of cattle. No wonder the Dutch Boer farmers, when they had first seen them, had named them *Wildebeest,* or simply wild cattle, for so they looked in their gigantic herds.

Frances stood in silence, knowing that she was witnessing one of the true marvels of the animal world. Even as she looked the gnus gathered and started on their way, leaving a trail across the plain where their hooves had thundered across the dusty ground. Once these enormous herds of animals had traveled right across the African continent, with nothing and no one to stop them. Now these were only a fraction of what once had been; but even so it was an impressive sight as they wheeled into line and followed their leaders out across the flat savanna, obeying some instinct as surely as their ancestors had done.

Another Land Rover drew up beside theirs and the driver got out and came and stood beside them on their narrow perch. He was one of the smallest black men Frances had ever seen, dressed in a white cassock and with a pair of dark glasses hiding his eyes.

"Dr. Whitney, I presume," he said with conscious humor.

She started. "Yes, Father," she said, though he was quite unlike any other priest she had ever seen, with his hair worn quite long in a full Afro.

Simon nodded a greeting and shook hands, going back to the Land Rover to leave them alone together.

"The *daktari* always escapes while he can," the priest said affably. "But you are one of mine, I believe?"

"Yes," she admitted.

"So I had heard, though I must say I didn't expect to see you before I am next due in Nguyu. You are very badly needed there, Dr. Whitney."

"I shall be here for the next two years," she said.

He turned his attention to the animals below them. "I shall do anything I can to help you," he said simply. "I am Father Kashioki, by the way." He pointed to some new arrivals who had only just come to join the main herd. "It is a magnificent sight, don't you think? It's a bit like the Church, with all God's children marching into heaven. It's part of my job to round up the strays that look as though they might get left behind."

Frances smiled at the thought. He was really very like her parish priest at home after all. "I haven't gone astray yet, Father," she said.

"I didn't think you had!" he protested immediately.

She met his bland stare, her own eyes amused. "Didn't you?" she accused him.

He shrugged endearingly. "The *daktari* . . . ?" He hesitated. "He is a very likable man," he observed quietly.

"Very!" Frances agreed. She sighed, abandoning all thought of pretense once and for all. "I am afraid of him, Father," she confessed.

He looked surprised. "Afraid?" he repeated. "Afraid of liking the *daktari*?"

"No," she said wryly, "not of liking him. Of loving him, and loving him not at all wisely but a great deal too well!"

To her surprise Father Kashioki only laughed. "That is the way life goes," he teased her gently. He escorted her over to Simon and helped her into the Land Rover, still laughing softly. "I shall look forward to seeing you both again," he smiled.

Simon nodded. "See you at Abel's wedding," he confirmed. He waited until they were out of sight of the priest and then he said, "He's a good priest, you know, and a fine man. I like him."

Frances studied the road ahead thoughtfully. "I rather think I do too," she said.

CHAPTER EIGHT

ELSPETH said, "You haven't been over for a bath for ages. How on earth do you manage to keep clean?"

Frances grinned. "I wash," she murmured impudently.

Then she relented. "Actually," she went on, "I find the shower arrangement I have out the back really quite adequate. Cain heats up the water for me and puts it in a kind of canvas bag that Mark rigged up for me, and I find it works very well."

"Did you ask Mark to fix it up for you?" Elspeth asked.

"No, he suggested it himself," Frances said carefully.

"Oh," Elspeth said. "Look, I don't want you to think I'm nosey, only Klaus made me promise to make sure you come over more often. You've made quite a hit there, haven't you?"

"With Klaus?" Frances repeated, almost as though she had never heard his name before.

"Oh, don't pretend!" Elspeth rounded on her. "He says you have the right kind of shape to go mountaineering! What higher compliment could you possibly want?"

Frances laughed, "Seeing that nothing would induce me to climb a mountain—"

"Really?" Elspeth interrupted her.

"Yes, really! I'd hate every moment of it."

Elspeth sighed. "He won't take me with him," she said, the words bursting out of her. "He'll take Mark, of course, *anyone*, but he won't take me!"

"But would you like to climb Mount Kilimanjaro?" Frances asked her, mildly surprised.

"I'd love it!" Elspeth exclaimed. She sighed again, dismissing the matter from her mind. "But what I really came to see you about was this party of yours. Wouldn't it be better to hold the thing at my place? We could lay on transport for the notables of Nguyu and the rest could walk, if they set out early enough. What I mean is, at least I have enough plates and glasses and so on, whereas you don't seem to have enough to entertain even one person properly."

Frances glanced with concern at the chipped cup that Elspeth held. "Oh dear," she said, "that does look a bit unhygienic. There's another one somewhere. I'll ask Cain where he put it."

"Three cups isn't going to take you very far," Elspeth began.

"No," Frances conceded, "but they can all bring their own."

"That will only lead to arguments if anything gets broken. No, it will be much better to come to my place I'll turn the whole garden over to you for the day. How's that?"

"It's nice of you," Frances said stubbornly, "but it's a Nguyu party and it has to be held here or it'll lose the whole point—"

"Oh, very well," Elspeth said crossly. "But it's going to be far more trouble bringing everything down here. And where are you going to put everyone?"

Frances refused to allow herself to be irritated. "I thought of taking over the marketplace," she explained. "At least it's more or less under cover if it rains."

"As it will," Elspeth said. "I don't fancy my china being exposed like that, you know. They're bound to steal odd pieces if all they have to do is to take it inside their houses."

"Yes," Frances said with resolution, "so it will be much better if they use their own."

There was a moment's silence; then Elspeth said in hurt tones, "Klaus said you wanted me to help you. I wouldn't have come otherwise."

"Well, yes," said Frances. She cleared her throat nervously. "I was thinking of having a barbecue—"

"But that will cost you the earth!"

"I thought you might be able to buy an ox for me," Frances went on.

Elspeth stared at her. "I have to hand it to you," she said, "you certainly don't do things in a small way!"

"Well, I did think they might like it," Frances said gently. "And they're doing almost everything else themselves. The women have already started on the *pombe*, and Mwete and Abel have stuffed the hospital refrigerator with canned beer and fizz. I haven't dared to ask where it all came from—"

"And what about the refrigerator?" Elspeth asked dryly.

Frances looked vague. "I keep the odd thing in it sometimes," she admitted. "It's usually full of Simon's beer. I wish he'd get a fridge of his own, but he hasn't yet."

"How cosy!" Elspeth drawled. "I suppose you see a lot of each other—Where is he now?"

"He's taken Abel to Arusha to bring home his bride. Abel was going to wait until Father Kashioki comes here, but the girl's father showed signs of finding another, richer son-in-law and Abel took fright."

Elspeth smiled. "Is he well enough to go careering around the countryside?"

"He'll be all right with Simon," Frances answered.

Elspeth raised her eyebrows, her mouth decidedly

sulky. "What would we do without him?" she muttered bitterly.

Frances could only wonder. It seemed to her that the whole of life in Nguyu revolved around him one way or another. "We would have to invent him," she said flatly. "Have some more tea?"

"No thank you," Elspeth said quickly. "I don't know what Cain does to it, but your tea tastes awful."

"Doesn't it?" Frances agreed. "I usually make it for myself at the hospital. I have a portable sterilizer that works splendidly as a kettle. Next time I'll ask you there."

"Next time you can visit me," Elspeth growled. "In fact why don't you come out now?"

Frances thought of all the things she ought to be doing and decided that for once they could wait. "Yes," she said. "I'd like that. I'll bring my washing things while I'm about it and have a lengthy bath at your expense—"

"Just so long as you find time to talk to Klaus," Elspeth put in. "He thinks you work too hard and need a holiday . . . with him, I presume."

"Climbing his wretched mountains?" Frances said lightly. "No, thank you very much!"

Elspeth looked decidedly more cheerful at the tone in Frances's voice. "Come on then," she said. "I'll drive you there and Klaus can bring you back!"

Frances was writing up her notes in the hospital when Abel brought his bride home to Nguyu. The rain was pouring down, hammering on the tin roof and forming pools of rust-colored water on the floor as it found the crannies around the nails that held the tin on to the wooden rafters. Every day now it rained a little longer, the leaden clouds gathering in the sky over the plains, and the thunder rumbling complainingly every now and then. Then, magically, the skies would clear again and the sun would shine as strongly as ever until the next day.

Frances would have welcomed the coming rains if it had not been for the illnesses it brought in its wake. The increase in stomach complaints was phenomenal, striking at adults as often as it did the children. It was the babies who really suffered, however, and one of them had even died without Frances having been able to do anything to defeat the onslaught of the agonizing stomach pains. Locally, people called the illness "the runs" and expected its attack, just as they expected the rains to come. She could only pray that Abel didn't succumb to it, so soon after his adventures with the rhinoceros, and took great care to supervise every morsel that he ate in the hospital. She would, she thought, have something to say to this new wife of his too and promised herself that she would say it as soon as possible.

Simon came into her office and threw himself into the nearest chair.

"Is she pretty?" Frances asked him without looking up.

"You'll be able to judge for yourself," he growled. "Apparently Abel wants her to doss down here until they're properly married."

"Here?" Frances said disapprovingly. "I thought they'd spend the day getting married."

"You've forgotten that Abel is a Christian," he reminded her.

"Oh," she said.

"Precisely. Is any of my beer left in the fridge, or is it totally taken up with provisions for your party?"

"Why not help yourself anyway?" she suggested helpfully, knowing that was what he was going to do whether it was his beer or not.

Simon did so, drinking the foaming liquid straight from the tin. "This getting married is an exhausting business," he told her. "Your patient stood up to it pretty well, which is more than can be said for me. I was given the most hideous things to eat and my stomach is upset."

"Shall I prescribe something for you?"

He looked at her oddly. "Will it do any good?"

"Probably not," she admitted, "but it might make you feel better."

"Then, no thanks," he said. "I'll put Abel's bride in my house and go out to Elspeth's. A bath and a comfortable bed will do me more good than anything else. Will you look in on the girl and make her welcome?"

"Of course," she said in stilted tones.

But she stayed at her desk for a long time after he had left. Elspeth would be very glad to receive him no matter how ill he was feeling, she thought. She sighed, feeling more than a little sorry for herself. She hoped that Elspeth would be kind to him. He had looked so terribly, terribly tired. But it hurt, all the same, that he should prefer to drive ten miles to Elspeth's, when he wouldn't even accept her pills and potions. It hurt badly and did uncomfortable things to her self-respect, but it didn't do to dwell on it. She would give herself something else to think about. She would go and meet Abel's wife.

Frances was glad she had done so. Simon's door stood wide open and muffled sounds of someone crying came from within. Frances knocked twice on the door and then went inside. Seated on Simon's bed was one of the most beautiful women she had ever seen. She was superbly built, with huge dark eyes above a wide humorous mouth that set off her dimpled cheeks to perfection. "*Jambo!*" Frances said inadequately.

The woman leaped to her feet, turning her back while she wrestled with her tears. Then, without warning, she turned and flung herself into Frances's arms, babbling out a tale of fright and disappointment that was quite clear even if Frances could barely understand a single word she said.

"I'll fetch Abel," she said.

But the girl only clung the harder. Frances eased her back onto the bed and poured out a glass of water for her.

"I'll get one of the other women," she said firmly.

The woman looked terrified at being left alone again, but Frances hardened her heart and went outside, shouting for Cain, who came running out of her own house, his face a picture of innocent inquiry.

"Fetch Mrs. Mbulu," she ordered him. "And Abel!"

"*Ndiyo, memsahib,*" Cain said at once. "I bring them to your house, yes?"

"No, to the *daktari's* house!" she retorted.

Mrs. Mbulu came first, bringing two of her children with her. She hesitated outside the door of Simon's house, trying to peer around the door at Abel's wife.

"*Mama,*" she whispered.

Frances urged her inside. "This is Abel's wife," she said in her slow Swahili.

"*Ndiyo, eko mama* Abel. *Bibi,*" she added in case the woman hadn't understood her. Mrs. Mbulu smiled slowly, turning to the young woman and pulling her off her perch on the bed with a torrent of scolding words. The girl responded in kind and Mrs. Mbulu laughed, though kindly.

"She cannot understand this husband of hers," she told Frances. "She thought that he wanted to marry her, for why did he go to Arusha and bring her home here? But now he doesn't want her. He has told her she must spend the night by herself—perhaps many nights—until the priest comes. She says she had better go home now before anything worse happens to her, and while her father will still accept her because he won't have had time to spend her bride price. She ... she is very unhappy, *mama!*"

Frances gave the girl an exasperated look. "What a fool Abel is!" she said.

Mrs. Mbulu laughed some more. "He has told her that now she must be a Christian and that this is what Christians do. She doesn't want to be a Christian. She wants to cook for Abel and bear him many children."

"Tell her that's what Abel wants too!" Frances said.

Mrs. Mbulu obligingly tried to translate this sentiment in terms that the girl would understand, but in the end she shrugged her shoulders and said, "She doesn't believe me."

"Why not?" Frances demanded.

"Because everyone will laugh at her because he makes her sleep on her own."

Frances saw Abel standing in the open doorway and her eyes kindled. "Abel," she began sternly. But she had reckoned without Mrs. Mbulu, who approached Abel like a veritable virago, berating him in his own tongue while he stood before her, looking like a small boy caught misbehaving.

Mrs. Mbulu ended with a yelp of triumph as Abel meekly nodded his head to everything she had to say. She snorted a last insult through her nostrils and turned back to Frances, her usual cheerful self once again.

"Abel will take her to his house," she said simply. "Father Kashioki will marry them when he comes, so what is the difference?" She picked up her children, balancing them easily on her wide hips. "She will also help us to make the *pombe* for your party," she said as she departed. "She has always worked hard and likes to make *pombe*, only Abel didn't drink much today and she is afraid he doesn't like her brew." She cast Abel a meaningful glance and swept out of the door, humming to her children as she went.

"I am very sorry, *mama*," Abel began. "I thought Mbella understood." He smiled sheepishly. "I am afraid it is her upbringing," he went on disparagingly. "She has had no chance to become Christian—"

"Abel!" Frances threatened him.

"Yes, mama?"

"Take her home. And, Abel, at my party you'll do your very best to get drunk on *pombe!* Understood?"

He grinned at her. "*Mama,* she won't know if I do or not, but I will tell her that her *pombe* is the best I've ever drunk!"

He clapped his hands together, regarding his spouse with a fierce frown that evidently delighted her. He stood up very straight and walked out without a backward glance. Mbella's eyes sparkled with delight. She smiled shyly at Frances, and then followed her husband, head bowed, down the path toward their own home.

Frances sat heavily on the bed and remembered that Simon had told her that getting Abel married had been an exhausting business. He hadn't known the half of it, she thought, still exasperated by Abel's treatment of his wife. And then, quite suddenly, she found that she was laughing.

The women made the *pombe* in large troughs dug out of felled tree trunks. They pounded away at the fluid that slopped back and forth, their arms rising and falling in perfect rhythm. Mbella, with nothing more than a cloth around her waist, looked like some lovely painting. She looked completely happy and, when Abel walked by, she pretended not to notice; but her eyes followed him for as long as he stayed in sight.

Simon was late returning from Elspeth's that morning. Frances tried not to notice, making sure that she kept busy at the hospital by holding the afternoon's clinic in the morning as well as her normal one for that time. She hoped that this would leave her free to make her final preparations for the party that evening.

When Simon did come, he was in a very bad temper.

"Next time you can fetch your own ox!" he shouted at her from the doorway. "Though why you had to ask Elspeth for it is beyond me!"

"I wanted to ask her to do something toward the party," Frances answered evenly.

"Having snubbed all her suggestions!"

Frances tried to hold her tongue. "I don't think it's any business of yours," she said, quite mildly.

"If you'd carted an ox around the countryside, you'd soon think it was your business!" he roared.

"You're frightening my patients," she said with dignity.

"Rubbish!" He lowered his voice a trifle. "Speak for yourself!" he added brutally.

"You can shout all you like for all I care!" she retorted, flaring up despite her very best intentions.

He smiled at her apologetically. "Where do you want this carcass?"

"I don't know," Frances confessed. "Somewhere where the flies can't get at it. If there is such a place."

"There isn't," he assured her cheerfully.

She looked around helplessly, peeping up at him through her eyelashes. "You find somewhere, Simon," she said. "Please?"

"What do you plan to do with it?" he asked her patiently.

"I'm going to barbecue it," she told him with renewed enthusiasm. "I couldn't think of any other way to feeding such a multitude."

"Well, at least that solves the whole problem," Simon said, relieved. "If we don't set it up straight away, it won't be cooked in time. Are you coming out to help?"

Frances shied away from the look in his eyes. "No," she said quickly. "I have to finish here first."

He smiled and thumped his chest. "I'm taking a holiday," he yawned. "Tomorrow I have to go off on safari again—"

"Tomorrow?"

He nodded. "It's a busy time for me when the rains come," he explained. "The carrion birds can carry diseases most easily at this time of year. And with foot and mouth about, I can't afford to take chances. It's only too probable that some vulture will feed on one of the dead cattle and then go to one of the new water holes to drink. We're beginning to think that's one of the ways these things are carried to the wild animals."

"I see," she said.

"Cheer up, I won't be gone long."

Frances stood up, turning her back to him, pretending to search her files. "I don't care what you do," she said.

She felt his hands on her shoulders and tensed up

against him. He kissed her softly on the back of her head.

"That's right, my love," he said. "Let the battle commence once more!"

"It never stopped, did it?" she said sadly.

"No. I'd be sorry if it had!" he smiled. "I enjoy sparring with you, Dr. Whitney. But, if you're really busy, I'd better go and roast your ox for you." He tweaked her hair between his fingers and chuckled. "An ox, I ask you! No wonder Elspeth thinks you're touched in the head."

"Does she?" she said indifferently.

He laughed. "Turning down her fine offer to hold your party in her garden! What next?"

Frances turned to face him. "It wasn't funny," she said. "She thought they could all *walk* there, if they wanted to come. I couldn't do that to them. Not even to please you!"

"It doesn't please me. I told you not to ask Elspeth to help you in the first place, that it wasn't her kind of party. Oh, Frances, really! Must you break your heart over a few people walking ten miles—most of them do that and more every day, you know."

"But I'm right!" she objected.

"Yes, you're right," he agreed. "I'll go cook your ox."

It was some time before Frances called in the next patient. Simon's irritation was at least something she had grown accustomed to, and he no longer looked as tired and ill as he had the night before. It seemed that his night in a comfortable bed had agreed with him—and it was that unpalatable fact that was so very hard to stomach.

By the end of the morning she felt quite light-headed.

She was conscious of a mild headache and a singing in her ears, but she was quite able to ignore these symptoms, for she knew that she was perfectly well and had luckily escaped the stomach complaint that had afflicted practically everyone else.

When everyone had gone, Mwete came in and helped her clear away the few pieces of equipment she had used. She liked to sterilize her own instruments so as to be sure that it was done properly. She kept them in separate packs that were easy to handle for any given occasion. It took her some time to do this and also check her bag for drugs or anything else that she might need if she were called out.

An elephant trumpeted not very far away, giving her a thrill of delight. Mwete made a pantomime of listening to it. "That is Abel!" he said.

"Have you met the bride?" Frances asked him, amused.

He nodded enthusiastically. "I have seen her!" He stopped smiling. "Cain has seen her also," he remarked.

Frances checked the temperature of the sterilizer. "Well, he is Abel's twin brother," she said.

Mwete's face puckered into a frown. "It is not good for him to look at his brother's wife," he said quietly.

This was a difficulty that hadn't occurred to Frances. "He ought to get married himself," she said.

"It will be many years, working for you," Mwete pointed out. "He wants to marry one of Mbella's sisters."

Frances made a face. "I'll think about it," she said.

Mwete shrugged. "Cain is not a mighty hunter like Abel," he muttered. "He is only a house and *shamba* boy."

"I'd have thought his wife would be glad of that!"

Frances exclaimed. "He's less likely to get himself tossed by a rhinoceros, or shot by poachers,"

"The *daktari* lives with the same dangers," Mwete pointed out, his eyes not quite meeting hers.

Frances began to take out the sterilized instruments and succeeeded in scalding herself as she did so. "Now look what you've made me do!" she said crossly. "Haven't you any work of your own to do?"

Mwete grinned at her happily. "*Ndiyo, memsahib,* plenty of work!"

"Then get on with it," she said.

Frances didn't feel like lunch. Thinking about Simon and his enjoyment of Elspeth's hospitality had left her feeling frayed around the edges. Without bothering to remove her dress, she sank onto her bed and fell asleep almost immediately. When Cain tried to waken her, she muttered a protest and slept some more. He left her to sleep for an hour and then tried to waken her again, bringing her some of his revolting tea to refresh her.

"*Mama,* you must get up!" he said. "Have you forgotten the party?"

She sat up and sipped the tea, wondering how he managed to make it taste like wet copper coins.

"How did Abel find enough money to pay the bride price for Mbella?" she asked Cain abruptly.

"The *daktari* paid his wages a long time in advance," Cain answered with a touch of indignation. "He made Abel a big man in her father's eyes!"

Frances drank some more tea and got off the bed to find herself an aspirin. Her head ached more than ever.

"Do you want to get married?" she asked.

For a long moment he said nothing. She turned and looked at him and saw that his eyes were round and anxious.

"*Mama* is not well," he suggested carefully.

"I am quite well!" she insisted. "I want to know if you want to get married like Abel?"

"Yes, *mama,*" he admitted.

"Then somehow I'll have to advance you the bride price," she said firmly. She worried about this for a moment, for the pocket money she received for her work in Tanzania had had to pay for the party; it would be some time before she would have enough to give Cain what he would need to pay for his bride.

"The *daktari* will not allow—" Cain began.

"It has nothing to do with the *daktari!*"

"No, *mama,*" he agreed doubtfully. "But I ask the *daktari* for money—"

"No!" Frances said, stung. "You work for me! It's my responsibility!"

Cain looked more bewildered than ever. "But, *mama,* the *daktari* is your man. You the *mama daktari,* like Mbella is *mama* Abel—"

Frances made a choking sound of protest. The tears flowed down her cheeks and her head pounded.

"It isn't like that," she said through her tears. "I wish it was!" She sniffed pathetically. "*I* am a doctor. *I* am the *daktari,* not Bwana Abbott—"

But Cain only laughed. "Everybody knows Bwana Abbott is *daktari!*" he said. He pointed a finger and laughed again. "You *mama daktari!*" He laughed all the way back to the kitchen, quite sure that *mama* had intended the whole thing as an elaborate joke. But there was one good thing that had come out of it, he thought. He would ask the *daktari* for the bride price for Mbella's sister, and then he would have a wife of his own and would be a big man like Abel. And he smiled happily to himself at such a pleasant prospect.

Frances finished her tea and took a cold shower to cool her burning skin. When she had finished, she was shivering, but she looked well enough. She stared at herself in the mirror and approved of the warm tan she had acquired. If she looked a trifle dark under the eyes, that was not to be wondered at. Everyone said that the beginning of the rains was a trying time. Everyone was on edge and irritable. Even Simon!

She dressed herself with enormous care in a long white kaftan that she had been saving for a special occasion. The hood gave the flowing lines of the robe a rather splendid look, for it was covered with bright embroidery, a feature that was picked up around the bottom of the skirt and all down the front. It was a modest garment, she thought with satisfaction, remembering Simon's comments on her black dress. And yet in its way it was as provocatively revealing as the other. She wondered if Simon would appreciate its more subtle challenge, and then wished crossly that she wouldn't keep thinking about Simon in this way. She told herself she was *glad* that he was going away on safari again!

He was waiting for her outside her door, carrying a vicious-looking knife, which he said he would use to carve up the ox.

"Well? Do you think I look nice?" she asked him.

He grinned at her, and it was she who looked away, annoyed to find that she was blushing.

"Absolutely stunning!" he drawled.

CHAPTER NINE

Mr. Mbulu stood under a multi-colored umbrella, looking about him in satisfaction.

"As headman of Nbuyu," he began, "I am making the speech on this auspicious occasion." He went on for a long time, with little choruses in which his audience joined, chanting their tribute to the beat of his right hand.

"*Uhuru!*" he said, using the word that could mean independence, or freedom, or almost anything else along the same lines.

"*Uhuru na* Tanzania!"

"*Uhuru!*"

"*Uhuru na* Nguyu!"

"Nguyu!"

The lilt of the chant caught up their swaying bodies into a kind of stately dance. But Mr. Mbulu was far from finished. He droned on, thanking everyone present for this happy, auspicious occasion, apparently unaware that his audience was slowly dissolving around him.

"How does one stop him?" Frances said desperately to Simon.

"One doesn't," he answered. "One cultivates patience and a pleasant expression. And just when I particularly wanted to talk to you."

"To me?" She swallowed. "What about?"

"Hush," he said. "He's about to come to his conclusion!"

Mr. Mbulu, unperturbed by the lack of interest in his speech, swelled importantly and graciously held his umbrella over Frances's head, "We have her to thank

318

for this auspicious occasion!" he beamed. "For *mama* is not only a good doctor, as you can see by the way she healed my foot, but she is a generous person who likes those about her to be happy. Hence this fine party!"

"But I shall enjoy it as much as anyone else," Frances said quickly, fearful that he would begin again.

Mr. Biboko, the schoolmaster, ousted Simon from his position beside her, ducking his head under the umbrella as well. It was, Frances realized belatedly, a symbol of prestige and dignity, rather than something to keep from getting wet from the threatening rain.

"This lady," Mr. Biboko said pompously, "is a very erudite woman. In the matter of the examination, we will all owe her much if I pass the English history, medieval period. We have studied all the Plantagenet kings and now we are reaching Richard III! It was he who began the system of bail for people who are awaiting trial—"

"Oh no!" wailed Frances.

"Is this not right?" Mr. Biboko demanded.

"Oh yes, I think it is," she assured him hastily.

He looked at her more closely. "Are you well, *mama*?" he asked her.

"I'm perfectly well!" she said firmly. "I feel fine!"

"Good, very, very good!" he said cheerfully.

Somehow or other, Simon managed to wrest the umbrella away from Mr. Mbulu and roll it up with care. Everyone stood and watched him, a little dismayed that their speech-making had come to such an abrupt end.

"You have all been so kind to me," Frances said rather tearfully, feeling their disappointment, "but it embarrasses me when you say such nice things about me when I'm only doing my job."

They accepted this as entirely understandable because she was, after all, a woman.

"This is a very fine party," they said formally. "Very, very."

"It will be finer still when we get some food inside us," Simon cut in forcefully. "I am definitely hungry. How about you, Fran?"

She shook her head. "Not very," she admitted.

He frowned. "Do you have a headache?" he demanded.

"It's only the rains," she said. "I had a headache this morning, but it seems to be going now."

"Then let's get this thing off the ground," he murmured with a curiously intimate smile. "Shall I carve?"

"Would you?" she chuckled. "I thought that was why you brought the knife!"

"It was. You're not the only one to have surgical skills. I want to show off what I can do, too. Dammit, woman, you offer more competition than I like!"

"I know that," she said.

"Has my jealousy been so obvious?" he asked.

"No. But you're not the sort of man who wants to compete with a woman, are you?" she asked gently.

"I don't know," he answered seriously. "I don't think I mind much as long as I remain the man—"

"That's what I thought!" she said quickly.

He laughed at her. "I don't think you have to worry," he told her. "You're far too feminine to want to take that away from me!"

"But I can't stop being a doctor—" She stopped suddenly taking a quivering breath, feeling suddenly dizzy and more light-headed than ever.

"I wouldn't ask you to," he said.

The ox was roasting over a charcoal fire in the center of the marketplace. The smell of cooking beef filled the warm, damp air. The children drew closer and closer to the fire, each of them carrying a plate, or a calabash, in which to put their slice of meat and the vegetables to go with it. Frances took some pleasure in watching Simon set to work on the large hulk of beef, cutting it into generous portions and laughing with each child as they received their share. The blue smoke rose into the evening sky, and the coals flared and spluttered as fat from the roasting ox fell onto the hot charcoal.

The women took up their stand behind one of the long counters, each with an enormous tin of homemade beer in front of them. The men passed by, sampling the *pombe* from each of the women they knew and complimenting the maker. Frances was relieved to see that Abel only tasted Mbella's beer, smacking his lips with every sign of approval.

Frances really was feeling most peculiar, so she found herself somewhere to sit and tried to concentrate on the interesting research Mr. Biboko had done on medieval England since she had last seen him.

Almost everyone had been served by the time Elspeth arrived, bringing her brother and Klaus with her in the back of her Land Rover. A fixed smile on her face, she hurried over to Simon and patted him familiarly on the shoulder.

"Simon darling, how the mighty have fallen!"

Simon shrugged away from her. "What do you mean?" he retorted. "This demands true skill, let me tell you. Have you brought your plate?"

"Of course not!" she smiled. "We didn't come to eat, but we thought we ought to make an appearance before bearing you off with us for a proper meal at home."

Simon grunted. "How about you, Mark?" he asked.

The young man looked embarrassed. "I'll go and find myself a plate," he said. "Fran will lend me one. I didn't realize we were supposed to bring our own."

"Nor I," Klaus put in. "Fetch a plate for me, too."

"Oh well," Elspeth said carelessly, "if you're all determined to ruin your appetites, I suppose I'd better do the same. Where is our hostess?"

"Around," Simon answered, irritably.

"Then I'll go and look for her," Elspeth went on, apparently unaware that she had annoyed him. "I hate you when you disapprove of everything in that superior way."

Frances, hearing every word from the precarious seat she had found for herself, knew that she ought to call attention to herself. It was strange that the man could be fond of someone and still find them irritating, she thought. If she hadn't known that it was so, she wouldn't have thought that Elspeth was Simon's type, for there was no doubt that she did irritate him often, just as she irritated Frances by her lack of sensitivity toward anyone's feelings but her own.

Elspeth saw her in the gloaming almost immediately and hurried over to her, sitting down breathlessly on the ground beside her.

"My dear, what a super dress!" she said by way of a greeting. "What on earth are you doing, sitting here all by yourself? Shouldn't you be accepting the kudos of the assembled community, or something?"

"Don't," Frances pleaded. "I thought the speeches were never going to end!"

Elspeth laughed. "Did you make one? Or Simon?"

"I thought the ones we had were more than enough," Frances groaned.

"But what would you have said?" Elspeth pressed her.

"I don't know," Frances said.

"They'd expect Simon to say it for you," Elspeth went on brightly. "I think he'd expect you to ask him to do it for you too, don't you? He always winces when he hears me giving orders on the farm. He's terribly old-fashioned, isn't he? I'm sure he'd prefer me to transmit my orders through Mark, though even he must be able to see that my little brother doesn't know a coffee bean from a groundnut!"

"I hadn't noticed," Frances said repressively.

"No," Elspeth agreed immediately. "You've hardly had time to notice anyone but Simon, have you?" She put back her head and smiled faintly. "Don't think I don't sympathize. He offers more than any other man I know!"

Frances regarded her with distaste. "To me he's just the vet," she murmured.

Elspeth laughed delightedly. "Oh, Frances, I think you're sweet!"

Frances felt that she could hardly return the compliment, though, under other circumstances, she thought she might have genuinely liked Elspeth. But now she could hardly bear to look at her, and she certainly couldn't bear to listen to her discussing Simon. It was plain, old fashioned jealousy, such as in the past she would have despised as unworthy and uncivilized; but now she had to face herself as both, and she didn't much like what she saw.

"I believe there are some sweet potatoes cooking in the ashes, and some corn on the cob, too," she said instead. "Would you like me to get you some?"

Elspeth shrugged. "If you're going to have some. I

must say, I always worry that native food will poison me, but you're the doctor!"

Frances went over to the fire and fished out some potatoes from the hot cinders. The heat from the smoldering charcoal seemed to reflect the heat that burned within her. For the first time she wondered seriously if she might be coming down with something. She felt terrible.

Klaus came and helped her with the hot potatoes, putting them in one basket and the maize cobs in another.

"Now everyone can help themselves," he said comfortably. He leaned a little closer to Frances. "Don't think I'm complaining, my dear, but is there anything to drink besides *pombe?* I have no taste for it."

"Oh yes," she assured him. "There's stacks of canned beer and bitter lemon in the hospital refrigerator. Mwete is supposed to be in charge of it."

She stood back from the fire and put a hand up to her throbbing head.

"What is the matter?" Klaus asked her immediately. "Have you been working too hard again? Why the circles under your eyes?"

Frances recovered herself. "It's only the heat from the fire," she prevaricated, almost sure that she was indeed unwell. "I think I'll go and sit down beside Elspeth."

"Ah now, that is something I wished to tell you," Klaus said softly. "Mark and I are going to climb Mount Kilimanjaro next week. I have every hope that I shall persuade Elspeth to come with us. Will you put in a good word for me?"

"She won't listen to me," Frances protested.

"I think perhaps she will." He hesitated. "You see, I thinks she wants to come, but she can't quite bring herself to admit it."

"What about Simon?" Frances said, despite herself.

"If she comes with me, I shall marry her," Klaus said simply. "That she knows. That is why she would like to be pushed a little, but I cannot push her. I have waited for a long time for her to make up her mind that she wishes to be Baroness as well as a coffee farmer, and I can't risk putting my foot wrong now."

Frances looked at him solemnly. "But what can I do?" she asked him.

He smiled, his eyes reflecting the light from the fire.

"The one thing Elspeth can never resist is a dare," he murmured, "She is convinced that courage is the highest virtue—"

"I know," Frances sighed.

"It is a little difficult when you are hoping that she might find loving somebody a more comfortable attribute," he admitted. "But I am hoping that she will one day see that that needs more courage than being boss of her coffee farm."

"And does it?" Frances returned doubtfully.

"I don't think so," he said honestly, "but she might believe it if another woman were to tell her it is so."

Frances thought it extraordinary that he could profess to love Elspeth and yet could know so little about her; but she agreed to do what she could to plead his cause, secretly hoping that it wasn't only because Elspeth married to Klaus would suit her so much better than Elspeth unattached.

But in the end she didn't have to compromise with the promptings of her better self, for Mark attached himself firmly to his sister for the rest of the evening, while Frances herself was taken up with the duty of apportioning her time equally among the Nguyu notables—only proper as she was their hostess.

"We have been saying that it is good to have a lady doctor here," Mr. Biboko told her with enormous tact. "It is better for the women, for we do not like them to go to a man for their doctoring. And with men it doesn't matter."

Much struck by this aspect of her work, Frances wished that Simon could hear them. If he did, perhaps he would have a greater respect for her efforts. And then there he was, slapping palms with all the men and drinking *pombe* with the best of them, carefully accepting a little from each of the women there.

"Now, at last, perhaps I can talk to you," he said, drawing her a little away from the others.

"I'm busy," Frances said. "I have to circulate."

He smiled. "I think you've come the whole circle, Fran. We're back to the beginning."

She blinked. "What do you mean?"

"It will take me a long time to tell you––"

"Then you'd better tell me tomorrow," she said with some asperity.

"Tomorrow I won't be here," he reminded her. "Look Frances, I wouldn't go if I didn't have to, believe me. Nothing would prise me away from you. Do you accept that?"

She nodded, not daring to say anything. She wished she could think, but her head ached abominably and her knees were weak, the latter symptom might very well have been because Simon was holding on to her arm as though he were afraid that she might vanish at any moment.

"I want to explain to you about Nairobi," he began.

"No, not that!" she protested.

"Why not?"

Her heart thudded. "Because I prefer not to think about Nairobi," she said with dignity. "I . . . I didn't behave very well."

She could feel his sense of shock in his tightened grasp on her arm, but when he spoke his voice was surprisingly gentle.

"Sweetheart, don't talk nonsense!" he said.

"But it's *true,* Simon! You could have . . . I mean, I opened the door again, but you'd already gone."

"I know," he said.

"But you can't know!" she wailed, her mind firmly set on making a full confession.

"Of course I know," he chided her. "If you hadn't been surrounded by such an obvious air of impregnable innocence, I might very well have come back—"

"Simon!"

"But," he went on, "I found to my surprise that I couldn't take advantage of you. I liked you too much."

"Oh, Simon!"

"What?"

"I didn't like you at all!"

His eyes gleamed with mockery. "No," he said dryly, "I was aware of that. My poor little innocent, you didn't know what had hit you, did you?"

"I still don't know," Frances sighed.

"That's what I want to talk to you about," he went on, looking rather white.

"But talking doesn't help!"

He grinned, "We'll try kissing too, if you like."

Her heart turned over. "I don't like," she said gruffly. "I wish you'd leave me alone!"

"Why?"

She pushed her hair back out of her eyes. "I don't

think you ought to ask me that," she reproved him gently.

"All right," said Simon.

"I . . . I think I'd better get back to the party," she mumbled. The buzzing noise in her head was almost deafening.

"All right," he said again. "But we can't go on like this—"

"And don't shout at me!" she pleaded.

"I am not shouting."

Frances didn't feel strong enough to answer. She glanced at her watch and wondered how long it would be before she could decently retire to bed. She longed for the comfort of cool sheets and a soft pillow beneath her throbbing head.

"Damn," said Simon.

"I'm sorry," Frances said uneasily.

"Oh, don't start apologizing," he advised her nastily. "That would be too much!"

"I'm n-not apologizing!"

"Then what are you sorry about?" he demanded impatiently.

"I don't know. I suppose because I can't do what you want me to do. I might have in Nairobi, but now I can't!"

"I see," he said.

"No, you don't!" she contradicted him flatly. "You don't begin to understand!"

"Then how about explaining it to me?" he suggested. She thought he looked unhappy and wondered why. At least he wouldn't be unhappy for long! He would go back with Elspeth and tomorrow he would be off on safari, and he would forget all about her, and she would be perfectly miserable! She was beginning to think she deserved to be unhappy because she could think of nothing she would like better than to be loved by Simon on any terms he cared to name. It had been like that right from the beginning. And yet, surely, one ought to have more self-control? Especially if one believed in any sort of morality.

"It's a question of survival." Frances said faintly.

Simon's hand bit into her arm and she could feel his tensed muscles beside her.

"Frances," he said, "will you marry me?"

The singing note in her head took on a new pitch that was as painful as a whining saw. Her knees and stomach turned to water and her heart pounded against an enormous lump in her throat.

"No," she whispered.

He clipped her hands into the small of her back, looking at her for a long moment until she struggled uncomfortably, uttering a faint gasp at the strength of her own feelings.

"It's the only answer," he told her. "I thought I could wait—"

"I know exactly what you thought!" she accused him. "You thought you could put up with my being here for two years, and that you could think of me as a doctor and not as a woman. And then you'd have a wild fling with me in Nairobi before I went back to England—"

He laughed shortly. "Just one in a long procession of women, I suppose?"

Frances bit her lip, unable to joke about such a matter. "It's the truth, isn't it?" she said tearfully.

He kissed her savagely on the mouth, holding her tightly against him. "That's the truth!" he said against her lips.

"I d-don't understand," she stammered.

"Frances," he said in despair, "I'm not asking you to think about it, because you're crazy enough to think anything. Do you want to marry me?"

"No," she said. "I won't ever marry you!" She swayed against him and began to cry. "And I have a headache," she added dismally.

Simon held her away from him, looking as though she had dealt him a deathblow.

"Why won't you marry me?"

She was too distraught to care what she said. "One's always hearing about this sort of thing," she said loudly, hoping that she wasn't going to disgrace herself by fainting at his feet. "It . . . it flares up, and then it dies away, and there's n-nothing left." She gulped. "Besides, I want my husband to love *me*, not half the women in Africa—"

"South of the equator!" he finished for her.

"Oh Simon," she wept, "please don't make me!"

He gave her a startled look; then his eyes narrowed. "No," he said in an odd voice, "I won't make you do anything—not tonight, anyway, sweetheart. You look as though you have enough to cope with at the moment. But I'm not giving up! One of these days you'll have to grow up and give up these romantic notions of yours."

"Wh-what about you?" she demanded reproachfully.

"I don't have any romantic notions about you," he told her wryly.

"Oh!" she gasped. "I thought you might pretend—"

"I don't need any," he continued calmly. "I know how it is between us, whether I like it or no—"

Frances made an abortive attempt to wipe away her tears with the back of her hand. "H-how is it?" she asked.

He put his arms around her, pulling her close to his chest. "I thought you knew," he whispered in her ear.

" 'While I am I, and you are you, So long as the world contains us both. . . . While the one eludes, must the other pursue. . . .' "

She laughed shakily. "I thought you were above romantic notions!"

"My love, that isn't a romantic notion; it's harsh reality. Why else do you suppose I want to marry you?"

She pulled away from him. "I can't imagine," she said. "But I'm not going to marry you, so you mustn't talk such nonsense."

Simon allowed her to escape from his restricting hands. "I'll say what I like to you!" he retorted. He smiled at her, his eyes kind and very lazy. "Don't make yourself wretched while I'm away. I'll ask you to marry me again when I get back, so all is not lost!"

"And I'll refuse you again!" she said, holding her head high, though it felt as though it were going to break in two at any moment.

"I think not," he said with such confidence that her own was shattered. "You see," he went on, a thread of laughter running through his voice, "I have a very unfair advantage. I shall simply kiss you until you say you will. Good night, Fran, sleep well. And thank you for having me at your party."

But Frances knew that she would never sleep well again. She would be far too busy steeling her resolution to go on refusing him, forever if need be! Because if she was unhappy now, how very much more unhappy she would be if she were married to him and had to share him with somebody else!

It was not Abel who got drunk on Mbella's *pombe,* but Cain. Frances knew that there was something wrong the moment she rejoined her guests in the marketplace.

"How could he do this thing?" Mr. Biboko demanded of no one in particular.

Frances tried not to laugh. "He'll feel terrible tomorrow," she said mildly. "I suppose Abel ought to take him home, but I'd rather he didn't start lifting heavy weights quite yet."

"Mr. Ndendulu will take him to the hotel," Mr. Mbulu commanded. "It is a very unfortunate happening."

"Poor Cain!" Frances said with determined sympathy.

Mr. Mbulu stared at her owlishly. "You are not minding?" he asked.

"Why should I?" she countered.

A smile of relief spread over his features. "We were afraid, *mama*, that you would think him a bad man and would not want him to work for you any more."

"Of course not!" Frances said with resolution. "I should miss the way he makes the tea, if nothing else."

They laughed appreciatively, dimly aware that this was a joke. "You are one of us, *mama*!" they said. "Nguyu would be very sad to have any other doctor!"

"Thank you very much," she said demurely.

She knew when Elspeth and the others left because she heard the Land Rover's engine backfire. The sudden noise was almost too much for her, playing on her nerves and resounding in her head. When she got home, she thought, she would take her temperature and decide what was the matter with her. Only she couldn't do that quite yet. She had to stay in the marketplace until the last of the guests left.

But eventually everything came to an end, and Mr. Mbulu and Mr. Biboko herded the final few out of the market square and back to their homes. Quite exhausted, Frances sagged against the nearest support, hoping that in a minute or so she would feel better. She didn't. If anything she felt worse. Then, quite suddenly, Mr. Biboko was at her elbow.

"You are not well, *mama*," he said kindly.

"I'm just a little tired," she said.

He nodded wisely. "Perhaps it is that," he agreed. "But you are very hot. I have been watching you, you see, and now that we have studied so much together, I see much that before I would not see."

Frances felt close to stamping her feet with sheer vexation. "I wish you'd all leave me alone!" she burst out.

Mr. Biboko clicked his tongue against his teeth. "I shall send for the *daktari*," he decided. "He will know what to do."

"No!" Frances yelped. "Anything but that."

"But you are sick, *mama*. . . ."

With an effort she calmed down, touched by his thoughtfulness.

"Yes," she said, "I think I am a bit off color. But it isn't anything serious, I'm sure of that! I'll be as right as rain after a good night's sleep. I think I may have a migraine, though I've never had one before, so perhaps it's only a bad headache."

"I will walk home with you," Mr. Biboko offered.

Frances heard him through a haze of pain and nodded vaguely. Her legs didn't work very well, but she tried not to lean on him too heavily.

"I don't know why you should be so kind—" she began, and stopped because saying anything made her head swim.

"It is you who are kind, *mama*," Mr. Biboko said simply, "Very, very! That is why I don't like to see you sick. I am glad you will be well again tomorrow. You must know because you are the doctor."

She only hoped he was right.

CHAPTER TEN

By morning, Frances was very ill indeed. She suspected that she had spent a large part of the night in a state of delirium that still came and went, granting her only a few sane and sober moments here and there. When she saw that it was daylight outside, she called out to Cain, but there was no answer. As he was always there first thing in the morning, she wondered where he could be. She tried to get out of bed, but her legs weren't strong enough to hold her. She eased herself into bed, feeling frightened at what lay ahead of her. She was sicker than she had thought.

She was only conscious for brief moments all that morning. She spent the time dreaming, violent dreams of a highly colored nature that left her exhausted and weaker each time she awoke.

She dreamed of the flamboyant tree. It grew and grew, its scarlet blossom engulfing her until she could scarcely breathe. Then the branches turned into Simon's arms and the relief was so enormous that all she could do was cry. When she awoke after that dream, she was almost sorry, for she remembered that Simon was away. She thought, too, that she would always connect the blossom of the flamboyant tree with Simon. It was as bright and as scarlet as the rush of feeling he inspired in her whenever they touched.

She dreamed too of Rodney. In her dream, she was back in the days before her finals, when she had imagined herself in love with Rodney. She remembered again, what she had since preferred to forget, how her father had stormed into the hospital to have a "little talk" with Rodney, to tell him to keep away from his daughter until she had qualified, and how her wretched, burgeoning feeling for the young doctor had been laid bare for all to see . . . and discuss.

And how they had discussed her! She lived again the humiliation of Rodney's open scorn, and the way that all the other young men had avoided her, knowing that her father had a great deal of influence in the hospital. She lived again the loneliness, the hurt, and finally the despair she had known then. In her dreams she qualified again without any particular relish for the life she felt was being forced on her. She worked out her year in the hospital, the loneliest year of her life, and decided once again to offer her services in the developing nations for two years, while both she and her home town forgot that she had once been silly enough to think that she had fallen in love.

Her dreams went around and around in circles, recurring again and again. The only interruption was a dream of Simon; and, always after she had dreamed of him, she would wake up, sweating and whirling in space, to find herself alone again.

"Cain," she murmured, forcing herself back to reality. "Cain!"

She listened to the rain pounding on the tin roof and thought perhaps he couldn't hear her above the din.

"Cain!" she called again.

He knocked on her door and came in, holding his head in his hands. "*Mama, mama,*" he said weakly.

Frances was too glad to see him to do more than give him the ghost of a smile. "Cain, find the *daktari,*" she whispered.

He shook his head. "*Mama,* I drink too much *pombe!*"

"Oh, Cain, please go," she moaned.

He stepped nearer the bed and took a frightened glance at her. "Mama, you sick?"

"Find the *daktari*," she repeated, and slipped back into the nightmarish dreams that came up toward her through the darkness.

When next she became conscious, she was alone. Her first thought was that the rain had stopped; it no longer pounded in her ears, adding to the discomfort of the pulsating headache that refused to relinquish its grasp. Then she heard a noise and came face to face with the baby rhinoceros, its ridiculous bump, where its horn would one day be, quivering as it snorted in her face.

"Oh, no!" she giggled.

The rhinoceros butted her in a friendly way, looking for chocolate. The motion caused a quiver of pain to go through her, but it all seemed a logical part of her dreams and she couldn't quite believe she was truly awake.

"Go away!" she shrieked. "I don't have any chocolate!"

Her bedroom door flew open and what seemed to her a dozen villagers chased the small rhino around her bed until she was dizzy watching them.

"He's hungry," she muttered. "He hasn't been fed."

She recognized Abel with a bucket of milk in his hand and tried to tell him that the rhinoceros would go anywhere for a piece of chocolate. Abel, however, seemed to know what he was doing. He lassoed the baby with a length of plaited rope and pulled at the other end, while everyone else cheered him on.

Frances felt more fractious than ever. "Stop him!" she pleaded with Cain. "He'll burst his stitches!"

But Abel only laughed. "Not me, *mama*! He'll be gone in a moment!"

Frances never knew what happened in the end, but the next thing she knew, she was alone again and the room had become unbearably hot and stuffy.

"Oh, Simon!" she gasped. "Why couldn't you be here!"

Cain came to the doorway and asked her if she would like some tea, but she shook her head.

"Where's the *daktari*?" she demanded.

"*Daktari* gone safari," he answered sulkily.

Frances opened her eyes and looked at him. He was still suffering from the hangover that Mbella's *pombe* had given him, and his dislike of the wet weather was just like a cat's. He plainly felt very sorry for himself.

"Cain," she said clearly, "you must fetch someone. Ask Mr. Biboko to telephone Memsahib Peissel. She will know what to do."

Cain was immediately suspicious. "The *memsahib* will take you away, *Mama* too ill to be moved!"

"Who said so?" she demanded.

"Mwete, he say so."

Frances considered this. Perhaps she was too ill to move. She certainly felt terrible.

"Telephone the *memsahib*!" she said loudly. "Now! At once!"

"*Ndiyo*," he said reluctantly.

"Now!" she said.

The dreams were becoming worse. They were bearable when Simon was in them, but he became more and more elusive. Only the humiliating incident of Rodney remained as bright and vivid as ever.

Frances felt completely exhausted when she next opened her eyes. She knew it was evening because of the long shadows in the room. It would shortly be dark, for in the tropics the sun sets quickly, falling out of the sky in a rush as though to keep ahead of the oncoming night.

She saw Mwete sitting beside her bed and tried to smile at him.

"Is Memsahib Peissel coming?" she asked him.

"No, *mama*."

Frances tried to turn over in the bed, but she was too weak even to do that. She had to get someone! They had to come!

"Why not?" she cried out.

"She has gone away with Bwana Mark and the other *bwana*."

"She can't have!" Frances nearly wept. "Not so soon!"

Mwete's eyes slid away from hers, betraying his anxiety, "We go to the hospital, *mama*, and you must tell me what to do to make you well again."

"Yes," she agreed. There was nothing else to do. A frivolous fear that she was going to die beset her; she cowered from the thought,

But she was not conscious long enough to have any say in her removal to the hospital. Dimly, she could remember a crowd of people in her room and Mrs. Mbulu chuckling as always at the sight of her. More dimly still, she was aware of being dumped onto a stretcher and carried along the street toward the hospital. The noises of the night were comforting. They made the world seem a highly desirable place to be and she felt more sorry for herself than ever, because now she was sure she was going to die.

They put her in the bed that Abel had vacated so recently. Mwete switched on the fan above her head, which sometimes went and sometimes didn't, depending on how much paraffin was available to drive it. Frances suddenly felt cold and began to shiver.

There was a great deal of noise all around her. She

plucked herself out of the highly-colored, nightmarish mists of her dreams and tried to concentrate on what the voices were saying.

"Mwete, you must take my temperature," she instructed harshly. "And find the book on tropical fevers in my house. It's in my suitcase."

He was glad to have something positive to do. He found the thermometer and stuck it under her tongue, frowning down at her. When he read it, he wouldn't tell her the result and she was left wondering if he knew how to read it at all.

"You must find the book, Mwete," she reminded him.

"Cain is looking for it," he reassured her.

She sank back, aching in every limb. "Where is it?" she kept asking. "It's in my suitcase."

"It's no good, *mama*," Mwete told her. "The white ants got into your suitcase. There are only little pieces of the books there."

"White ants?" Frances repeated numbly.

He held up the remains of the book, the cover completely eaten away, the pages yellow and still wriggling with live termites seeking any way to get out of the painful light. Frances took one look at it and turned away defeated. The tears came thick and fast and she was too weak even to wipe them away.

"What must I do?" Mwete asked her urgently, his distress growing as he saw her own.

"I don't know," she whispered.

"Mama?"

She tried to think. She suggested something that she thought would bring her temperature down, but Mwete was beyond understanding her. She knew that he was afraid of giving her something from the wrong bottle, a danger she herself had stressed to him again and again.

"Penicillin," she told him.

His hands shook as he gave her the injection, but she was no longer with him. The dreams had engulfed her once more.

Someone was cutting her hair. She tried to pull her head away, resenting the snipping scissors, but the hands that held her were strong and the haircut went on despite her.

"What are you doing?" Her voice sounded tired and scared like a child's. She didn't sound like herself at all.

"Hush, *mama*," a warm voice bade her. "Hush now, *mama*. Soon you will be well."

"Mwete?"

"I am here, *mama*. Soon you will feel quite well. You will feel much better very soon." But he sounded nervous and unsure of himself, and she didn't believe him.

The snipping stopped abruptly and pieces of her hair were carefully gathered up and taken away. Frances put up a hand and felt the stubby shortness that was all that had been left to her.

"I wish you hadn't cut my hair!" she said plaintively.

"It was necessary," another voice told her. She frowned, wondering what Mr. Mbulu was doing in the hospital.

"Mwete, get rid of all these people!" she demanded imperiously.

"Hush, *mama*," Mwete answered soothingly. "They are all here to wish you well."

"All of them?" she inquired.

She struggled to lift her head from the pillow and was surprised to discover that the small room was crammed with people. She collapsed back again, but not before she had beckoned Mr. Biboko to her side, whimpering under her breath as she did so.

"Mr. Biboko," she said to the schoolmaster, in a final, colossal effort, "Mwete doesn't understand. I must have air. All these people must go."

"They come to wish you well," Mr. Biboko said solemnly, regarding her owlishly through his dark glasses.

"I know," she muttered. "Very kind. But I don't want to die in public."

"Oh no, *mama* not going to die! What would the *daktari* say if he came home and found you dead? He would be very angry. Very, very! No, no, we see that you do not die. There is no need to be afraid. . . ."

"Is Simon coming?" she asked vaguely.

"Where he is there is no telephone," he explained slowly. "Mr. Mbulu has asked the game warden to contact him on the radio. He will come, *mama*, as soon as he hears. It is known that you are to be his woman. Why else would he bring you here? He will come!"

"And Elspeth?" she went on, shying away from the thought of Simon.

Mr. Biboko's mouth puckered up with disapproval. "She is away with her man. They are climbing Kilimanjaro—disturbing the gods!"

Frances giggled. "But you're a Christian."

"It was a joke," Mr. Biboko said pompously, but he didn't sound as though it were a joke to him at all; there was something in his voice that made Frances's blood run cold.

"Baron von Rahner has climbed it often," she murmured. "Haven't you ever been up there?"

Mr. Biboko shook his head, wiping his face with a snowy white handkerchief. "Never! They say it is very cold up there."

"It sounds . . . wonderful," Frances breathed through parched lips. "I wish it were cooler here."

"It will be, *mama*!" Mr. Biboko insisted importantly, recovering his spirits. "You will see!"

He went away and Frances shut her eyes, striving to hold on to reality, because she was afraid to go back to her dreams. The flamboyant tree stood high above her and she knew a great sense of relief that it was the tree that she loved and not Rodney who had humiliated her. The blossom of the tree danced in her eyes and she longed for Simon with a longing that tore her apart. She could almost laugh at herself for mistaking uncritical admiration for her senior for this soul-wrenching emotion. The blossom danced on and she allowed it to envelop her, while she sought Simon in the scarlet flowers.

She heard the drums from a great distance. The rhythm came and went, beating time with her pounding heart. She thought she was still dreaming, but the chants were none of her brain's devising. They began with a simple melody and grew more and more complicated, voices weaving in and out to the rhythm.

Many people were singing. They stood, swaying against each other, the sweat pouring down their faces, their eyes shut, feeling the emotion of the song through their entire bodies. The sound caught at Frances, carrying her up and away from her painful body. It was like the rhythm of creation itself.

Mrs. Mbulu came close to the bed and wiped Frances's face and neck with a soft cloth. Her hands were cool and gentle and kept perfect time with the beat of the drums. Humming through closed lips, she dipped the tips of her fingers into some ashes mixed with a little liquid and painted a pattern of lines on Frances's face and forehead.

Frances opened her eyes, very frightened of what they

were going to do to her. She felt completely helpless and horribly afraid. She had thought these people to be similar to herself, and now she knew they were not. They were strangers believing in magic and forces outside themselves, ignoring the logic of medicine. They were strangers and she was afraid of them.

For a moment her mind cleared and she was completely herself. If she allowed herself to be afraid of these people now, she would be afraid of them for all time. She could not allow that to happen. Somehow she had to retain her trust in them. She knew that they liked her, that they wanted to help her, and that would have to be enough. She had read somewhere that the African believed that the world had been created through rhythm, a creation that was reflected in their religious chants. Was that why the music sang in her blood and brought their disparate beings into one swaying entity? And herself with them?

The flamboyant tree came back to bewitch her, the scarlet blossom playing against her face. Then she realized that something was literally being dangled over her head, something warm and scarlet and smelling very much like blood.

Frances was dimly aware of someone in a grotesquely hideous white mask, carved of wood and fringed with what she recognized to be her own hair. Did she really look like that to them? If she had had the strength, she would have laughed, but at least she was no longer afraid. She knew all about masks, she thought comfortably, and wondered if it had been Simon who had told her about them. She knew that in the western world, they had largely lost their significance and were worn, when they were used at all, to hide behind. But in Africa they still retained their original purpose. They were not just some representation of the thing presented to the public view; they were the very thing they represented. She knew quite clearly that it was Mwete wearing the mask. His father was a witch doctor and he would have learned the skills, no matter how devout a Moslem he was in his everyday life. Faced with her illness, and not knowing what to do for her, he had made a mask of her own face and decked it with her own hair. By putting on the mask, he would put on her skills and medical knowledge, and all would be well.

Of course she would die anyway. It was strange how little she cared. She stared at the dancing mask that came and went in front of her face. It was strange, but it did resemble her. It wore her lipstick and a great deal of her face powder, and her hair flapped back and forth tickling her face and getting in her mouth.

"Mwete, take that ... thing away!" she demanded suddenly.

The mask hesitated, and then gyrated before her eyes more madly than before.

"Not be afraid, *mama*," someone whispered in her ear.

"I'm not!"

She became aware of several grinning faces "*Mama* feels better," they told each other.

Did she? She tried to remember how she had felt before, but only knew that she had been in the grip of a delirious fever that now, magically, had left her. She summoned up a small smile to reassure the anxious faces around her bed and fell immediately into the first natural sleep she had had for hours.

When she awoke she was confusedly aware that she had been shouting something in her sleep. She turned her head a little and saw Simon sitting on the chair beside her bed.

"Where were you?" she asked him sleepily.

"Perhaps I should ask you the same question," he said smiling.

"I've been going around in circles," she told him wearily. "I hope I never dream again."

"Mmm," he said. "You're tougher than you look. I half expected you to be heading for the nearest mental hospital—"

"Why?" she asked, bewildered.

He looked angry and she turned her face away, unable to cope in any other way than by bursting into tears.

"You should have seen yourself when I got here," he said dryly.

"Oh, that," she said.

"It was a good thing you weren't conscious," he went on.

"I was, some of the time," she told him.

He looked angrier than ever. "Why didn't you tell me last night?" he stormed at her.

Frances winced. "I . . . I don't know. I didn't want to be ill," she tried to explain.

"My God!" he said. "How you ever became a doctor is quite beyond me."

It was unfair that he could hurt her to the quick so easily, when she couldn't even touch him.

"Well, I did!" she returned sourly.

"Only just," he reminded her.

"How do you know?" she asked grumpily.

He laughed shortly. "After last night, there's very little that I don't know about you!"

She thought that she had plumbed the depths of humiliation in her life, but now she knew that she had only just begun.

"Indeed?" she said with a touch of dignity.

Simon's expression relented into a taut smile. "Don't look like that," he said gently. "We all say peculiar things when we're delirious."

Frances buried her face in her pillow, keeping back the tears with difficulty.

"I think I hate you, Simon Abbott!" she said bitterly.

He bent over the bed and kissed her on the cheek. "Hate away, my darling, as long as it makes you feel better." He kissed her again, ignoring her cold shoulder. "That's a small reward for high bravery," he added. "Go to sleep now, we'll talk again later."

She screwed up her face and pretended not to have heard him. They wouldn't talk again about *anything* until she felt a great deal better. Not if she could help it!

But Simon was always there.

"I think you'd better have a proper haircut," he said, when he brought her her tray at lunchtime.

For an instant she looked scared. "No!" she said.

"You look a fright."

"I don't care!" she retorted.

"I suppose it will grow again," he said. "I like it long and falling about your shoulders."

She looked down at the tray he had brought. "I . . . I don't feel very hungry after all," she said with distaste.

He looked at her sharply. "Frances, tell me about it."

"I can't."

His moment of patience evaporated. "Can't or won't?" he demanded.

"Does it matter?" she sighed.

Simon sat back in the chair beside her bed. "Look," he said, "I'm not trying to pry into your privacy, despite what you may think. I want to know what happened, my love. You were as stroppy as you always are when I left last night—"

"I was not!" she denied.

"Well, you said you wouldn't marry me," he reminded her.

She was silent.

"Stroppy!" he repeated.

"I would call it being sensible," she answered bleakly.

He smiled reflectively, enjoying some private joke. Call it what you like, but if I had stayed any longer we both would have regretted it!"

"Yes, and I know where you went!"

"I told you where I was going," he agreed. "Not that I was much use to them when I got there. I left them trying to talk some sense into those nomads—"

"Before that!" she interrupted him.

His eyes gleamed. "That reminds me," he said. "Where the hell is Elspeth? Why didn't you send for her?"

A glow of pleasure spread through her body. She was shocked that she could feel so triumphant. How could she feel like that when she knew that she was about to hurt Simon badly? She blinked, astonished at herself. She had been a stranger ever since she had come to Tanzania—a primitive, female stranger, quite unlike the timid, repressed, almost sexless doctor she had been at home. She ought to be ashamed, but she wasn't. She was exultant.

"She's gone climbing with Klaus," she said demurely.

"She's *what*?"

"Mark has gone with them," she went on, not daring to look at him. "She had already gone when I tried to get someone to send for her. She must have left pretty early . . . but then, I expect you would know about that."

Simon looked at her thoughtfully, saying nothing. "It wasn't because you don't like her?" he asked.

"I'm not a complete fool!" she said. "I thought I was going to die," she added on a different note.

His hands clenched. "And I thought you were dead when I got here!"

Frances jumped at the fury in his voice. "Oh?" she said inadequately.

"Well, what was I to suppose? All I could see was the blood and ashes all over your face and neck, and—" He broke off, his anger burning itself out. "All I could think of was that you might come to and see that ridiculous mask and be frightened out of your wits."

"They were doing the best they could," she said gently.

"*You* can say that?"

"Besides," she went on, pressing home her advantage, "what right had you to be worrying about me?"

He gave her a mocking smile. "Turn the knife in the wound all you like," he invited her. "My chance is coming—"

Her courage died at the look in his eyes. "It wasn't as bad as you think," she told him quickly. "It might have been if I hadn't understood about the mask. But I knew Mwete's father had been a witch doctor and I knew they were as frightened of my dying as I was."

"Frances—"

She rushed on, determined to convince him. "It isn't quite the sort of thing one would expect in a hospital ward, but I found it rather reassuring. There was something about the chanting and the rhythm that really did make me feel better. At least, it made me mind dying less—"

"Frances, what was all that about a tree?"

She blushed as scarlet as the blossom of the flamboy-ant tree. "How ... how should I know?" she asked faintly.

"And another thing—"

"Y- yes?"

"I don't want to hear any more about Rodney!"

Her eyes widened "But I've scarcely mentioned him," she protested.

Simon gave her a rather bleak smile. "We heard all about your singularly uninteresting schoolgirl crush on the dear doctor all night long—"

"I can hardly remember what he looks like" she said, lowering her eyelids to hide her embarrassment. "You don't have to *mind*," she added uncomfortably.

"I do mind," he said flatly. "I'd like to punch him in the nose!" He laughed suddenly. "No, I'm not jealous, my dear. You'd never have given him another thought if your father hadn't trodden all over your sensibilities. But did you have to choose someone who was so damned hopeless?"

CHAPTER ELEVEN

SIMON went away again, back to his nomads and their disease-ridden cattle. It should have been a relief to her, Frances knew, but she hated every moment of his absence. The books he had found for her didn't interest her, and the instructions he had left as to what she could eat meant that she was given nothing but slops and taste-less whites of eggs, which she disliked at the best of times.

Mr. Biboko came to see her, his textbooks under his arm, and began to talk about English history just as though nothing had happened.

"I am going to Arusha for the examination tomorrow," he told her. "I have been allowed to take the time away from school." He wiped his face with his handker-chief, looking suddenly nervous. "Do you think I will pass, *mama*?"

"If they ask the questions I think they will," she reassured him.

"It is not just for me," he explained earnestly, "it is for the prestige of Nguyu."

"I don't think you'll have any trouble," she said.

"I hope not," he said and departed.

Mwete was the only one who actually referred to his attempt at following in his father's footsteps for her benefit.

"The *daktari* was very angry," he told her sadly. "He made us all go away. He said you would never want to see any of us ever again—"

"He thought I might be frightened," Frances soothed him.

Mwete frowned. "I was very frightened," he confessed.

"When I became a man my father told me many secrets about his craft, but I am a good Moslem. I have never tried to use them before."

Frances laughed. "I think you were rather successful," she said dryly. "The fever was broken and I feel a great deal better."

"Yes, mama, but the *daktari* he says it was the medicine he gave you when he got here!"

"Perhaps it was a bit of both," Frances suggested.

Mwete's face cleared. "*Mama,* were you afraid of *us?*"

She bit her lip. "I was at first," she said, determined to be honest with him. "But I knew you wouldn't deliberately hurt me. In the end, I decided I had to trust you." She kept to herself the fact that she had thought she was going to die anyway, despite their efforts.

"The *daktari* said it wouldn't work with a white woman because she has not been born with the rhythm of Africa in her blood. I have never seen the *daktari* so angry. He didn't understand that we wanted you to be well again."

"I think he did," she told him. "It was the blood. . . ."

Mwete nodded sadly. "He washed it away himself. He wouldn't let any of us touch you again."

Frances blinked and was annoyed with herself for being embarrassed at the thought of Simon's nursing her himself.

"I don't think he's angry any more," she said aloud. "He didn't mind leaving me on my own here, did he?"

"No, *mama,*" Mwete said with feeling. "But if you don't get better while he is away, he will make all Nguyu suffer. I think he is still a little bit angry."

Frances chuckled suddenly. "I don't think he likes my

new hairstyle," she grinned. "I'll have to do something about it before he comes back."

Mwete nodded solemnly. "Mrs. Mbulu will like to help you," he said. "She often helps the other women with their hair and she has never seen hair like yours. She will help you."

Frances thought she would prefer to deal with her own hair, but when the smiling Mrs. Mbulu was led to her bedside, she found it unexpectedly pleasant to have nothing more to do than allow the woman's soft, capable hands do what they would.

Mrs. Mbulu cut her hair, washed it and rubbed it dry, turning it into a bright cap of hair about her face that suited her more than Frances herself had expected.

"It shines in the sun," Mrs. Mbulu said brightly. "It will frighten all the bats out of your house. They don't like to see the light of day."

Frances accepted the compliment with a slight shiver. "Is Cain keeping my house clean?" she asked her, trying not to imagine half a dozen bats in the rafters.

"Very clean," Mrs. Mbulu answered serenely. "He and Abel make Mbella clean it every day."

Frances frowned. "But it isn't her job," she protested.

Mrs. Mbulu shrugged. "Abel has no garden and so there is not much for her to do. He won't allow her to work in Cain's *shamba*. He says Cain must have a woman of his own, but there is too much for one woman to do on Cain's land."

"Oh?" said Frances, intrigued.

"He will marry Mbella's sister, and later he will marry some other woman to do the work," Mrs. Mbulu informed her indifferently.

"But isn't Cain a Christian like Abel?" Frances asked.

"Sure," Mrs. Mbulu agreed.

Frances tried another tack. "Won't Mbella's sister object?" she demanded.

Mrs. Mbulu giggled. "At first she will object," she said placidly. "But she will be glad to have help with the work and she will find a friend who will be modest in the house and not make trouble." Mrs. Mbulu's eyes flashed suddenly, "It is Cain who will have to walk softly with two women to keep satisfied!" she added maliciously and, rearranging her capacious garment, sailed out of the room.

Frances began to feel rather sorry for Cain. He was not as clever or as charming as his brother. Abel strode the savanna after Simon, whereas Cain only tilled his garden and worked for a woman inside her house. But perhaps Cain would end up rich and the father of many children, and he probably wanted no more than that. It was those who wanted the sun, the moon and the stars who suffered in this world—people like her, haunted by the memory of a scarlet blossom. But she wouldn't think about Simon. She would not! He could rush around the countryside after his beastly cattle all he wanted to, and she wouldn't care in the least!

Simon had been away three days when Frances put a first tentative foot to the floor. She was feeling much better, but the weakness of her body told her how the fever had taken its toll of her health and energies.

"I think I'll sit down for a while and then go back to bed," she said to Mwete. "And I'll have something decent to eat!"

He grinned broadly. "At once, *memsahib.*"

Frances sat bolt upright on the hard wooden chair and tried to will herself into not only feeling better, but also into looking better. Her painful thinness shocked her.

But when Mwete returned, it was not food he brought her, but a strange man, a white man with a large red face and sandy hair.

"Dr. Whitney?" he greeted her, smiling. "I'm from the Flying Doctor Service. Sorry I couldn't get here before. It was some time before we heard that you were ill. Fever, wasn't it?"

She nodded, struggling to her feet, only to collapse back onto the hard chair. "This is my first time out of bed," she told him, feeling a little foolish.

"Hmm," he said. "You were lucky Abbott caught up with you in time. I hear you underwent some rather macabre doctoring before his arrival?"

"Everyone was very kind," she defended them stubbornly.

"That wasn't quite Abbott's story," the doctor said dryly. "I'll help you back into bed, and then I'll take a look at you. I think you're over the worst from a physical point of view, though."

Her eyes widened. "What do you mean?" she asked quickly.

She saw the regret on his face. "I'm sorry, Dr. Whitney, but I thought you may have already heard. The Society are sending you back to England—"

"I won't go!" she said passionately.

"They always do, you know, if any of their medics fall ill."

"They can't make me go!"

The doctor smiled. "I think they can as long as you remain with them," he murmured, rubbing his hands together so that they would feel less cold. "You've had a bad time. You might not be so lucky another time."

Frances bit her lip. "There won't be another time!"

The doctor raised his eyebrows. "You know as well as

I do that you're more likely to get another dose after the first time—"

Frances was silent for a long moment, breathing in and out as he directed.

"You said as long as I remained with the Society," she said thoughtfully at last. "What happens if I resign?"

The doctor flushed. "I was thinking we might fit you into the government service. I mean, I hear that you're going to marry Simon Abbott, so you'll be staying out here anyway—"

"But could I stay on here in Nguyu?" she interrupted him.

"That was the general idea."

Frances thought about it for a moment, then said, "I'll write my letter of resignation at once."

"No hurry," he assured her. "You won't be going anywhere for a while, not even back to England!" He grinned at her. "What does that Society of yours pay you? Pocket money? Well, I think we can do better than that. Mind you, it's government policy that nobody is paid well enough to swan around in expensive cars while the bulk of the population has less than nothing, not even the politicians! Not that I imagine that's your style. Anyway, Abbott put in a good word for you with the authorities. I gather you've been doing an excellent job here and can't be spared. Useful, of course, being a woman doctor in the bush. You can do much more with the women and children than they'll allow us to do, God bless them."

"Simon suggested that I should stay?" Frances said in a stunned voice.

The doctor laughed. "He has quite a lot of pull with the powers that be. He's a citizen to begin with, and then he understands what they want to make of the country.

He isn't one of the 'here today and gone tomorrow' types."

"But he isn't a doctor!"

"He's a damned good vet."

"That isn't quite the same," she muttered.

"At least he knew what to do with you, young lady," the doctor teased her. "You can be glad he didn't panic at the sight of you. Many men would have, if they'd been in love with the woman."

Frances laughed shortly. "But then Simon has loved so many women!"

The doctor stared at her. "He hasn't married any of them. If you're not going to marry him, you'd do better to go back to England. Nguyu is his territory. You can't expect him to leave, and it wouldn't be fair to stay here yourself if you're not going to marry him."

Frances thought of Simon as she had last seen him, cool and casual and hardly shouting at her at all. Almost as though he didn't care any more . . .

"Well?" the doctor said.

She thought about England, and about life—any-where—without Simon.

"I . . . I want to marry him," she said meekly. "Even if it means giving up m-my job, I want to marry him."

"Good," the doctor said briskly. "Then I think we can consider that settled. I'll drop by in a month's time and sign you up. You won't feel like doing anything before then, and it takes time to get the details through the right channels. Sometimes I think the whole world will end up tied up in a welter of red tape!"

Frances thought about Cain's marriage. "Doctor. . ." she began.

"Yes?"

"I will end up with some money of my own, won't I? I

mean, I bought an ox and I haven't paid for it yet, and now the man who looks after my house wants to get married—"

"Dr. Whitney, are you asking for an advance against future earnings?" the doctor asked, grinning.

"I suppose I am," she admitted.

"Will 50 pounds be enough?"

"Oh, but I don't need all that!" she protested.

But he only laughed and shook his head. "Getting married is an expensive business," he told her. "You'll want a new dress and a new nightie or something, I expect." He sat down and pulled out his wallet, counting out the notes. "A check isn't much use to you here, so I always carry quite a lot of cash with me on jobs like this." He smiled at her. "I thought you might need a bit of money, but don't expect to get away with it once you're married. Abbott can advance you any money you need then!"

"Yes, doctor," she said quietly.

He shook her outstretched hand. "Nice to meet you, Dr. Whitney. Simon Abbott is a lucky man!"

Frances blushed and lowered her lids, peeping up at him through her lashes. "I think I'm a lucky girl," she murmured. "You're not going to see Simon before I do, by any chance?"

"No, I don't expect to. Do you want me to get a message to him?"

Frances sighed with relief. "No," she answered. "I'll give him my own message."

"Very romantic!" the doctor approved. "Be seeing you, Dr. Whitney."

Frances clutched the roll of notes he had given her and waved the fingers of her left hand. How on earth, she wondered, was she going to explain this to Simon?

Simon was home. Frances made herself look as pretty as possible to receive him, but he didn't come near the hospital. The only person who came to see her was Father Kashioki, his white cassock covered with red dust from the road.

"My, my, doctor," he said, "what have you been doing to yourself?"

"I'm *much* better now," she assured him.

"Splendid. I'll be holding mass in the marketplace tomorrow morning. Will you be able to get as far as that?"

"I'll try," she said.

He chuckled. "I hope you will be there. There are one or two marriages I have to see to." He produced a piece of paper from his pocket. "Mbella wishes to be baptized first of all, I see. Do you think that's her idea or Abel's?"

"Abel's," Frances said without hesitation.

The little priest sighed. "I think you may be right. I see we have two weddings down for tomorrow."

"Two?" she repeated.

He handed her the list, his face puckering with laughter. Frances recognized Simon's writing and even such a small thing as that gave her heart a jolt of swift pleasure. The list was headed by Mbella's baptism, followed by her marriage to Abel. But then Frances saw her own name linked with Simon's.

"But I said no!" she said foolishly. "I told him I wouldn't marry him! How dare he?"

The priest merely looked at her and waited.

"Father, I *can't* marry him! They say he's kissed half the girls south of the equator—"

Father Kashioki scratched his nose with one finger. "I

think that such a reputation must be a little exaggerated," he put in.

"Not with Elspeth!" Frances retorted.

The priest looked dismayed. "Perhaps you will want to discuss it with Simon first?" he asked her.

"I can't discuss anything with him," she moaned. "He shouts at me all the time."

Father Kashioki went back to first principles. "Doctor, Miss Peissel is going to marry Baron von Rahner in a few weeks' time. The question is do *you* want to marry Simon Abbott or not?"

Frances caught her breath in the back of her throat and choked. "Oh yes!" she gasped as soon as she could, her voice breaking. "I want it more than anything!"

"Then that is all that matters," he told her. "If you are not well enough to come to the marketplace tomorrow, I will come here and marry you." He stood up and blessed her. "Pray God you will make him a good wife. He is a fine man!"

But still Simon didn't visit her.

Mr. Biboko came back from Arusha reasonably certain that he had passed all his exams.

"It is all thanks to you, *mama,*" he said gratefully. "It was just as you said it would be, with all the questions you said they would ask. All Nguyu is thankful that our school will have the prestige of a fully qualified headmaster!"

"Congratulations!" Frances said warmly. "You've worked so hard, Mr. Biboko, that you deserve to pass . . . with honors!"

His owlish face lit up. "So the *daktari* said!" he gloated.

"Where is the *daktari*?" she asked lightly.

"He has Father Kashioki staying with him," Mr. Biboko replied. "He often stays with the *daktari* when he comes. He will say mass first thing tomorrow, and then he will be gone again for another few weeks. He has a very big parish."

"He must have," Frances said.

Mr. Biboko looked at her closely. "*Mama* is tired," he said. "You must rest a great deal and get strong again. Mwete told me that was what the doctor said you should do. Then in a few days, you will be able to go back to your own house. When you are well again," he went on importantly, "you must come and talk to my school about the matter of hygiene. I have been promising that you will come very soon!"

Frances summoned up a smile. "I'll come as soon as I can," she agreed, then dismissed the whole thing promptly from her mind.

Where was Simon?

He arrived just as she was finishing her evening meal. He stood in the doorway and watched her as she struggled not to let the cutlery rattle against her plate, giving away her nervousness.

"How are you?" he asked her.

"B-better," she said.

He sat down on the edge of her bed, still looking at her. She pushed the tray away. He took it from her and put it on the chair beside the bed.

"I see you've had your hair done," he remarked.

She nodded eagerly. "Do you like it?"

"It looks better than it did!"

Frances grew restless under the fierce look in his eyes.

"S-Simon . . ." she began.

"What is it?"

It was clear that he wasn't going to help at all. "Father Kashioki. . . ."

"Well?"

"Are you really going to marry me tomorrow?" she burst out.

He grinned at her. "No, tonight," he said.

"Tonight?"

He was very gentle with her. "Father Kashioki won't be back here for another few weeks. He thought you'd prefer to do it in front of the whole town tomorrow, but you're not up to that quite yet, my love—"

"But I said I wouldn't marry you!" she protested, her heart thudding.

"I know you did," he said lovingly.

"Then—"

"Don't you have a prettier nightgown than that?" he interrupted her. "I always imagined my bride being married in something white and fluffy."

"Oh?" she breathed. "I . . . think there's a clean nightie in that drawer."

He opened the drawer and pulled out the practical cotton nightdress. "Clean," he agreed, "but hardly what I had in mind."

"Oh," she said again. "I'm afraid it's the only one I have apart from the one I'm wearing."

He looked faintly guilty. "Actually," he said, "I brought you one back with me. I couldn't choose it myself, but—"

Frances felt as though she was being carried along on some irresistible tide. She tried to summon up some kind of independence and command over her own fate, but she couldn't. All she could think of was Simon, and she couldn't really think about him properly. She was bemused, exultant and peculiarly shy.

"Who did buy it?" she asked him.

"Not Elspeth!" he teased her. "So there's no need to look like that." He pulled the nightdress out of his pocket, holding it up for her to see. "Like it?"

It didn't seem to her at all the proper kind of garment to get married in. It was shiny white satin edged in scarlet, quite definitely a nightdress. But she couldn't help feeling that once she was wearing it, remarkably little would be left to the imagination.

She swallowed. "I . . . I'd rather save it for—" She broke off, completely embarrassed.

"Later," Simon supplied helpfully.

"Yes," she said with relief. "For later."

He grinned. "I can hardly wait," he said dryly, watching approvingly as the color fled to her cheeks. "If it weren't for the aftermath of that fever of yours, I'd take a foretaste here and now!"

"It isn't catching!" she assured him, wishing that she didn't feel quite so exhausted.

"No, but I'm more than half-afraid you might break in two, you're so thin. I prefer my women to have a little flesh on their bones."

Frances pulled her sheet more closely about her. "Father Kashioki thinks that your reputation in that respect is grossly exaggerated!" she said.

"I don't think I'll tell you what he said about you!" he retorted, trying not to laugh.

"No? Tell me!" she demanded.

"He thinks you'll be a great deal happier when you have a couple of children pulling at your skirts. I wonder what you said to him, my love, to give him that impression?"

Frances struggled valiantly to find something snubbing to say. "I wish you wouldn't call me your 'love'!" she murmured sulkily. "You've had so many!"

"I'll call you what I like!" he said, pleased with himself. Then he saw the shadows on her face and his expression softened. "Don't worry so, Fran. It will all work out."

Her eyes pleaded with him. "Will it? I wish I could believe that. But marriage is something different from an affair, isn't it?"

"Very different," he agreed.

The small room was uncomfortably crowded once again. Frances refused to stay in bed for the ceremony and had dressed very slowly, making herself look as nice as possible for Simon. Now she stood beside him, surrounded by the people of Nguyu, feeling a stranger even to herself as they both faced the little priest in his gold and white vestments.

Mr. and Mrs. Mbulu stood side by side, their faces completely blank as they watched the ceremony. Mr. Biboko, more than a little distraught, had taken upon himself the duties of best man, but as he hadn't the faintest idea as to what these duties were, he could only stand directly behind Simon and hope for the best. Cain and Abel and Mbella were squashed into the corner beside the bed. Of the three of them, only Abel looked as though he was enjoying himself, probably because he was thinking happily of his own wedding in the morning. Everybody else had to stand in the doorway, taking turns peering in through the open door, constantly changing places and arguing with one another in loud and increasingly angry whispers.

It was so far removed from any wedding of Frances's

imaginings that the whole thing seemed quite unreal to her. She exchanged her vows with Simon and received his ring, a little surprised at the way his hand trembled as he passed it over her fingers. He was actually nervous, she thought with wonder, and liked him all the better for it. And then it was all over and she was Simon's wife.

Father Kashioki smiled at her and shook her by the hand. He pulled off his gorgeous cloak and laid it carefully on the bed, folding it with a fierce concentration. When he had done, he nodded briskly. "I'll bring you communion in the morning," he told her, as though he hadn't just married her to Simon at all. "I take it you'll be staying in the hospital for a while yet?"

"I . . . I suppose so," she said.

She began to wish that she hadn't used up so much of her strength getting dressed. She had not realized that she was still so weak. She felt that if anyone spoke to her she would burst into tears.

Everybody shook hands with her, giving little courteous bows to show their respect, and she was touched by their good wishes and their dignified manners. They were her people and she belonged to them in a way that she had never felt during her training in the hospital in England. She felt a rush of affection for them all as they went on to slap palms with Simon, calling him brother and making jokes. At another time, explicit jokes would have shocked her, but now she was too weary to take them in, or do anything other than smile vaguely and hope that everyone would soon depart.

Afterwards she could hear the drums beating outside and the lilt of chanting; she was grateful that they should make music and dance in her honor. She tried to say as much to Simon, but he wouldn't listen to anything she said.

"Simon, I want to go home to my own house," she pleaded with him.

"Not tonight, my love," he said.

He pulled her clothes off over her head and helped her into the despised clean nightdress, tucking her firmly into bed.

"But, Simon . . ." she protested.

"I'm due to have a drink with Father Kashioki," he said tautly. "He's staying with me overnight."

"Oh, I suppose Elspeth is still away."

She was so appalled that she could have put such a thought into words that she couldn't even begin to meet Simon's eyes.

"Go to sleep, Frances," he said wearily.

"Oh, Simon, I'm sorry! I shouldn't have said that."

"No, you shouldn't," he agreed sternly. "Forget it, Fran. We'll work it all out in the morning."

She leaned up on her elbow, wondering what demon could have possessed her. Somehow she had to persuade him that she was bigger than that small-minded, hurtful exclamation.

"Aren't you going to kiss me good night?" she asked him, wretchedly.

"No, I'm not! Go to sleep, Frances. I'll see you in the morning!"

He switched out all the lights and closed the door with depressing finality after him. Frances buried her face in the pillow and found that she was too tired even to cry. She was married to Simon, whom she loved more than life itself, and she wished she were dead!

CHAPTER TWELVE

To Frances's surprise, she slept better that night than she had ever since the fever had first gripped her on the night of her party. At intervals she stirred and heard the drums still beating through the night and, comforted by their rhythm, slept again. In the morning she felt stronger, more her old self, and more eager than ever to leave the hospital and return home.

Father Kashioki came and went.

"Well, Father," she rallied him, "I'm still on the march like your migrating gnus. If I fall by the wayside now, it will be partly your own fault!"

But the priest only smiled. "I think Simon is strong enough to make you keep up," he answered. "I have no fears for you now."

Frances sighed. "I wish I could say the same," she said wryly.

"Do you fear that he doesn't love you, or that you can't make him do so?" he inquired gently.

"Both," she said. "I think he—he wants me, but I don't think marriage was precisely what he had in mind."

"And you?"

"I love him so much it hurts," she answered passionately. "But I'm jealous, too. I don't think I'm strong enough to share him with *anyone,* even a passing fancy that we both know won't last. It isn't very nice to feel like that about someone, is it?"

Father Kashioki smiled faintly. "Why not?" he countered.

She hesitated. "I thought I was a civilized person," she

said, "with nice, civilized emotions, all beautifully under control. And then along came Simon!"

"Africa is not yet a very civilized place," the priest told her. "I think you have discovered that."

She was silent, listening to the drums still beating outside.

"Does it mean anything to you?" she asked curiously. "Is that rhythm a part of you too?"

"Why not?" he said easily. "I am not yet so sophisticated that I can't appreciate the primitive urges that drive all of us, even a young Englishwoman like yourself!"

She smiled ruefully. "You think I'm being silly," she accused him.

"No, no," he denied, "I should never suggest such a thing."

"Then you should! I am being silly, and you are probably right and a couple of children will cure me of it. But I'd never been in love before, though I thought I was once, and it isn't in the least bit like I expected."

"The *daktari* should not have repeated that to you," he said with disapproval. "I think you are a good woman and a good doctor."

Frances was unexpectedly and completely flattered by his opinion of her. "Father, do you think I will be able to make Simon happy?" she asked him urgently.

He laughed. "Why don't you ask him that?" he answered blandly. "He can tell you much better than I can."

"But I don't know if he will," she sighed. "I said something stupid to him yesterday, and I've been regretting it ever since."

Father Kashioki shook his head. "I would tell him so," he advised.

Frances pleated her sheet neatly between her fingers. "I'll try to."

He picked up the suitcase, containing his vestments that he had brought with him. "Good," he said. "I'll be back next month, but if you want me before that, the catechist knows how to get hold of me. God bless you, Frances."

"Thank you, Father," she said.

When he had gone, she went back to sleep, although she had meant to stay awake and listen to the racket going on outside in celebration of Abel's official wedding day.

She probably would have slept all morning if Mwete hadn't come in, the responsibility of running the hospital heavy on his shoulders no matter what was going on outside.

"Oh," he said, looking pleased. "*Mama* looks much better today!"

"So I am," she assured him. "I'm going to get dressed and go home to my own house."

He looked a bit doubtful at that. "Cain is celebrating Abel's marriage," he mentioned slyly. "Who will make your food in your own house?"

"I'll get it myself!" she said gaily. "I feel strong enough for *anything* today."

But Mwete was still anxious. "I'll tell the *daktari* and he will take you home," he said.

"No!" She saw his eyes open wide and hurried on, "I want to go by myself."

"Why, *mama*?"

She shrugged her shoulders. "I want to look at my flamboyant tree ... and the rhinoceros *toto*," she explained. His complete mystification as to why she should want to do anything so crazy made her want to laugh. "They may have grown while I haven't been looking," she went on with a chuckle. "Why, the *toto* may have forgotten how much he likes chocolate, it's so long since he had any!"

"I tell the *daktari*," Mwete said again stubbornly.

"When he's busy drinking *pombe* with all the other men at Abel's wedding?" she asked.

Mwete blinked thoughtfully, shaking his head. "I tell the *daktari*," he reiterated.

Frances was cross with herself for telling him what she meant to do. "Can't you understand?" she demanded. "I want to be alone for a little while."

"Yes, *mama*," he said consolingly.

"The *daktari* can wait," she added forcefully.

Mwete shook his head, eyeing Frances reproachfully, while she became more annoyed than ever.

"All right," she said. "Tell him, then. But I'm still going home by myself."

He grinned reluctantly at her. "Yes, *mama*," he said.

Frances began to dress herself as soon as he had gone. Her clothes hung on her as though they had been made for another person. She looked plain, she thought, as she studied herself in the mirror. She had never wanted beauty, but she would have liked to have felt its aura now, if only because she felt she owed it to Simon. Her stupid tongue! How could she have mentioned Elspeth at such a time?

There was no sign of rain when she stepped out of the main door of the hospital. The sky was a clear blue, with small, fluffy clouds strung out across the horizon. It would come though, later on in the day. She had learned that the rains were like that. They began slowly, lasting for only a few minutes, but they built up until much of the day was wet and sticky. Then the whole process would go into reverse and the long dry season would begin again.

Frances walked home to her house along the shady side of the road. There was no one to be seen for everyone was in the marketplace, dancing and drinking and making merry in Abel's honor. Her house looked blessedly familiar and she stopped for a moment to stand and look at it, together with its close neighbor that belonged to Simon. It would be easy enough to knock the two into one, she thought happily. They would need more room eventually. Why, they might even be able to persuade Mark to build them a proper bathroom of their own. He might do it for them as a wedding present.

Her flamboyant tree had grown a good inch. She knelt beside it and saw the first buds of the scarlet blossom about to break open at the end of the young, spindly branches. A shadow crossed her path and she looked up. It was Simon.

"Oh, Simon!" she exclaimed, her pleasure reflected in her face. "Do look! It's going to flower already."

He bent down and examined the tree, a slight smile just curling his lips.

"So I see. Tell me, Fran, what was all that about the flamboyant tree?"

It was pleasant sitting on her own front doorstep with Simon beside her. Frances eased her back against the door and fed the rhinoceros *toto* more chocolate.

"I thought you never wanted to hear Rodney's name ever again," she answered at last.

"I was wrong," Simon said. "I find I want to know every detail about your misspent past."

She laughed, blushing a little. "There isn't much to know—"

"My dear, you don't have to tell me that!"

She gave him a reproachful look. "It seemed very important to me at the time," she remembered with dignity. "Though I think you were right. He was hopeless . . . , as a man, I mean. He was a very good doctor in his way. I'd like you to believe that."

"I do," he said promptly.

"Yes," she went on, "I admired his work. And then he asked me to go to the hospital dance with him and I was walking on air!"

"Because you admired his work?"

"I was very keen," she answered, nettled.

"You must have been," he commented unkindly.

"He wasn't as bad as that," she protested.

Simon grinned. "I could cheerfully wring his neck. Poaching on my preserves!"

"They weren't yours then."

"Meaning that they are now?"

Frances blushed. "I thought you wanted to hear about Rodney," she said waspishly.

His eyes grew lazy and, therefore, dangerous. "I want to hear about the tree," he said.

"Yes," she agreed. She swallowed. "I'm coming to that. If you wouldn't keep interrupting—"

"Sorry. You were walking on the air at the prospect of going to the dance with your Rodney."

"Well, he kissed me!" she explained.

"Very understandable," Simon drawled. "But if you were telling the truth the other night, you didn't like his kisses very much."

She stared at him. "D-did I say that?"

"And a whole lot more!"

Frances wondered exactly what she had said. The old familiar feeling of humiliation threatened to swamp her.

"It isn't fair!" she said grimly.

"No, it isn't," he answered promptly. He touched her cheek very gently with his forefinger. "I wasn't going to tell you, sweetheart, but everything you said that night only made me admire you more. I swore to myself that I wouldn't walk all over that sensitive spirit of yours with my own hobnailed boots, if I can help it. But," he added wryly, "you look so much better that I'm finding it remarkably hard to concentrate on your beautiful spirit!"

She chuckled. "I'd noticed," she teased him. Then her laughter died. "Not that I have a beautiful spirit. Simon, I'm so sorry for what I said last night. It was stupid—"

His lazy look flickered over her face. "Tell me about the tree," he said.

"I'm trying to," she protested.

"Is it so difficult?" he asked, and suddenly his eyes weren't lazy at all.

"I don't know what I said . . . that night," she prevaricated, knowing that she was being silly. Why should it be hard to tell him about a simple dream? Only it sounded so very much like a romantic flight of fancy that she was afraid that he would laugh at her . . . or worse.

"You wouldn't say anything about the tree," he snapped, making her jump. "I tried to make you tell me about it then, but you kept going back to Rodney and how nobody was going to hurt you in that way again."

"I don't think Rodney meant to hurt me. I think he thought it was expected of him to kiss his partner at the hospital dance. I never thought about it before, but I don't suppose he welcomed the publicity that being caught necking with my father's daughter brought him any more than I did."

Simon took her hand in his and squeezed it. "I would have thought it worth it," he said gently. "*More* than worth it."

"I suppose you would have!" Frances said honestly. "Rodney and I didn't even enjoy kissing each other much." Her eyes glinted with laughter. "You see, I do know the difference!"

His grasp on her hand tightened. "You will when I've finished with you."

"That . . . that was where the tree came in. My parents didn't mean it, but I didn't much like myself by the time they'd finished threatening Rodney with what they would do to his career if he didn't leave me alone. I began to think I didn't like medicine much either."

"So you came to Tanzania to be yourself?"

She nodded. "It sounds ridiculous put like that."

"You said it, my love."

"Did I?" She shut her eyes, enjoying the dappled sun and shade on her face. "But at least I looked sophisticated. You have to admit that."

"It was some dress!" he agreed readily.

"The tree had something to do with you," she said shyly. "I kept dreaming about the hospital . . . and Rodney; it was all rather horrible. The tree was strong and cool and held me tight. It kept me alive, because I knew that if I could just keep going for long enough, it would come back and turn into you."

"I see," he said, looking rather white.

Frances opened her eyes and looked at him. "Do you? Oh, Simon, I think I love you—"

"One day I'll try to deserve that," he said kissing her lightly on the cheek. "Come inside and I'll make us both something to eat. I think I love you too!"

It was all very disappointing.

Simon was an excellent cook and Frances enjoyed the ham and eggs he produced for her, followed by a fruit salad of bananas, pawpaw, pineapple and passion fruit. But the passion fruit was the only passion around, she thought, wondering what had gone wrong. There had been no trouble in that way before, between them. She wished she knew how to put things right.

"As a matter of fact," she said suddenly, "I had to marry you. I was going to be shipped back to England, you know."

"Perhaps that would have been the best thing for you," Simon returned.

She was bitterly hurt. "If you felt like that, why did you put in a good word for me with the government service?" she asked him sharply.

He shrugged. "A bad bout of fever can have very nasty after effects—"

"Much you know about it!"

He laughed. "At least my book on tropical fevers hasn't been eaten by white ants."

She was immediately interested. "You have a book on tropical fevers? May I borrow it?"

"I don't think so," he said. "You're always thinking you know best as it is, without the written word to prove you right."

She was afraid of annoying him by going on about it, so she lapsed into silence again.

"By the way," he said flatly, "Elspeth is back from her mountain. She's getting married to her baron next month and we're both invited."

"Oh," Frances said inadequately. "I'm sorry."

"Sorry?"

"Well," she went on uncomfortably, "you'll miss her, won't you?"

"Not particularly. She'll still be around. He's going to help her with the coffee farm."

Frances considered this. "But it won't be the same," she said unwisely.

His eyes became lazier than ever. "In what way?"

She swallowed. "I know I shouldn't have said it," she began in a rush. "But you don't have to pretend. I know you often spent the night there."

"You spent a couple of nights there yourself," he reminded her.

"Yes, but I went to have a bath—"

The sound of his laughter shook her badly. "And just what do you suppose I went for?" he asked her sweetly.

"Elspeth!"

His eyes never left her face. "*Very* ignoble!" he said.

She blushed, feeling very small. "I know all about you!" she claimed wildly.

Simon was silent for a long moment; then he asked, "Do you intend to be jealous of every woman I've ever kissed?"

"No!"

"Only of Elspeth?"

She could feel the color storming up her face. "That's different," she maintained. "You see, I couldn't give myself lightly ... to ... to anyone! I suppose it's different for a man. . . ."

"Very ignoble!" he repeated, his voice as unyielding as granite.

Frances tried to retrieve the situation. "She ... she couldn't have been much in love with you if she's going to marry Klaus—" She broke off, catching sight of his expression. "What I mean is—"

"I think you'd better shut up! If you want to know if I've ever been to bed with Elspeth, I haven't," he said slowly and clearly. "I can't say the same for all other women—"

"I should think not!"

This wasn't the way she had wanted it, but anything was better than the considerate indifference she had been treated to for the past few days.

"But that was before I met you," he went on relentlessly.

"But you would have—" She stopped, blushing.

"Yes, I would have," he said deliberately. "I had it all worked out, only you were so obviously the original little innocent abroad that I had to change all my plans. But now that you're my wife, I fully intend to, as soon as you look a little less like a bag of bones—"

"I do not!" she protested, trying not to laugh.

"So you can dream about that tonight, Dr. Abbott. It's been some time since I could think of anything else." He grinned at her. "Stop laughing, woman! How was I to know what one dance with you would do to me?"

She chuckled. "I'm not laughing. But oh, Simon, I'm so *glad*!"

"Daktari! Daktari!"

Simon stood up reluctantly. "Very opportune," he remarked. "Why don't you have a rest while I'm gone?"

"It might be for me," she reminded him pertly.

"If it is, I'll send them away!"

But Frances wouldn't allow that and she went to the door herself. A bright-faced girl stood outside, her face gleaming with excitement.

"Come quickly, *mama*. There is a new baby coming!"

Simon came to the door also, pushing Frances to one side. "The *mama daktari* is not well," he said abruptly.

Frances put her hand on his arm, "Nonsense, Simon," she said. "Of course I'll go!"

"But you're not well enough!" He looked as anxious as a small boy watching someone else play with his most treasured possession, almost sure that they would break it before he could get it safely back into his own hands. "You ought to rest."

"I'll rest when I get back," she promised.

"Fran!" He sounded desperate and she turned back, looking up at him inquiringly. "Have you no idea of your own limitations?" he asked in distracted tones.

"I think I must be tougher than I look," she answered him, meeting his eyes straight on. "I did try to hint as much—"

"I'll come with you!" he said.

She hoped she didn't look as relieved as she felt. "You can carry my bag," she smiled at him.

"Thanks very much," he said gratefully.

His humility bothered her. "Darling?"

"Yes, doctor. You can call me darling later!"

The child rattled on, telling him about each member of her family and the best way to reach her father's compound, which was some distance from Nguyu. Simon drove the Land Rover, with the child perched up in the seat beside him. Frances sat in the back, where she could watch Simon as much as she wanted. It was a small luxury, but one she found she enjoyed very much. It was restful, too. She was glad of that, because it was one thing to prove to Simon that she was well enough to be kissed by him without falling apart, but it would be quite another if she found that she wasn't as strong as she thought and had to spend another night alone.

There were three huts inside the compound. The child led them to the one in the centre, pushing past an old woman who sat in the entrance, defying anybody else to enter.

Frances smiled at her. She wore the most enormous metal earrings in her distended earlobes, and some tribal markings had been cut into her face. Because she had no teeth, her cheeks had fallen in, giving her a sour look that changed to laughter as she peered back at Frances.

"Aiee," she murmured.

The child ran out of the hut again. "Come in, *daktari*, come in! My mother has need of you!"

It was very dark inside. A small fire crackled and smoked in the center, heating up a pot of water. A woman was squatting beside it, poking at the fire with a long, charred stick. She jerked her head toward the darkness behind her, not bothering to look up.

Frances took a deep breath, distressed by the heavy atmosphere of smoke and badly cured skins. She made a quick dive for the entrance, banging into Simon as he was ducking his head to come in.

"I have a flashlight in my bag," she said crisply. "I think I'm going to need it. I can't see my hand in front of my face in there."

He steadied her, snapping open her bag and producing the flashlight, checking the position of anything else she might need.

"How's the mother-to-be?" he asked her.

"I don't know," she answered briefly. "Simon, would you mind holding the light?"

"Try and stop me."

He did quite a lot more than hold the torch. Frances

marveled as she saw the gentleness with which he received the newborn baby from her.

"You've done this before!" she accused him.

He grinned. "Animals go through much the same processes, you know," he chuckled. He added something in Swahili to the mother, whose eyes lighted up. "I'll give this young fellow a wash, before his mother sees him. He's her eighth baby, but only the second son. I think she's waiting for you to congratulate her."

Frances did so, her tongue tripping over her carefully learned Swahili. Now that it was all over, she was glad to sit and do nothing for a few minutes. By the time Simon had finished giving the baby his first bath, the woman by the fire had pressed a tiny garment into her hands. Simon silently handed her the child, and she slipped the robe over the baby's head and placed him in the crook of his mother's arm.

It was lovely to be out in the fresh air once again. Frances saw the steel-gray clouds gathering in the sky and hoped that they would reach home before the rain began again.

"I was wondering why she sent for me," she said as Simon joined her. "I didn't recognize her at first. She came to the first clinic I ever held, just for the fun of it, because she's never had any trouble with any of her babies."

"You're going to be kept pretty busy if they all call you out," he warned her.

She smiled warily. "I hope you aren't going to object," she said, "because my doctoring has to come first."

He smiled back at her. "I'll let you know when I object. Meanwhile, madam, can I drive you home?"

She put her hand in his. "Yes, please, Simon," she said very gently. "Home and beyond!"

The drums had stopped beating when they drove back into Nguyu. The streets were deserted and muddy from the rain that poured down over the tin roofs, dripping onto the hard earth.

"Tired?" Simon asked her.

"A little," she admitted. "I'm glad I have short hair now. I'm wet through!"

He cast her an anxious glance. "You'd better dry off while I put the Land Rover away."

"All right," she agreed.

She would have liked a hot bath, but she made do with a kettle of boiling water and a bar of her favorite soap. When she was both warm and dry, she flicked a comb through her shining hair and dropped the scarlet and white nightdress Simon had bought her over her head.

She heard his footsteps in the sitting room and, catching a glance of herself in the mirror, thought she looked every inch the bride he wanted.

"Simon?"

She noticed at once that he had taken the trouble to go to his own house for a shave and a quick shower.

"Do you approve?" she asked him, her voice trembling.

He took a quick step forward and she tumbled into his arms.

"Fran, I love you so much!"

She reached eagerly for his kiss, answering his own need with her own.

"I love you too," she whispered. "Simon, I love you so much it hurts! Please—"

He silenced her with his lips. "This is better than Nairobi," he said.

"Much better!" she agreed.

The rain clattered down on the roof, but neither of them heard it. This, Frances thought, was what she had been born for. Simon's arms tightened about her as he led her into a realm of glory to which the scarlet flower of the flamboyant tree was only a pale sentinel standing guard outside the door. The reality was better. It was Simon himself.

BLACK NIALL

BLACK NIALL

Mary Wibberley

"You didn't buy me when you bought Courthill!" Alison snapped at Niall MacBain. "And you didn't buy this house either, so I'm perfectly entitled to tell you to leave."

But, after he'd gone Alsion began to wonder if everyone else was right and Niall actually was charming and wonderful. Maybe she was just seeing him through a distorted lens — one warped by an old family feud and a humiliation she had endured at Niall's hands a few years earlier. Perhaps I'm only a frustrated schoolteacher after all, she thought miserably.

She had believed she hated Niall MacBain, but soon Alison began to realize it was really herself she disliked.

CHAPTER ONE

NOBODY knew that Niall MacBain was coming home to Shielbaig until the stormy summer day he arrived.

Alison Mackay was sitting in the classroom, when her attention wandered from the laborious account of Robert the Bruce that Willy MacLeod was giving to his six fellow pupils. From behind her desk, she saw a flash of blue through the trees and rain, and something made her go to the window.

"Carry on reading, Willy," she told the boy as he faltered. "We're all listening." She waited for the car to reappear. It was difficult to see anything, for the driving rain gave the village below the school a misty appearance. And what would anyone be wanting there midweek in late June? They were off the beaten tourist track, completely isolated except for the mobile stores that visited twice a week, and even they would be parked somewhere safe in this. Thunder rumbled distantly, threatening, like a growling dog half-asleep.

Then she saw the blue car again, as it came halfway up the village's only street and stopped almost on the beach of Loch Shiel, now gray and leaden in the strange half-light. Alison shivered, some premonition of trouble making her cold, although the small classroom was warmed by the peat fire that glowed in the corner. She watched the faint, blurred figure of a man leave the car and run across the street, then vanish into one of the cottages. She wasn't sure, but it appeared to be the one belonging to old Fergus MacBain.

A waiting silence made her turn. "Fine, Willy, that was fine." She looked at her watch. A quarter to four.

No more work would be done today, for the storm was making the children restless, one or two even frightened. Alison crossed to her desk. "Get your coats, children. I'll take you all home." She smiled at the ensuing hubbub, thankful that she'd come in the car that morning, for even though she lived barely a mile away, she would have been drenched after walking only a few yards.

Checking to see that the firescreen was secure, Alison switched out the light, plunging the place into premature gloom; then she had the students wait on the porch while she dashed around the back for her car.

As they drove down the hilly street, she deposited the giggling children one by one at their doors. Fiona Stewart lived next door to old Fergus MacBain, and Alison said casually, as she leaned back to open the door for the child, "My, it looks as if Mr. MacBain has a visitor."

She felt rather than saw the odd look the girl gave her. Fiona was very mature for a ten year old, and everybody knew about the feud; it had passed into village folklore. Now all she said was, "Aye, miss."

A light was on in Fergus MacBain's cottage. Alison pretended to watch Fiona as she stood on the porch, but it was the glow of the oil lamp from the front window of the other cottage that really fascinated her. And even then, some presentiment of who it could be was hovering tantalizingly at the back of her brain.

Alison had so many other things on her mind that she had forgotten the incident by the time she reached home. Jessie heard the approach of the car and she hurried outside to open wide the garage door.

"Come away in, child," she called, her white hair forming a fuzzy halo around her from the light behind.

"What a day, Jessie! Is there tea in the pot?" Alison ran in thankfully and smiled.

"I have the kettle on now. Sit ye down. I want a word with you."

"I'll make it," Alison protested, but Jessie waved her away and sniffed.

"No, you won't. There is only one person knows how to make tea in this house, and that's me."

Alison grinned at her from the rocking chair as she coasted gently backward and forward. "Yes, Jessie, sorry, Jessie. I don't know what we'd do without you." More than jest was in her words. She meant them quite seriously. She watched the old woman, her bony hands confident and capable as she lifted the heavy kettle from where it bubbled on the range. She had been with the family since before Alison was born; even before her brother Alec, who was five years older. And now, with their father dead, Alec married and living in Canada and their money gone like a will-o'-the-wisp, Jessie was still with them, firm and immovable.

A tower of strength, she had kept Alison's mother going during that difficult time three years before when Mr. Mackay's plane had crashed into the sea as he was on his way to Yugoslavia for a business conference. He had been on the verge of a breakthrough in his engineering firm in Inverness, one that would mean new wealth and security, sadly depleted because of a trusted partner's dishonesty.

What little they did have had been swallowed up in death duties after the tragic blow. But Jessie had remained, and, Alison hoped, would for as long as she lived. She loved the old housekeeper dearly.

Jessie put the teapot firmly on its stand, then glanced at Alison. "It's your mother. She's acting strange again, wandering around getting in my way instead of doing her painting. And she's got that dreamy look on her face— the one she gets when she has an idea fixed firmly in her mind. I don't know what it can be, but I have a pretty good idea."

Alison nodded, her heart plunging to her shoes.

"The house?"

"Aye." Jesse watched Alison shrewdly, her blue eyes bright and youthful in her wrinkled, beautiful old face. "She's been going on for the past few months about it being too big, too expensive to run, and all sorts of things—"

"I know," Alison interrupted miserably. "But she always does in the summer, when the sun shows up all the faults. I . . . oh, Jessie, what can we do?"

Jessie looked around the huge high-ceilinged kitchen. "God knows, child. She's right. What can three women do in a house this size? There's your money, and the bit Alec sends, and what your mother makes from her paintings—such as *that* is, but we all know it's not enough—"

"She can't sell the house. It's been in the family for generations," Alison said desperately. "And anyway, who'd buy it? We all know these big houses are a glut on the market. Oh, Jessie!" She put her hands over her eyes for a moment. "I hope we're wrong."

"Aye, but we ought to find out. You had better ask her . . . and be kind, Alison. You know how upset she gets at any unpleasantness."

Alison managed a smile. "I should know by now. Thanks for telling me, Jessie. Perhaps we can work something out, who knows?" She said it lightly, but her heart felt as heavy as lead. She loved her home with a fierce pride. It was a large, beautiful granite building facing the loch, capturing all the sun, shielding them from the wildest storms and rains, and surrounded by trees and mountains in Wester Ross, the loveliest part of Scotland. As Alison walked from the kitchen to the hall, a flash of lightning illuminated the gloom for a second and she shivered.

It was much later that evening before she learned the truth that ended her speculations.

Alison was curled up on the sofa in the living room marking exercise books, when she looked up and caught an odd, almost furtive look on her mother's face. The woman was normally so open, almost transparent, that Alison could bear it no longer. She put down her book.

"Mother," she said gently, "tell me . . . please."

Mrs. Mackay blinked, opened her eyes wide, and looked more guilty than ever. Alison felt a surge of love for her and a lump in her throat that she quickly swallowed. Her mother was so fragile and helpless looking that she had to make a conscious effort to remember that this slender, dark-haired woman had in her younger days been a successful interior designer and traveled around the world before being swept off her feet by Alison's father, who was on vacation in Australia. She had come home, married him and settled down to being a laird's wife. And no one had ever heard her utter a word of regret for the fame that could have been hers if she had gone on with her career. Now she confined herself to doing oil paintings of the Highlands, and occasionally sold some to Murdoch Imrie, an old friend of the family who owned an expensive antique shop in Inverness.

"Tell you what?" But her hand went to her cheek in a curiously fluttering gesture that gave her away.

Alison went over and sat at her feet, resting her head

on her mother's knee. "Oh, Mother! Both Jessie and I are concerned for you. There's something on your mind. You're going to have to tell me sooner or later. Why not now?"

Mrs. Mackay sighed, and stroked Alison's hair gently. "All right, I know. Oh, Alison, it's something I should have told you before, but because I don't like to be underhand, and you should know, above all—" her voice broke; then, as if gathering her courage together, she went on; "Things have reached the stage where it's impossible to go on much longer. We'll have to sell the house."

Alison looked at her, blinking back tears at having the fears finally confirmed. "That's what we thought. But I love it so."

"So do I," her mother answered softly. "Oh, I've given it a lot of thought, and maybe I should have talked about it with you sooner, but . . . well, I kept hoping . . . you know how I do." Alison nodded, unhappy for her mother as much as for herself.

"I've already had a word with Mr. Stewart—" Alison looked up sharply. John Stewart had been the family lawyer for years; he was almost like an uncle. It was the sensible thing to do, she knew, yet talking to him made it so definite.

"What did he say?"

Her mother gave a faint smile. "You won't believe this, but there's someone interested in Courthill. He wouldn't tell me who it was, but apparently a person—I don't even know if it's a man or woman—contacted him a year or so ago and asked to be told if Courthill ever came up for sale. It must be someone who's seen it. He phoned me yesterday. This person will be contacting us soon." She looked at the fireplace, where the peat fire glowed dully, nearly out. "That's why I've been on edge these past few days." She squeezed Alison's shoulder. "Forgive me. I have no choice."

"No." Alison shook her head. "There must be something we can do!"

"What? I wish there were. You know what it's like here in winter, when we practically hibernate because the house is like a refrigerator. We should have had central heating put in years ago. It was all right when we had visitors all the time and fires in every room, but not any more. There are only the three of us, and Jessie is old. How long do you think she can go on working in that huge drafty kitchen? She never grumbles, she's an angel, but it's going to tell on her."

The storm had died away. It reflected Alison's mood, which was quieter and suddenly resigned. She sighed and turned her head. Rusty, their golden labrador, lay stretched out fast asleep in front of the fire and Alison reached out a hand to stroke her. The old dog stirred slightly.

"Mother, where will we go?"

"I've been looking at the cottage. It's been so long since we had a gardener that it needs a lot of fixing up, but it could be done. And it's big enough for the three of us, plus Rusty."

"Rusty," Alison echoed. "But can you do that? Sell the house and not the cottage?"

"Of course." Her mother looked surprised. "It's practically separate anyway. We'll keep the small garden around it and we'll have the same view of the loch as we have from here."

All she said was true. But would she be able to stand living so close with someone else in her house? That was the question, and there was only one way to answer it.

They went to bed. Alison still hadn't told her mother about the other thing that was bothering her, but it was just as well. Mrs. Mackay had enough on her plate. Alison's burden was doubled, however. It was almost certain that the school would close after the fall semester. Of the seven children she taught, five were almost 11 years old and would be going to boarding school in Dingwall. The other two would then be transferred to the school in Strathcorran, 15 miles away. Since there were no other children above the age of one in Shielbaig, the school would stay closed for four years, if not forever. Alison knew too well how the school officials worked: she might be transferred to a school far away. She still hoped for a miracle—much, she thought wryly, as her mother had done. If only a couple of families with three or four children of school age would move into Shielbaig. Then her job would be safe!

Alison sighed, turned out her bedroom light, and tried vainly to sleep.

The next day, Friday, was so bright and sunny that the storm might never have happened. Alison was supervising in the playground early that afternoon, when she heard the roar of an engine and saw the same blue car that had arrived during the storm slow down and stop again outside Fergus MacBain's. Since yesterday, she had completely forgotten about the old man's visitor. She went over to the low stone wall that protected the children and the playground from a sheer drop to the village below, and looked curiously at the silent car. She could see it perfectly now: an old Ford Cortina. A man got out, and before he crossed the road he looked up toward the school. It was a fleeting glance, but it made

Alison feel foolish, as if she'd been caught peeping at a window. She turned away, chiding herself for having too vivid an imagination. Yet she was curious to know who the visitor was. If one of old Fergus's sons had been coming home, the news would have been all over the village, but she hadn't heard a word. Nor had she had a chance to see the stranger's face, but there was something disturbingly familiar about the way he walked. She looked again toward the little cottage where Fergus MacBain lived alone. He had had four sons, Alistair, Ian, Duncan, and Niall. The two older ones lived in New Zealand; they were sheep farmers, if rumor was to be believed. Duncan and Niall had both left home years ago to join the navy. Duncan and Niall . . . Black Niall, the wildest one in a rough, tough quartet of boys, belonging to a family that had had a bitter, silent feud with the Mackay family for more than 100 years. Alison only remembered Niall, because he was the youngest and practically the same age as Alec, her brother. They had been in school at the same time. At the same time, but not together unless they were fighting.

It must have been in their blood, thought Alison, this urge to be constantly at each other's throats, born in them from the terrible time in 1869. The two families had been the chief ones in the village and surrounding crofts, and the names Mackay and MacBain were said in the same breath. But one day Hector MacBain and Domnuil Mackay had had the misfortune to fall for a fiery-eyed village beauty who'd led them both on. The tale had become embroidered throughout the years until it seemed that the two youths were tragic victims of a cruel Jezebel. Whatever the truth of that, the fact remained that one day the two young men had gone off into the hills to "settle their differences." They were never seen again.

A few days later a shepherd had come down from his bothie, wild-eyed, and telling a terrible tale. He had been searching for stray lambs on a rough part of the mountain, near some high cliffs, when he saw the two men locked in fierce combat. The ground was covered with loose stones and as he watched, they had slipped and gone hurtling over the edge, still fighting.

By the time he reached the spot, it was too late. Far below, the white foamy sea crashed against the rocks. Sick with shock, he had turned away.

When the shepherd told his tale, bitter unforgivable words had been spoken. And from that day on, hatred sparked like a live wire whenever a Mackay and a Mac-Bain met. There was more too, but the tales were vague, hinting of smuggling, gambling and illicit whisky stills.

No one ever told Alison exactly what had happened. Perhaps there was shame of a different kind on both sides, she thought. When she was a child, she had never dared ask, and now it was too late. Sometimes she wondered if Alec had ever found out.

Alison lived at Courthill, the family home since long before the feud, and Fergus MacBain, the last remaining member of his family in the area, lived in a small cottage that had been his father's and grandfather's before him. The big MacBain house so near Courthill, had been destroyed by a terrible fire in 1872, and all their money, so the story ran, had gone with it. A few heaps of stone were all that remained to tell that there had once been a house.

Alison shivered, suddenly cold at the memories revived, and joined in the children's exercises with such enthusiasm that her pupils were startled and couldn't keep up with her pace. Her mind refused to join in with the later lessons. She was weighed down with an intense feeling of depression. It was probably the knowledge that the school might have to close, or it could have been caused by the thought of leaving her home.

In any case, it brought on a headache that persisted even after she had taken two aspirins, and by four o'clock she was so wretched that it was a relief to see the children go. She sat very still at her desk and watched them run shrieking and shouting down the hill.

Distantly, on the other side of the loch, she could see home. Just the roof and part of a bedroom window over the thick trees, but it was enough to bring a lump to her throat. How can I leave it, she thought. Tears of pain and fatigue sprang to her eyes. She was being childish, she knew. Her mother was right. They could not go on living there, managing as they did, and expect the house to maintain itself. She wasn't so blinded by love for it that she couldn't see the window frames that needed fixing, or the shingles missing from the roof. Even the grounds had deteriorated rapidly since they had laid off the gardener. Alison and her mother did their best, but it was a losing battle against the acres of rich vegetation that ran riot, sheltered as they were in the curve of the bay.

She sighed, picked up her mirror and dabbed carefully at her eyes. There must be no trace of tears when she reached home. She looked at herself coldly and critically, seeing only the damp smudges on her cheeks. She was not aware of what others could see, the inner beauty that shone through, lighting her features so that everyone she met was immediately drawn to her. Her mouth was full and feminine, softly curved; her eyes an attractive shade of deep blue, fringed by long lashes, with finely shaped brows slanting serenely above them. Both brows and lashes were thick and dark.

She put the mirror away and flicked a comb through rebelliously curly hair; then she went around checking that all was safely in its place. The school was silent and lifeless without the children.

Alison's headache disappeared as she walked down into the village a few minutes later. She had to stop at the post office to pick up some airmail forms for Jessie, who carried on a prolific correspondence with nieces and nephews all over the world. It was pleasant to greet the friendly-faced villagers as she went along, feeling at home there as she knew she would nowhere else.

The post office, which also served as grocery store, newsstand and hardware store, was at the end of the village around a bend in the road. As Alison reached it, she half turned to wave to Mr. MacIntyre, who was repairing his nets on the beach. Turning back, she crashed into a man who was coming out of the post office. For a split second she was winded with the impact. She felt two strong arms steadying her and looked up. And in that startled instant of mutual recognition she gasped and pulled away as if from the embrace of a snake. The man she had cannoned into so violently, and who was looking at her with the strangest expression, was none other than Niall MacBain. Black Niall himself! Recovering, Alison moved to one side and hurried into the dark store, her heart beating violently. She was acutely aware that he still stood outside, looking through the window.

"A dozen airmail forms, please, Mrs. Finlayson," she said. Her arms still burned from his touch and her skin crawled at the memory. Of all the sons—that it should be *him*, the one she loathed most, who had come back home to his father's house!

Mrs. Finlayson regarded Alison with bright, beady eyes, her head slightly tilted to one side in excitement, and a flutter in her voice.

"There now, Miss Mackay. Did you not see who was just in here? Fergus MacBain's youngest, Niall!"

"I saw him, yes," Alison answered.

Mrs. Finlayson clicked her teeth. "Ach now, I was forgetting! It is so long since the boys were home, and your brother away to Canada, that it seems as if the feud has been forgotten." She chuckled, the malicious gleam in her bright eyes belying her next words. "But there, now. It is nothing to do with me at all, is it?"

"Oh, that!" And Alison laughed, determined not to let the other woman see that anything was wrong. "That was long ago."

"Aye, no doubt." As Alison paid for the blue airmail forms, Mrs. Finlayson said, "Ach, I must away and send this telegram. Eh, Rio is in South America, is it not?"

"Rio? Yes, Brazil." Alison took her change, smiled her thanks, and escaped. There was no sign of Niall MacBain when she got out into the fresh air, and she took a deep breath. It was bad enough to see him, but to have bumped into him as well! She rubbed her arm as if to erase his touch and walked quickly homeward, trying desperately to push to the back of her mind the humiliating memory of the last time she had met him, nine years before. It was no use. As she walked down the familiar forest road with no sound except her own footsteps, the picture she had tried so hard to forget came bustling forward as if anxious for release.

It had been so near there too. Alison was almost 16 at the time, and Alec 21. There had been a dance in Shielbaig on Saturday night, and their parents had let her go, provided that she came home with her brother. There had been a big crowd in the Institute Hall, and the night had been hot, noisy, and tremendously exciting. Alison had discovered, to her delighted surprise, that she was much in demand for all the dances, and had spent the entire evening being swept, almost literally, off her feet on the waxed floor. Another thing that gave her secret pleasures was the glimpse she had, early in the evening, of Niall MacBain standing by the door. He wore an ill-fitting blue suit and looked desperately uncomfortable. Alison knew he was watching her, and it made her all the more determined to let the world see what a wonderful time she was having. Some instinct of female coquetry, one she barely understood, must have been at work, for each time she whirled past and looked ever so casually at him, his eyes were on her. She laughed, eyes sparkling, into her partners' faces, and more than one tried to steal a kiss in that dismal shed that had become paradise for one magical evening.

Like Cinderella's ball, the evening had to end, and, when Alison tried to find Alec, he was nowhere to be seen. As people drifted away, she looked around, wishing she had kept a closer eye on him. But she had been having too good a time to bother, and now . . . . "See you home, Alison?" A voice came from the darkness, and she whirled around to see one of her more enthusiastic partners, a handsome boy from Strathcorran named Johnny Gordon, watching her.

"N-no, thanks." She was suddenly uneasy. It was one thing to flirt with gay abandon at a dance, but quite another to be walking home with a young man who had a reputation as a wolf. "I'm meeting Alec down the road," she lied, and with a careless wave ran off into the darkness. Where, oh, where was he?

Once away from the hall she slowed down. She wasn't

frightened of the dark and enjoyed walking. She was busy planning what she would say to her brother when she sensed she was being followed and began to walk faster. She was near a short cut that lead directly into the grounds of Courthill, so she scrambled over the low stone wall, breaking a fingernail in her haste. Then she was among the thick sweet-smelling pines. Branches caught spitefully at her hair as she half ran, half walked through the moonlit gloom. Something made her turn and stop; she heard unmistakably, from somewhere close behind, the sound of fighting. There were grunts and cracks, as if of fist meeting face, followed by the obvious sound of crashing, in the undergrowth as someone went sprawling. Then she heard voices, low and urgent. Running footsteps faded into the distance. Alec? Could it be Alec who had seen someone following her and had caught up with him? Alison wondered. She waited, but there was no further sound.

"Alec?" She said it quietly at first, then louder when there was no reply. Quickly she retraced her steps, came into the clearing by the trout stream and stopped dead in utter astonishment as she saw her arch-enemy, Niall MacBain, standing with his back partially to her, rubbing his knuckles. Knowing how he and Alec spent their lives battling, she dashed forward immediately.

"What have you done with my brother?" she demanded, so angry that she caught his arm.

He turned around slowly, and she remembered thinking how different he was. He had been like a fish out of water in the crowded hall. Now he seemed to have grown and was no longer ill at ease. He looked down at her, and even in the misty, cold light of the half-hidden moon, Alison saw the contempt on his face.

"I've done nothing wi' your brother," he said, shaking

his arm free. "The one who's just now run away like a rabbit was Johnny Gordon. He was following you."

"I don't believe you!" But she saw the blood on his chin welling from a cut under his mouth even as she said the words.

He shrugged. "Do you think *I* care whether you believe me or not?" His mouth twisted. "The way you were behaving tonight, it's a wonder you didn't have a few more after you!"

"What do you mean by that?" she demanded, glad that he could not see the hot color rushing to her cheeks.

"You're almost 16, you should know," was the brutal answer.

Alison drew her breath in sharply. "How *dare* you speak to me like that! If Alec was here, he'd soon—"

"Aye, but he's not, is he? And do you think I'm scared of him?" He gave a mocking laugh. "You should see what I just did to Johnny."

Fighting's all you think about, isn't it?" she ground out furiously, and at the same time angry with herself. "You're always fighting."

"I wouldn't say that . . . not all the time." He grinned suddenly and reached out to touch Alison's face. Startled, she hit his arm and backed away a few inches.

"Don't touch me!" she said. "Don't ever do that again!"

"You didn't mind everyone else doing it at the dance," he retorted. "In fact, I'd say you looked as if you were enjoying every minute of it." He suddenly pulled her toward him, catching her off balance and so much by surprise that she was in his arms before she knew what was happening.

"Let's see what everyone found so wonderful." And he kissed her hard on the lips, taking her breath away.

Just as abruptly he released her and stood before her, his chest heaving.

Sobbing with the shock of it all, and deeply disturbed at her own reaction, Alison slapped him hard across his face. Before she could turn to run, his hand shot out and held her arm. She gasped with fear, suddenly remembering his fiery temper, and tried to pull away. Then he laughed. "You're safe enough," he might have read her mind. "I never hit girls. But I don't like being slapped by them either."

"Let me go!" She suddenly realized something else. "You . . . you were following me as well." Her teeth began chattering as she realized the implications, and she twisted desperately, trying to free herself.

"Aye, but I was coming this way anyway." He released her abruptly. "I fancied taking home a few trout for supper, so . . ." and he looked from the stream to Alison as if challenging her to say anything. She couldn't meet his glance and looked away. Shame mingled with the impotent rage she felt at his bold, rough manner. They had seldom spoken before. The feud was like a shadow between them, one that colored Alec's and her lives, and she hated him for forcing her gratitude. She hated him also for that rough male kiss, taken so abruptly and cruelly. It had been her first kiss. . . . She had not imagined it would be like that, or from him.

"That would be poaching," she said eventually, trying to sound firm and authoritative.

"Poaching?" He threw back his head and laughed. "Poaching, eh? Well, *Miss Mackay*, it won't be the first time I've poached here . . . or the last."

"You— What do you mean?" Astonishment had replaced fear. A deep instinct told Alison that he would not harm her, though she did not know why.

"What do you mean?" he mimicked cruelly. "Are you crazy? What do you think I mean? I've been here hundreds of times. Aye, and my brothers too. And your precious gardener, and Alec, even your dogs—they've never known."

"I'll tell them," she said. "I'll have you arrested!"

"Och, you'll have me trembling in my boots! Try it, and you'll all be the laughing stock of Shielbaig. Where's your proof?"

"I'll tell them what you said."

"Will you now?" He cocked his head to one side. "And have them ask me how I got this cut on my chin?" He dabbed at the dark patch with a handkerchief. "What will you have me tell them, eh? That *you* were fighting me? Or the truth?" A smile broadened his mouth and Alison clenched her fists, hating him more than ever. He was loathsome! He had an answer for everything and she was only wasting time talking to him; worse, being made to look foolish. She stood up straight and glared coldly at him.

"Take your trout," she said clearly, "and go. You must feel entitled to some payment for your so gallant rescue."

She knew that her words had stung him by the quick darkening of his face as he spat out, "It's a pity someone can't take you down a peg or two, Miss High-and-Mighty."

"Who, you? Don't make me laugh!" She turned and began to walk away. His voice came after her, harsh with anger.

"Aye, maybe . . . one day."

Alison ran home then, but she never told anyone what had happened. Not even Alec, who had been flirting around the back of the hall with a girl and who received a tongue lashing from their mother for not bringing his sister safely home.

She had passed the trout stream now, and she bit her lip at the memory of those last bitter words of Niall MacBain's. They had obviously been said in a fit of temper, for shortly afterward he had left home. She had not seen him since.

The contrast between the thin, long-legged, gangly youth with his fiery temper and the man she had bumped into was enormous. He had filled out, his shoulders becoming broad and powerful. The dark, intense boy was now mature. His deeply tanned face was a mocking reminder of the youngster she had so hated, but the lines of experience lent an interest to what before had been the promise of good looks. All this Alison had seen in that split second of mutual recognition. The eyes . . . she would never forget his eyes as he had looked at her. They were changed: older, wiser, more cynical. Deep gray, the color of the loch in winter, there had been a disturbing expression that had worried her and made her pull away so quickly.

Lost in thought, she walked on homeward, knowing that Jessie at least would be interested when Alison told her whom she had seen. The feud had always fascinated her. Not so Alison's mother, who had always been distressed at Alec's eagerness to fight with the youngest MacBain and couldn't see why something that had happened so long ago should affect their lives as it did.

But when Alison went into the house, she forgot everything at the sight of her mother's face. The older woman came running down the stairs as Alison pushed open the heavy front door. There was an air of suppressed excitement about her as she greeted her daughter, and Alison said, "Mother? What is it?"

"I've just had a phone call from John Stewart. The man who is interested in buying our house is coming to see it tomorrow!"

Alison's heart gave an unpleasant lurch and she looked at her mother in dismay. There was something else about her mother too, something puzzling. "Oh, I see," she said.

"And Alison—"

"Yes?"

"Oh . . . er . . . nothing." But her hand went to her face and Alison sensed sudden distress.

"Mother? What is it? Have you had second thoughts—"

"No, no . . . it's . . . I don't feel very well." And she ran up the stairs as if someone were after her. Alison thought her mother had had an attack of nerves. She didn't know what had caused her distress. She was to wish later that she had asked.

She woke with leaden heart next morning and bathed and dressed with the feeling that execution was imminent. Her mouth and eyes felt dry and gritty. She had slept badly. The previous evening she had made such a determined effort to be cheerful that reaction had set in.

The stranger was coming at ten. At nine-thirty Alison forced herself to drink a cup of black coffee. Her stomach rebelled at the thought of anything more. She found the tension of waiting unbearable, and at half past nine told her mother she would take Rusty for a walk in the grounds.

As they set off she looked back to see the house, grand and immovable, facing the loch with the calm and serenity it had had ever since the day it was built. A lump came into her throat. Her father had been born in that house, his forefathers before him, and both Alec and Alison herself. It was unthinkable to sell it. But barring a miracle, they had no choice.

Alison and Rusty walked slowly, for the dog was old and not interested in anything more than a gentle amble through the trees, with much sniffing at interesting smells in the thick undergrowth. Alison had no particular destination in mind, but perhaps because of the memories revived the previous day she found herself heading toward the old trout stream, already faintly audible in the distance. Thin shafts of sunlight pierced the thick greenery overhead. The entire wood had an aura of warm greenness, as if underwater. It was a slightly eerie atmosphere, and her heart began to beat faster as she neared the stream. In a minute now she would see the clearing where that fateful night. . . .

She came past the final obstructing tree and gasped, her hand going to her mouth in horror at the sight of the ghost who stood looking at the water. Then he turned; it was no phantom, but a solid, flesh-and-blood man, larger and more confident than the last time she had seen him in the very same spot. The same place, the same person, but nine years later—Niall MacBain. He stood watching her, waiting, almost as if he had known she would come.

CHAPTER TWO

ALISON walked slowly toward him, motioning a curious Rusty to her side. Her first childish impulse was to shout, "Go away!" but she was no longer a child. Nothing, however, could make her welcome him, and as she neared him she said, "What are you doing here?"

"Just looking and thinking." His voice was disconcerting, as was the expression in his eyes. In those few words and the way he said them was a world of difference from the rough, quick-tempered boy Alison remembered. This was a man, and one who was fully aware of it. His hair was different, his face and eyes, all so devastatingly masculine as to be an affront to her peace of mind. She was, after all, facing a trespasser, yet it was difficult to keep calm as his eyes raked her from head to toe, subtly appraising her.

"You still enjoy trespassing?" Alison was stung to retort.

"You're mistaken . . . Miss Mackay." The pause was deliberate and faintly insulting. It made her feel curiously on the defensive.

He went on, "I'm here by invitation." His voice was soft.

"Invitation? Never! I wouldn't—" Alison stopped, seeing his smile. And still she didn't realize.

"Your mother's. Didn't she tell you?"

"No! It . . . you c-can't." She was stammering, so took a deep breath to steady herself. Now was the time for self-control. If the nightmare words he was saying were true, it meant that he was the "stranger" who was coming to see her home.

She said more calmly, "Are you telling me that you are the person who wants to buy Courthill?"

"I am." He looked at his watch. "I arrived sooner than I expected, so decided to walk this way to the house. It seemed the natural thing to do, and after all it will save you showing me around the grounds if I've already seen them, won't it?" There was a gleam of mockery in the dark gray eyes that touched a raw nerve in Alison.

"I'm sure you already know every inch of them," she retorted. The shock had not subsided. A kind of dismay had her in its grip. Now she knew why her mother had been so distressed the night before. Mrs. Mackay had been frightened of Alison's reaction, nervous that she would be angry. It was too soon, and the shock was too great for that . . . yet. Anger would come later. Just at the moment all she felt was a sick numbness. She watched as if in a dream as Rusty ambled over to him. The dog half wagged her tail, unsure whether the man was friend or foe until he stooped and patted her head after letting her sniff his hand. As the tail wag increased rapidly, Alison called, "Rusty, come here girl!" Niall looked up, the corner of his mouth quirking slightly. Unable to stand there a moment longer, Alison turned away and began to walk back home. Perhaps it was a bad dream. Perhaps he'll vanish if I ignore him completely, she thought wildly.

She heard footsteps behind her, his voice saying, "It's almost ten. I'll come to Courthill now." And something snapped inside her. Whirling around, seeing him only inches away from her, she said, "The joke's over. You've had your fun. *You* buy my house? I'd rather die!"

A muscle tightened in his cheek, a dangerous sign that should have warned her. But his voice was quite calm as he answered softly, "It's for your mother to say yes or no, not you."

Then Alison said the unforgivable. Looking straight into his eyes, she retaliated, "She wants to *sell* it, not give it away. For money . . . if you know what that is!"

Under the tan, his face went white with anger, but she was beyond caring. Recklessly she spat out, "So don't think you can waste our time. All you want to do is gloat over our misfortune." Her eyes sparked fire, her fists were clenched tightly for control.

"For your information, I have the money to buy Courthill, with enough left over to do all that's necessary to it. If what I hear about your home is true, it's certainly been allowed to deteriorate these last few years. Your spirited defence of it might be more credible if you'd taken the trouble to maintain it properly."

Alison felt as if he had struck her. The hammer blow of each word struck more forcibly because of the expression in his eyes. She was helpless in the face of it, more so because she knew instinctively that he spoke the truth. There was superb confidence in his bearing, in his manner, in everything about him; the confidence that comes from wealth. She should have known, for it made even greater the contrast between the young aggressive fighter she remembered and the man he was now. His temper was equally fiery, although clearly under control; yet as she watched him, she felt fear. He would be a formidable opponent because of all these factors. Losing her own control would only do her harm she knew. She took a deep breath, fighting for calmness.

"If it's in such poor condition, why are you interested?"

"I've always been interested, all my life. I made up my mind even before I left home that when I made a fortune, and the house came up for sale, I would buy it.

I've made not a fortune, but enough, and Courthill is now on the market, so—" he shrugged "—I want to buy."

"S-suppose my mother refuses to sell?" Alison asked.

He lifted one eyebrow a fraction. "Why should she? You can't afford to live here any more. My money is as good as anybody's. She'll sell."

"Perhaps not to *you*."

"And how many more do you think you'll have interested, eh? I'll tell you . . . none! Beggars can't be choosers," he finished cruelly.

Alison flinched. "How dare you say that!"

"I haven't even started yet. And I'd have to go a long way before I could be as appallingly rude as you." He was still angry. She could feel it, and something more that she didn't understand. It was as if, somehow, he was actually enjoying himself. Alison knew she could only make things worse, so she turned away. "Come on, Rusty." She began walking home, and there was silence behind her. Before the clearing vanished completely, she had an overwhelming, irresistible urge to turn around. He stood there, perfectly still, tall and erect. And he was watching her.

"What are we going to do, Jessie?" Alison implored her, watching the old woman as she bustled about the kitchen preparing lunch.

"What can we do, child?" Jessie answered. "Your mother, bless her, doesn't have a choice." She looked up from the pastry she was making. "You should be away in there with them, you know."

Alison shook her head. "I couldn't, really. I don't even want to speak to him, let alone sit in there drinking coffee like old friends. I'd throw it at him, saucer and all, or be sick!"

"Aye," Jessie gave her little smile. "You always did have your share of the Mackay temper." She shook her head wonderingly. "Ach, but he's grown up into a good-looking devil, I'll say that. So dark, just like his father was when he was a young man."

"Good-looking!" Alison nearly spilled her coffee. "He's hateful, like a . . . a pirate! Black Niall, they used to call him. It suits him more than ever now. He's loathsome."

"You think so? Aye well, maybe you're right. But you cannot deny he's a powerful figure of a man. He's broken a few hearts in his travels around the world, I'd wager."

Something struck Alison, and she asked, "Jessie, how do you think he's made enough money to buy our house? He's been in the navy all these years, hasn't he?"

"That he has. As for the money, it's as much a mystery to me as it is to you. I haven't heard anything in the village, and that's unusual, but then the old man has never been one to talk about his sons."

The faint jangle of the bell in the corner made the two of them look at one another. Jessie said quietly, "That's for you, lassie. Your mother said she'd ring when she needed you."

Alison stood up and smoothed her skirt, suddenly nervous. It was frightening. She was in her own house, where she had lived all her life, and yet she was shaking at the thought of going into her own living room to face a man she disliked. The worst aspect of it was the awful feeling of helplessness that filled her.

She walked across the hall and opened the door. Her mother was sitting on the sofa by the fireplace. Dressed simply in a beige sweater and brown skirt, she made a small appealing figure. Alison felt a surge of pity that her mother should be reduced to being nice to this awful man because of their financial situation. Then she looked reluctantly at him. He turned at that moment, and their eyes met in silent hostility across the room.

"Alison, dear," her mother held out her hand to Alison, and she clasped it, dismayed to feel the fine tremor. So she too was nervous! "I'd like you to show Mr. MacBain around the house and grounds—"

"Mother—" Alison began, agonized.

"Please, Alison." The pressure of her hand increased slightly, and Alison subsided. "All right. Now?" She looked at him.

He bowed his head slightly. "If that is convenient for you, Mrs. Mackay." Alison might just as well not have been there.

"Of course." Her mother gave him a smile, but it looked strained, and Alison felt a quick rush of temper. She wondered what he had been saying to her. Had he been bullying her?

"Are you all right, Mother?" she asked quietly.

"Perfectly, dear. I just want a little time to think."

About what? Alison wondered. Before she could lose the resolve, she turned back to the dark silent man. "Will you wait in the hall, please? I'll be with you in a moment."

He went out without a word, moving quietly and easily across the room. As the door closed behind him, Alison knelt down. "Tell me quickly. Has he been awkward? Is he trying to force the price down?"

Her mother shook her head, fine lines round her eyes emphasizing the delicacy of her features. "No, Alison, it's nothing at all. He hasn't said one word out of place. I just have to consider things for a little while. I'll tell you later, I promise. And please, dear, for my sake, try not to make it so obvious that you dislike him."

"You don't expect me to hold hands while I'm showing him around, do you?" Alison asked bitterly.

"I don't think he'd expect that." Mrs. Mackay gave her a little smile, more herself. "But be civil. He's not as bad as you think."

He is infinitely worse, Alison thought, but she said nothing.

"All right, I'll try. Do . . . do you think he'll buy it?"

Her mother nodded. "Yes, I think he will. I'm sorry, but there it is. I'd be silly to turn him down."

Alison went unsteadily to the door.

She hadn't realized how shabby the house was until she saw it through the eyes of a stranger. As they went through each of the seven bedrooms she saw him glance around, saw his hard incisive look as he examined windows, floors and walls. She was filled with shame. That this day should come was bad enough, but to know that he was examining every crack and crevice and filing it away in his mind was too humiliating.

He took a small book out of his jacket pocket and began making notes as they went along. Alison was too choked up to speak, only managing the briefest of comments as they went into each room. The furniture in the unoccupied rooms, sheeted and ghostly, was a reminder of days long gone, and the faded elegance of the high-ceilinged upstairs corridor seemed to hold the echoes of laughing voices as they walked along it.

She paused at the foot of the twisting, uncarpeted staircase to the attic. "Do you want to see the small rooms upstairs?" she asked.

"If it's no trouble." There was a hardness about him as he stood there waiting for her to lead the way up. Alison shivered inwardly. It was no use, she thought wryly, seeing his face. He had won.

The accumulated rubbish of many years lay under those sloping ceilings. Boxes, trunks, piles of magazines, cases of books too precious to throw away but too numerous for the library downstairs, an old rocking horse from the nursery—all these reminders of the past lay in the first of the five large attic rooms. Alison looked around, realizing that everything would have to go. There wouldn't be any room in the cottage for it.

Niall seemed oblivious of the clutter, striding over objects to reach the window and look out. "Hm, I think these will do," he was speaking to himself, and she wondered what he meant. He turned to her. "How many more attic rooms are there?"

"Four," she answered. "All the same as this."

He wrote something down. "Right. I'll see them some other time. We can go down now." He came back toward Alison, and they went out. His words had puzzled her. There had been an expression on his face almost of satisfaction, as he had looked around the attic—as if confirming something he wanted to know. But what? Nobody, unless they had lots of children, or servants, could possibly need attics. As far as Alison was aware, he was possessed of neither, but then he was a man of mystery.

She took him through all the downstairs rooms except the one where her mother sat with Rusty. When she took him into the conservatory he nodded approvingly. "This is fine—very interesting. Who looks after all these plants?" His gesturing arm took in the green wilderness of potted plants all around them, the ivies and cyclamens, a tall philodendron that curled all over the glass roof, threatening to take over, and the various cacti and succulents that Alison tended so carefully in her spare time.

"I do," she answered briefly. "I'll show you the studio. This way, please."

A passage led off from the conservatory, with its permanently damp, earthy smell. They walked along flag-stones to Alison's favorite room. This, her mother's studio, was a large, airy stone shed that had been added to the side of the house years ago. The light and the views from all the windows were exhilarating. Paintings were propped against the walls and on the easel was one, not yet dry, of the loch at night. Niall stopped to look at it, backing away slightly to get it into better perspective. Alison wanted to pull him away so he wouldn't look at anything so intensely personal. But she had to stand there, her hand gripping the door handle so tightly that her knuckles were white. She felt physically exhausted from the stress of resisting all the natural primitive urges to send him away. He looked at her after a few minutes.

"Now, may we go outside?"

"You've seen the gardens before," she answered stiffly.

"But not properly. Mainly at night." A slight, mocking smile lit his face briefly and was gone. "I would like to look around in daylight. And see the garages, and the chapel, of course."

Alison looked sharply at him. "That hasn't been used for years."

"I'd still like to see it—if I may." The last three words left no doubt of his intention to get his own way. She shrugged, and he opened the door for her to go out in front of him.

The nightmare was over half an hour later when they went back to the house. The tension and strain had left Alison feeling so weak that she stumbled on the bottom step as she went up to the front door. Immediately he shot out a hand to steady her, and the touch was like fire on her arm. She regained her balance and moved quickly away. "Thank you."

"A pleasure." A warm rush of color surged into her face at the mocking words. She could sense that he hated her as much as she did him. She wondered if he remembered the incident after the dance nine years ago; as she did, she recalled his last words, spoken in anger, of "taking her down a peg or two."

Could this be it? His revenge, cruel and subtle? Alison looked quickly at him as she opened the front door, and their eyes clashed for one awful moment. The look in his made her shiver—a look of suppressed, smouldering anger. She took a deep breath, suddenly afraid. If this was his way of doing it, he was choosing a superbly refined way of torture. One that would go on and on. For as long as she lived, Alison knew she would not forget the man who was depriving her of her home.

Alison had thought that nothing could be worse or more distressing than having to show Niall MacBain around her home. She was wrong. When they returned to the room where her mother waited, Mrs. Mackay looked up—at him, not at Alison—and something, passed between them some unspoken question, Alison glanced quickly at Niall.

"Have you said anything?" her mother asked him. He shook his head.

"No, I thought it would be better if you did that, Mrs. Mackay."

"What is it?" Alison's heart began to pound.

"Wait, Alison. First, Mr. MacBain, you've looked around now. Does your offer still stand?"

He walked slowly from the door to Mrs. Mackay and stood in front of her. "Yes, Mrs. Mackay, it does. Say the word and we'll go to the lawyers on Monday."

"Mother, before you say anything else, please—what should he have told me?" Alison was breathless, as if she had been running. She knew that in another second a final irrevocable act would take place—a handshake of agreement.

Her mother looked at her almost sadly. "Mr. MacBain is going to turn Courthill into a hotel."

"Oh, no!" Alison closed her eyes, shocked beyond measure. Again she could see him looking around the chapel, nodding approvingly, saying, "This could be repaired quite easily." And in the attic too. . . . Now she knew why. Her home, a hotel, with loud strangers walking in and out as if they owned it, going out in boats from the private mooring, walking through the woods, fishing. . . .

"No, you can't do it! Don't let him!" She looked at him standing there, and for the first time in her life wished that she were a man. She wanted to knock him senseless, to fight him, punish him in the only way he understood, by brute force. Almost shaking, she said. "Don't sell to him, Mother. We'll find someone else—" He turned and looked at her, and she saw a puzzling expression, almost of pity. A second later it was gone, to be replaced by studied blankness, as he said, "Maybe I should leave you alone for a while to discuss it."

"That won't be necessary," said her mother. "Alison, calm down, please." Alison sat down beside her, wanting so much to cry, but holding herself in check by a strong effort of will. Of course she could do nothing. Her mother had already decided. That was what she had wanted to think over. There was worse to come, but Alison didn't find out what it was until later in the day.

She watched their handshake. Then her mother said, "Sit down, please, Mr. MacBain. There are one or two things we must discuss."

He sat down opposite them, and Rusty ambled over and collapsed at his feet in a pleading heap, her tail wagging. He bent and began to scratch her ears idly as he said, "The cottage you want to live in. Is that the one by the loch?"

"Yes. It's quite separate, and we could probably fence off a path to the main road."

"Whatever you like, it doesn't matter to me. You can use the grounds as you please." He paused, then added, "And, Mrs. Mackay, your studio—I wouldn't want to take that from you. If you want to keep using it, it's yours."

Alison heard her mother's sharp, incredulous intake of breath, then, "Why, that's—very kind of you. Are you sure—?"

"Quite sure. We can easily put a door in the studio and block off the one from the conservatory, so that no guests will wander in. You'll have your own key, of course."

"Thank you. There really wouldn't be room at the cottage. I was wondering what on earth I would do."

You'd think he was doing her a great honor, Alison thought bitterly.

"And the island, Mrs. Mackay. When can I see the island?"

"Mother! You're not selling the island too?" Alison gasped.

Her mother looked at her, "Of course. It goes with the house, you know that. What use would it be to us?"

"I go all the time and you're always painting there—"

"I'm sure Mr. MacBain wouldn't mind us going." She turned to him. "The views from it are magnificent. Really inspiring for a painter."

"I'm sure." He smiled at her. "I might fix up the cottage on it—maybe rent it out as a honeymoon island—"

"How romantic!" Mrs. Mackay clasped her hands to her breast. Alison looked stonily at him. His eyes had flickered toward her as he had almost said the words mockingly. By now she was almost past caring. She didn't think anything else could happen to affect her. She found out how wrong she was later.

"Alison will take you there this afternoon."

"You know your own way there, don't you, Mr. Mac-Bain? I'm sure you'll manage better on your own," Alison said, knowing she was being appallingly rude.

"I would prefer you to take me," he answered calmly. "After all, you know your own boat best, and I'd hate to damage it."

Her mother looked doubtfully at them both, fully aware of the charged atmosphere and torn with indecision. Alison stood up.

"I'll take you. And now, if you'll excuse me, I have a lot of work to do." She went out quickly and shut the door behind her. Her destination was the kitchen, where she could pour out her feelings to Jessie. She would understand more than her mother who, in the last few minutes, had seemed almost visibly to go over to the enemy side. It was, thought Alison in horror, almost as if she *liked* him.

Under any other circumstances the boat ride to the island at the mouth of the loch would have been enjoyable. It was a warm afternoon laced with stiff breeze, and the boat sped across the calm deep loch with hardly any effort. Alison sat in the bow and watched it cleave through the black waters, but her heart was heavy. She looked back to see her home and the village receding rapidly. It was a beautiful sight, but spoiled by the man leaning against the stern, hand on tiller as he guided them along.

He had come back after lunch, having changed into a thick white sweater, gray leather jacket, and tight-fitting gray slacks. Binoculars were slung on a long cord around his neck. The sweater accentuated his tan and the jacket matched his eyes. If Alison hadn't loathed him so deeply, she would have admitted that Jessie's assessment, "a good-looking devil," was an almost perfect way to describe him. He was more than six feet tall, towering easily over her—long-legged, slim-hipped and broad-shouldered. So that was what life in the navy had done for him, she thought: turned him into a tough-looking giant. But how had he made his so-called fortune?

Alison turned away, her eye caught by a shiny black shape that heaved itself up out of the water, then vanished. A seal most likely, or a porpoise. Both were common in the loch during the warm summer months, and curious enough to come up to a boat.

Niall and Alison hadn't spoken since they left the house. She had nothing to say to him, nor he apparently to her.

She looked toward the distant schoolroom, now

smaller than a matchbox, and thought with bitterness how only two days ago she had wondered who the stranger's car belonged to. Her premonition had been right. The car that had carried Niall MacBain back home to Shielbaig had brought trouble with it.

They were nearly there. Alison turned back again to see the island looming before them, spreading and widening as they came into its shadow. It wasn't large— a quarter of a mile long, and the same width, in a very rough square shape. It was big enough to have deep caves, plentiful trees and shrubs and a cottage, the roof of which was faintly visible through the trees as Alison bent to see where the treacherous underwater rocks were.

"Left a bit," she called, and felt the boat surge left as they coasted gently in, bumping a little in the waves that lapped against the shore. Niall switched the motor off and it put-puttered into silence. There was only the creak of the wood as the boat's keel touched the gravelly beach. Niall climbed swiftly past Alison, jumped out and pulled the boat up onto the shore.

Before he could offer her his arm, Alison jumped out too, glad that she'd worn wellingtons instead of shoes with her outfit of rust-colored sweater and pants. Their footsteps crunched on thousands of tiny shells and pebbles, and Niall looked around him appraisingly.

"Marvelous." He turned to her. "Don't you think so?"

"Yes," she answered briefly. "Where do you want to go first?"

He gave her an odd, very level look. "The cottage, I think."

Alison shrugged. "As you like."

"Can you manage the climb? Do you want help?" he asked.

"From you?" She looked at him, not bothering to conceal her feelings. "No, thank you. I'm fine."

There was silence for a moment, then he said slowly, with a hard cutting edge to his voice, "Let's get one thing straight. If you think you can, by your childish and silly behavior, make me back out of buying Courthill, you're very much mistaken. In fact, it only makes me more determined to have it."

"Does it?" She faced him then, breathing fast as if she had been running. "Or did you make up your mind years ago? You've chosen a cruel way to have your revenge, haven't you? Oh, don't think I don't know. I remember."

He looked puzzled. "Revenge? What the hell are you talking about?"

"Don't look so innocent. I have a good memory."

"Better than mine, I guess." He stared steadily at her, and his eyes were like chips of granite. "You'd better tell me."

So she reminded him of the words he had spoken at the end of the evening nine years before, and when she finished, he nodded.

"So that's what's eating you?" He gave a wry smile. "And you think that something I said when I was mad would make me alter my life, just to have revenge on a girl? My God, you're sillier than I thought." And for a moment she believed him—almost.

She turned toward the rocks to begin the climb to the cottage. Anything to get away from him. She was seething at his manner, the way he had an answer for everything. He had always been the same, arrogant and sure. The only difference was that he now had the appearance to go with it. No longer the shabby boy in baggy hand-me-downs, he was now so well dressed and assured that it seemed to her he could get away with anything he chose. He had already won her mother over. It was a fact Alison had to face. And Rusty too, dear old Rusty. Who next, she wondered bitterly as she scrambled up the rocky track to the cottage. Not Jessie, surely? She shivered, afraid. It would be unbearable to be entirely alone with no one to confide in. Alison had a good friend, Meg, living near Inverness. But even with her it wouldn't be the same, for she could not know of the emotions that had built up over the years—smouldering hatred fanned by all the incidents of childhood now, years later, brought to the point of explosion by this one man. No one could understand, except Alec, and he was too far away to do anything. Married with two children, he worked on a hydro-electric system in Canada's icy north. He would feel like Alison did about his home going to Niall MacBain, especially when she told him that it would be opened as a hotel.

As her fingers scrambled for a handhold on the roughest part of the path, her foot dislodged a stone that went hurtling down. She turned instinctively to shout, but it was too late. She saw the piece of rock land squarely on Niall's hand as he held on to a clump of grass, and then the blood spurted out and she turned away, sick and faint.

At the top, she leaned over to help him the last few feet, but he ignored her hand, whipped a handkerchief from his pocket, and bound it around his wound.

"I'm sorry," she said. "It was an accident."

"Was it?" He gave her a smouldering look and began to walk toward the cottage that was visible through the trees. Alison ran to catch up with him, sick with regret for what, after all, had been a genuine accident, yet stirred to anger by the utter contempt in his voice.

"Yes, it was." She caught up with him at last. "You must have seen me going up. I couldn't have foreseen—"

"Forget it," he cut in, and stopped walking to look down at her. "You've been up that trail often enough to know the dangers of loose rocks and stones, I'm sure. And to know how to avoid dislodging them. Instead, though, you charge up like a child of five, with no sense of danger—"

"If you're so clever," she was stung to retort, keeping her eyes averted from the widening patch of red on the white handkerchief, "why didn't you wait until I reached the top before setting off?"

"Because you looked as if you could fall the way you were going. Better to catch you halfway down than to let you roll all the way."

Alison's eyes blazed back into his, "I would think you'd be only too glad if I had!"

"My intentions are to buy your house, not to kill you off," he replied softly, with ice in his voice. Something warned Alison not to go any further—an inner voice telling her what she already knew, that this man's patience was dangerously near breaking point.

She drew a deep breath, unable to take her eyes from his lean, attractive face. It was slightly pale now, but whether from pain or anger, she did not know.

"Would you like to go back, and see the island tomorrow?" she asked quietly.

"No. Why?" He looked down at his hand. "I've had worse than this. I'll probably survive."

"I have a kleenex somewhere," she began.

"It doesn't matter." He walked on and left her standing there. When she reached the cottage he was walking slowly around it, looking up and down as if picturing it redecorated. Then he went in, and Alison waited.

It was coming to her that she was fighting a losing battle against this formidable man. Wouldn't it be better, she reflected, as she saw him pass a window, if she just let everything happen? It seemed inevitable that the sale would go through. Her mother would be crazy to refuse a cash offer. They had no money to live on if they stayed there, and even a hotel would be better than seeing their once lovely home deteriorate rapidly, as it soon would. Alison loved it dearly, but she wasn't blind to its defects nor did she expect a miracle. This was probably the best chance they would ever have. Maybe when it was finished he would go away, leaving someone else in charge. He was a sailor, they seldom settled easily on land. It might be possible to forget, again. . . .

"I'm going to look around. Coming?" His voice was a harsh intrusion into her thoughts.

Numbly she nodded. He had insisted on her presence. She might as well see it herself while they were there—see what they were losing. I'm growing sentimental, she thought wryly, as they scrambled down through the thick pines, with the strong tangy scent all around them. The path was easier on the south side of the island. She should have remembered that, but her thoughts had been chaotic since his arrival that morning. It was not surprising that she had forgotten the obvious. Alison watched him as he went nimbly down ahead of her, never once looking behind him or offering to help. His back was straight, his shoulders broad. A powerful and determined man, and so vastly different from the boy she had known and loathed, that she could still scarcely believe it. And yet could she not admit it at last? Under the dislike, mingling with it even, had there not been some trace of admiration for such a free, reckless spirit as he? Frightened of nothing, going anywhere he chose and getting himself in and out of trouble the only way he knew—with his fists. Was there not an element of devilry there that had fined down, become tempered in the man? And did it not make him more worthy of attention because of that? Reluctantly, Alison admitted the truth of her thoughts. And knew too, in that moment of revelation, that if he opened a hotel, it would be a good one. There would be nothing second rate for Niall MacBain.

He reached the stony shore and partly turned.

"This way." He set off in a westward direction, and Alison followed. This was perhaps the best side of the island, for from the beach they could see Skye in the distance, with the ghostly gray-blue sweep of the Cuillins, mistily beckoning yet seemingly unapproachable. Alison stood still, looking at them with the sense of wonder that always possessed her.

Niall turned impatiently and she hurried after him. The day was a terrible one, and she wanted to go home. She shivered. He wanted this island, this small wooded piece of land at the mouth of the loch. She felt as if he were trying to take everything away from her; all the security she had known in her life seemed to be crumbling away like fine sand washed by the sea. And soon all they would have left would be the small cottage that had once belonged to the gardener and his family. And the studio—she had almost forgotten that. Why had he made such an apparently generous gesture?

As they came to the jutting rocks on the far west of the island, he stopped and put the binoculars to his eyes as he gazed toward Skye. Alison decided to ask, "Why did you let my mother keep her studio?"

The binoculars wavered, then he turned and looked at her. He lifted a quizzical eyebrow. "Don't you ever try a little subtlety in your cross-examinations?" Alison felt herself go pink, for a gleam of amusement lit his dark face.

"I don't think you appreciate subtlety," she replied, "I haven't been aware of any in *your* behavior so far."

"True," he shrugged, and turned away, lifting the glasses again to his eyes. Then casually he asked, "Do I have to have a reason?"

"Yes, I think you do," she answered, keeping her voice level. "But I can't see what it is."

"No, you wouldn't." He lowered the glasses, and made as if to take them from his neck. "Do you want to look?"

"No, thank you." He was going to tell her something she knew. She wanted no distractions.

"Very well. It's quite simple. Your mother used to be an interior designer. I want her to help me plan the layout and decor of the hotel."

So that was it! Alison gave a disbelieving laugh. "And do you honestly think she will? You must be crazy!"

"You think so?" he answered softly. "Why?"

"Because she feels like I do. She won't want anything to do with you once we've sold Courthill. You must be very insensitive to think otherwise!" she retorted. "And you thought you'd bribe her by letting her keep the studio. When I tell her, she'll throw it back at you!"

"On the contrary," he smiled slightly. It was almost as if he was enjoying himself, and perhaps it should have warned her. "That's where you're wrong. I've already asked her—before I thought about the studio—and she agreed. Your mother, Miss Mackay, is going to be working for me!"

CHAPTER THREE

THAT night, for the first time in years, Alison cried herself to sleep. The nightmare was endless. Niall MacBain, for all his protestations to the contrary, was exacting a subtle and terrible revenge against his family's old enemies. And Alison seemed to be trapped in the middle of a giant web, becoming more tangled with every slight effort to get free.

After Niall's awful words she had walked away and gone back to the boat while he finished his tour of the island. She no longer wanted to speak to or look at him.

When they landed she had gone straight into the house, leaving him to tie up the boat. That too would soon be his, she thought, as she made her angry way to Courthill. She couldn't even face her mother, for she knew she might say things she would regret. Instead she went straight upstairs, after telling Jessie she had a headache and was going to lie down. Something about Jessie's face made her want to break down and cry, then and there, in the kitchen. But she managed to resist.

On Sunday she got up early and packed a picnic lunch. She wanted time alone to think, and the best way was to find somewhere quiet, far away, with only Rusty for company. She got home late, tired but still confused, and went straight to bed.

Her mother, so Jessie told her, had been working all day in the studio.

Next morning Alison breakfasted alone. It was her mother's turn to have a headache. Alison didn't even know how long Niall had stayed on Saturday, or what had been said. She preferred not to know.

As she passed the MacBain house on her way to school, it was the hardest thing to keep looking ahead. It was as if a magnet drew her eyes to the tiny house. The car was standing outside, so Niall was at home. Alison wondered if he had told his father everything, and felt her throat become constricted. How the old man would chuckle! He had always hated them, even more than his four sons did. Revenge must be that much sweeter for him. She blinked furiously, for a sharp breeze blew specks of sand into her eyes, stinging them. Whatever happened, she must not let any of her feelings show in front of the class, for they were bright youngsters, alert to the slightest sign of anything out of the ordinary. She knew that if she wasn't careful, it would be all over town that "Miss" was upset.

She managed to put everything to one side and concentrate on the work. She even managed to run down the hill with the children at lunchtime, so that as she ran through the woods toward home, flushed and breathless, her troubles were nearly forgotten.

Then she saw the car stopping outside the front door as she approached and she slowed down. Niall MacBain got out and opened the car door for Alison's mother, who seeing her daughter said, "Heavens, is it that time already?" and looking at him, added, "Will you come in for a coffee?"

"No, thanks, Mrs. Mackay." He was watching Alison steadily. "I'll get on home. I'm going to Inverness later, and won't be back until Thursday. Is it all right if I come over then?"

"Yes, of course. Goodbye, Mr. MacBain."

Alison turned away and ran up the steps. A moment later her mother followed, and as she shut the door, they heard the car go down the drive.

Before Alison could speak, her mother said, "Why are you so rude to him?" Alison looked incredulously at her. She was watching Alison with a puzzled look on her face.

Stunned, Alison answered: "Rude? I can hardly look at him, let alone speak. He's taking our home away from us, and our island—and you—even you, Mother. You're going to work for him, aren't you? Why, oh, why?"

Mrs. Mackay nodded. "He told you about it. I would have preferred to explain to you myself, but there—" she made a little face. "I'm sorry, darling, but how can I turn down good money?"

"We're not that desperate," Alison muttered. "And there'll be his money for the house—"

"Don't you see?" her mother was genuinely upset. "I love this old place as much as you. Oh, Alison, if I can by my effort and designs bring it to life again, even if it's for someone else it will be worth it. He has the money. I'd be silly to let someone else decide what colors for this room, or the hall or the bedrooms, when I know them so well." She looked around and lifted her arms wide in a sweeping gesture. "Can't you see it all?"

Alison nodded reluctantly, glad that she hadn't approached her before. They would both have regretted it . Yet it was frightening how each of his moves could be made to seem so logical.

"I'm sorry, Mother," she said. "But I just feel as if he's taking everything away from me."

Mrs. Mackay looked at her, and compassion shone in her eyes. "Oh, darling, you mustn't think like that. He's not wicked. There's something very . . . well, nice about him. I can't explain it." She smiled. "Dear me, I'd better not let him hear me. We've been to the lawyer's, by the way."

"I guessed that. So it's definite, is it?" Alison's heart twisted inside her. He had cast a spell over her mother.

"Almost. There are the usual legal proceedings to go through, of course, but they won't take long, two or three weeks at most. And then the house will belong to him."

"And we will leave it," Alison said softly.

"Yes. It will be difficult at first, I know, but we'll soon settle down." She took Alison's arm. "Come on, we'll see what Jessie has for lunch, and then you have to get back to your children."

The week dragged by. On Thursday when Alison returned home from school at four, there was a little man from the County Council going around with a tape measure and notebook. He gave Alison a slow smile and politely tipped his hat, assuring her with grave Highland courtesy that he'd be "no sort of a nuisance at all."

She was sufficiently interested in what sort of plans Niall had for her home that she asked him if she could watch him at work. He seemed pleased at her interest, clearly mistaking it; she left him with the wrong impression, hoping thereby to discover more.

As they went along she got a picture of what Niall had in mind. There was to be no major resculpting of Courthill, in fact he didn't intend to touch the exterior, but inside most of the larger bedrooms were to be divided in half. In each case they had more than one window anyway. A small room on the first floor was to be made into a bathroom, as was one of the attic rooms. The only thing that would show on the outside was a fire escape from the top floor to the ground, but the little man assured Alison it would be at the side of the house and scarcely visible. He spoke knowledgeably of gable ends and gyprock, while Alison nodded and hoped that her lamentable ignorance didn't show.

When he had finished, she saw him to the door. He made it clear that there would be no difficulty in the planning permission coming through, and it was with a heavy heart that she bade him goodbye. Soon there would be an end to their peaceful existence. The place would echo to the sound of hammers on wood and the tramp of heavy boots on bare boards. And it would never be the same, ever again.

She went to her mother's studio and knocked.

"Come in." Her mother looked up, focusing her eyes to the present from the world she occupied when painting. "Has he gone?"

Alison nodded, and her mother smiled at her. "Good. I couldn't bear to stay. Is it . . . is he going to do a lot to the house?"

Alison told her as well as she remembered of the alterations planned for all three floors, and when she had finished, her mother gave a sigh of relief. "Thank God! He's not going to ruin it."

"Did you have doubts?" Alison asked curiously.

"No, but . . . well, one never knows."

"It's still not too late," Alison said quietly.

Her mother looked at her oddly. "You really do hate him?"

"Yes, I do."

Mrs. Mackay's eyes stayed on Alison's face. "I've never seen you like this. I always thought you were too sensible to let a family feud go to such lengths, but I believe you mean what you just said. Why?"

Alison shook her head. Some things went too deep for

words. She could no more have revealed her innermost feelings and fears than she could fly. Even to her mother, warm-hearted, understanding and loving—even to her it was impossible to explain the extreme aversion that she felt whenever Niall MacBain was near. She didn't want to try. Instead she answered, "Maybe it's in my blood, Mother. Like it was in Alec's, remember? Only he could fight it out . . . I can't." She tried to laugh, to make light of it. "Heavens, can you see me having a brawl with Niall MacBain?"

But her mother didn't laugh. She looked down at the paint-covered palette she held, and she spoke softly, as if to herself. "I think he'd be a difficult man to get on the wrong side of. Don't push him too far."

"Are you warning me?" Alison pretended to be alarmed, her eyes wide.

Her mother shook her head, a faint smile on her lips. "Just giving you a motherly word of advice, Alison. I don't want to see you hurt. Men like him can be ruthless. He had a hard childhood, don't forget, and since then he's traveled the world and made money. That's a dangerous combination in any man. I sensed his vibrant power when I met him the other day. It's well concealed, but it's there all right—a hard core of steel beneath the velvet exterior. It's in his eyes and in his face—a remarkable face really, in one so young. I'd like to paint him."

Alison heard a distant bell, the front door, and said, "That may be him now. I'll go see." She turned and went out before her mother could see the effect of her words. They had disturbed Alison deeply, confirming what she already knew about him. He could be a dangerous enemy. But if her mother thought she would meekly acquiesce because of those words, then she didn't know her daughter as well as she apparently knew Niall MacBain, thought Alison wryly.

Jessie had let him in when she reached the hall. She was just saying: "I'll fetch Mrs. Mackay," when she heard Alison and turned.

"It's all right, Jessie," Alison said with a warm smile. Then she looked at the waiting man and removed the smile slowly. "I'll take you to my mother, Mr. Mac-Bain," she said, "if you'll follow me."

"Thank you." He gave Jessie a friendly nod, and Alison turned and started to go back the way she had come, leaving him to follow.

She walked steadily, feeling his eyes on her back and resisting a primitive urge to hit him. She wondered why he always made her feel so breathless, as if she had been running, whenever he was near.

She tapped on the door and opened it. "Go on in, Mr. MacBain."

He looked straight into her eyes and she flinched at the cold grayness of them. But all he said was, "Thank you." He went in and she shut the door, her hand suddenly trembling as she turned the handle. As she moved away she heard him say, "I've just come back from Inverness, Mrs. Mackay. Did someone come . . . ?" His voice faded as she walked quickly out of earshot. Alison knew now, partly anyway, why her mother found him so interesting. His voice just then had been full of warmth and charm. The perfect gentleman, she thought wryly as she made her way through the damp greenness of the conservatory. Perhaps when the house was his, and she was actually working for him, some of the charm might wear off, and her mother would see his true nature. But by then it would be too late. Much too late.

That evening Alison's mother told her that over the weekend Niall wanted to come to the house and take measurements for all the wood and other building materials that would be needed. Alison looked at her, aghast. "And you said yes?"

"Of course. I'm sorry, darling, but there it is. You'll just have to keep out of the way." As Alison nodded her mother added, "Look, why don't you phone your friend Meg? You haven't seen her for ages, and she's always asking you over. See if she and Bill will put you up for the weekend."

Alison looked at her. "Of course! I'll phone her now. It'll be good to see her again," and to tell her all about *him,* and get some of the growing heaviness off my chest, but she added that only inwardly. She prayed, as she dialed the number, that Meg hadn't decided to go camping with Bill and the children that weekend. Her prayers were answered. When she got through, and asked her question, Meg squealed with delight.

"Alison, of course. I'd love to see you. When? Friday evening? What time? And you're coming in the car? I can't wait!"

It was so nice to hear her friendly warm voice and to know that there, at last, she would be able to talk freely that Alison came away from the phone with a light heart, planning what she would wear.

"Alison, he sounds *awful*! A veritable monster!" Meg watched her wide-eyed over the coffee cup she held. She shivered deliciously. "I mean, it's too rich for words. I'm sure you're exaggerating!"

Alison laughed, happy for the first time in a week. It was Friday, nearly midnight, and she and Meg were sitting by the fire in Meg's bungalow on the outskirts of

Inverness. They were both in their dressing gowns and holding coffee cups, while outside the rain lashed mercilessly down. In one of the nearby bedrooms slept Meg's three-year-old twin sons, in another her kind and witty husband, Bill, who had told them as he bade them good night. "I'll leave you girls with your gossiping—and please don't wake me with your giggling, or I might get mad. I'm a tiger when I'm aroused!"

That had started them off laughing at the thought, and somehow it had set the mood for their talk. Strangely enough, in that warm room, Niall MacBain and all he represented seemed so far away that Alison almost felt as if she really was exaggerating. Meg was the ideal confidant. The perfect listener, she never interrupted and had listened agog from the beginning of Alison's tale until she finished with her mother's words of warning the previous afternoon.

Meg leaned over to refill their cups from the coffee pot. Alison watched her with affection, feeling much better than she had ever thought possible. They were both the same age, and had studied at teacher's college in Edinburgh together. Meg had gone to Dingwall after qualifying, Alison to Shielbaig. Meg had been teaching only a year when the handsome young sports teacher, Bill Graham, had swept her off her feet. They had married, although Meg intended to go on teaching for several years. But nature decided otherwise, and within a year of the wedding Alison had been godmother at the christening of their month-old twins. Meg was auburn-haired, calm-faced and, since the birth of her babies, slightly plump, which added to rather than detracted from her pleasant looks. The two friends kept in touch by phone and letter, and many times Meg and her husband had spent weekends at Courthill camping in the woods. They always refused offers of beds in the house, but gratefully accepted Jessie's culinary hospitality, for Bill kept saying she cooked like an angel, and insisted that he only came to eat her fluffy scrambled eggs for breakfast!

Now Meg, having refilled Alison's cup, looked up, a glimmer of light dawning. "MacBain?" Didn't you once tell me something *awful* about him? Something happened after a dance, you know—and he gave a boy a black eye—"

"That's him!" Alison burst out. "The family feud. So you see—"

"But quite frankly, I can't connect the two. Honestly, you remember how we used to talk it over in our room when we were at college, and to me it was almost—well, you know—romantic."

She went a little pink at Alison's disbelieving gaze, and persisted, "Yes, it was. You know, deadly enemies, but he rescues you from the clutches of a veritable wolf then kisses you—" here she fluttered her eyelashes, "I mean, it's the sort of thing we used to love reading about when we were younger. Don't you remember, Alison?"

Alison did. She was silent for a moment, thinking of the pleasure the telling and retelling of the incident had given them both at college. Strangely, seen through Meg's eyes like that, Alison could appreciate her meaning. There *was* a romantic flavor about it. But now—she shivered and pulled closer to the fire.

"Well, Meg, you'd have to see him now to know what I mean. He's utterly different, obviously. There's something about him that's almost frightening."

"Mmm, well," Meg looked severely at Alison. "I can see there's only one thing to do. I'll have to persuade Bill to load up the tent, and we'll sort of mosey over your way and pitch camp for a few nights. Then I'll see for myself."

"Would you? I believe you would!" Alison stared at her, then began to laugh. "Oh, Meg, you do me good. Why don't we live nearer to one another?"

Meg smiled. "Maybe we can arrange to have Inverness moved a little closer to Shielbaig."

The following Monday was cold and wet. The children were fretful, and Fiona Stewart, usually quiet, hit Willy MacLeod with a ruler and started a free-for-all that took Alison several minutes to quell. She sorted out their grievances, discovering that Fiona had caught Willy bullying one of the younger boys and had exacted her own justice. By the time all was peaceful it was four o'clock, and Alison dismissed them, quite sure that the quarrel would break out again once they were away from the school.

She crossed to the window and watched them run helter-skelter down the hill. A man stood aside to let them pass, a familiar figure . . . Alison's heart skipped a beat. It was Niall MacBain, and he seemed to be walking toward the school! He looked up, and must have seen her at the window. She was about to move away almost guiltily, when she stopped herself. She had every right to be there, she decided. And so she waited. It was possible that he was going to one of the two houses that lay past the school. Possible, but highly improbable, for both were occupied by elderly single women who owned lots of cats and rarely spoke to anyone.

Alison stepped back slightly as he looked up again, then chiding herself for silly curiosity, went back to her desk. She tidied everything, found a paper she had been looking for for a week and then stood up. Her coat hung in the corner at the end of a row of pegs. A solitary unclaimed scarf was the only other occupant. She picked up her coat, put it on, and was about to go to the door, when it opened and Niall MacBain walked slowly in.

"May I come in?" he asked.

"Yes," she had to swallow. "What do you want, Mr. MacBain?"

"To talk to you for a minute." He spoke quietly, and Alison looked at the middle button on his jacket, for she knew what she would see if their eyes met and she wasn't ready for that cold look. In a minute she would be, when the shock of his arrival had subsided.

She took a deep breath and slowly met his glance. "I think anything you have to say is better said to my mother. You are dealing entirely with her. I'm sorry."

"No," he shook his head very slightly. "This has nothing to do with Courthill. This is your business. School business."

"I don't understand." Alison's puzzlement showed on her face, and his own face suddenly relaxed its serious expression as he said, "I assure you this is no joke. I've come to see if you have room for another pupil. Have you?"

"Why, yes." She hid her astonishment as well as she could. "There are only seven at the moment. Are . . . are you telling me you want to enrol a child?"

"I am." He stood there watching her, and Alison turned away and went to her desk. She pulled out her large notebook, opened it, and pressed the page flat with her hand. And all the time that she did this, a sense of unreality filled her.

"May I have the child's name and age?" She looked up at him.

"Yes. André Luis Garcia. He's six years old."

She wrote the name and figure six, then said, "And his address?"

"His present one doesn't matter. When he arrives here, he will be staying at my father's home in Sheilbaig, with me."

"I see." She wrote "Shielbaig, Strathcorran, Rosshire." Then she looked up again. "I gather he isn't British. May I know his nationality, and the length of time he'll be here?"

"He is Brazilian. He . . ." Niall paused, and Alison saw and odd expression on his face. He noted the glance, and looked slowly around the classroom. For a moment there was a tense silence, so taut that she feared to break it. Then he spoke again. "He will be staying here for good. This is his new home." His voice had gone harsh, as though it was an effort to speak.

"Thank you." She carefully wrote "Permanent Resident," then, closing the book, said, "I'll have to inform the authorities, of course. When do you want him to start?"

"He's arriving Wednesday. Is next Monday all right?"

"Monday is fine." She bit her lip. "There's something I'd better tell you. The school may have to close after Christmas. There will be only two—or rather three—pupils left. They will have to go to school in Strathcorran."

He nodded. "That's something I'll worry about when the time comes. Meanwhile, he is registered?"

"Yes, he is."

His eyes went around the small room again, with its walls covered by the children's paintings and poems, and their plants on the windowsills. A friendly, homely room, it had changed little since the day 20 years before when he had left it. Even the desks were the same.

Deeply scratched and scarred, they stood square and solid, having withstood battering from dozens of small bodies, elbows, and well aimed ink darts.

Alison wondered if the same memories were going through his mind. At that moment he looked up, and his eyes, fractionally, had lost some of their hardness.

"Well, is that all?" He made as if to move toward the door.

"Yes, it is. Except . . . oh yes, one more thing. I must know André's legal guardian." She leaned over to pick up the book again.

And she waited. For a moment there was silence, then he said, "I am."

She swallowed. "I see," and began to write "Guardian, Mr. Niall MacBain," but even as she finished the last word, he interrupted her.

"Wait, I should have said 'Father,' not guardian. And add 'MacBain' after Garcia. André is my son."

Strangely shocked, Alison said the only, absurd thing she could think of. "I didn't know you were married."

He looked at her, and a muscle moved and tightened in his dark jaw. "Why should you know?" He turned and strode out of the schoolroom.

CHAPTER FOUR

A<small>LISON</small> found herself waiting for Wednesday, when she would see this child, the son of Niall MacBain. He must not have mentioned it to anyone else in Shielbaig, for, although news had gotten around in its usual magical way about the sale of Courthill, nothing was said about him being married with a child. He hadn't mentioned his wife, but that now seemed the logical reason for him to buy Courthill. His father's cottage was very small, only two bedrooms—certainly not big enough for a suddenly expanded family. Alison was curious about his wife. Would she be some exotic Brazilian beauty? She imagined that nothing but the best would do for Niall MacBain. If, too, she were rich, it would account for his apparent acquisition of a fortune. Yet, mused Alison, if she really was an heiress, would she be able to settle in such a quiet backwater town as Shielbaig?

She set out from school toward home on Wednesday afternoon. She was in the car, because the day was heavily overcast. Niall's car had been missing from the front of his father's house since the previous evening. Maybe his wife and son had flown from London to Inverness the day before, and he had gone to meet them and to spend a night there with them before beginning the last stage of their long journey. Maybe he wanted to prepare them. Maybe. . . .

Alison shook herself mentally, and swung into the drive from the road. All this supposition, about a man who had upset her life so abruptly. He didn't matter. She must make him not matter, for if she was to live any sort of normal life in the future, it would be with him as a neighbor. Alison knew that the strange mutual hatred would only destroy her, if she allowed it to. In an odd way, the fact of his being married might help, she thought.

She heard a car's engine, and through her rear view mirror saw his car go past. During that second, it seemed as if he were alone.

By Thursday evening the news was all over the village. The different versions of the story were numerous, and would have been almost funny if Alison hadn't caught a glimpse of the child at the front window when she passed on her way home from school Thursday noon. He was small and pale, a little figure holding onto the curtains as if for protection, wide-eyed, solemnly watching her as she walked past. His face haunted Alison.

When she entered the post office after school that afternoon, a sudden silence fell, broken by Mrs. Finlayson who quite unabashedly called out, "Ach 'tis only Alison. Tell us, is it true that Niall MacBain is married to a Brazilian coffee millionaire's daughter?"

Alison looked at her with genuine amazement.

"I don't know, I don't imagine so," she answered, very conscious that as the future teacher of his child, she shouldn't indulge in gossip. "I haven't seen his wife yet."

"We haven't either," chorused Daisy and Doris, two sisters who lived a few doors away from Fergus MacBain. They always wore pixie hoods, winter and summer, and spent so much time at the front window, that they missed nothing that went on.

"But he arrived with this wee laddie yesterday, and the luggage—" said Daisy.

"—beautiful," said Doris. "All new, with big labels on—"

"—so we got out the glasses, and we could just read—"

"—as large as you like: "RIO-LONDRES. Can you imagine?"

Conversation with them was difficult, for they constantly interrupted each other; but their meaning was clear. The little shop was so small that the village women nearly filled it, and they were all looking at Alison expectantly, as if she would know everything. The reason became obvious the next moment when Doris said: "Didn't he come to see you at school on Monday—"

"—saw him. So he was going to register the child—"

"—and must have told you his name. Is it—"

There was another silence as Doris stopped in mid-sentence, not because of interruption, but because the door behind Alison opened gently, and Niall MacBain eased himself in. Doris and Daisy squeezed past, chorusing their greetings, which he returned quietly. Then Aggie murmured something about seeing to the tea, and Alison was left to order her groceries very conscious of the big, silent man behind her.

She heard the rustle of paper, then the scratch of a pen. Mrs. Finlayson pursed her lips and nodded as if her worst suspicions had been confirmed. Alison wanted very much to escape from the shop, which had suddenly become too close for comfort. As she thanked Mrs. Finlayson and turned to go out, she saw that he was filling out a telegram form. And she remembered the other one.

Outside in the fresh air, Alison took a deep breath. All this speculation was infectious. Because so little ever happened, every new occurrence was talked about and threshed over for weeks. The villagers were getting plenty of tasty morsels to keep their appetites whetted, and Alison, who tried to keep detached from rumor and gossip, was finding herself fascinated with news of the mysterious boy, and the even more mysterious, but as yet invisible wife.

Her mother and Jessie each had heard various versions of the rumors about Niall MacBain. He was divorced, he was widowed, his wife was coming next week, she was a Brazilian film star, an opera singer; the boy was unable to speak a word of English, he spoke it fluently . . . the stories were endless, all conjured up from the fertile minds of a few villagers with too little to do and too much time to talk about others.

It was Jessie who spoke the first sensible words on the subject, of which Alison was rapidly tiring.

"And what," she demanded, as they ate supper together in the kitchen, "will the poor laddie do when school's over each day, and his father's working here? That wife of his had better turn up, or there will be one very lonely boy in that house. Can you see old man MacBain looking after him?" she demanded, looking at Alison and her mother. "He'll be off on that bike of his to the pub in Torrie, come what may. That's all he thinks about these days!"

The two of them looked at one another. Alison was beginning to see that Jessie was right. And the question persisted. If Niall's wife was coming, why hadn't she arrived at the same time as her son?

Alison wondered if Niall would send the boy to school alone on Monday morning. She hoped not, knowing how overwhelming a strange place and new faces could be to a young child.

As nine o'clock came, she looked at the seven shining, expectant faces, and she said, "You all know we have a new boy beginning today. He's a lot younger than most of you, and he's from South America. I hope you'll all do your best to make him feel welcome."

There was a murmured chorus of assent, above which rose Fiona's clear voice.

"I've already met him," she announced, looking around. "He's staying next door, and he's a shy little thing, so I'll help look after him, Miss." As Alison was about to thank her, Fiona added, "He's cried himself to sleep every night since he came."

The words had the strangest effect on Alison. They were like a hammer blow to the heart, hardly bearable. She took a deep breath and said quietly, "He's probably homesick, so we must make extra sure to be kind to him." But inside her heart cried out at the cruelty of an insensitive father to let his child suffer so. How could he? A little boy of six, scarcely more than a baby, to have come alone from so far away to live in a house with two men. No warm feminine arms to comfort him and soothe away the tears; just a cold bed in a small room, and perhaps not even a toy for company.

There was a small stirring of excitement in the class, and Alison looked up as the door opened to see the little boy come in, his hand held firmly in Niall's. The picture they made at that moment so deeply etched itself into Alison's brain that she knew she would never be able to forget it as long as she lived. On the left the small, pale-faced child, dressed in a pullover, short pants and a jacket. Beside him, towering over everyone and filling the doorway, his father, looking toward Alison with no trace of the arrogant power in his features, but almost as if, for the first time, he were human.

She moved forward, her limbs acting mechanically, and as she reached them, held out her hand. "Hello,

André." She waited, hoping desperately that he would respond. He did. His right hand came up into hers, and as she took it, she found herself looking into a pair of gray eyes so incredibly like his father's, yet with a strange defenselessness about them, that it caught her breath in her throat.

He was pale, his hair dark like Niall's but soft and babyish, his nose small and straight, and no smile about his mouth, only the frightened look of a child who is trying very hard to be brave but not quite succeeding.

Something of her feelings revealed themselves, for Niall gave a slight puzzled frown, then said, "Is there anything you have to ask me, Miss Mackay?"

"No, Mr. MacBain. André will be all right here, don't worry. And I'll see him safely home at lunchtime."

"Thank you." He turned to his son, detaching his hand gently, and touching the boy's head. 'Bye, André. Be good." He was gone, moving silently across the room and out the door before Alison could speak or think.

This first morning at school would be vitally important, she knew. The wrong impression now would adversely affect him for the rest of his schooldays. She looked around the class with a bright smile, grateful that she had a nice group of children. Rough though the boys undoubtedly were, they were kind-hearted and living in such a small community there was a kinship about them that was heartening. Alison looked at Heather, who at eight was the nearest in age to the new pupil. "Heather, André will sit next to you—you can move your desk nearer. Fiona, come with me to the stock room, and we'll fetch all the things André needs for lessons."

"Yes, Miss." Both girls stood up, Heather to go over to André and take his hand in a motherly way, Fiona to come to Alison's side.

As she saw the two children walk to the desks at the side of the room, she felt lighter. She had done the right thing, she knew. Heather was a tall sturdy girl with a pretty face and a kind heart. Between her and Fiona there would be friendly rivalry as to who could look after the new arrival best. And both, in their own ways, were adept at lavishing scorn on any boy who might be tempted to bully their protégé.

The morning went well. Alison avoided André, preferring to let him find his ground with the children in his own way. She soon discovered that he was bright and intelligent. He spoke English with a quaint accent, but sufficiently well to make himself understood by the others.

At recess she remained behind in the classroom and watched curiously to see how this small edition of Niall MacBain would mix with the rough older boys. He wisely decided to play safe, and remained with the two girls. Alison turned away, smiling. He was doing well enough for his first morning.

And so his life at Shielbaig school began. A turning point for him, and although she did not know it, for Alison too.

She did not see anything of Niall for several days after that. His car was always outside his father's house at lunch and in the evening, and André seemed, as each day passed, to be settling in better. He even began to smile when the others spoke to him and showed him their playground games. Alison was aware that he was painfully shy, deeply aware too that there was nothing she could do to help, except to try and protect him from the unconscious cruelty of children when they tried to ask him questions about where he had come from.

She said goodbye to him on Friday with a heavy heart, praying inwardly that Niall would let him play with the other children at the loch side on the weekend. He looked as if he needed fresh air and good food to build him up, and Alison knew, from casual remarks made by the other children, that once home from school each day, he wasn't seen out of doors until the following morning.

She told Jessie about this while they sat in the kitchen drinking tea after she reached home that day. Jessie was busy making crowdie, the soft white cheese they loved to eat on jam-covered biscuits at weekends. The old housekeeper looked up from her vigorous beating with the wooden spoon in the basin.

"Ach, you've taken to that bairn, haven't you?"

"I ... yes, I have," Alison admitted, warmly aware that little escaped Jessie's eye.

"Hmph! Considering your feelings for his father, I call that rather strange!" she said.

"My feelings toward Niall MacBain have nothing to do with it," Alison answered. "You'd know why, if you met him. He's a poor little scrap of humanity, dragged halfway across the world on his own, and wanting nothing as much as a woman to cuddle him." She bit her lip, aware that she was giving herself away.

Jessie sighed. "Ach, Alison, I'm sorry. If you could see your face, child! There's only one thing for it, that I can see. You must, for the boy's sake, tackle MacBain when he comes again. Ask him when his wife is coming ... and tell him why."

Alison looked up from her tea, aghast. "Jessie, I couldn't do that! I can barely talk to him without ... why, he'd jump on me like ... oh, no!" She shuddered.

"For the child's sake," Jessie looked at Alison. Some-thing showed in Jessie's eyes that struck an instant response in hers, and they understood one another per-fectly. Jessie, peaceable and good-humored, would, if she saw any injustice, turn into a raging tigress. And in that moment of mutual comprehension, Alison saw the spark that told her Jessie spoke the truth.

She stood up slowly, and she smiled. "Yes, Jessie, I will," she said.

Jessie smiled back. "Aye, that you will," she answered. "And it can be tonight, for he's coming over."

"Why, you—" Alison began to laugh. "You crafty old woman!"

"Me?" Eyes wide with innocence, the housekeeper looked around, as if Alison must be talking to someone else.

Then it sank in. "Why is he coming?" she asked.

Jessie shrugged. "Just a few details to sort out, I sup-pose. The building materials will be arriving next week, and then the work will be starting, once everything is signed."

"First we'll have to move out," Alison said very quietly.

"Aye, that we will. But there is someone coming to decorate the cottage next week, before we move in."

"What?" Alison whirled around. "When was that decided?"

"Ach, I don't know. They talked it over. Your mother is probably wanting to surprise you—so don't let on I've told you, for heaven's sake."

"No, I won't. Don't worry, Jessie." But she felt strangely hurt that all this should be going on without her knowing. It was almost as if her mother was in conspiracy with Niall MacBain, and Alison was gradually being shut out. It was probably her imagination, she knew, but already there seemed a difference in her mother. She walked and talked with new purpose in her, as if she were coming to life again, and Alison knew that it was because of the work she would be doing for him.

When Niall MacBain arrived, Alison was sitting in the living room with her mother, watching television. They heard the doorbell, and she jumped up. "I'll let him in. I want to talk with him a second."

"Alison—" her mother began.

Alison looked at her. "It's all right. It's about his son."

She opened the door to see him standing there, larger than life and very formidable; she quaked inwardly. He would not tolerate interference. Then, as she remembered André's wistful face at the window, Alison found her voice. "Mr. MacBain, before I show you in to the living room, may I have a word with you?"

He came into the hall, his gray eyes looking at her and narrowing slightly at her words. "Yes, what is it?"

"It's about your son," she began. She wished they were anywhere but in the hall. It was so vast. A smaller room would have been less overpowering, but she had begun, and she had to go on before her courage evaporated in the face of his overwhelming hostility.

"You'll think I'm interfering, and for that I beg your indulgence, for I'm thinking only of André." As she spoke, she regained her composure, and met his cold glance with the clear gaze of complete frankness. "It's this. He's so young and so helpless. I wonder if I might ask when your wife will be coming? And also—will you please let him play with the other children after school?"

His face had gradually darkened as she talked, and

when she stopped there was an awful silence. When it was stretched to breaking point, he said softly "Is that all?"

Alison swallowed. "Yes."

"Then I'll take your second question first. André is a delicate boy, not used to playing games. He has been a sickly child, and is just starting to get stronger. When he's more used to school, yes, I will let him play out, for I realize, as you do, the value of fresh air. As to your other question, what reason have you for asking it?"

"If *you* have to ask that," she burst out, "you wouldn't understand when I told you."

"Try me," he suggested, steely hard.

She took a deep breath. "All right, I will. I'm speaking as his teacher now, so this has nothing personal in it at all. Do you understand?"

"I think so," and those gray eyes never left her face for a moment.

"He ... he needs a woman's love, someone to be there, to comfort him when he's homesick, or lonely, as he undoubtedly is at times in such a completely different country. He's little more than a baby to be without his mother, and I—" she paused, blinking back the treacherous tears as she went on, "I heard from a pupil who lives next door to you that he cried himself to sleep the first few nights, and it was like a pain in my heart to hear it, Mr. MacBain. Oh, I know it sounds awfully stupid and sentimental, and men like their sons to grow up tough, but please, he's such a lovely little boy, I can't keep silent any longer." She closed her eyes.

"I believe you care."

"Yes, I do, very much." She could meet his gaze again, in a strange kind of temporary truce. And she saw his lowered glance, as if he was unsure of himself.

"Then I'll tell you. His mother won't be coming. She's dead. She died a short time ago, in Rio de Janeiro. All he has now is me."

The words sank in slowly. As their full impact struck her, Alison gasped, "Oh, no! I'm so terribly sorry. I didn't know."

"How could you? I've told you now only because I believe you are genuinely interested in the boy's welfare. For that I thank you. But you see, there's nothing I can do. He's going to have to grow up the hard way, as I did."

Alison shook her head. "Please forgive me for asking. I'll take you to my mother now." Just before he reached the door, a thought struck her. "What's going to happen when you're working on the house? Who will look after him then?"

He stopped. "I hadn't looked that far ahead. My main concern was to get him here before—" he paused, then went on, "I'll think of something. My father is at home, and there will be other men working here as well as me. I don't have to be here all the time."

"I see." But as she opened the door, she wondered what he had been about to say. "Here's Mr. MacBain, Mother."

"Thank you." He stepped past her and went in, and she moved away. So André was truly alone. Poor child, no wonder he looked so sad and lost. Her arms ached to comfort that tiny frail body.

The building materials began to arrive the following week. A truck was parked by the garage when Alison went home on the Monday afternoon, and two men were unloading wood and bags of plaster. She recognized them as two brothers from Strathcorran and greeted them, wondering if they would be coming to do the work. Alison knew them to be good craftsmen. Niall MacBain,it seemed, knew what he was about.

Jessie greeted her with the words "Your mother's at the cottage. She asked you to go there as soon as you come in."

Alison put her bag down on the rocker. "I'll go now."

She wasn't prepared for what she saw when she reached the cottage, an L-shaped bungalow. The door was open, and, hearing voices, she assumed that Niall was there with her mother. But it wasn't he who stood in the living room with Mrs. Mackay. It was someone she remembered very well from a fateful dance—who was now a man and good-looking in a very different way— Johnny Gordon.

Hiding her astonishment as best she could, Alison went forward. He turned and smiled, then held out his hand.

"Hello, Alison," he said, in his slow quiet voice.

They shook hands, and all she could think of, in that moment of utter astonishment, was, surely this man isn't the wolf that Niall MacBain fought with after that memorable dance? It seemed incredible. Gone was the brash, hot-eyed boy. In his place was a tall, well-built man of about 30, dressed simply in jeans and dark fisherman's sweater. Sandy-haired, blue-eyed, he was tanned and healthy. She smiled back. "Hello, Johnny."

"Johnny is going to decorate for us here," her mother said. "I thought we might talk it over at the house. He can get the paper and paint from Inverness tomorrow."

"Aye, and then I'll work at Courthill next week, with the Cameron brothers. Well, I think I have all the measurements I need." He tapped an old notebook in his hand. "Look through the pattern books I left at the big house and decide what you want."

"You'll stay and have some tea?" Mrs. Mackay asked.

He smiled. "That's very kind of you."

He looked across at Alison, and she saw a spark of something that made her go warm. Her mother said, "Let's go now. You know, I'm thinking this old place won't look so bad at all when it's fixed up."

They walked slowly back, and Alison wondered at Niall MacBain's choice. She knew that Johnny Gordon had his own small business near Strathcorran. He did general building work and repairs, and, presumably, decorating as well. Niall couldn't have known this, for he had been away for nine years. Alison didn't imagine old Fergus was fond of letter writing, which left her with one conclusion. All this had been in Niall MacBain's mind for a while, and maybe he had asked John Stewart, the lawyer, to look around for him. It was almost frightening, as though there were an inevitability about everything. Things were happening so swiftly, too, that Alison began to feel as if everything was slipping past her rapidly. Already, at night, when she went to bed, her head was a whirl of thoughts, ideas, and fears, so that she could hardly sleep. One thing above all disturbed her. More than the fact of losing her home—she was becoming reconciled to that—or her mother's deciding to work for the "enemy," more even than the feud itself and the mutual dislike between her and Niall— overriding all this, one fact was constant. The small, wistful face of Niall's son haunted and disturbed her. She wanted so very much to help him. She could do it only during those few precious hours he was in her charge, and she made the most of them. Gradually, as the days passed, she sensed a response from him, an opening of spirit, like a flower to the light. She wanted so desperately to succeed to have him be a normal happy boy. And she knew she must, for her own peace of mind.

Something was to happen that following week to help Alison in her personal task, though she did not know it.

On Wednesday, Niall took André to school after lunch. Alison had gone back a few minutes early, and was alone in the class, looking through various drawings from the past term's art lessons. She looked up as the door opened and the two walked in. She stood up and went toward them, and as she did so, a strange thing happened. André pulled away from Niall and came to her with a smile.

"Hello, André." She took his hand, then looked up, surprising a rather odd expression on Niall's face. "Yes, Mr. MacBain, is there something wrong?"

It was strange, but at the times when André was with him, they seemed to have an unspoken truce, almost as if they both knew that it was important to tread carefully.

He shook his head, and a slight smile lifted the corners of his mouth. "No, but I have a favor to ask. Would you be good enough to take André home with you at four o'clock? I have to go to the lawyer with your mother. I went to see her this morning, and Jessie told me that she'd look after him until we get back to Courthill."

Something made her answer more hotly than she intended. "I'd look after him."

There was a small silence. Then he said, "I'm sorry, I didn't mean it that way. I imagined you'd be busy after school."

His apology shook her. She hadn't thought him capable of anything so human, nor had she intended answering him so sharply. But she had been stung by the implication that she wouldn't want to take care of André outside of school hours.

"I usually am. But I'm sure André won't be any trouble." She ruffled the boy's hair. "Will you like that, coming home with me and meeting my dog?"

He looked up, smiled, but said nothing. He had the disconcerting habit of occasionally not answering questions, but giving a smile instead. Alison had already decided he understood quite well, but just didn't feel like making the effort to speak. For the moment, she wasn't prepared to correct him. They were learning gradually to get on, she and André, and to understand one another.

"Then that's settled." She looked at his father. "He'll be well taken care of until you return. Jessie will give him something to eat if you'd like. We generally have a light meal at four-thirty."

"Thank you." He turned to his son. "You hear, André? Be good. I'll come for you at Miss Mackay's. Goodbye."

After he had gone, Alison said, "That will be fun, won't it?"

He thought about that for a moment. She had also discovered that he took every question very seriously and weighed it carefully before he answered. Now, after a few seconds' thoughtful silence, he said, "I don't know if I like dogs."

"Oh, I see!" She was relieved. "Well, you'll like Rusty. She's a nice old dog, and very kind to little boys."

He gave that remark some frowning consideration, then nodded, and without another word trotted to his desk and sat down.

The arrival of the other children was heralded by scuffling and muffled laughter as one of them fell outside; then the door burst open, and the afternoon began.

"We have a rocking horse in the attic. Would you like to see it?" Allison was showing André around the house. At her question he looked up and smiled. She took this for assent, and they climbed up the steep attic stairs hand in hand.

She watched his face at the first sight of the huge dappled horse with the brown leather saddle well worn but still showing faint traces of a shine, its eyes as bright as ever, even after years in the dusty attic.

"May I touch her?" André asked, after studying the horse for a few moments.

"Of course. His name is Pegasus." As he made his way over the jumble of years, she added, "You may ride him if you want to."

André stood beside Pegasus for a moment; then he reached out his hand and carefully, very gently, stroked the rough mane that had so fascinated Alison as a child. The horse rocked very slightly, a mere stirring at his touch, and he turned a startled face to her.

"It's all right." She crossed quickly to his side, and pushed the large wooden creature. "See—he goes up and down. Watch."

She climbed on, held the reins, and rocked to and fro as she said, "Whoa, Peg, old boy!" She looked up to see the boy laughing delightedly, his small white teeth like little pearls.

"Oh, she . . . he is good. He is good. I like."

Alison slid off his back. "Then try. I'll hold you."

Gently she lifted him on, a gossamer weight in her arms, put the reins in his hands, and holding him securely, started to rock the horse gently. After the first startled moment when he clutched at her in fright, she felt his small body relax, and eased her hand slightly away. He chuckled with pleasure, making clicking sounds with his teeth, oblivious of her and of everything except the horse. This was a different child altogether from the one she had seen looking out of the window at his grandfather's house. And she knew that Pegasus should belong to him. It would be fitting in a way, for the horse would then remain in the house it had stayed in for more than 50 years.

Something, perhaps a slight sound, made her turn and she started as she saw the movement in the shadows of the doorway. Niall MacBain was watching them. He came in then.

"I didn't mean to make you jump," he said. "I was watching André ride the horse."

"Have you been here long?" She felt slightly confused, as if he had eavesdropped on her thoughts.

"A minute or two, that's all. I didn't like to disturb you."

Alison had to take a deep breath to curb the odd breathlessness that had begun. She looked at her watch. "We'd better go down now. Jessie was making some sandwiches for André."

"Yes. She sent me up to get you." His eyes were very still upon her, very level. She turned and lifted André from the horse. "There now. Did you like that?"

He looked up at her, eyes shining. "I like her very much."

"If your father will let you have Pegasus, he's yours." Alison looked at the man as she said it, realizing that she should have perhaps left it until André wasn't there, in case. . . .

"Are you sure? It must have been in the family for years—"

"Quite sure," she answered. "We won't have room at the cottage. I would truly like André to have it." She looked down at the little boy, and was startled to see tears well up in his eyes. Then suddenly he put his arms up to her, and she bent instinctively to feel them slide around her neck. As she straightened, she lifted him with her. He was so small, but his arms were strong as he squeezed them around her neck, and whispered fiercely, "You are a good lady. I would like very much—" then he stopped, as if remembering his father was there. "*Papa,* may I, please?"

"Yes, André, you may. Say thank you to Miss Mackay."

"I thank you, Mees Mackay."

"You're very welcome." She began to walk to the door, still carrying him. She stepped very carefully over the piles of books and magazines, but André obscured her view, and as she put her foot down hard on a book, it moved slightly with the weight and she lost her balance. Niall moved in that instant of time before she fell—one hand to André, steadying him, the other around Alison's waist. It was only for a moment. She regained her balance and he lifted André from her and put him on his feet at the door with the words, "Down you go."

Alison couldn't have put it into words, nor would she have wanted to, but something changed in that moment. The atmosphere was charged with a tension so brittle that it seemed the air crackled with it. She said breathlessly, "Thank you," and went past him as he stood back in the doorway. She had never been so sharply aware of another person's nearness before, so strongly conscious of the masculinity of the tall powerful figure standing so still beside her. Then she was going down the stairs with André, and it was as if nothing had happened. It had been her imagination, of course. She was tired, she had not been sleeping well lately, not since knowing they were moving. That, and the worry of school. . . . But she knew it wasn't only those things. She had, in that moment of startled awareness, been conscious of an overwhelming desire to have Niall go on holding her. Absurd, of course. How Meg would laugh when she told her, Alison thought. She would put it all into perspective. The poor frustrated teacher who swoons when the parent of a pupil touches her! Alison could imagine her witty interpretation of the situation, and smiled reluctantly to herself. It was funny, really funny—for they didn't even like one another.

It was all settled. The house—her home—was no longer theirs. It belonged legally to Niall MacBain. Johnny Gordon was working in the cottage, wallpapering, painting, and repairing and the wood, plaster and other supplies needed for the alteration of Courthill were stored in the garages at the back of the house. There was a lot of work to be done, but it would be completed eventually. Then the strangers would come, and perhaps part of her would die. It would take months before that happened, and meanwhile she would have to learn to live with the fact. Alison blessed the day she had decided to become a teacher. There was such infinite variety and hard work in teaching even a small number of children that she had less time to brood about Courthill. And there was André. Every day he was creeping further into her heart, and every day she watched him become a little stronger, a shade less dependent on others. She had to stop herself from feeling proud. It was not her doing, it was his own. He was a clever, sensitive child, and knew immediately what was wanted of him. She liked him so much, yet she had to hide her feelings, had to remind herself whose son he was.

Her mother was rarely seen. She was so busy in her studio, designing the layout for the hotel that Alison scarcely saw anything of her. She admitted, reluctantly, to Jessie that it was a change to see her mother so purposeful. She had seen some of the drawings, and they were very good. The hall had been transformed, on paper, into a modern reception area that would do justice to any hotel in the world. As she looked at the drawings, Alison could see the love and skill that her mother was putting into her work. A stranger could not have done nearly so well, however clever.

Jessie agreed with her. It was after school two days later, Friday. They were in the kitchen, Alison with her cup of tea, Jessie busily sorting out drawers for the move the following week. Alison looked around the enormous room and sighed. "Oh, Jessie, he'll have new stoves here soon, and a new sink. It won't be the same place."

"That it won't," Jessie agreed. "Ach, and I would not mind doing the cooking for him!"

"Jessie!"

The old woman began to chuckle at Alison's gasp.

"Well, your mother is already working for him. My guess is he'll find something else for her to do when the place is completed—after all, there is always a lot to do in any hotel."

"But you . . . you'd work for him, here?"

"Aye," Jessie pursed her lips. "Only on a part-time basis, of course. I wouldn't ever leave you or your mother, for we are like a family. But he'd be fine to work for, fair and just."

"How do you know?" Alison asked derisively.

Jessie nodded. "I know! I'm old enough to weigh people up. Yon Niall MacBain is a bonny man right enough. Make no mistake about it."

"You surprise me." Alison looked at her in amazement.

"Aye, well, maybe I do. But it's the truth. And can you not see yourself what he's like?"

Alison pretended to shudder. "Yes, I can. The less I have to do with him, the better."

"And his son?" asked Jessie softly.

"That's not fair!" Alison protested. "He's a child. As far as I can see he's not a bit like his father, except in looks. He's certainly not like *he* was as a boy, thank the lord!"

Jessie looked at Alison shrewdly, then gave a little smile. "That's a fact." Suddenly realizing that she was wasting time, she began pulling out drawers. "This won't get the place empty, will it?"

Alison stood up. "No. And I'd better go and do the same thing in my bedroom. Oh, Jessie, do you think we'll be happy in the cottage?"

"Of course we will." Jessie laughed. "It'll be warmer, and cosier—we won't know ourselves in winter."

Alison smiled. "I hope you're right. And there'll be no guests at Courthill in winter—come to think of it, I can't imagine so many in summer either, yet he seems to know what he's doing—" and as she said the words, an odd expression flitted across Jessie's face, and was gone. Alison stopped, some instinct forcing her to say, "Jessie, what is it?"

The housekeeper shook her head. "Nothing—nothing much."

"Yes, there is. Just now, when I was saying about guests, you looked almost as if you knew something."

"Aye, well, it was just that I was hearin' a wee rumor, that's all." And she turned away, busying herself rummaging in the old knife drawer.

"A rumor about what?" Alison persisted.

Jessie looked at her, "I won't tell you, for it may not be true, and I'm the last one to want to cause trouble. I'm sorry, Alison, but that's that."

And she would not say another word.

The following day Alison found out for herself what Jessie meant. It happened in the shop, where she had gone to buy vegetables and canned food for Jessie. While Mrs. Finlayson was serving her, another woman walked in. Alison recognized her as a niece of Doris and Daisy, named Alice. She lived in Strathcorran and came regularly to visit her aunts. She was a small woman with birdlike eyes that constantly darted about in a disconcerting manner, as if she might miss something. She greeted Alison with, "Well, it's the teacher, is it?"

Alison agreed that it was, and said hello as pleasantly as possible. Alice was nosier than her aunts, and not so harmless.

"Ach well, 'tis a shame you have to leave the big house after all these years. A hotel, is it, that it will be?"

"Yes," Alison said shortly. "Mrs. Finlayson, did I ask you for sugar?"

"Aye, he knows what he's about, that young fellow, does he not? I said to my aunts just now, I said, 'He'll go far, that one.' There'll be good money made with the new road opening, and the skiing too. Fancy it! This old place will be like Aviemore in a few years."

Alison had to put her hand on the counter to prevent

herself from falling. The shock was so intense that she felt herself go white, and heard Mrs. Finlayson's voice as if from a great distance saying, "Why, what is it? Shall I bring you a glass of water?"

"Please." Her lips felt dry. She took the glass and drank thirstily. At all costs she knew she must not show her feelings to these women. It would be all over the village in five minutes. She managed to smile. "Thank you. I had a sudden dizzy spell. I must be anemic." She looked at Alice, and said lightly, "You were saying about the new road. Yes, it certainly will make a big difference here. I didn't think many people knew about it."

Alice smiled smugly. "Aye, well, it's supposed to be a secret, but my brother works for the council, so *he* gets to know these things."

Mrs. Finlayson decided she had been silent long enough. "Aye, and young MacBain would know, for his uncle works in the Highway Department in Inverness and you can be sure he'd pass on a piece of news like that." She smiled at Alison. "You maybe should have held on a little longer. There would have been more interest in Courthill with it being right in the centre of everything. Aye, we'll be busy here soon enough."

Alison managed to escape eventually. In the safety and coolness of the woods on the way home, she stopped and put down her basket. She was trembling with a mixture of shock and rage. Shock at hearing news so startling yet having to hide her natural reaction, and rage with the man who had coolly bought their house from them, knowing that he was practically stealing it. With a new road, and a ski resort planned, its value would at the very least double within weeks of the news getting out.

Oh yes, he had been clever all right, very clever, she

thought bitterly. How he must have laughed all the time he was ushering her mother to the lawyers, and asking her to design the layout. That was to keep her quiet and happy, Jessie had heard, and knowing she could do nothing, had kept quiet. Alison felt almost ill at his treachery. He had certainly had his revenge with a bonus.

Just days ago, when she had been with André in the attic, she had sensed a difference about him, seen another side to his nature. How wrong I've been, she thought. He hasn't changed at all! The years had made him more cunning, that was all. She bent to pick up the basket, and heard his voice say, "I'll take that." Alison whirled about to see Niall walking toward her.

CHAPTER FIVE

ALISON waited for him to reach her. As she watched him, the loathing she felt filled her eyes, and spilled out in tears.

He stopped and frowned. "What's the matter?" And as he spoke he held out a hand to take the basket. She moved it away, and saw his face change. Eyes narrowed, he spoke softly. "All right. You look as if you want to hit me. Out with it." His gray eyes met Alison's challengingly, and she knew that this was the moment of truth.

"I've just heard that there'll be a road coming by here, a major road from the south—a new direct one that will bring lots of people to the new ski resort that's planned."

"Well?" His voice was level.

"Did you know about it?" Alison tried to keep her voice even, but with the greatest difficulty. Then she saw him smile slightly, and clenched her hands on the basket handle to keep control.

"So that's it!" He spoke softly, as if to himself.

"Did you know?" she repeated, her voice rising slightly.

He looked down at her, his eyes very steady on hers. "Maybe."

"Then you stole Courthill from us! You knew, and you let my mother sell it to you at a low price because—" Alison's voice broke, and she felt stifled. "You're no better than a thief!"

She saw the muscles tighten in his cheek, saw the flare of anger in his eyes match her own. But he kept his voice still low as he answered her. "I would choose my words more carefully if I were you."

468

"Why? There are no witnesses to hear us," she spat back. "I'll say what I like to you. You're a cheat! You gambled on my mother's not knowing about the road, and won. She didn't know, so you got the house cheap. Are you proud of yourself?"

"So you think that's what happened? Everything is so clear-cut to you, isn't it? Either black or white, no shades in between. I bought the house, I knew about the road, therefore I'm a thief and a cheat. You haven't called me a liar yet. Did you forget that one?"

She spun around to move away, and his hand shot out and closed over hers, making her drop the basket, which fell to the ground and toppled on its side. He pulled her slightly toward him.

"Don't walk away when I'm talking to you. You started it, remember? Never walk away in the middle of a fight or you'll lose."

"Let me go!" Furiously she tried to pull her arm free, but his grip was like steel. "You're too despicable to speak to!" Her chest heaved with the effort to breathe, and she felt weak. "There's nothing more to be said. The house is yours now, so you've won."

"But I haven't finished with *you* yet," he said. "You seem to think you can make wild accusations about me any time you like with impunity, just because you're Alison Mackay. Get that out of your head right now. I will not be called a thief by you or anyone. Just for the record, I don't tell lies either. I didn't when I was a boy, and I don't intend to start now. I bought your house at a fair price, and if you don't believe me, you can ask your mother."

Something in his tone made her pause in her efforts to free herself. He hadn't denied knowledge of the road, but some assurance in his voice puzzled her. There was no guilt on his face, as there should have been. And then Alison remembered something that she had known subconsciously all along. A faint memory dredged from the mists of the past; childish words said in anger after a fight between Alec and Niall, witnessed by her. Words soon forgotten—except by her.

"You said just now that you never told lies," she managed to get out. "Then something you said years ago, when you were about 11, must also have been true."

"What did I say?" He had not once raised his voice, and it was somehow more frightening than if he had shouted. Yet she had to go on, had to know the truth, at whatever cost to herself and her peace of mind.

Running her tongue over suddenly dry lips, she said, "You told Alec after a fight that Courthill was really yours—that you and your family should be living there instead of us—" she winced, then gasped as his hand tightened on her wrist, and suddenly she was frightened. "Let go of me!"

Abruptly he did so, and she saw the expression, almost of pain, on his face. It was gone in an instant, and his eyes hardened as he looked down at her. "You have an even better memory than I thought."

"What did you mean by it?"

He shrugged. "It doesn't matter now."

"Yes, it does. If—as you say—you never tell lies, then that must have been the truth as you knew it. So what did you mean?"

"I said forget it. It doesn't matter now, because Courthill is mine." For the first time his voice reflected his anger, no longer quiet, but harsher.

For some reason she had touched him where it hurt. And because she still wanted to hurt him, she said. "Then I must draw my own conclusions. I can only assume that we stole Courthill from the MacBains at some time in the past. Perhaps before the feud? Is that it? Tell me—is it?" Her voice had a ragged edge to it, as if she had been running, and the odd breathlessness was back. There was something far deeper than she had suspected here, she knew, and as he turned away, it was her turn to stop him. She reached out and gripped his arm with all her strength. "Answer me!" she cried. She felt the hard muscles under her hand as he turned, and she gasped at the expression on his face. She saw it only for a second, for the next moment everything was blotted out as he bent and kissed her with brutal hardness. She was too stunned to move, then realized what was happening and pushed him away.

"How dare you do that!" she gasped. This had happened before, in nearly the same spot, nine years ago— but what a difference! Then his mouth had been boyish, the kiss clumsy and breathless. Now, a hardness, a taste of the experience that had gone into the years between, left her feeling weak and confused.

"That's all the answer you'll get from me," he said. "And what have you got to say to that?" His voice had lost its quietness; he spoke more quickly, and Alison suddenly realized that the kiss had had more of an effect on him than he had intended. His eyes went darker, shadowed, and as he stood watching her, the air seemed to crackle with electric tension. It was all around them in that cool green light, the trees silent witnesses to a kiss that had been a surprise to both of them.

"If that's the way you deal with questions you don't like," she said shakily, trying to dispel the tension, which was making her terribly uneasy, "it must make life very difficult for you. Don't ever do it again," she took a deep breath, "or you'll be sorry."

"Threats?" he asked, and a muscle twitched at the corner of his mouth. "I react differently to threats than most people. To me they're a challenge—you might do well to remember that, Miss Mackay." His eyes flickered down to the basket which still lay on the ground. He bent down and picked it up, then handed it to her. "I don't offer my help twice, either." And he strode off toward Courthill, leaving Alison standing there. Her heart thudded rapidly, and she was more confused than ever before. She had the obscure feeling that she had just lost an argument.

And so the work began at Courthill. They planned to move the following Wednesday, the day after Johnny finished decorating. He had done a good job, inside and out, and the white walls of the cottage gleamed in the afternoon sun as Alison walked to it on Tuesday after school. The front door was open and she went into the small hall. The smell of paint still lingered in the air, even though Johnny had left all the windows open. The large living room was to her left. This, with pine walls and ceiling, had been left as it was, the beauty of the wood brought out by Johnny's skilful polishing. The kitchen, on the other side of the living room, gleamed warm honey gold; through the window was a breathtaking view of the loch. The cottage was L-shaped, so Alison had the same view from her bedroom window. She smiled to herself, wondering what Rusty would make of the move. She decided to move the dog's basket into her room for the first few nights.

"Anyone here?" It was a man's voice, and she stiffened, fearing Niall MacBain. She hadn't seen him since Saturday, she didn't want to see him, and the fact that he had paid to have their new home decorated only added fuel to her burning resentment. Her mother was delighted and had expected Alison to be equally impressed. She can't see his motives as I can, she thought. Even when Alison tackled the subject of the new road with her mother on Saturday evening, Mrs. Mackay had insisted that all Niall's actions had been fair and above board. The road wasn't definite, it was all very much a gamble whether it was ever built, and everyone knew they took years to actually *do* anything, she had argued. Clearly, he had hypnotized her well. Alison gave up and went to bed, seething with anger.

Now she turned and saw with relief that her caller was Johnny Gordon.

"I was admiring your work," she told him. "You've done a wonderful job. Especially here." She waved her arm around at the kitchen, where the smart white cupboards and gleaming sink were ready for them to move in. He grinned and looked at her, and what she saw in his eyes made her suddenly warm. She knew that gleam of masculine admiration when she saw it—and something more—but she was no longer a foolish teenager and it didn't bother her. He spoke quietly, never taking his eyes off her.

"Aye, it's not bad," he admitted, and Alison wondered why she had thought that he was changed the other day. It was still there all right, but more subdued—perhaps more dangerous. She might have to watch Johnny Gordon, she decided. He was no longer a boy.

"You're moving in tomorrow, Alison?"

"Yes. If I could get the day off school I would, but it's impossible. There's no supply teacher for miles."

"Well, the Cameron boys will be here, and me. We'll

bring everything over for your mother. And the furniture staying at the big house for use in the hotel will be stacked in one of the bedrooms that's not having any alterations done."

Alison bit her lip. When her mother had told her that Niall wanted to buy their surplus furniture, she had had mixed feelings. It seemed on the surface an ideal solution, for seeing it sold at an auction would have been heartbreaking. It was old and solid and good, and wouldn't fetch anything close to its value. Now, that wouldn't have to happen. Yet it seemed as if he were taking more and more all the time, taking everything she knew and loved for his own.

"So I might come home from school to find the work all done," she said lightly, forcing a smile. He wasn't so easily fooled, though, for he gave her a shrewd look.

"Aye, that's true. It will be a jolt for you, living here I mean, instead of Courthill."

"We'll get used to it." She opened a cupboard door. "Jessie will find it easier, I imagine. The other kitchen is enormous."

He nodded. "That it is. Well—" he looked at his watch, "I should get going. We'll be starting early in the morning. The sooner everything is moved out, the sooner we can begin the work there."

"Johnny," she said, and he turned slowly. "How did Niall MacBain come to ask you to work for him?"

"Mr. Stewart arranged for all of us. Didn't you know?"

"I know very little of his plans," she answered, and there was a trace of bitterness in her tone.

She saw him glance sharply at her before saying "So it's like that, is it?"

"Like what?"

He shrugged. "Och, word gets around. The feud's never been forgotten around here. People have long memories, you know."

"I've lived here all my life, Johnny. I know."

"They say he's changed. They say he goes all out to get just what he wants."

Alison shivered. So it wasn't only her. "And what do you think?"

Again the shrug. "I think they're right. But he's a good man to work for, I'll say that. There's no nonsense with him. He tells you what he wants doing—and he expects it to be done." He paused, then added, "He's paying me well. He'll get a good job done by all of us."

"I'm sure he will." Alison began to walk to the door. "Will you come home for a cup of tea before you go?"

He grinned suddenly. "I was hoping you'd ask."

They began to walk back to the house, Johnny beside her as they went through the tall thick trees. So lost in thought about the move was she that she didn't look where she was going, and a jutting twig caught in her hair as she passed it, jerking her to a standstill as she gave an exclamation of surprise.

Johnny turned and saw her predicament. "Stay still," he ordered, and pulled the offending twig free. "You should look where you're going," he told her, amused, and put his hand to her hair. "Mind now, your hair is full of twigs and leaves—you'll be full of tangles."

But he seemed to be taking his time, and Alison moved away with a laugh. "I'll manage," she said. For she guessed what was in his mind, and she had already had enough trouble in the woods; she wanted no more.

He caught up with her and touched her arm lightly. "Did you think I was going to kiss you?" he asked, in a curious voice.

"Not at all!" Alison tried to sound astonished, but kept on walking.

He began to laugh. "Well, I was. So don't say you've not been warned. I may try again."

"Will you now? Thank you for telling me." As they came in sight of the house, she added "I'll have to keep out of your way, won't I?"

"Will you?" He gave her a slanting sideways look. "No, don't do that, please, Alison. You're one of the reasons that I took the job."

"Oh, really, Johnny!" she burst out in amused disbelief.

"It's true! I wanted to see what you were like, after all these years. Och, I've seen you, yes. But only from a distance, never to speak to. And I'll never forget that night of the dance—"

"No!" she whirled around on him. "Don't mention that. It's one night I want to forget."

He backed a few inches, pretending alarm. "Hey, I'm sorry—" His eyes became wary. "What did he do?"

"Niall? Nothing! Why do you ask like that?"

He grinned reminiscently, and stroked his jaw. "Because I followed you, hoping for a kiss, and got a punch on the chin for my pains. Perhaps I have a right to ask."

Alison tried vainly to keep her face straight. "I'm sorry, Johnny, but it was your own fault." Laughter bubbled through. "He ... he'd only come to poach trout!"

"That's not what he said to me."

Suddenly sobered by something in his voice, Alison stopped laughing. "Why, what did he say?" she asked.

He looked at her almost regretfully. "Och, it doesna' matter. It's too long ago—"

"Then tell me . . . please."

"He said, 'She's mine, boy, not yours—mine.' And I shall not forget the look on his face when he said it, ever."

Those strange words of Johnny's and the way he'd said them came back to Alison the following night. It was late, and both her mother and Jessie had gone to bed exhausted after the move. She looked around her new bedroom, and Rusty, from her basket in the corner, looked up and thumped her tail sadly as if in sympathy. Alison swallowed hard, wondering if she would ever sleep. The room was so much smaller than her old one. Brightly decorated with a sprigged paper she had chosen herself, it gleamed in the overhead light, and it wasn't home. She switched off the light and went to the window to look out over the still black waters of the loch. Nothing moved; everyone was long since in bed and asleep. A white moon rode high in the sky, and Alison turned to Rusty. Only the soft gleam of her eyes betrayed where she lay and watched her mistress.

"Rusty, do you want to go out?" The magic word sent her up and quivering for action, and Alison laughed. "Come on, girl, let's take a little walk by the loch."

They crept quietly out, like two thieves in the night, and Alison left the door ajar so as not to disturb the others on their return.

It was cool, and she reached into the closet and lifted the nearest jacket from a peg. Old and worn, it smelled of heather and tweed and fish, evoking instant memories of childhood fishing trips. She slipped it on as they went down the narrow path to the water's edge. Rusty, pleased at this unexpected treat after what must have been, to her, a very puzzling day, ambled along sniffing without much hope for rabbits. At the water's edge Alison sat down on a giant stone and waited for the peace and stillness to transfer itself to her. She needed something that would soothe away the restlessness of the day, and as they sat there, the calm and tranquility reached her. She looked around.

The loch was beautiful by day. Now, with the night upon it, it was breathtaking. The hard, clear moon bathed everything with its cold unearthly light, lending a shimmering beauty to the water and etching the trees in stark blackness against the backdrop of the sweeping hills. Everything was contrast—deep, deep shadows, ghostly whiteness. And the only sound was the faint shush of the water, so near that Alison could reach out and touch it if she wished. She sat and looked, and knew that, whatever else happened, nobody could take this away from her. This she would have, locked away in her heart, for the rest of her life.

It was time to go. It was gradually getting colder, and the jacket was too old and worn to give much warmth. Alison stood up and called Rusty softly. The dog ambled to her side. As she started walking, she found they were heading in the direction of Courthill.

"Why not?" Rusty looked up startled as she said the words aloud. One last look around, with the house empty and waiting, might be what she needed to shake herself out of any self pity. Just one last look to say goodbye as well. After tomorrow it would never be the same again.

Gently, footsteps quietly crunching on gravel, they

made their way along, and Courthill loomed up gray and ghostly in the moonlight. The windows, cold and yellow, caught the reflected light with blank expressionless eyes. It looked deserted, as if they had run away and left it alone. Alison walked up the steps to the front door, which opened at her touch. They walked in, and the door creaked slightly, a lonely sound. The bare boards looked dusty in the gloom, and Alison walked quietly across and opened the living room door. Here the moonlight slanted in, showing the shabbiness and emptiness starkly. Something had gone with the moving out of the furniture, some spirit that had kept the house alive.

It was like an empty shell. She looked at Rusty, and then knelt and buried her face in the dog's fur.

"Oh, Rusty," she whispered. "It's not ours any more." Rusty whined softly, and her tail drooped. Hot tears filled Alison's eyes, and spilled out into the dog's golden coat as she held her. She should not have come, she knew. It had been a mistake to return. It was all over. The memories came jostling then, of Niall MacBain's words so long ago, words that he had tried to pretend didn't matter the other day—that the house should really be his. And now it was. And after that came the other more recent, even more painful and puzzling memory: what Johnny had told her of Naill's words to him on the night of the dance. They had meant nothing, said by a youth as an excuse to fight, and yet somehow they had been frightening, almost prophetic—almost as if. . . . She held her breath, shocked at the thought of what Niall might have intended Johnny to think, then she closed her eyes in despair.

It was best forgotten now and put to the back of her mind with all the other memories.

"Come on, Rusty." It was time to go, and this was goodbye. Unsteadily she rose to her feet, and then Rusty growled low in her throat. Alison froze as she heard the soft opening of the front door, footsteps across the bare board in the hall—

"What on earth!"

Her first thought was, *how absurd that he always turns up just as I'm thinking about him!* The thought was followed quickly by revulsion.

"I'm just going," she said coldly. She wished that she hadn't been crying, but at least he couldn't see.

"Come on, Rusty." He stood in the doorway, and she could see him only hazily because of the shadows and because her eyes were sore from weeping. Then, as she saw him reach out a hand toward the switch, she said "Don't . . . don't switch it on, please."

His hand paused, he let it fall to his side, and perhaps he guessed, for he said more softly, "I wasn't sure if they would work anyway."

"Oh no . . . yes, I mean," she stammered. "They're coming to read the meter tomorrow." She went toward him. "Excuse me."

"What's the hurry?"

His voice held a note of grim amusement, as if he knew, and she answered, "I can't stay."

"Can't—or won't?"

She began to experience that odd breathlessness again, almost a feeling of claustrophobia. It made her angry—with herself mainly, but with him as well, for it was as if he had a measure of control over her actions, and she resented that. She snapped, "It doesn't matter, does it? I'd just like to get off *your* property."

"Then why come on it in the first place?" he asked quietly.

"I don't expect you to understand, so I don't intend to explain. Will you please let me pass?"

"In a minute. I came to see if everything was locked up. There's a band of gypsies camping by Donnie's Barn, with some rough-looking ones among them. I thought maybe it would be safer to lock the door in case one of them was out looking for rabbits."

"Then lock up. I'm going."

"I'll walk back to the cottage with you."

Alison moved away quickly, not knowing why. "I'm not afraid of the gypsies. They're harmless enough," she said.

"Are they? Have you met any at night?"

She laughed. "No, and I won't now. Anyway, I'd feel safer with them than with *you*." And she went past him, pleased with her parting shot, clicking her fingers for Rusty to follow. As she ran down the steps, she saw the light go on, and turned her head to see him standing in the middle of the room, hands in pockets and looking around as if he was thinking. The encounter, plus the shock of his sudden arrival, had left her feeling weak. And she disliked him more than ever. What's the matter with me, she wondered. She wasn't normally so childish, yet with Niall MacBain it was as if she was constantly on the defensive. Alison recalled again the words Johnny had told her. They must have been deeply etched on his brain that he hadn't forgotten them. Niall MacBain, who never told a lie, had said them. He had taken everything else from her. In a curious, cruel way, she could almost believe that he would want her too. There he would be thwarted. Alison vowed silently that she would not allow him to touch her again, ever.

The days passed, and the cottage began to seem almost

like home. The weather was bad, and as the men were working inside the house, there was little to be seen. Niall was there with them every day. Sometimes he got home in time to greet his son, and sometimes old Fergus had to look after him. It distressed Alison to think of him being alone in the house with the old man—not that she imagined he would harm André. Rather, he was morose and spent his days checking the racing results or walking to the phone booth to call a bookmaker. She felt sure André would be lonely. It was too wet to play outside. The fine misty Highland rain, more penetrating than a downpour, had been coming down for days.

One particularly bad day made Alison decide. She stopped outside Niall's home and looked at the boy beside her. Niall's car was gone, a sure sign he was out.

"If your grandfather will let you, André," she told him, "you may come home with me."

He looked at her, and some of the silent misery went from his eyes. "I will ask her?"

"Yes. 'Him,' André, not 'her.' Go on now."

She watched him slip in the open door, and waited. Alison had never spoken to Niall's father in her life, but she was shrewdly aware that he would allow her to look after his grandson if it meant a bit of peace for him.

A few moments later the boy ran out and got back in the car.

"She—he says it is all right. My daddy is at the big house. I may go."

"Fine." Alison started the car.

Her first task was to let Niall know where his son was, to save him a fruitless journey home. She stopped the car by the back door of Courthill and, telling André to wait, she went in.

It was strange to see the kitchen bare, without Jessie working away, and all their possessions gone. The only evidence of occupation were milk bottles, glasses and sugar on the bare table.

Faintly she heard a tuneless whistle, and even more distantly, the sound of hammering. She went into the hall and called "Anybody here?" The whistling and hammering stopped; then there were footsteps, and Johnny appeared at the top of the stairs, wearing plaster-covered overalls. He began to walk down, his heavy shoes clattering on the uncarpeted stairs.

"Hello, Alison. Did you want something?" his smile was pleasant and warm.

"Hello, Johnny. It's your boss I'm after. Is he here?"

"Och, him." He nodded behind him. "Aye, he's away up in the attic. Can I give him a message for you?" He stood at the bottom of the stairs very close to her, and Alison was strongly aware of his eyes upon her. She smiled at him. He was good-looking, nice and so different from the brooding man who had taken over her home that he seemed, in contrast, positively delightful. And one more thing her instinct told her. He was very much attracted to her. It was useless to try and ignore it, for he made it very clear. There was nothing wrong, she told herself, in enjoying it and basking a little in the warmth of a masculine smile.

Then a strange thing happened. Johnny had a smear of plaster on his forehead, and a trace of it over his eyebrow. Alison blinked and lifted her hand. "Stay still," she said, and brushed it away. As she started to take her hand away, he put his own over hers.

"Thank you," he said softly, and bent to kiss her palm. She was about to pull her hand away when a movement caught her eye and she saw Niall appear silently at the top of the stairs. Suddenly, on an impulse she couldn't explain, she stopped resisting, and as he kissed her hand, laughed lightly and looked up. She caught sight of Niall's face, and drew her breath in sharply. Anger flowed out of him in almost visible waves—and she suddenly remembered that other time so long ago.

Then he broke the sudden silence. His voice was quite calm and level, deceptively so, for Alison seemed to detect a ragged edge of anger in it.

"Did you want me? I saw your car."

Johnny turned slowly, realizing they weren't alone, and she answered "Yes. It was such bad weather, I brought André here with me."

"Thank you. I hadn't realized how late it was. I'm sorry." Everything was well under control again.

"He'll be safe at the cottage until you want him. Your father knows."

"Right. If you're sure—if he's any trouble, bring him over, I'll mind him here."

"He won't be." Alison turned to Johnny, and saw the spark in his eyes as she smiled at him and said "If you'd like to come over in a few minutes, I'll make you all a pot of tea."

"Och, that will be fine. All right with you, Niall?"

Niall nodded, then vanished, and Alison realized something at that moment that gave her an indefinable sense of well being.

That innocent, harmless gesture of Johnny's had made Niall angry. Alison didn't know why, yet it was true. He disliked her, yet he objected to the other man's mildly flirtatious action. As she went out through the kitchen, she smiled to herself. If she was right she had a weapon—a small one, but a weapon for all that—in her battle against the loathed intruder. She liked Johnny, and there would be no harm in flirting a little with him. His cast-iron heart was virtually indestructible, if the various village girls that Alison had gossiped with at different times were to be believed. As she ran out to the car, she thought of Meg. How she would enjoy hearing about it all! Alison began to hope that she and Bill would come up soon to Shielbaig. Meg would appreciate the slight tinge of irony so well.

Somehow, imperceptibly, it slipped into a routine, Alison's bringing André home every day. She didn't mind at all. Nor did Jessie or her mother, who both liked him in their own different ways. Jessie had decided when she had first met him, that he needed fattening up—and had set out to do just that. Both Mrs. Mackay and Alison had to admit that it showed results. His thin cheeks grew plumper and more colorful, and he enjoyed her fussing. Her mother constantly sketched him in her spare moments, thought his bone structure was "superb" and determined to paint him when she had time. Alison just watched, knowing yet not daring to admit, that she was growing to like him a little more with each day that passed. She hated herself for her weakness—it could only lead to unhappiness when the inevitable separation came, as come it would—yet she could not deny her feelings, which were matched only by her dislike for the person closest to André—his father.

Another problem approached—the holidays. For six weeks the the school would be closed, and André would be alone, for Niall was now working hard every day at Courthill and certainly could not spare the time to look after his son as he should be looked after. Alison mentioned her fears to Jessie on the Thursday before school finished. André was outside in the garden, throwing a stick for Rusty to retrieve—without much success, for although the two were now good friends, Rusty made it plain that collecting sticks was beneath her dignity.

"Well, child, what do we do?" Jessie asked, busily making sandwiches for the workers. Since the day Alison's encounter with Johnny had so displeased Niall, Jessie had kept the men supplied with hot lunches, and tea and sandwiches at four-thirty. Niall insisted on paying for this service, saying that it saved them a lot of time, which it undoubtedly did. Yet Alison felt slightly uneasy about it. It was one more small encroachment into her life. Jessie enjoyed looking after them. She liked both Johnny and Niall, and Alison, having seen the way they behaved toward her, knew why. She had come in late for lunch one day, and was at the kitchen door before she realized that Jessie wasn't alone.

As she was about to go in, she heard Niall's voice, "You cook like an angel, Jessie. If only I were twenty years older—" and Jessie's rejoinder, tart, but with that slight hidden laughter Alison knew so well. "Ach, away wi' your flattery!" She had gone in then, obscurely angry, and had seen Jessie's sparkling eyes as she had handed Niall the lunch. They had both looked around, and the smile had slowly vanished from Niall's face at the sight of Alison.

He'd nodded, said coolly, "I'll go now. Thank you, Jessie," and had gone. Alison came back to the present to realize that Jessie was waiting for an answer.

"What will we do?" she shrugged. "What can we do? You know I'd love to have him here, but—"she stopped and bit her lip, unable to finish.

"Aye, I understand." Jessie's eyes were kind as they

rested on her. "It's difficult for you. Still, if your mother or I were to suggest we'd have him—"

"Would you?" Alison's face gave her away.

Jessie nodded slowly, "I will. Alison, you mustn't let yourself get too fond of the boy, you know—"

"You don't need to tell me. I've already worked that one out for myself. How can I be like this, Jessie, tell me? Hating his father so, and yet with André—oh, I don't know." She leaned on the table and put her hand on her chin. She sighed heavily.

Jessie's blue eyes were bright with concern, and something more that Alison didn't understand. "Are you sure?" she asked softly.

"Sure of what?" Alison was puzzled.

"That you really do hate Niall MacBain. Hate is a very strong word, you know."

"Then dislike intensely will do. Yes, I am sure." She looked up at Jessie, startled, as the meaning sank in. "What exactly do you mean?" she added slowly.

Jessie gave a small shrug and busied herself cutting the sandwiches. "Ach, well, never mind, just an old woman's fancy. Only—" she stopped and pursed her lips.

"Only?" Alison asked suspiciously, and something in the air brought a catch to her breath. "Tell me, please."

"Well, it's just that—I don't think Niall dislikes you quite as much as you try and make me believe—"

Alison gave a disbelieving snort, but Jessie went on, "No, it's true. One day he came in to return the tea things, and you were playing in the garden with André."

She paused, and Alison said, "Go on."

"And he went to the window and watched you, and I saw—"

"Yes?" Alison could hardly breathe.

"I saw the expression on his face. He didn't look hard any more. He looked almost gentle." Jessie gave a little smile. "And he looks very nice when he's gentle."

"It was André he was looking at," said Alison firmly.

"No. That's what I thought, until I went over to the window. He was watching you."

"Then he must have had a mental blackout," she said cruelly. "He loathes me as much as I do him, Jessie. Believe me, the feeling is mutual." But something had stirred inside her at the words, something she could only suppress, and bury in the farthest recesses of her mind. I don't want him looking at me at all, she said inwardly. Gently or otherwise.

Jessie finished the sandwiches and slipped them into a large plastic bag. Then she picked up the teapot, and Alison said, "I'll take them over."

"But—" Jessie's eyebrows nearly vanished in surprise.

Alison laughed, back to normal again. "I'll give them to Johnny or the Camerons. I like Johnny." She picked up the things before Jessie could say any more.

There was no need to call out when she went into the hall at Courthill. Johnny was coming down the stairs as she pushed the door open.

"I was just coming over," he said. "Here, let me take that heavy teapot." And he reached out and took it from her hands.

"Where are the mugs?" she asked.

"In the kitchen. I have a notion they need rinsing," and he looked hopefully at her, making Alison grin.

"All right, I'll do them."

"Come on, then." He strode off and she followed. She could hear distant hammering from upstairs, and wondered how the work was going.

As they reached the kitchen, she said, "I'll help you carry these up. I'd like to see how much you've done."

"That will be a pleasure," he smiled slowly, watching her as she carried the mugs to the sink. "I'll show you around."

Alison returned them to the table, while he added milk and sugar and asked as he did so "Are you going to the games next week?"

"I wouldn't miss them for anything. And you, Johnny, are you going?"

"I am. There's a dance afterward. You haven't forgotten that?"

Alison smiled. "No." She knew suddenly where his questions were leading. To give herself time, she said "What are you entering for?"

"The field hockey match for one, of course. We're a player short. What sort of shape are you in?"

She shook her head, laughter bubbling. "No, thanks! I played it once and was covered in bruises for weeks after. That's one game I prefer to watch."

He smiled, his eyes never leaving hers. "I was only joking, Alison. It is too rough. But you'll maybe go in for something?"

"Maybe. I usually do. I have seven small supporters, even if I don't win anything."

"Then you'll have another," he took a sip from his glass. "Unless I'm in the same race as you, of course, in which case it's every man for himself! And the dance—you'll save some for me?"

"All right," she smiled. "If you want."

"I do want." He picked up two glasses and the package of sandwiches. "Let's go, or I might forget my promise."

As they went to the door she looked at him, bewildered. "Promise?"

"My promise to myself. Not to kiss you without invitation."

"Oh!" She went through the door first, saving herself the necessity of hiding her grin. It seemed that she would have no need to maneuver Johnny into anything if she wished to test her theory about Niall MacBain. In fact— and the thought came to her suddenly, startlingly—he was already well ahead of her. She would have to be very careful not to burn her fingers, she decided, playing with that fire.

CHAPTER SIX

NIALL was working with the Camerons on the first floor. Alison and Johnny brought the tea and sandwiches in to them, and she looked around at what had once been the largest bedroom, the one shared by her parents until three years ago. Now it was different.

Devoid of furniture, it looked very bare; a dividing wall made it into two rooms. The walls were stripped of wallpaper, and had a curiously naked air. The elder Cameron, Laurie, was smoothing plaster over the newly bricked fireplace, while his brother Ian burned paint off the window frames with a blow torch. They looked around as she entered, and stopped work to greet her with shy nods.

When Johnny called out to Niall, the hammering from the next room stopped and he came in, running his fingers through his thick black hair.

"Hello," he said briefly, then seeing what she had brought, "Thank you."

Before Alison could say anything, Johnny asked him, "Can I show Alison around? She'd like to see our work."

Niall moved toward the tea, then looked at her, his glance devoid of expression. "Of course. Watch the door to the kitchen upstairs. It needs tightening."

"I will. Come on, Alison." As he went through the doorway, Johnny's hand rested for a moment at her waist, as if to guide her into the corridor. Alison wondered, childishly she knew, if Niall was watching.

They went up the stairs and into the first attic room off the small narrow corridor. She stood still and looked around, seeing it empty for the first time in her life—

empty except for Pegasus, the old rocking horse that now belonged to André, draped with an old sheet in the corner. Without the rubbish that had filled it for years, the room was larger.

Here again the walls were stripped bare, the fireplace was bricked in and plastered, and the windows were devoid of paint. Alison looked at Johnny. "It's so different somehow," she said.

He nodded, and gave a little smile. "Aye, it is. Wait until you see the rest." He took her arm. "Come and look."

Dazedly she followed his lead into the other rooms. It was the last one which showed the most startling change. They had just come out of the fourth attic room, already almost transformed into a bathroom, when Johnny carefully eased open the last door and said, "This is the kitchen."

Then Alison realized. As she looked around the room, now with sink unit, built-in cupboards and cabinet, she asked. "Is this where Niall and André are going to live?"

He nodded, looking at her coldly. "Aye. Didn't you know?"

"No. I thought . . . I imagined he might let someone else manage it for him—"

"Ach, no. He'll run the place himself all right. This floor is self-contained. He'll have a baby-sitter for André, to live in—" her head shot up involuntarily, and anxiety flared in Alison as she thought of Jessie "—and he'll be downstairs looking after the guests. I think he'll put this place on the map."

He paused, then added quietly, "And whether that's a good or a bad thing remains to be seen."

"Well he should have no trouble when the road's built," she said. "Look at Aviemore."

"It's not definite," he watched her as if slightly puzzled. "It's little more than a rumor, and you know how long anything takes up here."

Alison looked around. "It doesn't seem to take him long to do anything."

"That's true." He began to laugh. "You hate his guts, don't you?"

"Do I make it so obvious?"

He shook his head, his smile dry. "No, but I'm perhaps more sensitive where you're concerned. I like him—in spite of the fact that he beat me up years ago—over you." The last two words were so softly spoken that she barely heard them. She looked at him, a brief flare of anger sparking in her eyes.

"I asked you not to mention that again."

He put up his hand as if to ward off a blow. "Whoa, sorry," he gave a low whistle. "My, but you're pretty when you're in a temper!"

"I am not in a temper," Alison said very slowly.

"No, of course not," he grinned. "I never argue with a lady."

"Oh, Johnny," she was unable to hold back the smile, "you're incorrigible!"

"If I knew what that meant, I might feel insulted, so I won't ask." He held out his hand. "Come on, I'll show you what we've done downstairs."

"I'll follow you in a minute." Something had just struck her about all the cupboards, and she wanted to examine them more closely.

"Then I'll drink my tea before it gets cold." He went out, and added, "Watch the door."

"I will," but she wasn't really listening. She was crouching down by the long row of superbly finished cupboards with sliding doors. Gently she pushed one open, and it slid smoothly along the groove. Alison moved her hand down its surface, admiring the craftsmanship that had gone into them. Then she knew what had made her pause. There was no maker's label anywhere, and she wondered if Niall had made them himself. He had always been at the top of the class in wood shop, much to Alec's chagrin, and even Alison had secretly admired the things he had made and painted himself. Intricate cigarette boxes, carved stools, even a child's chair had come from those skillful boyish hands. She stood up and turned to go out, taking one final look back as she opened the door wider—and remembered Johnny's warning just a fraction of a second too late. Even as she realized that no door should feel so loose as this and tried to step out of the way, it toppled toward her. She screamed as the weight came down, pushing her over backward so that she sprawled full length on the floor with the heavy door on her legs.

As she lay there dazed, she heard as if from a great distance the sound of steps pounding up the stairs. She tried to pull herself up, but in vain. The next moment Niall's face swam into view, then Johnny's, and the weight disappeared as if by magic. Tears of pain blurred Alison's eyes so that she couldn't see clearly, but it seemed to her that it was Niall who knelt beside her, saying, "Alison, can you hear me?"

She blinked rapidly several times, and stiffened at his touch, feeling his strong arms beneath her back as he eased her up.

"Yes, I'm . . . I'm all right."

He turned his head slightly. "Johnny, a cloth . . . plenty in the third bedroom . . . soak it well. . . ." Johnny had gone before he finished speaking, and Alison frowned. "But I'm not—"

"Ssh! All right, stay still. I've got you. How did it happen?"

"I told Johnny to go. I wanted to look at the cupboards, and he w-went. He warned me about the door, but I d-didn't listen, I'm sorry."

Then, to her utter dismay, she burst into tears. Loathing herself for the show of weakness in front of the enemy, she tried to gulp them back, but it only made things worse.

Then she saw her leg and gasped at the sight of blood welling out and spreading over her ankle.

"No, don't look. It's not as bad as it seems. You must have caught it on the lock." Suddenly, he put a firm hand on her chin and twisted her to face him. "Can you sit up?"

Alison nodded, one half of her mind registering the rather surprising fact that Niall MacBain was not being hard or ruthless, or anything else she associated with him, but unexpectedly gentle.

The other half was busy with the pain from her leg, pain that throbbed mightily, making her gasp.

Johnny appeared carrying a wet cloth. Niall looked at him. "Wrap it around her leg. It will do until we get her home." He lifted her up a little more, his hand firmly around the middle of her back. She winced as the cold cloth touched her, but it was over a moment later, and Niall nodded. "Right. Now, get over to the cottage, and tell Mrs. Mackay or Jessie that I'm bringing Alison over—and to keep the boy out of the way."

Johnny looked at him. "Do you want any help?"

"No, I can manage. Just prepare them. I'll follow in a minute." Johnny vanished, and they were alone.

"Sit up," Niall ordered. "I'm going to tie that cloth so that it doesn't fall off," and he pulled a handkerchief out of his pocket and bound it around the makeshift band-age. He looked at Alison with a grin. "I'm not a doctor, but it will do." Then, more slowly, "Alison, I'm sorry this happened."

She shook her head, still fighting tears, not knowing why. "It was my own fault. I was careless, that's all. Don't b-blame yourself or Johnny, please."

He stood up and looked down at her. "I'm going to carry you home now. Just lie still—I won't drop you."

He bent and eased his arms carefully under her knees and back, then picked her up as easily as if she weighed as little as his son. In a very impersonal voice he said, "Put your arm around my neck. Comfortable?"

She obeyed him and answered, "Yes, thank you." It was odd, but now that the immediate urgency was over, so was the temporary truce that the emergency brought about. Alison tensed up as she realized just what was happening.

Then his voice came abruptly, "Relax." There was a trace of harshness now. So he had noticed it too! She tried to relax but a silent promise she had made to herself returned to mock her. She had vowed never to let him touch her. Alison breathed deeply, trying to control the weakness that threatened, and they made their slow way down the stairs. She was aware of the utter silence as they passed the room where the Camerons were. They would be watching and wondering.

Then slowly down another flight of stairs and into the hall, bare and empty. He glanced at her as they neared the front door. "Are you all right?"

"Yes," she answered, but she could scarcely breathe. Odd how it was starting again, but he was so close—too close for comfort. His face was only inches away, the face that she had told Jessie reminded her of a pirate's.

She tried to slow her breathing, but it was difficult, and she prayed that he could neither hear nor feel the pounding of her heart. Deep tan, and dark hair, so dark, so near she couldn't take her eyes away. His chin was stubborn. She had never noticed before, never wanted to, just how obstinate and strong it was. He had cut himself just underneath it, she could see that clearly—dried blood in an inch-long line. Cut himself shaving that morning, and already a faint shadow of beard showed again through the tan. He was so dark; that was why they had called him Black Niall. The name suited him now more than ever. Alison began to shiver helplessly as they went outside, and he mistook it and said, "We'll be home in a minute. You need a warm drink." She couldn't tell him that it wasn't cold that made her shake—it was fear. Fear of this dark stranger who had come back into her life so suddenly and was threatening it in so many different ways.

Jessie was so concerned about her that Alison had to reassure her that she was fine, and that there was really nothing wrong with her at all. Niall, seeing the old woman's anxiety, had taken complete charge, asking for bandages, antiseptic, and water. As Alison protested, weakly, that she would manage, he looked at her once with that level gray glance and she subsided. Useless to fight him. The only thing he allowed her to protest about was Jessie's decision to go and fetch her mother from the studio. "No," he said, smiling a little as if to reassure Jessie. "Alison says her mother doesn't need to come back, and I think she's right. But please, Jessie, I think a cup of tea would be a good idea." And he bent down and removed the blood-stained cloth from Alison's leg, glancing swiftly at her as she drew breath. She was on her bed, and he had had Jessie bring in a towel so that the blood from the cut wouldn't mark the coverlet. Now, as he hesitated, she looked at him.

"What is it?"

He gestured with his hand. "Your stocking."

"They're not stockings," she answered, "they're tights." And some spark of mischief drove her to add, "What are you going to do about it?" And let me see you get out of *that*, she added silently, waiting for his discomfiture. He knew. A glint of that quick temper showed for an instant, but was swiftly repressed.

"Lie back." She did, waiting for him to leave the room, knowing that he wouldn't dare. . . .

The next moment the unbelievable happened. Alison felt Niall's hands slide under her skirt to her hips; and then the tights were being pulled gently down, down her legs. Gasping, she struggled to sit up, hot color flooding her face as she stared first at him, then at her tights, now over her ankles. "Oh! How dare you do that—you— you—!"

Niall looked at her, unmistakably smiling. "You dared me, remember? I've already told you how I react to threats—and dares." He deftly eased the tights off, but she winced with pain.

"Sorry." He flung them over a chair and began to clean the cut on her leg. Alison lay back, her heart thudding, her face still burning. It was she who was embarrassed, unbearably so. Her sides were on fire where his hands had touched—only lightly, but nevertheless in a most expert manner. She turned her head away, hearing Jessie come in, hearing her say, "Shall I phone the doctor?"

She felt cool ointment being put on her leg as he answered, "No, Jessie. It's a shallow cut, a clean flesh

wound. The antiseptic and the ointment will be suffi-
cient." Then he was tying the bandage, and Alison
opened her eyes to see Jessie hovering over her, her lined
face filled with worry and love.

Alison smiled at her reassuringly. "I'm fine, really I
am. And I'd love that cup of tea."

"Aye, well, come on now, sit up." She put the steam-
ing cup on the bedside table and plumped Alison's pillows. "There now! And there's a cup for you in the
kitchen, Niall, and a very worried little boy."

"Let me wash my hands, and I'll go get it." He picked
up the bowl of water and went out. Jessie looked at Alison and nodded, an ominous gleam in her eyes.

"Mmphm!" she muttered. "Well, I've seen some enemies in my time, but that one takes the cake." For a
dreadful moment Alison thought she had seen him take
off her tights, and began, "What do you—"

"You know very well! Poor man was worried sick
about you, and you say—" she stopped as the bathroom
door opened, then put a finger to her lips. "I'll go see to
him. Have your tea, there's a drop of brandy in it to
warm you." Then she was gone. Alison began to drink.
Would she ever forget the humiliation?

She phoned Meg later that evening, after having had a
short sleep. It was difficult to talk freely, for the phone
was in the hall, near where her mother and Jessie sat in
the living room. Alison needed someone to talk to,
badly.

Her main purpose in phoning was to ask Meg to come
and visit the following weekend. They had come the previous year during the week of the games, and they had
all enjoyed themselves tremendously, leaving the twins
in the care of Alison's mother the evening they went to

the dance. Alison had already mentioned the plan to her mother, who was pleased at the idea, and said it would do Alison good to have an interest. Almost, Alison reflected as she picked up the phone, as if she thought I was bored.

Meg was delighted with the invitation. Bill was out, but she said she was sure he would say yes, and that she would call Alison back. Then she added, "And how's the monster?"

"Well, it's a little difficult," Alison began.

"Aha! You mean you can't talk freely?"

"That's right. We've moved into the cottage now. It's a lot smaller."

"I get you, loud and clear. Well, I'll phone you later, but I'm looking forward to it already. And we'll go to the dance in the evening?"

"Yes."

"Marvelous. I love the atmosphere in that village hall. Can't wait! 'Bye, love, I'll call the minute Bill gets in."

Alison put the phone down thoughtfully. She wondered what Meg would make of Johnny, who would undoubtedly be with them at the dance. She looked down at her injured leg and wondered if the bandage would be off before the following week.

The phone rang just as she was going to bed, and she picked it up, sure it would be Meg. But it was Johnny.

"Sorry to call so late, Alison. I wanted to know how you were."

"Oh, Johnny! Thank you for phoning. I'm fine now."

"Good. I was so sorry, Alison. I shouldn't—"

"Nonsense. It was my own carelessness in not listening. You mustn't blame yourself."

"Ach, well, it's nice to hear you're all right. I'll sleep

well now! Shall I come over early tomorrow and drive you to school?"

She smiled. "That's very kind of you, but really—"

"It's the least I can do. I insist—and I'll be at your home at quarter to nine in the morning. Sleep well, Alison, good night." And giving her time only to answer his farewell, he hung up. Alison was oddly touched by his gesture. It was nice of him to offer, and it was clearly something that wouldn't have occurred to Niall Mac-Bain, she thought wryly.

But there she was wrong. She went to tell her mother who had phoned, and why, and Mrs. Mackay looked worried.

"Oh dear," she said.

"Why? There's surely nothing wrong—" Alison began.

"Oh no, it's not that, but Niall came over when you were asleep. I'd just got back from the studio. He offered to pick you up in his car in the morning, and I said you'd be all right. I hadn't realized—" she looked doubtfully at Alison's leg. "Dear me, I hope he doesn't see Johnny taking you. It will look so bad."

"Is that all?" Alison laughed. "I don't mind if he does see me. I don't mind at all." But as she said the words, she wondered if she was trying to convince her mother or herself. The telephone's shrill ring saved her from further introspection.

It was Meg, whose words made Alison forget all about Niall's probable annoyance, as she assured her that she and Bill would be delighted to come down the following Thursday with the twins for a long weekend.

Alison went to bed happier than she had been for a long time.

There was never any work done on the last day of term. The prospect of six weeks' freedom was too heady to bear, and the children were full of mischief and fun as they all played "Guess Who?" in which they took turns posing as famous people and answering questions about themselves until their identity was revealed. Alison smiled to herself a little as she sat back in a corner of the classroom and listened, for once an onlooker. They didn't know it, but this too, in a way, was helping them to learn. As each "character" whispered his identity to her beforehand, she was able to correct any glaring inaccuracies. She thought back to Johnny's arrival at a quarter to nine that morning. He had said he would come for her again at noon to take her home, then back after lunch as well. He drove a battered Land Rover, and as noon approached, Alison watched for it to come up the hill. But it was Niall's car that she saw, and it stopped outside the school in a flurry of tiny stones from the road.

"Go to lunch now, children" she told them. "André, wait here. Your daddy has come for you." They ran out, and she walked carefully to her desk for her bag as the school door opened, and Niall walked in.

She looked up as if surprised. "Hello. You've come for André," she said brightly.

"And for you," he answered.

"Oh, but Johnny said—"

"He's very busy painting cupboards and fixing a door," he answered. Then he looked at his son. "Hello, André, have you been good?"

"Sim, Papa—"

"English, André. We must remember to speak English." Their voices faded away as they went out, leaving her on her own. His tone when he spoke to his son was

kind but impersonal. There seemed no warmth, no love.
A fine tremor ran through Alison. It was as if they were
strangers. How could Niall be so cruel to a little boy?
And something else she had noticed subconsciously,
which now came forward. When he spoke about André
to Jessie or Alison, he always referred to him as "the
boy" or "André," never "my son." As she went to the
door after a last quick look around, something more disturbing clamored for her attention. Niall had never once
spoken of his wife. If ever he had to refer to her, he said
"André's mother," but that was rarely. Surely, she
thought, he could bear to speak of her now? But to do it
so impersonally seemed heartless.

With a faint sigh, Alison closed the door and went to
the car.

"Can you manage?" Niall asked.

"Yes, thank you," she answered stiffly. She would
have preferred to walk, but her leg was sore, and she
wanted it to be all right for Meg's visit and the games.

They drove home without speaking, except to André,
who seemed unaware of the brittle atmosphere. Alison
couldn't, even for his sake, force conversation with
the impossible man who sat beside her, his hands that
had. . . . Stop it! she told herself fiercely, hating him and
herself. She must have stirred slightly in her seat, for his
glance flickered and he said, "Leg hurting?"

"Yes," she answered, regretting the lie immediately.
But it made her scalp prickle, the way he seemed able to
read her thoughts. Almost as if he *knew*—oh, how she
loathed him! And, too, for the casual way he treated
André. He might have had a rough childhood, but that
was no reason to inflict a similar one on his own flesh
and blood. She wanted to say it out loud—you are not fit
to have a child—but she didn't dare to. Some things had

to remain unsaid. Once spoken they could never be retracted, and nothing would ever be the same again.

She turned to look out of the window as they swept along the drive toward Courthill—his house. Instead of stopping at the back, as she expected, he took the narrower path to the cottage. Stopping outside, he turned to André. "Jessie has told me she will give you some lunch—or will you have it with me in the big house?" As he spoke he was getting out, and Alison hastened to open her own door, unwilling to let him help her, or touch her again.

As she got out, so did André, who put his hand in hers, as he looked up at Niall. "Please, I like to have with Mees."

A muscle tightened in Niall's cheek, but he merely nodded. It's all right, she thought wryly, I'm not going to try and take him from *you*.

They walked in the front door, Niall behind them, and Alison called out to Jessie, who answered, "I'm in the kitchen, Alison. You mother's gone to Strathcorran, picking material for the—" she came in wiping her hands on her apron, and saw Niall. "Ah, you've come back. Good. You can take the food back to Courthill." To Alison she added, "Sit you down and rest the leg. I won't be a moment." Alison walked into the kitchen after her and sat by the table. Niall remained in the doorway, watching André, who had sat down beside her. She hardened her heart. It was his own fault. Why should she feel sorry for him? But most oddly, she did. There was something in his face as he looked at his son that mystified her. Then, as Jessie handed him the huge covered dish and the plates, he became the hardened man again.

"I'll be back at one-fifteen." He glanced at Alison.

"Yes. Thank you for the ride," she said. But he had gone.

And so school closed for the holidays. That afternoon Jessie told Alison that André would be coming every day while his father was working. Her heart lifted absurdly.

"How did you ask him?" she said, wonderingly.

Jessie smiled, then chuckled. "I came straight out with it. Told him he had to think of his son, and should I mind him. He asked me if it would be too much trouble, because he intended having him at Courthill. I told him it would be a crime, and that anyway we had friends coming down next week with two young children, which would do him good." She stopped to draw breath, then went on, "And he insisted that he had to pay me, so I told him you'd be helping me and I was sure you wouldn't accept any money—" Alison nodded vigorously, "—and he said I was right there, and you were marvelous with him; he could see the difference already." She looked sternly at Alison. "So he does appreciate something you do."

Alison gave a little smile. "He has a funny way of showing it." André came in from the garden at that moment, carrying a bunch of assorted grasses, which he presented to her with a funny little bow before running out again. She sighed, looked at them, and went to fill a milk bottle with water. The subject of Niall was dropped, but she felt a small glow at his words.

The holidays had begun, and they would have André, and next week Meg and Bill and the children would be coming to stay. The world began to look a little brighter.

Thursday dawned bright and sunny, and Alison awoke feeling full of energy. Her leg was almost better. She had discarded the bandage the previous day, and as she dressed she looked critically at her leg. Only a slight scab was left of the cut. She began to look forward to the games on Saturday, and the dance in the hall afterward. She had not seen much of Johnny during the week. Either Niall or the Camerons came over for the men's meals, and she had thought nothing of it. Then, on Thursday afternoon, she decided to take the tea over herself. She had made up, and wore a slim-fitting sleeveless dress in burnt orange that fitted her to perfection, in readiness for her guests' arrival. On her feet she wore fawn sandals, and on her wrist a white bracelet that showed off her slight tan. She was breathtakingly beautiful—but quite unaware of the fact.

"My leg's fine," she told Jessie as the housekeeper protested her offer. "And I need some exercise." She picked up the sandwiches and teapot. "I'm off." She didn't see Jessie's amused smile as she went.

She walked in, heart beating a little faster than usual. The sounds came from upstairs, and she called, "Tea's here," and waited.

She hadn't expected to see Niall appear, and for a moment was silenced. Then as he came toward her, she said quickly, "I wasn't sure if the cups would be upstairs."

"No, they're in the kitchen." He reached the bottom of the stairs, and his eyes were upon her as he walked nearer, softly taking it all in—the sandals, dress, hair, everything. She was suddenly embarrassed. The expression in those gray eyes was disconcerting, as if he were taking her apart and reassembling her, and deciding whether or not he liked the result. His hands came out and took the heavy teapot from her, and he said quietly "I'll take that."

Alison turned to go toward the kitchen, very conscious of him following her, and of his eyes on her back and legs. She should not have come. She was making herself look foolish—the thought made her walk taller. Why should she give a damn about him? She marched into the kitchen, banged the sandwiches down on the table, picked up the mugs and went across to the sink. After rinsing them, she took them back to the table, said, "There you are. I hope you can manage to carry them upstairs. I'm going now." She wanted to hit him and she wanted to cry, and above all, she wanted to get away. And he *knew*. She could tell by the smile that touched his mouth.

Then he said, quite softly, "Or shall I send Johnny down to help you pour?"

"I don't think you'd be able to spare him from his work, would you?" she managed to say.

The smile broadened slightly. "Not really, but I'm sure you don't want to waste that dress on *me!*"

She walked quickly past him, leaning slightly to avoid any contact. She was determined not to start another argument, because with a man like him she couldn't win and if she spoke she would only lose her temper, she knew. He had that effect on her. That and the stifled breathless feeling she hated, and which was coming back so strongly that she just had to get out in the fresh air.

He caught her just before she reached the door, and put his arm in front of her. "What is it, Alison?"

"I didn't say that you could use my Christian name," she answered. "And will you let me pass, please?"

"Forgive me, Miss Mackay. It was a slip of the tongue," he bowed mockingly, but still blocked the doorway. "Have I said something else that offends you?"

"Everything about you offends me," she retorted. "Don't worry, I won't bring your tea again. I'll concentrate on looking after *your son* instead."

She knew that she had hit the target by the expression on his face. He moved his hand, said, "I'm sorry," and turned away to go back to the table. Alison hesitated a moment in the doorway, then went out, back to the cottage. He'd asked for it, but having said it, she wished she hadn't. She tried to tell herself that it didn't matter, but she knew that it did. Somehow in those eight short words, she'd touched something deep inside him, had wounded him in a way she could only guess at. She looked back just before going out. He stood very still by the table. She had been wrong in one respect. Somewhere he had a heart, after all.

It was like old times, like so many visits of Alison's to Inverness, but now they were in her own home. It was late on Thursday evening, and she and Meg sat by a warm fire in the living room drinking cocoa and toasting their toes on the hearth. Bill and the twins were fast asleep in the tent outside. Alison had said that they would house the children, but Meg had refused. Having seen the inside of the tent, Alison wasn't surprised. It was warm and cosy, and the boys lay sleeping snugly in their sleeping bags on low camp beds.

It was late, and both women were tired, but there was so much that had to be told. Alison was nearly at the end of it.

Meg listened, completely fascinated, her cocoa growing cold. As Alison reached the last, bitter words she had said in the kitchen of Courthill, Meg bit her lip.

"Was he angry?"

"No—it would have been better if he had been. I'm used to that," Alison answered wryly. "But he just turned away. Somehow I'd hurt him deeply—and it was almost frightening. I rushed out, and when he came for André later, I kept out of the way. Childish of me really, I suppose."

"Mmm, well, he did ask for it." Meg drank the remaining cocoa, and smiled. "Enough of him. I'm dying to meet Johnny. He sounds a bit—well, you know!" And she raised one eyebrow meaningfully, making Alison laugh.

"Oh, he is," she assured her friend. "You'll see him on Saturday if not before. I'm glad you're here, Meg. And the twins can play with André. He'll like that. He's a lovely boy."

Meg gave her a look similar to one of Jessie's and Alison smiled tightly. "All right, don't say it, I know. Don't get too fond of him—I won't, don't worry." She looked at the clock. "Heavens, have you seen the time? It's nearly one. Bill will lock you out if you're not careful." Giggling like schoolgirls, they went into the kitchen, and Alison watched Meg arrive safely at the tent before closing the door and going to bed.

The next morning when André arrived, Ian and Andrew, the twins, were playing ball in the garden with Bill, and Meg was with Alison in her bedroom experimenting with perfume. Niall had gone when they went into the kitchen, and Jessie nodded toward the window.

"Look at them," she said. They watched the red-haired boys, still only three years old, talking to André while Bill waited in the background, arms akimbo, smiling at the serious manner in which his sons introduced themselves.

"Why, he's not much bigger than my boys," Meg whispered.

"I know," Alison answered softly. "Jessie's fattening him up, she says." She looked around and grinned at Jessie, busily occupied with preparing lunch for 12 people. That was the wonderful thing about her. The more she had to cope with, the better she enjoyed the challenge. Now she was quietly humming under her breath as she peeled the potatoes. Many a time Alison had offered to help, only to be given a firm "no." Jessie worked better alone, and the results always justified her obstinacy. She did allow the women to go to the village store, however, and Meg and Alison set off, leaving four males playing in the garden with Rusty watching and Mrs. Mackay busy at Courthill in her studio. The only time Alison saw her mother was in the evenings, unless she came home for a cup of coffee during the day. She had changed. New purpose lit her life as she matched and compared fabrics and samples for soft furnishings and carpets. Niall, it appeared, had given her a free hand in every way, and the confidence it had filled her with was good to see. Good . . . and yet again Alison felt as if he were intent on taking everything away. It wasn't something she could explain to anyone, even Meg. It was such a deep, intensely personal emotion that she could scarcely have put it into words. How much more would he buy? She still didn't know where his money— this fortune that had irrevocably altered her life—had come from. Meg was as fascinated as Alison about it. They didn't know then, as they walked to the shop in Shielbaig, that they were soon to discover the answer.

That evening they drove in Bill's station wagon to have a drink at the hotel in Strathcorran. The twins were safely tucked in Alison's bed, already in their sleeping bags for transfer on their return. The first person Alison saw as they walked into the hotel was Johnny, about to buy a drink. He crossed the crowded cocktail bar to greet them, a grin on his face. Alison introduced him to Meg and Bill, and was amusedly aware of Meg's subtle weighing up. She would, she knew, have a full report on the way home.

Soon they were sitting together in a comparatively quiet corner, Bill and Johnny discussing soccer and cars, while Meg and Alison chatted and occasionally joined in. It was pleasant, and rare, for her to have an evening out, and she was enjoying it more than she imagined. Then suddenly the conversation changed, and the men were talking about Courthill. Bill was interested in the work, so Johnny began to explain, drawing diagrams on the table with a forefinger as he described the layout of the house Meg and Bill knew so well. Bill nodded, interested, and gave a low whistle as Johnny told him about the conversion of the upper floor into a self-contained apartment. "That alone will cost a lot," he commented dryly.

"Och, he's loaded," Johnny winked at Alison. "I wouldn't mind a small share in that mine, would you, Alison?"

"Mine?" she echoed stupidly. "What mine?"

"Do you mean to say you don't know about it?" It was his turn to look stunned. "It's one of those tales that you wouldn't believe—except that it's true."

Seeing their intent faces, he laughed. "I'd better tell you, but first another drink. My round, I think," and he vanished toward the bar, leaving the three of them looking at one another. A few minutes later he returned, sat down and looked around.

"Are you sitting comfortably? Good," he grinned. "I've never had such an attentive audience. I—"

"Johnny!" Alison said warningly.

"Och, all right. Well, apparently Niall and his brother and two other sailors found themselves in a bar in Rio one hot summer evening several years ago. They were slightly . . . er . . . merry, and they got talking to a nice old man who told them this tale about the iron mine he owned, somewhere in the wilds of Brazil. But hard times were forcing him to sell, et cetera; a real con story. As I said, Niall admits they were all sort of tipsy, and loaded with money after months at sea. The long and short of it is that they chipped in and bought this mine for a ridiculous sum—something like 200 dollars in our money. The old man gave them some impressive documents, wrote them a receipt that was almost illegible, and remembered a very urgent appointment elsewhere. Of course they discovered they'd been had, the next day when in the sober light of morning they took the certificates to a police station."

He paused, took a deep swallow of lager, and then went on, "There they were told, with great amusement, that the mine was in fact a genuine one—but had been closed for years and was certainly worthless." He stopped and looked at them, and Alison knew by his smile that something big was coming, but couldn't see what.

"Go on," urged Meg impatiently.

"Niall hung onto the papers, more for a souvenir than anything else, and as a reminder not to talk to strange men in bars. Then about three years ago, some prospectors opened up a rich new vein of iron in a mine a few miles away from theirs—and suddenly it wasn't worthless any more. It was in all the Brazilian papers. The owners of the other mine were looking for the owners of their mine. Duncan was in Rio at the time, having left the navy, and he contacted Niall, who went there with his worthless bit of paper, and they sold their mine for a terrific sum—Niall didn't say how much—and the four of them shared it among them."

He stopped and looked at their astonished faces. "Yes, I know it's fantastic—but it's true."

"So," Alison breathed out slowly, and looked at Meg. "So now we know!" All the suppositions and rumors had been nothing compared to this modern fairy tale. And it was due to some old man in a bar that Niall now owned Courthill. Fantastic, as Johnny had said, but true. She wondered again about his wife. He must have already been married when the fortune came, and André would have been a baby. Yet apparently he was still in the navy, sailing the seas. Something, somewhere didn't make sense. Alison knew she would probably never know. André never spoke about his life before coming to Shielbaig, and she would never ask him. Soon afterward they finished their drinks and left, promising to see Johnny at the games the following day.

There was excitement in the air as they walked the following afternoon to Shielbaig for the games. These were held about a quarter of a mile past the village in a huge open field, and people came from miles around to compete, to meet old friends, and to indulge in that favorite Highland pastime—a good gossip.

The twins ran on ahead, full of energy, jumping and pushing one another like a couple of puppies. Alison wondered if they would see Niall and André. The men had not been at Courthill that morning, but his car was outside his father's as they passed.

Cars, bikes and vans passed them, and Alison waved to everybody she knew, while Meg beside her kept saying "Don't forget now, when you see the monster—tell me."

"I will. Besides, you'll know him from my description."

Meg began to laugh. "You made him sound like a black-bearded pirate! I keep looking for someone with a patch over one eye, and waving a Jolly Roger, but so far, I must admit—"

"You're an idiot," Alison stifled her laughter. "Can you just imagine!" she looked sideways at her friend. "Oh, Meg. I'm so glad you're here. You can't think what it's like, having no one to confide in. Jessie and my mother have gone over to his side, there's no other way to put it. Of course I'm glad that Mother has a new interest, but it's so—"she stopped, unsure of what she wanted to say.

Meg squeezed her arm. "I know, Alison. I understand, truly I do. And I'd feel the same way about him, but—"and she bit her lip, her pleasant face troubled "—but even so, he sounds so—intriguing, somehow. Not like an ordinary man, but—well, larger than life."

"He's that all right," Alison agreed bitterly. "And if you dare say he's good-looking, I shall personally strangle you!"

Both laughing, they walked into the field where already nearly a hundred people were gathered. More were coming all the time. Some were in small groups, others walking idly about, inspecting the various parts marked-off for the different races. The highlight of the afternoon would be the field hockey match, after every-

thing else was over. At the back of the field a large tent
had been erected, waiting for the rush of people wanting
refreshments. The twins ran off screaming delightedly at
having such a large field to play in, and Bill paused to let
the girls catch up with him.

"I might have a go at the bicycle race," he said with a
grin, pointing to the pile of ancient bikes leaning against
an old oak. Alison's mother and Jessie had said they
would come late, and Alison looked around from their
vantage point near the tent, wondering how long they
would be. She wondered idly if they had decided to
come earlier than usual because of Niall. It would be the
ideal place to let the whole world know that the feud was
dead. And so she waited, watching, talking and listening
to Meg and Bill, and keeping an eye on the twins who
had been roped in for a jumping game with some children in another part of the field.

More people came, car doors slammed, supplies were
carried into the tent by self-conscious youths followed
by giggling girls. It was the same as every year—yet
there was one thing different, and so she waited and
watched.

Then she saw him. He stood by the entrance to the
field with André, and Alison touched Meg's arm lightly.
"He's there." She saw Meg turn slowly, not making it
obvious, saw her looking, then Meg turned back to Alison, her eyes wide. "I don't believe it!"

"Don't believe what?" Meg had her back to him, and
Alison could still see him as he was greeted by one person, then another.

They stood talking until André, seeing Alison, said
something and tugged at Niall's arm, then began to run
toward them.

"André's coming over, be careful what you say," Alison warned, as the little boy reached them and looked up smilingly at her.

"Hello, André. The twins are over there," she pointed. "Do you want to go and play with them?"

He regarded her thoughtfully, then nodded, and streaked off to join the laughing crowd of children.

"I can't believe I'm really seeing *him* at last." Meg looked casually around, then at Alison. "Will he come over and speak to you?"

Alison pulled a face. "Not if he can help it, but if my mother—" She stopped and waved, seeing them by the gate. "She's here now with Jessie—and we'll soon see."

It happened about half an hour later, when the games had begun, and everyone was crowded around the perimeter of the field. The children's events were first, and they all clapped and cheered, laughing at their efforts. Jessie was beside Alison, very smart in her best blue hat lavishly decked with flowers. Mrs. Mackay stood beside her, small and elegant in a blue trouser suit. Alison saw her wave, then heard her greet someone, and she knew it was Niall.

So it had happened. She had been right. And Meg would have her wish. Alison looked at her friend, oblivious to what was going on beside her as she watched Ian and Andrew hopping madly along in the race for tiny tots. She suddenly wanted very much to know what Meg thought about Niall MacBain, but she couldn't understand why.

CHAPTER SEVEN

MEG told Alison much later, at the dance, when Bill and Johnny had gone to join the line-up for refreshments. It was the first chance they had had to talk together since the games.

The noise around them was so deafening that anything they said would be private. Meg leaned across and said in Alisons's ear, "About you-know-who."

"Yes, what about him?"

"You really think he's not attractive?" Alison looked at her. There was one thing about her friendship with Meg. The two of them had never been able—or wanted—to be less than truthful in anything with each other. Now was the test.

Grudgingly Alison admitted, "Well, I suppose he's got a certain something."

"I'll say he has! Honestly, Alison, you must have your head examined! Here was I imagining something really awful—you know—but he's so charming. You know when your mother introduced us?" Alison nodded, silent, waiting. "Well, he looked at me with those gray eyes—it's immoral for a man to have eyes as sexy as that—and I had to try hard to remember that I'm a respectable married woman and mother!" Her eyes sparkled with humor, and Alison forced a little smile. "And he was so—well, nice when he spoke that I had difficulty in reconciling him with this ogre who's so utterly vile to you." She gave Alison a very keen look. "In fact, if I didn't know you so well, I'd have thought you were making it up."

Just then the men came back, effectively bringing an

end to their conversation, but for the rest of the evening, as Alison danced with either Johnny or Bill, she remembered Meg's words. So her last ally had gone! She began to wonder, quite seriously, if there were something wrong with her. Perhaps they were right, and he was charming and wonderful, and it was Alison herself who saw him somehow through a distorted lens—one twisted by the feud, what had happened in childhood, and a thousand other things that went to make a person. She remembered too the time in the attic, when he had steadied her with André, and the ridiculous sensation she had experienced then, of wanting him to hold her. That, too, Alison had told Meg, and she hadn't laughed, as Alison would have expected, she had given a little mysterious smile. Perhaps I am a frustrated school-teacher after all, she thought miserably.

Johnny's voice broke into her thoughts.

"A penny for them." She looked back at him, aware that she had been miles—no, only one mile away, in that attic at Courthill.

"Sorry, Johnny. I was daydreaming."

"At eleven at night?" His arms tightened around her. "You'll have to do better than that." He skillfully avoided collison with another couple on the hot, crowded floor, and swung her towards the door. "Let's go outside for a breath of fresh air."

"All right." She knew it wasn't fresh air that was on his mind, but a numbness had come over her and she didn't really care.

Outside it was cool, and she shivered. Pitch blackness was all around them, but faint murmurings and stifled laughter told Alison they weren't alone. Johnny put his arm around her. "Cold?"

"A little." She knew he was going to kiss her, and she

willed herself to enjoy it when it happened. They began walking around the side of the hall which vibrated with the enormous volume of sound. There was a bench somewhere around the back, and she imagined they were making for that, when ... Suddenly his mouth came down on hers, his arms slid firmly around her, imprisoning her, and she found herself pressed against a tree. Johnny leaned on her, wordlessly kissing her and pausing only slightly for breath. Alison tried hard to respond, to enjoy the warmth of his embrace, but in vain. Something froze her, held her back from answering the primitive emotions he tried so hard to arouse. After a few minutes, she pushed him slightly away, pretending to be flustered.

"Heavens, Johnny, you took me by surprise."

"Oh, Alison, don't torment me ... you're so beautiful, come here ..." and he tried to kiss her again, but she wriggled away.

"You're too dangerous," she said, praying that Meg would look for them and knowing that she wouldn't. "A woman's not safe with you," she protested, as his hand began moving up from her waist. She took hold of it and returned it to its original position.

Johnny's voice was husky with emotion. "I've been wanting to kiss you for weeks, ever since that day, remember?"

"I remember." If she could keep him talking and lead him gently back to the hall. ... It had been a mistake to come out. There was no magic cure here for whatever ailed her, she realized. Nothing to take the ache from her, the pain of hating someone that everybody else thought so marvelous.

"And I've been wanting to ask you out, but I was afraid—"

"You afraid? I don't believe *that*." They were moving in the right direction.

"Yes, I was. Och, I know what you're thinking. I'm no angel. But you're different, Alison. There's something about you—remote somehow. You're more beautiful, more wonderful than ever . . . och, I'm no good with words." His hand tipped her chin and he kissed her more gently this time, almost somberly. Then he released her, and, although it was dark, she sensed the sadness about him as he murmured, "You're not for me, I know that now, Alison. You are . . . I could fall in love with you. Perhaps for the first time in my life, I could truly love someone, but I know now—" and he stopped, gently tracing a line on her chin. She knew he was deeply sincere. It moved Alison so that she softly kissed his cheek. There was no need for words. And she did not ask him what he had been about to say.

Slowly they walked back to the hall. Alison knew that Johnny would be different. He had changed in those few minutes outside—something had made him say what he did—and she realized there was more depth to him than anyone knew. Alison hoped sincerely that he would find happiness with a women who would be able to love him as much as he deserved. But for her there would be nothing—she knew that now, quite suddenly.

Niall had told Bill on Saturday at the games that he was welcome to see the work at Courthill, and on Sunday morning the three of them went over. Alison's mother still had a key to let herself in, for the new door to the studio was not yet done and her only entrance was through the house. Everything was quiet, almost eerily so as they walked through the hall, and Meg whispered, "It's so different now," looking at the high bare walls, the uncarpeted staircase with its delicate wrought-iron work, and the various doors leading off the hall.

Silently Alison agreed. Some of the pain had gone, and she could come into the house more easily every time. Soon she might be able to enter that front door, and it would be like going into a stranger's house. Maybe. . . .

She showed them the attic, knowing Meg's reaction to the conversion. She stood in the kitchen doorway and turned back to Alison. "This will be really marvelous when it's finished—better than mine!" This with a sly look at Bill, who grunted, too busy examining the cupboards to comment.

"I know," Alison answered. "It will be virtually a house. I admit he's clever. He made those cupboards too."

Meg looked at the door. "Oh! So this is where—"

"Yes," Alison pulled at the door. "They fixed it straight afterwards. It was my own fault." And suddenly she didn't want to talk about it any more. They went through the bedrooms, and then down to the ground floor, which was as yet unaltered. That would be done last, she knew. Bill was very impressed with the quality of the work. She then took them into the studio and showed them her mother's designs.

Meg gazed wide-eyed at the picture of the reception hall as it would be. "I'd be tempted to come here myself for a holiday," she told her. "Honestly, Alison, this place will be something special. Really, I mean it," she emphasized, seeing Alison's face, which showed her disbelief.

Alison shrugged, said carelessly, "Perhaps you're right. We'll see soon enough." But inside, a pain stabbed her.

They went back home for lunch. Meg and Bill were leaving for Inverness the following day, and the friends had their last gossip that evening by the fire. They were both tired after the dance the previous night, so it was only eleven when they said good night to each other and went to bed. Alison was exhausted with something more than just a late night. An incredible weariness overcame her as she lay in bed looking up at the ceiling. What was the use of fighting any longer? She felt as if she were being swallowed gradually into a giant whirlpool. Nobody would ever understand how she felt. It must be her. Something must be wrong with her. She turned her face into the pillow and wept.

The next two days were spent quietly at home. Some of the life had gone with Bill and Meg's departure on Monday, and Alison felt restless, as if she wanted to get away. She avoided going near Courthill, and stayed away from the kitchen the times Niall came for their lunch or tea. She took André for walks with Rusty, and enjoyed listening to his quaint accent. He had begun to speak more, as if emerging from his shell, and told her a little of his flight to Scotland. But of his life before, he would not or could not speak, and Alison, longing to know but not daring to ask, remained silent. It had nothing to do with her, she knew, yet there was a strange fascination in thinking of André's mother, and of what she had been like.

They walked for miles some days, and the weather remained sunny and pleasant. Everything would have been perfect it if hadn't been for the shadow that remained at the back of Alison's mind like a small dark cloud. There was nothing that would make it go away.

Niall MacBain had come back for good. There was only one solution—for Alison herself to leave, and she loved Shielbaig too much to want to do that—yet.

On Wednesday she left André playing with Rusty while she went to the store for Jessie. When she came back, he had vanished with Rusty and she set off to find them, knowing they would not have gone far. She set off down the garden, opened the small wicker gate at the bottom, and followed the route they usually took on their walks, the path that followed the loch to Shielbaig. She stopped after only a few yards when she saw the tiny figure standing by the boat, which was pulled up on the shingle. Rusty sat patiently beside him, and then, seeing Alison, got to her feet and ambled across wagging her tail.

"I didn't know where you were, André," she said. "You mustn't leave the garden without asking."

He looked at her, gave a little shrug, then said, "But it is so quiet with no one to play with. I come only to see the boat. I like her very much."

Alison smiled, "Maybe your daddy will take you out in her to the island over there." She pointed toward the tree-covered mound set serenely in the dark water.

"You will come if I do?" he asked, his eyes anxiously upon her. She ruffled his hair. How could she tell him?

"Perhaps," she answered. "Some day." But she knew she would not. She held out her hand. "Come on, we'll go back. Jessie will be worried about you. I think she's made some scones. You like those, don't you?"

He nodded, and they set off home. As they passed Courthill something made her look up, and it seemed as if a man was standing at the upstairs window watching them. The sun reflecting off the glass made it impossible to see exactly who, but she had a feeling it was Niall. Without knowing why, she released the boy's hand. Deep down the memory of those cruel, hurtful words she had said stirred and returned to torment her, and she wanted him to see that she knew André didn't belong to her.

The next morning a letter arrived from the Education Committee. Couched in official language, it told Alison that at Christmas, the school would close "until such time as circumstances permit its reopening." The remaining children would be taken by school bus to Strathcorran. Alison would teach there temporarily, until a transfer could be arranged. Even though she had half expected the news, it still came as a considerable shock, and her mother saw her face as Alison read the letter at the breakfast table.

"Why, Alison, what is it?" She gave the letter to her mother, who read it twice, as if disbelieving it. Then she looked up, her face distressed. "I'm so sorry. Did you know before?"

"I had a good idea, but I didn't want to worry you about it. You had enough to think about a few weeks ago, and I tried to push it to the back of my mind."

"You should have told me, even so. Heavens, child, no wonder you looked so unhappy! Still, Strathcorran's not too far away. It's just that this is such a nice school."

"Maybe a miracle will happen before Christmas," said Alison lightly. But she knew it wouldn't, and so did her mother.

She saw Johnny later on that day for the first time since the previous Saturday. Alison was coming out of the store as he went in.

"I won't be a moment," he said, touching her arm lightly. "Wait, and we'll walk back together."

A minute later he caught up to her, and stuffed two packs of cigarettes in his pocket.

"Now if I'd known you wanted them," Alison told him, "I would have got them for you."

"Ach, never mind. And how would you have known, eh? You've been keeping out of my way all week," he answered, grinning. He took the basket from her and held her arm.

"Johnny!" she protested. "Be careful! Carrying my basket, and linking arms! Everyone will have us engaged if you don't watch out!"

"Let's give them something to talk about then. It's little enough they've got to do. Shall I kiss you as well?"

She quickened her step, well aware of watching eyes as they passed the last few cottages. "You wouldn't dare."

"Wouldn't I?" he gave a low growl in his throat. "Wait until we're almost home, then see."

She looked at him and smiled. Had he forgotten those words so softly spoken at the dance? She doubted it. Perhaps he had meant them at the time. They had left her with a pleasant afterglow, which came back as they walked slowly along the road to Courthill.

His arm was warm in hers, his manner quieter than usual. They talked about the work, and of Meg and Bill, and the games. But one name wasn't mentioned. It was as if Niall MacBain didn't exist.

Through the greenness of the sheltering trees, along the narrow path to Courthill they went, and then, by the back door, they stopped.

"I'll come over for the lunch today, if I can," he said.

Alison opened her eyes wide. "Such an honor!"

Something sparked in his own eyes, and as she half turned, putting our her hand for the shopping bag, he said softly, "Alison?" and still held on to the bag.

"Yes?" She turned back, and his free arm came around her as he bent his head and gave her a slow gentle kiss.

As they broke apart she saw Niall MacBain come out of the garage, his arms full of wood. He looked, but said nothing, and then went into the house.

Johnny, gave a low whistle, and smiled softly. "Bye for now." Then he too was gone, and Alison went on home. She was left with two questions to tease her. Had Johnny known that Niall would be in the garage? And had he then kissed her deliberately? There was no one to answer her.

For the rest of the day she busied herself making a dress. She had had both the pattern and the material for a while. André was fascinated watching Alison as she snipped away at the material, a rich, dark blue cloth, then began to sew on the ancient but reliable machine. She was so busy that she almost managed to forget the letter in the buff envelope behind the clock on the mantelpiece. Everything was so normal, uneventful, perhaps a little dull, that the work was an enjoyable change, and as she went to bed that night, she decided that she would finish the dress the following day. She couldn't know that her life would never be the same again after tomorrow.

There was nothing to warn Alison when she woke up on Friday that this was the day of destiny. André arrived at the usual time, and she caught a glimpse of Niall's back as he vanished out the kitchen door. André ran to her and flung his arms around her legs in a burst of delighted laughter.

"My *papai* will take me to the island tomorrow," he told her; his accent was stronger in his excitement. "She see us looking at the boat, and she will take."

"There you are," Alison smiled at Jessie, who watched them benignly. "I said he could." So it had been him at the window. Perhaps he had seen, or sensed, the longing in his son's eyes as he watched the boat.

"I ask her—him—is she take you, Mees, but she say no, Mees Mackay is too busy to come."

Alison saw Jessie purse her lips and turn toward the work that waited for her. And Alison smiled brightly at the boy, annoyed at the tremor near the corner of her mouth. "Yes, I will be too busy, but maybe one day I'll be able to." She ruffled his hair. "Well, do you want to take Rusty out, and then we'll start on my dress again?"

"Please, yes." His eyes shone, and she stifled the lost eerie sensation that suddenly plagued her. She was pleased that Niall was beginning to take his duties as a parent a little more seriously.

The morning passed as did every other morning of the holidays. And every day André eased himself a little further into the fabric of Alison's life. Perhaps, she thought, wryly, as she drank her coffee at 11 and watched him trying to make Rusty sit up for a biscuit, perhaps Niall will be glad that the school is closing at Christmas. She bit her lip as the coffee cup jerked sideways, spilling the hot drink on her work table. She quickly mopped it up. What is the matter with me, she wondered. Alison knew she was tired, for she hadn't slept as well for about a week. Her mirror showed that she looked pale, with faint smudges of fatigue under eyes. A holiday away from Sheilbaig and everybody would do her good, she knew. But she didn't want to leave, for fear of what might happen while she was gone. It didn't seem possible that Niall MacBain could rob her of much more, but with him nothing was certain. An unpleasant dream she had the previous night returned suddenly with dreadful clarity as she finished the last of the coffee. She had dreamed that she came home from school to find the cottage cold and empty. When she called out, an answer came from Courthill, and she had walked over, trying to go fast, but feeling as if weights were dragging her feet back. It was a struggle to reach the steps, to climb up . . . and then she had seen her mother coming to the door, as in the old days, to welcome her. She had run in, sobbing with relief, to look around at the newly decorated reception hall. There was a desk, and phones and her mother was dressed in a smart uniform. Even as Mrs. Mackay smiled and shook her hand, Jessie had come from the lounge, dressed identically, and asked Alison if she would like a cup of tea in the restaurant . . . and then she woke up, drenched in perspiration.

Of course it had only been a dream but it was still too real for comfort.

Her mother, yellow overalls spattered with paint, came in for lunch and they all ate in the kitchen.

"They'll be knocking a hole in the studio wall," she told Alison as they finished their dessert. "Then I'll have my own door. I've been trying to move all the paintings out of the way."

"Can I help?" asked Alison. "André and I could come over this afternoon if you like."

"Would you dear?" She looked vague for a moment. "There are so many to be moved—yes, that would be fun. I don't see half as much of you as I'd like to lately."

"And I'll bring you some tea at three-thirty," added Jessie. So it was arranged. When lunch was over, the three of them went back to Mrs. Mackay's large, untidy studio at the side of the big house.

They were so busy that Alison lost count of the time until André said, "Please may I have a drink?"

"Why, of course." She looked at her watch. It was almost four o'clock. "It looks as if Jessie has forgotten us. Come on, we'll go and bring something back."

They set off through the conservatory and across the hall. At any moment she expected to bump into Jessie gossiping with one of the men as the tea grew cold, but the sounds of work continued upstairs, and they saw no one. As they neared the cottage Alison began to run, hearing the faint whistle of the kettle, and sensing that something was wrong. The kitchen was filled with steam, which billowed out through the open door. For a moment she thought it was smoke, until she realized it was coming from the kettle.

Heart thumping in sudden fear, she ran in, leaving André outside. She could see nothing for the steam that filled the entire kitchen and curled its way into the living room. "Jessie!" she shouted, pulling the hot kettle from the stove and switching it off, then flinging open the window.

Then Alison heard a faint moan and her scalp prickled. As the air cleared she saw Jessie lying awkwardly on the floor, a fallen footstool beside her telling its own story.

She knelt and touched the old woman's forehead gently. "Oh, Jessie dear! Don't try to move or talk. I'll get help."

She ran outside to the frightened boy. "Go and fetch daddy," she said. "And my mother. You understand?"

"*Sim.*" Eyes wide, he turned around and scampered off. Rusty came out of the living room whining softly. Alison knelt beside Jessie again, pulling a cushion from the kitchen chair and easing it beneath her head. She didn't dare look at Jessie's left leg, which was twisted beneath her at an awkward angle, for fear that the dismay would show in her face. She prayed that Jessie hadn't broken it, and that help would soon come.

Jessie clutched Alison's hand, her eyes filling with tears. "I was getting down the box of scones," she said faintly. "The stool wasn't steady, and the next thing I knew, I could hear the kettle whistling away."

"I know." Alison squeezed her hand. "André has gone for Niall and my mother. I'll fetch you a blanket and some brandy."

She covered her up and helped Jessie sip the warm liquid, and at that moment Niall, followed closely by Johnny, came in. It was so much like history repeating itself that Alison had a strange feeling everything had happened before. It had, but very differently. Hers had been a trivial accident. This could be serious. And she saw by Niall's face as he knelt beside her that he thought the same. She stood up and went to Johnny. "Does my mother know?" she asked, stiff-lipped.

"Yes. André went there after telling us." He came to Alison's side.

"You look white, Alison."

"Yes. It's her leg. Look at her leg," she whispered. Niall, kneeling beside Jessie, looked up at Alison.

"Is there a doctor still at Strathcorran?" he asked.

Johnny answered. "Aye, shall I go get him?"

"No. We'll take Jessie in my car to save time. Drive it up here, Johnny, as near as you can to this back door.

Alison, I want blankets and pillows." And then to Jessie, he added. "Don't worry, love. You'll soon be all right. I'm used to this." The faint answering smile on her face, twisted by pain, wrenched at Alison's heart. She hurried to do Niall's bidding.

Ten minutes later they were gone. Mrs. Mackay had insisted very firmly on going with them, and Alison was left with André to await their return.

She made a cup of tea for the Cameron brothers, and took it over, glad of something to occupy her mind. She could see Niall and Johnny carrying Jessie out to the car as carefully as if she were made of glass, and she knew that Niall was right, as always. He had taken charge as if he was used to it, and everything had gone smoothly. She had watched the car roll gently down the path, and had then gone back to reassure André.

That was the worst part, waiting for someone to come back and not knowing what was happening. Half an hour later the phone rang shrilly, and Alison went to pick it up, her hands suddenly clammy.

CHAPTER EIGHT

JOHNNY'S voice came over the line. He was phoning from a telephone booth in Strathcorran.

"I've just seen them off to Inverness," he told Alison.

"Where? What happened?" She could scarcely hold the phone.

"We went to the doctor's, but he was out on a maternity case and couldn't be reached. His wife gave Jessie an injection of pain killer and asked if she should call an ambulance—but you know how far it has to come, and it meant waiting, so Niall decided to take her to hospital himself."

"And my mother?"

"She's gone too. Listen, Alison, she told me to tell you she'll phone from the hospital as soon as she knows anything. But it might be hours."

"Yes, I know." She thought of them driving Jessie the seventy odd miles to Inverness, and caught her breath.

Johnny's voice came again. "And Niall wants to know if you'll keep André until he returns. His father is away to visit a relative near Torrie."

"Yes, of course I will. Your Land Rover's here. Will you come back for it?"

"No. If you'll ask Laurie to drive it to Strathcorran for me, and have Ian follow in theirs, it will save me coming back. The keys are in the ignition." And then he added in a very odd tone "In fact, Niall insisted on it. I wonder why?" But Alison was too worried about Jessie to be puzzled at the meaning of his words. Only later did she remember, and wonder.

After he had hung up she went to tell the Camerons

the news after first reassuring André about Jessie and his father. Then she made them both a meal and switched on television for him. She was restless and unable to settle down and found herself watching the phone. It was silly, because working out the distance to Inverness and allowing for traffic and Niall's having to drive carefully, it would be eight o'clock before she could expect to hear from her mother, she knew. She looked at the dress material and bundled it away. She tried reading but in the end she watched the television with André, who remained glued to the screen since it was first switched on.

Then at eight-thirty the phone rang again. Her mother's voice crackled faintly across the hilly miles between them.

"Alison, I'm sorry, love, I couldn't phone before. I know how you've been waiting for news, but we've just left Jessie tucked up in a lovely comfortable bed."

"How is she? What's the matter?"

"They don't know yet. They've taken X rays of her leg and left arm. They'll know soon enough, and, Alison. . . ."

"Yes?" Alison thought she knew what was coming.

"I've decided to stay here overnight. I've just phoned Meg, and she's told me to come over as soon as I finish here. It's the least I can do. Jessie has no one."

"Of course you must. Shall I put André to bed here?"

"Do you want to talk to Niall? He's outside the booth."

"No," Alison said hastily. "Just tell him André will be safe here. Give Jessie all my love, and try to phone me tomorrow."

"I will, goodbye—" The phone went dead, and Alison put it down slowly. At least she knew where to reach her mother if she wanted her. She told André he could stay the night, and his eyes lit up.

"May I have Rusty on my bed?" he begged.

Alison laughed. "I'll have to see. And now, I think it's time you went. Come on, I'll give you a good wash, and tell you a bedtime story."

As they went into the bathroom, it began to rain.

The fire was dying down, and Alison was warm and glowing after a hot bath. It was past eleven, and she sat curled up on the sofa watching a late movie on television, aware of the rain lashing heavily against the windows and drumming on the roof. The lamp glowed in the corner, and Rusty lay stretched out on the rug in front of her, her paws twitching as if she was dreaming of rabbits. Alison had already moved Rusty's basket into her room where André slept soundly, his arms tucked under his head and his face a picture of sweet innocence. Alison had stood watching him for a few moments before coming back into the living room. Niall would be coming for him in the morning, to take him to the island. She would have to make sure she was very "busy," so as not to disillusion the little boy. She turned away, her contentment vanishing, and went to fix her supper.

The movie came to an end, and she stood up yawning and switched it off, looking at the clock as she did. It was five minutes to 12. Suddenly there was a knock at the door, a low insistent rat-tat-tat. Rusty jumped up growling, and Alison went to the window but could see nothing.

Taking Rusty's collar, she went to the door, heart pounding, and called, "Who is it?"

"It's me, Niall MacBain," was the reply. She opened

the door to find him standing on the porch his wet hair shining in the light.

Her heart lurched, and she spoke the first words that came into her head, "I'm just going to bed."

"I won't keep you. I've just come to return the blankets," he answered. "If you hold the door open a moment, I'll get them from the car." His voice was curt, clearly resentful at her reluctance. She held the door wide, watching him splash to his car, then come back carrying the bundle. He wiped his feet on the mat and went into the living room where he put everything down on a chair. Alison followed him in and said, "It would have waited till morning."

"Perhaps, but your mother asked me to make sure you were all right," he answered. His gray eyes never left her face. It was disconcerting, and she felt a trace of embarrassment, clad as she was in her nightie and dressing gown. She wanted him to go away.

The memory of what had happened when he had caught Johnny kissing her came back strongly. He had looked just like this then—cool and faintly contemptuous. It was none of his business what she did, she thought rebelliously. He had no right to condemn her behavior, and yet she was tremendously uneasy.

To hide the awkward tension that seemed to grow with every second, she said, "I'm fine, thank you, and so is André. I'll have him ready in the morning, for you to take to the island." And then, because of something she herself didn't understand she added, "Don't worry, I'll make sure I'm very busy when you come." And the quick flash of understanding in his eyes was matched by the spark of anger in her own.

Then he smiled. Very slowly, he said, "Don't tell me you wanted to come too?"

She caught her breath at the sight of his smile, cynical and almost mocking. It stung her to retort, "With André it would be a pleasure. I've already been there with you." And she smiled back.

"And you wouldn't care to repeat it?" he asked.

"It was hardly the most enjoyable trip of my life. I love the island, but it's no longer ours." She took a deep breath. "I'm very tired."

"And you'd like me to go?" His mouth quirked. "Since we can't seem to have a civilized conversation, I think it would be better if I did. After all, I'm not Johnny, am I?"

His long glance at her from head to toe, expressed his meaning very clearly.

A warm tide of color surged into Alison's face. "What exactly do you mean by that remark?" she asked, breathing hard, fighting an awful sensation of overwhelming anger.

"You can take it to mean what you want," he answered coolly. "If your behavior in public is any indication—"

"If you're referring to yesterday," she shot back, "that was hardly in a *public* place—though I'm quite sure that when the hotel is swarming with your guests the gardens will be like Princes Street on Saturday morning. And if you have to sneak in and out of garages, you should expect to see things occasionally that you're not supposed to."

One eyebrow lifted fractionally. "Hardly sneaking. I was working."

Then Alison recalled Johnny's words on the phone and said, "I suppose that's why you insisted on the Cameron brothers taking Johnny's Land Rover to Strathcorran—so he wouldn't come back here?" The tightening of the muscles in his cheek told her she had hit the target, and she went on, "I must thank you for your keen desire to protect me—but I assure you I don't need protection from *Johnny. He's* a gentleman."

"And I'm not?" His voice, though still level, had a hard edge to it now. It gave her a small stab of satisfaction to know that she had managed to shake him.

"You asked for it," she glared defiantly up at him. "Take it any way you want."

"And how does a gentleman kiss, then?" he asked harshly. "Like this?" His fingers tightened on her shoulders as he pulled her quickly towards him. His mouth came down on hers, not roughly but strangely gentle.

For one absurd moment she tasted the sweetness of his lips, and allowed her body, her treacherous body, to relax as she responded, unwilling yet unable to prevent the surge of strong emotion that swept through her. It hadn't been like that with Johnny. She had felt nothing then. Now—so different—it was so very different. She realized why and with a faint gasp, managed to wrench herself away. Her mouth trembled uncontrollably as she gasped shakily, "Get out—*get out!*"

"When I'm ready to," his eyes had gone very dark. "I haven't finished with you yet."

"Don't touch me again!" she hissed.

"Frightened?" he taunted. "Why? I may not be a gentleman, as you pointed out so clearly a moment ago, but I don't use force on a woman, ever."

"You just did," she retorted, "when you kissed me."

"I got the strong impression you enjoyed it. At least you didn't stop me," was the soft answer. "In fact, you were asking for it."

"You have an odd idea of what constitutes an invitation if you think that," she retaliated sharply. "You didn't buy *me* when you bought the house. Try to remember that in the future." She moved toward the door of the hall and held it open. "And you didn't buy this house either, so I'm perfectly entitled to tell you to leave. Now, will you go?" Then as he turned slowly around, she added, "You haven't asked to see your son yet. Shouldn't you make sure he's safe?"

His eyes raked her face, and she was startled to see in them that expression she didn't understand, couldn't fathom. As he went into the hall she said, "He's in my bed."

Alison tried resolutely not to watch as he walked silently into her bedroom. A moment later he came out. Driven by the desire to hurt him, because he had hurt her and exposed some inner emotions she wanted hidden, she said breathlessly, "After Christmas the school will close and André will have to go to Strathcorran. I won't be teaching him any longer—*that* will make you happy."

He stopped in his tracks, stopped on his way to the front door, his wet hair still faintly glistening in the soft light of the hall. He turned very slowly, and something told Alison that she had gone too far.

"Make me happy?" he repeated, in an odd, harsh tone. "Why?"

"Don't think I haven't noticed the way you are when he's with me. I've seen you. You—you were watching only the other day, when we were on the beach. I saw you. I'm not like you, trying to steal what *you* hold dear. You've taken everything of mine, because that's the way you're made. I'm not like that. I love André because he's a wonderful little boy. It's a pity you don't."

He looked as if she had hit him hard. An icy cold wave of something akin to fear filled her. She gasped and moved into the living room and he followed her, closing the door behind him.

"You had better explain that remark." His face was white with anger. "Because I don't intend to leave until you do."

Alison backed away. He was too close and too tall. And filled with cold rage. All the pent-up frustration of the past weeks, all the resentment she felt about his treatment of his son, bubbled to the surface.

"I'll tell you," she said. "You're like a stranger to him. You're so wrapped up in your work you can't see how unhappy he's been, or how pathetically grateful he is because you, at last, have deigned to take him out somewhere with you. Even when you speak of him it's 'The boy,' or 'André,' never 'My son.' Do you think he doesn't feel it? He has a heart, you know, a small one, it's true—but it's full of love. He needs affection—he needs cuddling and h-hugging occasionally, but you can't see—" she broke off, tears perilously near. But she had to go on, had to finish saying what was on her mind. She took a deep breath. "And you never speak about your wife. If you have to refer to her, it's always as 'André's mother'—"

"Maybe it's because she was not my wife."

The words didn't register for a few moments. Then she realized what he had said. "You mean you weren't married to her?"

"No." He stood perfectly still, watching her.

"Then he—" Alison stopped.

"Then he's illegitimate? Are you frightened to say the word? You surprise me."

"Oh, I see."

"I don't think you do at all. In fact, it's time you learned a few basic facts of life, Miss Mackay. One of which is that things aren't always what they seem. And now I'll tell you something else that is absolutely no business of yours, but maybe you should know. It might give you something to think about." His words were rapier thrusts of anger, sharp and wounding. "André is my adopted son. His real father is Duncan, my brother, who had an affair seven years ago with a Brazilian woman in Rio. He was already engaged to someone else, when he discovered he was to be a father. He paid money for André's support after that—and never told his wife, who belongs to a wealthy Brazilian ranching family. Then, a few months ago, he heard that André's mother was ill and asked me to go see them. He had heard the news too late. She was dead, and André had been sent to an orphanage. The girl's family didn't want anything to do with André; they were poor and he was just another mouth to feed, although they had every intention of continuing to take the monthly allowance. It sickened me, this callous indifference to a child, and I made them let me take him from the orphanage. Money still talks, you know. I'm not a sentimental man, but he is my own flesh and blood—and once I'd seen him, I knew—" he stopped and ran his hands over his face. Then he looked at Alison again.

"And you think I neglect André, am like a stranger. That's because, in a way, I am. Or was at first. I'm learning, slowly but surely, to be a real father to him. But you wouldn't understand that—you with your clear-cut instant solutions for everything. I seem to have failed, in your eyes. I'll try and remedy that. And I'm going to take him with me now."

He turned as if to go to the bedroom. Alison put out her hand.

"Please don't." It was an effort to speak. "Please—let him stay. He's sound asleep. You can't disturb him." Tears were near, but his glance was stoney. Then he nodded.

"Very well. But I'll be here first thing in the morning." He walked out, his back broad and straight and unyielding.

Alison crawled to bed in her mother's room, and she couldn't even cry.

CHAPTER NINE

THE next morning Niall came at nine o'clock sharp,
dressed in a sweater and jeans, and carrying a pair of
wellingtons for André and a basket of fruit.

He nodded formally to Alison as he came in. "Thank
you for keeping my son. André, say thank you to Miss
Mackay for letting you stay."

He was as remote as a stranger. As he and the excited
boy went out, he took his son's hand, and André skipped
happily along.

Alison stood at the kitchen window and watched them
make their way to the boat. Inside her was a leaden gray
despair. She had thought she hated Niall MacBain. It
had taken a child of six to show her it was really herself
she disliked.

Her mother phoned from Meg's to tell her that the X
rays had showed no broken bones, but that Jessie had
wrenched a muscle in her leg and would have to rest for
a while. Then she hesitated, and Alison sensed her reluctance to say something else. Gently she asked "What is
it?"

"Well, Jessie can come home on Tuesday. I was wondering if you'd mind if I stayed on at Meg's until then?"

"Why, of course not." She had a sharp pang of inner
dismay. Was her mother so nervous of her reaction that
she had dreaded telling her? More quietly, she added
"You've been working so hard. A few days away from
home will do you good—and I'll manage fine."

"You will, dear? That's a load off my mind. You'll
explain to Niall?"

"Of course. And I'll phone you this evening. Give Jessie all my love, and will you take her some flowers from me?"

They spoke for a few minutes more, and then Alison chatted to Meg before hanging up thoughtfully.

She was having her eyes opened about herself, and she wasn't sure if she liked the experience. It was rather sobering to realize how selfishly she had been behaving. She had fought against her mother selling the house— even more so against the man who was now transforming it: Niall MacBain, who had adopted his brother's son because nobody wanted him. That would be a big step for anyone to take, but he hadn't hesitated. And Alison had accused him of not caring. Truly she had a lot to learn, and her first lesson had taken place the previous night. The first — and undoubtedly the last, for something told Alison there would be no more talking with Niall MacBain. She could not erase from her mind the expression he had worn when he finished telling her about André. There was a certain pride, a look almost of nobility.

Niall was a true man, a gentle man in the best sense of the word. All her scorn had been wasted against his strength of purpose and his sense of honor.

She walked into the living room and looked around her. Her face was drawn and tired, for she hadn't slept much after Niall had gone. There was a yawning emptiness about the house that had nothing to do with her mother or Jessie being away.

The room was untidy. Jessie would have to rest, and would be unable to do housework. And Alison, with the days stretching blankly ahead, had to do something to fill the vacuum. She collected all the cleaning materials, dressed in old clothes, and began to clean the house.

At six o'clock she sat down in the kitchen for a welcome cup of tea, tired both physically and mentally. She had worked so hard she'd managed to keep from thinking, but now, as she tried to relax, the thoughts came rushing back.

Alison drank the tea and pushed the cup away restlessly. If only she could go somewhere to sort everything out in her mind. If only . . . then she saw the boat bobbing gently on its mooring. They had returned and gone home without a word. She stood up impatiently. What had she expected? Niall to come and tell her how the picnic had gone? She smiled bitterly and went to the window. The boat looked inviting, and the outboard motor still attached. Why not? She looked at it again then at Rusty. A boat ride to the island would clear her head and maybe help her to sleep when the night came and she was utterly alone.

"You want to come?" Alison asked the dog, and Rusty wagged her tail and stretched. They went out, and as they passed she felt the line of washing billowing in the breeze. It was nearly dry. When they came back it would be ready to take in and iron—something else to help pass the long evening.

The sky was bright, with clouds hurrying past. Gulls were crying harshly as they wheeled overhead. They would be watching her, beady eyes on the boat as she started the motor, pulling the string to whirr it to life. Some would follow them to the island, anticipating fish for supper. But Alison wasn't going fishing. There was something she had to think about and she could do it better on the island—might remember what it was that pressed at the back of her mind as irritating as a speck of sand in an oyster. As they set off Rusty crouched down to avoid the stiff breeze. She preferred to lie as flat as possible until they reached their destination. Rusty loved the island, for it had new smells to sniff out in the undergrowth. The journey infinitely long as it must have seemed to her, was well worth it.

Alison looked back, saw in the distance Niall's car, several children playing on the shore, and a dog barking furiously at the gulls, the noise carrying clearly over the surface of the water even above the put-put of the motor as they sped along. She sighed and turned to look ahead. The island loomed closer and darker as they neared it. She wondered what had been in André's mind as he came for the first time that morning. Excitement, naturally, perhaps tinged with fear, for it did look rather grim and forbidding from this side. But with Niall he would have known that he was safe. And he would have scampered out to the beach and run about excitedly, waiting for the picnic to start.

So vivid were the pictures conjured up that Alison blinked hard. She hoped that he had enjoyed it. She wanted so very much for him to be happy, and perhaps he would be now, after such an unfortunate beginning. For whatever Alison had said and thought about Niall MacBain there was one thing she knew deep down. That was that what he'd said so bitterly and forcefully the previous night had been true. He was learning to be a father to André, a real father. He would be a good one, just and fair, and never cruel, for even as a boy he had had a strong sense of justice, and. . . .

Alison drew her breath in sharply as the boat bumped against the beach. She knew now what had been nagging at the back of her mind for days, knew in a blinding flash of revelation exactly what she had been fighting all these weeks. The knowledge flooded her mind, pushing everything else out, and she jumped from the boat after Rusty, skidding on the slippery sand as she landed. She got her balance, then walked quickly along the beach, away from Shielbaig, to the other side of the island.

She knew it, yet still she would not put it into words. Knew why, now, she had fought so hard to prevent Niall from coming into her life, knew why she had always had the breathless, heart-stopping sensation whenever he was near. The prickly antagonism had been a defense— and a poor one—against her woman's heart, the foolish heart that had finally betrayed her. And now she could say the words. As she went the last few feet to the warmer, Skye-facing side of the island, she said them out loud "I love Niall MacBain."

Rusty looked up from her eternal sniffing and wagged her tail as if in agreement. Tears filled Alison's eyes. She loved a man—had done, she knew now, for years, and he despised her, thought of her as selfish and spoiled. How he would laugh if he knew! How ironic that he should in the end take her heart, after she had fought so bitterly against him. She went and sat on a flat rock, still shaken from her belated discovery. All the little things she had tried to ignore came strongly to the fore as she gazed out over the sea, and she remembered the one thing that she had deliberately forgotten for so many— too many—years.

It had happened at school when she was nearly six and Alec and Niall were eleven. Miss Carmichael, their stern but much loved teacher, had gone out to talk to the mailman, leaving the children working. An ink bomb had landed on Alec's desk, and he had immediately gone over to Niall and accused him of spoiling his exercise book.

Inevitably, a fight had started, and Alison, fearful that Miss Carmichael would come back, had rushed impulsively to stop it. Too impulsively, for a flying fist had caught her ribs and sent her staggering back. As she cried out, the boys had stopped and, seeing her white face, had come shamefacedly to their feet.

Then a strange thing had happened. Niall, the sworn enemy, had come to where she stood crying and holding her side, and said, completely ignoring the astonished stares of Alec and the other children who surrounded them, "If it was me that hit you, Alison, I'm sorry. It was an accident." There had been only concern on his face, nothing else. She had remembered it because of that, and the look in his eyes had remained locked away in some secret memory chest ever since. Perhaps because, even at six, she had recognized true gallantry when she saw it.

She bent restlessly and picked up a few pebbles, and began to flick them into the water as she watched the black waves rush up the sand and recede with a slight shushing sound. A gull swooped down then rose again, soaring effortlessly upward with sad harsh cries as if disappointed at seeing no fish.

It was no use. The closure of the school would give her an opportunity she must take: to get away from Shielbaig. She would apply for a transfer immediately, perhaps to Inverness or Edinburgh, and there she would try and forget what had happened; maybe in time she would forget Niall. For she would not be able to bear the bittersweet agony of seeing him every day, of living within a few hundred yards of him and André, of wondering what he was doing, where he was going, and why . . . she would come home on weekends, but if she was careful she wouldn't have to see him. She would tell her mother and Jessie. Jessie, with her shrewd mind, probably wouldn't be surprised at all. Several things she had said recently now seemed in the light of Alison's newfound knowledge, to have been remarkably astute. Perhaps she guessed Alison's feelings, and had wondered. . . .

Alison looked up as she felt a heavy drop of rain on her hand. The sky had grown darker, and some of the warmth was gone. She looked toward the Cuillins, but they had vanished in a grey mist.

"Come on, Rusty!" she called, and the dog galloped up to her. They set off back. It had been a mistake to come, she knew, for the bitter realization of her feelings had brought only sadness with it. She walked around the bend and saw the beach. It was empty. Alison stared in disbelief, wondering if she had made a mistake. Then she saw the boat bobbing all alone out in the lake. In her haste to land, and with her troubled mind, she had forgotten to tie it up. She had no way of getting home. Even as Alison stood there watching helplessly, it drifted farther away. Then the heavens opened and the rain lashed down.

CHAPTER TEN

Alison stood in the shelter of the trees, wondering if she could swim as far as shore. Even as she debated, knowing the dangers, she realized with sinking heart that it was no use. The current was too strong. She would be exhausted before she was halfway there, and if Rusty decided to follow her. . . . Already the leaves were heavy with rain and beginning to tip over. She looked up at the steep slope behind her.

"Rusty, come on, girl," she commanded, and began to scramble up the rocky incline toward the cottage. There was no thought in her mind other than the immediate problem of shelter. She dared not think ahead yet.

It was only as Alison stood in the open doorway looking out at a dripping wet world of green and gray that she realized the full gravity of the situation. There was no one at home to miss them. It was Saturday night, and growing rapidly darker with swollen rain clouds overhead. She shuddered, in the face of an overwhelming sense of loneliness, and thought of her mother who would phone, and phone again, and wonder. . . . She had no matches to light a fire, and no food. Alison swallowed hard, and looked around her. It was no time for tears or self-pity, and she couldn't stand up all night, so she might as well try and see what advantages were to be gained from her shelter before the light grew too poor to see.

The cottage had a stone floor, littered with dead leaves and twigs. There were four rooms altogether, two upstairs and two down, connected by a crude wooden staircase. She looked around, but because there was nothing to sit on, she went to the stairs, sat on the botton one, and drew Rusty to her.

"Well, old girl, you'll go hungry tonight," she whispered, "I'm sorry. But I'm glad I brought you with me." Rusty's soft brown eyes gazed up into Alison's, and she bent impulsively and hugged her. The dog's coat was still damp from the rain, and she whined softly as Alison held her.

She would remember this day for the rest of her life, she knew. Not only for the awful sense of being marooned, but because she had discovered the overwhelming fact that she was in love, painfully in love, for the first time in her life.

They sat there quietly, listening to the rain because there was nothing else to do. The image of Niall's face was everywhere. Alison dared not close her eyes because she knew she would see him as he had been the previous night, lashing her with his contempt. She moved awkwardly as the hard stairs pressed into her back. No, she wouldn't forget this.

She wasn't afraid of the dark, nor of being alone, yet there was an indefinable sense of eeriness about the place, some atmosphere dredged from the mists of the past. It was nonsense, of course, but it seemed almost as if she were not alone, as if others, long-dead Mackays, waited with her.

She must eventually have slept, for she had an odd dream, in which she heard someone call her name again and again. So vivid was it that she awoke and sat up to find Rusty gone. Heart hammering against her ribs, she stood up a little shakily and found her shoes, then went to the door.

"Rusty, Rusty!" she called, and heard a faint answering bark, then a voice shouting, "Alison!"

She hadn't been dreaming, it was real! She ran out of the cottage, into pitch blackness, the rain lashing down heavier than ever as she sped along the path heedless of the danger. The rain mingled with the tears that coursed down her face—tears of joy that blinded her so that she ran straight into the darkness. Then she was held tightly in a pair of powerful arms as she heard a most familiar voice say, "Thank God! Thank God! I thought you were dead!"

She opened her eyes, and it was Niall who held her. She gasped painfully, whispered, "Oh, no, it's you!" and tried to pull herself away.

"Don't. Don't fight. Let me hold you." Strangely, his voice trembled. Alison gazed up at him, saw his hair and face running with water as he looked down at her, and she took a deep breath. And then she knew.

They looked at each other, there in that bleak coldness of pouring rain, and he lifted his hand gently to touch her face.

In a voice that shook, he said, "I thought you were dead."

"I was here . . . in the cottage . . . the boat . . ." she began.

"Yes, I know now. I saw it drifting . Then I saw your washing hung out in the pouring rain and I knew something was terribly wrong." His arms tightened around her. "I had to make sure, so I went to the cottage—and it was cold and empty, and your cup was on the table, and Rusty was gone—and I knew." He suddenly bent his head, burying it in her hair. "Oh, my God, that was when the nightmare began. I took a boat, I don't know whose, and set out. I was hoping you'd be in the other one, but when I saw it empty—" he stopped.

They were so drenched with rain that their clothes

were sticking to them, but Alison couldn't have moved away for anything on earth, nor did she want to. A growing wonder filled her heart, swelling every moment as she heard his words. She hastened to tell him "I'm sorry, it was all my fault. I'd come here to think, and didn't tie it up, and—"

"No, it doesn't matter. Don't you see, Alison? It doesn't matter. All that counts is that you're safe." Trembling like a man possessed, his mouth found hers and for endless seconds they clung together, filled with a kind of precious wonder. The rain was sweet on his lips, sweet and cool, and the kiss was warm, and of such infinite tenderness that she could scarcely breathe or think, only know the ecstasy of his mouth on hers.

Then shakily he said "We should go. You're soaked to the skin. We must go home now."

"Yes." Her teeth were chattering with the cold, and with her feelings. She could not believe that it was happening. It wasn't possible. Yet the rain and the cold were painfully real. They made their slippery way down to where the two boats were tied together. Rusty woofed apologetically, as if for leaving her.

"We'll go in ours, it's got a better engine," Niall said, as he helped Alison in. It seemed odd to her that he said "ours." It was his boat now. Rusty sat beside her in the bow, Niall started the motor, and they set off through the icy driving rain, now intensified in force because of their speed. The island receded, and they were alone in a vast gray wilderness of water. Niall stood in the stern guiding them, his eyes never looking away from Alison's face. She looked back at him, and something sparked between them. Almost electric, like fire, their glances met and held. There was no need for words.

She was shivering violently when they beached the boat outside Courthill. Niall swung her up into his arms and carried her home. In the kitchen he put her down.

"Go and get yourself dry," he ordered. "I'm going to Courthill for my work clothes."

"Yes—yes, I will." She went to do his bidding. When she padded into the kitchen after changing, he was wearing his old jeans and a paint-spattered sweater, and briskly rubbing Rusty with an old towel.

He looked up, saw Alison, and gave Rusty a smack. "That's enough for you, old girl." Then he stood and came towards her, and Alison waited. Slowly he took her hands in his. The clasp was warm and firm, and her heart beat so fast that she could scarcely breathe.

"Alison," he said.

"Yes, Niall?"

"You know, don't you?" His voice was low and gentle, and she couldn't take her eyes from his face, his dear sweet face, which she saw in so many dreams.

"Yes, I know," she answered, and his face became blurred. Suddenly, wordlessly, they were clinging together in the warm haven of the kitchen, and their mouths told them what words could not.

And later, after they had eaten toast and hot soup, an ordinary enough meal yet with him a banquet, they sat on the sofa in front of a roaring fire in the living room. Rusty lay sprawled out on the rug at their feet, fast asleep. Niall's arm was tightly around Alison, as if he would never let her go. And that was right.

"When did you know?" he asked.

"This afternoon. I went to the island to try and think, because after last night I knew—at least I thought I knew that you despised me, and I had to get away. I was planning how I would get a transfer and work in Inverness—or Edinburgh—anywhere to get away from you."

He groaned and turned toward her, his face softer and gentler in the glow of the fire. "And I would have let you go. My stiff-necked pride would have let me watch you go away—oh, Alison, I've been a brute and a swine, I—"

"No," she put a finger to his lips. "No, you haven't, it was me. I hated you because you were taking everything from me—but I didn't realize, all the time, that I was fighting this growing attraction to you, this awareness of everything you were and did. It wasn't until I reached the island this afternoon that I finally knew I loved you." She paused. "I was so stunned by the realization that I forgot to tie up the boat."

He began to laugh softly, his fingers playing lightly up and down her arm. "And it wasn't until I saw the boat that I realized you were the whole world to me—" He suddenly sobered, and went on more quietly. "All the time, these past years, you've been in my mind, just there, quietly at the back of my thoughts. And always I remembered our last meeting, in the woods."

He must have felt her stir uneasily, for he drew a deep breath. "You hadn't forgotten it either, had you?"

"No, how could I? Perhaps that was where it began, there by the trout stream that night."

"Yes, I think it did. You were so beautiful, Alison, so proud and defiant as you told me to go away. I wanted so desperately to kiss you." He seemed faintly surprised, as if the memories were rushing back faster than he knew. "Somehow, the thought of you was always bound up in the house, as if you belonged together. I always loved Courthill, always envied you and Alec for being able to live in it, especially when—" he stopped.

"Go on, please," she prompted.

"Well, you know that time you asked me why I'd said it should really be mine?"

Her heartbeat quickened. "If you don't want to tell me, it's all right—"

"No, I can tell you now, Alison. There are no secrets between us any more." Their eyes met and held, and Niall's were so full of love that she almost cried out.

"I learned when I was a boy that there was more that had been kept well hidden. There had been smuggling, and whisky-making—on the island, I believe—more than 100 years ago. Our families were tied up in more ways than one. Two of our great-great-grandparents were inveterate gamblers. Only yours wasn't so lucky, and when he was on a bad streak one night, he staked Courthill and lost. But before the deed could be transferred to the MacBains, someone gave the game away about the whisky and the smuggling to the customs man—and my ancestor went to prison. Yours didn't. Nobody ever found out how it had happened, but you can imagine the rumors flying around. Then when the two boys fell for the same girl—everything erupted. The feud was on."

His story shook Alison. She raised anguished eyes to him.

"Then all this time—"

"No," his lips silenced her worried question. "What's past is done. How can we *know* the truth after all this time? But it's something I believed when I was a boy, and you know how a child's mind works. It helped to feed the fires when I wanted a scrap."

"I know," she smiled. "You were always fighting, both of you. Perhaps, without the feud, you might have been good friends?"

He grinned. "Perhaps. But life wouldn't have been

half so much fun. I'll never forget those days—nor you. Oh, Alison, I've been so jealous every time I've seen you with Johnny—I just wanted to hurt you."

"And I you. And all the time, as I grew more fond of André, I thought how I mustn't because he was yours, and—oh, Niall, I was jealous too, in a very different way."

"He loves you, Alison. He's always talking about you, asking if you'll look after him when he's older."

She drew breath sharply. "And I was going to—"

"No, don't say it. I need you, Alison, very much. I've never wanted anyone as much as I want you. Everything about you—you drove me mad at times, until I couldn't stand it any more, which is when I did the only thing possible—kissed you!" He laughed, and held her tighter, joyously. "But I didn't realize the effect it would have on me!"

"Oh, Niall, don't worry. I'll work at Strathcorran school as long as I can, and look after—"

"I don't mean teaching. I mean as my wife, with André and me, at Courthill, to be together for always."

"Oh, Niall darling, I love you so much. Yes, oh, yes!"

And his kiss was more wonderful than anything else in the world.